Bonnie,
I HOPE YOU ENJOY
THIS BOOK-IT IS SET
IN SONOMA COUNTY &
HAS ROMANCE & ADVENTURE
Martha

Hard Destiny

William W. Winamaki

Chapter 1

Dominico Londi, everyone called him Dom, was sixty years old when he boarded a ship in Naples bound for New York. He had spent all his life in Florence. Being the son of a competent cook, he had followed in his father's trade, working for many years in some of the finer restaurants in Florence. He had never married, though he had enjoyed playing the field when he was younger. There were so many pretty women in Florence, from dark-eyed, black-haired ones to blue-eyed, reddish blondes—who could pick just one?

The sea of time moved swiftly in the warm Tuscan air, and it seemed that before Dom knew it, he was old. His parents were gone, and having no wife or children, he decided to see the world before it was too late. Everyone was talking about America. All said it was a land of true beauty and opportunity. Living somewhat but not too frugally, he had managed to put away quite a little sum of money. Being still a spry and robust man for sixty, he decided to make the journey across the sea. Why not, after all, he had nothing to lose, and surely anyplace in the world could use a good cook.

Dom had heard that of all the different states in America, California had the finest weather and exceeded all in natural beauty. Being a profound admirer of beauty, that is where he decided to journey. After landing in New York and going through the necessary procedures of a new arrival, he boarded a train that would eventually take him to California.

Many days later, tired and stiff, though still optimistic and of a light spirit, he arrived early one morning in the city of San Francisco. It was a cool, clear day in April with a brilliant sun when he stepped off the train, dressed in his finer set of clothes. He asked, in the broken English he had picked up over the years in the cosmopolitan restaurants of Florence, directions to the Toscano Hotel. Dom even knew where to go. A friend of his cousin's was already living in San Francisco. Dom had written him several times, and the man, Primo Nuti, was expecting him sometime this month. He had told him to go to the Toscano Hotel and book a room. After rest and refreshment, when he felt up to it, he was to ask the clerk, a recent Italian arrival himself, for directions to Primo Nuti's residence. The following day, after a good sleep in a comfortable bed and a hot bath in a room down the hall, Dom dusted off his finest, and going downstairs, received the directions to Primo's house. Though tired and a little overwhelmed, he had noticed the day before that many of the establishments in this part of town were run by Italians—and now, in walking less than a block, he encountered many Italians going to and fro or standing here and there talking to one another. *This is kind of a Little Italy*, Dom thought. He knew that New York had such an area, as did the Irish, the Germans, and many of the other Europeans. For some reason, though, maybe just because he had always heard so much about New York and its make up, he was pleasantly surprised to find such a distinct taste of Italy here in San Francisco.

Dom was hungry, and he noticed a small café across the street called Angelina's. Waiting for a pause in the horse-drawn traffic, he crossed the street and entered the establishment. It was not very crowded and pretty much looked like the inside of many cafés throughout Italy. Not the outside, though. The outside was made of some reddish type of wood. A few pieces of the horizontal siding still had some fuzzy, hairy red bark clinging to them. The whole building looked like it had recently been thrown together with little detail or craftsmanship. No one, at least in Florence, would dare build such a thing and call it a café. *Oh well*, Dom thought, *America is still such a young country*. It was clean and comfortable inside, and Dom took a seat at the polished counter.

An Italian-looking, middle-aged woman, still very attractive, he couldn't help but notice, came to wait on Dom, and speaking in Italian said, "Would you like some breakfast, Joe?"

"How'd you know I was Italian?" Dom asked.

"What do you think? The gray mustache, the hooked beak, the fine expensive suit, the wondering look of the eye—I bet you just stepped off the boat."

"Well, not exactly," Dom said, "I just stepped off the train." And both of them laughed.

"I'd like three eggs lightly scrambled, a nice slice of bread with butter, and some coffee please. And, why did you call me Joe?"

"Now listen carefully, and I'll give you your first English lesson. Repeat after me, 'What's up Joe?'" Dom promptly repeated the words.

"That's perfect," she said. "Whenever you meet an American and want to break the ice, just say, 'What's up Joe?'" And off she went to get the breakfast. She came back shortly with the eggs and a wonderful chunk of crusty bread.

"*Dio Bono*," Dom said. "This bread is delicious. What do you call it?"

"We call it San Francisco sourdough French bread. Some miner during the gold rush came up with this special yeast. It's that yeast that gives it the flavor. Lots of people around here make the bread with the original yeast they've preserved and passed on over the years."

"Truly an amazing bread," Dom said. "I've seldom tasted finer." Over coffee he was able to chitchat with the woman during breaks between customers. Indeed, she was Angelina, and had recently opened the café following the death of her husband in a construction accident. They were throwing up buildings so fast in the city and building many of them on unstable landfill, that often during construction they simply collapsed, taking many a worker with them, as was the case with her husband.

"I'm so sorry," Dom said upon hearing that. "To lose a husband at such a young age is a terrible thing."

"I'm not that young, and you know it," she shot back.

"Nonetheless, you must have been devastated. And your children?"

"We had none. I'm probably too big a sinner," Angelina said.

"I would imagine your sins to be petty, and anyway, some of the biggest sinners I've met have had the largest families. Who knows what God's intentions are," he said.

"Hey, what are you, a priest in hiding?"

"No, just a simple cook."

They talked on until the little café suddenly began to fill up and Angelina began working non-stop. He had one brief opportunity to talk to her again, and he remarked, "This building that houses your café looks like it was thrown together pretty fast too. Some of the boards still have bark on them. What do you call that wood anyway?"

"It's redwood. These huge redwood trees grow someplace around here. Someone told me that they can grow to forty-five feet in circumference."

"I know when someone's pulling my leg. No tree could be that big. If someone told you that, he must have been feeding you a line," Dom said.

"Think what you like, Joe, the counter is made out of that wood too."

Dom had been admiring the counter. Over the years he had done a little woodworking and appreciated well-made things. The counter was made out of what looked to be a single three-inch-thick, two-foot-wide reddish board, sanded very smooth and oiled to bring out a beautiful grain pattern. If such large trees truly existed, Dom placed it at the top of his priority list to search some out. He was beginning to think that this new land could daily have the potential to surprise him—and that was just what he needed. His world had become just too routine in Florence.

Dom finished his second cup of coffee, but before he made his way out the door, he was able to catch Angelina alone and said, "Say, I'm on my way to a relative's friend who evidently lives close by. His name is Primo Nuti. Do you know him?"

"Why sure," she said. "He's the biggest crook in town." And off she went to wait on customers.

Dom found her remark quite interesting as he stepped back out into the bright light. She had said it with a slight smile on her face. Dom walked on for perhaps ten minutes, and after turning down a side street, he came up to a detailed wrought iron gate with a copper plaque hanging near the top that bore the address he had been searching for. The plaque was emblazoned with a medieval Italian coat of arms. Dom could tell by the little trees planted near the house and remains of construction debris scattered about that this house too was recently erected. But what a house. It was huge. Three stories of stucco and brick, it had a concrete-pillared colonnade out front and many gothic-shaped windows of different sizes reflecting the sun's light. Dom couldn't help but notice the two massive front doors. They looked to be made out of the same wood as Angelina's counter. Each door was at least three feet wide and each milled from a single plank. Dom unlatched the gate and walked up the steps to the heavy iron striker on the door and clanked it down three times. Almost immediately, the great door opened, and a small white-haired man said in English not much better than Dom's, "Can I help-a-you, sir?"

Well, well, another Paisan, thought Dom, and replied in Italian, "My name is Dominico Londi, and I'm here to see Mr. Nuti."

"Ah yes, Mr. Londi, we've been expecting you. Won't you come this way, sir?"

The little man had replied in Italian but in a dialect much different than Dom's. *Must be a Sicilian,* he thought. Sicilians came to the Florence restaurants now and then, and Dom sometimes had a little trouble understanding them.

"My name is Pietro, sir. Don Nuti is in the music room with his daughter."

The house was truly beautiful inside; high ceilinged with thick maroon curtains, paintings, and tapestry on the walls, polished floors, oriental carpets. He noticed a wide, curving stairway leading to the upper floor with an intricate banister of what looked to be that redwood again. The door to the music room was partly open, and Dom could hear the clear notes of a violin playing, hesitatingly yet adequate.

Pietro, with Dom a short step behind, opened the door fully and, after a slight cough, announced, "Pardon me, Don Nuti, but Mr. Dominico Londi is here and wishes to see you."

Good grief, Dom thought. His cousin had told him that his friend Primo had moved to California and was just starting to do well in the business world, but Dom had imagined him to be, as Angelina would have said, just a regular Joe. And from several letters he had received in Florence from Primo, nothing had led him to expect all this pomp and finery. Why, the way the house looked and the way

Pietro was acting, Dom thought that he was being introduced to one of the Medicis. A mischievous-looking little girl of around ten quit playing her violin.

Don Nuti turned away from a music stand and, looking at Dom, said in the same dialect as Pietro's, "Oh boy, Dom Londi. From what I hear the finest chef in all of Tuscany." And coming towards Dom, he grabbed his hand and shook it firmly, a beaming smile on his large face. Dom noticed a missing front tooth when Primo smiled. He also had a scar running down from the corner of his eye to the bottom of his jaw. Other than that, Primo could be called a handsome man, a little taller than medium stature, of around forty-five years.

Pietro suddenly started laughing and said, "Hey, Dom, maybe you could cook us up some donkey balls tonight with a little vermicelli?"

"Hey, Mister." The little girl put down the violin and, grabbing her chin, began pulling up and down on it, braying like a donkey. "Hee, haw, hee, haw," she said, and began circling Dom in a little dance.

At first he thought he had entered a crazy house, but now, looking at them all, he could see that his leg was being pulled since he banged on the door.

"Sorry, Dom," Primo said. "My uncle regrets that he missed his calling as an actor—occasionally when one of the wealthy Americans pays a call, Unc plays the obedient servant up to the hilt. I guess he just couldn't resist practicing on you.

"The business has been going great, and the dough's been rolling in. We just finished with the building and furnishing of this fancy house and have begun to put on airs like high society folk are supposed to. I even go to the opera, and Maria here takes violin and music lessons, and by golly, she's really taking to it. But enough about us— let's have some coffee, or perhaps you'd like something stronger. I want to hear about your plans and how the trip over went. Follow me into the kitchen. It's very sunny and warm in there."

As they approached the kitchen Dom detected the aroma of a marinara sauce with a hint of meat to it, simmering. Sure enough, a savory tomato based sauce was slowly bubbling away in a cast iron pot on an obviously new, elegant wood stove in a spacious well-appointed kitchen. Dom knew kitchens, and he was pleased with what he saw. There were many pots and pans of various sizes and metals hanging from hooks along one wall on both sides of the stove. Glass-doored, spacious cupboards took up most of the remaining wall space. A large, beautifully polished wood ice cooler with intricate brass hinges was against a wall next to a counter, and there was a sink with hot and cold water faucets. Primo saw Dom staring at the sink.

"Yep," Primo said. "We have hot water furnished by a coal fired boiler in the basement. Bathrooms are that way too. Sure beats boiling water," he added.

Dom walked over to the sauce and took a good whiff.

"Oh no," he said. "Don't tell me all the Italians are doing that over here too."

"No one can resist, Dom. There are so many robins around, the supply seems inexhaustible," Primo said.

"Yea, that's what they used to say around Florence. Now, it's rare to spot a nice fat one."

Dom thought about how his grandfather and friends used to supply the restaurants with robins. They used to watch them in wooded fields, then throw rocks to see which way they would fly. After doing this a few times over several days, they would string a large net between two trees in the flight direction. They would leave the net lying on the ground between the trees, a rope attached to the bottom and top of the net, with two men at the end of each rope, hiding quietly at a distance in the brush beyond the trees. One man would suddenly startle the birds.

Two men on each side would draw the bottom rope tight. The upper ropes, looped high and resting in the crotch of an upper branch, would be drawn tight by two other men simultaneously. The robins would fly mostly straight into the net. Money would be made, and the restaurants would have plenty of fresh robins for the sauce.

Primo set out coffee cups for everyone, including Maria, and they sat at the cozy table in the center of the kitchen while Primo poured coffee that had been kept warm on the back of the stove.

"Half cup for me, Pa," said Maria.

"No," her father said. "Quarter cup with lots of milk."

"And lots of sugar," she said.

"Little sugar, and get us the raisin bread, please."

She moved fast to the counter and set down a knife and plate filled with a large loaf of bread stuffed with almonds, raisins, and dried cherries.

"Raisin bread," Dom said. "What a surprise!"

"That's one thing you'll find about San Francisco," Primo said. "The breads here are delicious."

"I'm beginning to see that," Dom said. "Say, my journey here was wonderful and actually went quite smoothly, but please tell me about yourself and how you've come to do so well in this new country."

Maria walked away carrying her coffee and bread, saying, "I'm going to practice the piano."

Primo watched his daughter leave and said, "That little girl is the heart of my life, Dom. I only wish her mother were here. Has your nephew, Mario, told you much about me?"

"No," Dom said, "only that you two were friends at University in Verona and that you were studying law when your wife died. You moved to America shortly after," he said.

"I hate that damn word *death*. As long as you're alive, it forces you to have new dreams. And I wanted no new dreams. I wanted to practice law in Verona and live simply with my wife and child. When Sophia fell sick, they called it the galloping consumption. I wanted to leave the world with her. I knew I couldn't, for the sake of Maria. I left University and my part time job as a bricklayer's apprentice, and we booked passage, along with my uncle, for this new dream of America. My dreams died in Verona."

Dom could understand broken dreams. Age and routine, after all, had prompted him to board ship.

"What did you do when you arrived in New York?" Dom said.

"I immediately, after finding a place to live, enrolled in a New York university that specialized in law. I worked on the docks unloading freight three days a week and attended classes Thursdays and Fridays. Most of my weekends were spent in the city library. Little Maria was watched over by a Genovese family that was kind to us. I obtained my law degree, and we moved to California, where I heard that there was a great opportunity to be made for lawyers on this new shore.

"Oh, by the way," said Primo. "How's your English? If you plan on staying here, you've got to pick it up."

"I'm an old man," Dom said. "But if I decide to stay here, I am not without learning skills."

The kitchen was quiet for a moment. Pietro had been moving about stirring the sauce.

"My nephew is a lonely man," he suddenly announced. "A man with a daughter needs a wife."

The air had been quite heavy.

"Yea," said Dom, "couldn't we all use a wife?"

Pietro suddenly approached the table and laid his hand hard on it and said, "I've never married, and for good reason. I've read about that Helen of Troy. A woman is to be appreciated and used, but never to be venerated. Women are placed in this world for one reason—to steal your soul."

"Possibly, but maybe when one is truly in love the soul can be big enough for two," Dom said.

"Philosophers," Primo said. "Go sit on your mother's lap. Let's have some wine; to hell with all this coffee."

Thus began the friendship between Dom Londi and the Nutis.

Dom found the room at the Toscano Hotel adequate for his needs and rented it on a monthly basis. With a little help from Primo, he soon found a job in one of San Francisco's finer restaurants and was amazed at how soon he was piling up money. He learned that Primo was making all his money by representing mostly the Italians who needed legal aid. They trusted Primo above all others. Not all the immigrants who left Italy were impoverished economically. In fact, many of them were quite wealthy and started successful businesses that were growing rapidly. Primo's talents were constantly in demand. Many of the Chinese also sought his aid. His first Chinese client had been treated fairly and with great respect, and after that the word got around, and his downtown office was always full.

Dom also found out that Primo was a pretty tough customer. The scar on his face was the result of a knife fight in Monte Lepre, Sicily, where he grew up. The missing tooth happened only recently. San Francisco was a tough town. A judge, ruling in favor of a case involving one of Primo's clients, had angered the opposite side, and one night two thugs, who must have been following him, jumped him down a narrow side street and began working him over. Primo was strong and fought them off, but not before losing the tooth. He was going to be getting a new gold one any day. Dom found that Primo also followed an older, more traditionally Sicilian way of life. When charges failed to be brought against the son of a prominent businessman who had violated the virtue of an Italian baker's daughter in a violent manner resulting in her hospitalization—the father had come to Primo pleading for justice.

"The courts have turned a deaf ear," Primo explained. "The boy comes from too prominent a family. Money in high places must have been exchanged. In the old country there were ways to deal with such instances. Allow me to think on it for a few days," Primo said. "The ways of justice may enfold in unexpected ways." And he assured the father he would do his best.

Primo was well known among the Italian fishermen moored up at the dock. During the off-season many were willing to pick up a few dollars any way possible. When Primo explained, to a group of those he knew best, what had happened to the baker's daughter, most were immediately ready to go uptown, find the young man, and feed him to the fishes.

"Hold on. Hold on," he said. "If things are too obvious it won't go well for the baker and his family. We have to make a sly plan. Here's my idea: four of you are not going to cut your hair for a month. Have some of the women go shopping and come back with some hair dye, bleach, anything to turn your hair blonde. Next, you have to get your hands on some of those coats and caps the Swedish fishermen wear—even if you have to go away from here, maybe Monterey, and rob them from some guys, it shouldn't be a problem; you have a month. Start listening to the Swedes, learn how to say this in their accent, 'Ya, ya, you betcha. Ya, ya.' Near the end of the month, if there are any Swedish ships at the docks, try to encourage them to leave. Tell them there's great fishing either to the north or south. If any Swedish vessels try to enter the bay on the appointed day we are to act, have one of your own patrolling and go out to meet them and say, 'Cholera, cholera at the docks, go back.' You see what the plan is—you're going to pretend to be Swedish fishermen who get in a fight with this *animale*. You'll give him a beating he'll never forget—have both his legs and one arm broken. The baker's family will have at least a sense of satisfaction."

"It would be appropriate for us to slit his balls for him," one of the men said.

"I feel the same way," Primo agreed, "but it might seem obvious if his sexual apparatus were compromised. In the meantime, I will show one of you where this bastardo lives. You will slyly stalk him and learn his routine. He likes to drink and has several favorite saloons; that's where you end up in a fight with him and administer the revenge. Don't beat him until he's unconscious. He must hear you talk like a Swede.

Make sure he hears you say, 'Back to the docks.' You have to get away quickly and cleanly. If there are too many witnesses, they may catch you as you make your getaway. Have a covered coach nearby for the escape. Or arrange to enter a nearby friend's house unseen through a side door. I leave much of this up to you—you've got to make your plan as fool proof as possible. If for some reason it looks like everything won't go off as planned, abandon your mission. Try some other night. At your first opportunity, cut your hair, burn your clothing or sink it in the bay. Dye your hair black, and no one should be the wiser. You will also have to try to keep an eye on what's going on at the Oakland docks. We wouldn't want any boats full of Swedes docking up here that night. We would be defeating our purpose if anyone innocent took the blame for this. But are we not 'sneaky dagos' as some of them call us? With precise planning and execution it should be a cinch. Agreed?"

They all agreed, and actually couldn't wait for the day when that young rich fellow would get what he deserved. The result of stalking their prey revealed the arrogant chap to be a creature of habit. Most days and evenings he frequented the same saloon. On Saturday night, after heavy drinking, he would stumble out of his favorite one, The Palace, and head around the block to a nearby brothel. They decided to nab him when he turned the corner towards the brothel. The appointed night arrived and all was ready. It was off-season for many types of fish. No boats of Swedish fishermen were moored at the docks. It didn't take long for the men to see, after observing their victim, that he had a nasty temper when drunk and enjoyed bullying people. Saturday evening, when he left the bar around midnight, he rounded the corner heading towards the brothel and ran directly into a small blonde Swedish fisherman.

"Watch where you're going you little flat-head," he slurred, and landed a punch to the man's stomach.

At that moment, three other Swedish fishermen rounded the corner and, coming upon the scene, said, "It's Hans, you betcha. It's Hans."

And pushing past the attacker, they came to their comrade and helped him to his feet, and then they suddenly turned on the arrogant rapist and rapidly administered a severe beating. Positioning his leg in an awkward angle, one of the men stepped down on his knee with all his force. They could hear the snapping of the bone. They did the same to his other leg. It was simple. The man was so drunk that after the first volley of blows he could offer no resistance. They broke his right arm at the elbow, and then they took off running, saying, "Back to the docks!"

The man's screams had brought several people out of the bar to investigate, but after they rounded the corner, all they could see was what looked like men in fishermen's dress moving away. The men rounded a corner, and slowing to a walk, entered a dark alley where a covered coach was waiting to take them to a friend's house about a mile away. Once there, they changed clothes, cut and dyed their hair black, put the old clothes in a sack, spent the night there, and during the morning bustle, were driven to their respective homes. The sack of clothes was weighted and tossed into the bay.

The police searched the docks looking for Swedish fishermen. None who fit the bill were found. After a while, Primo heard news that the elite man's son would probably forever walk with a limp in one leg. The baker said he was to be forever grateful to Primo, and assured him that if there was anything at all he could do for him in the future, it would be his pleasure. Dom came to know that this was not the only instance when the laws had failed and people had sought out Primo's help.

At least several times a week, Dom went to Angelina's for breakfast. She served some of the best sausages he had ever tasted, full of various spices, and the eggs were always fresh, brought in daily. But what Dom enjoyed the most was talking with Angelina. She had a confident manner, almost a swagger, but it didn't take him long to see that she used this front to hide a serious, somewhat sad demeanor. She would joke, banter, and even flirt with some of the customers, but Dom would often see her from his seat at the counter, standing at a small window in the back room staring pensively out.

"Angie, a penny for your thoughts," he would say.

Immediately, the smile would return to her face.

"I wouldn't give a penny for your thoughts, old wolf, but tell me, aren't you getting a little old for those types of thoughts?"

And back to the cheerful world she would return, seemingly without a care. Dom liked the way Angelina looked. She wasn't thin, and she wasn't fat, just about right, he thought. Her hair was dark and luxuriant, sprinkled with gray. And she always wore it tied up in a bun, but Dom could tell it was quite long. She had large, dark eyes and full lips, her nose was large and straight with a slight hook, and dressed in her usual black with gold crucifix around her neck, she looked just like the many women seen strolling the streets of Florence.

"Tell me," Dom said. "Your husband, he must have been a nice man, huh?"

"Ah, so you're getting personal. Oh well, I don't mind. No, he was not so nice of a man. I thought he was when we married, but I came to see he appreciated drink and the company of his buddies more than he appreciated me. He was an American, a native San Franciscan. I met him shortly after my brother and sister and I arrived. I immediately found a job in a restaurant, and I met him while serving tables. He pursued me relentlessly and passionately. My brother and younger sister soon moved down the coast to Monterey where my brother, Mario, went in as partner on a sardine boat. I think I married him partly out of loneliness. True, he could be funny and was handsome, but mainly I just got tired of refusing him and figured what the heck, I'm not getting any younger. I could always do worse. So we married, and all went well for the first few months. Roger was a hard worker and brought home good money. On the weekends he would like to drink and hang out with his friends. I didn't begrudge him. Men can be that way. Most evenings we had fun. He would teach me English and would laugh at my attempts. We would play cards, and we went out to dinner a lot. He enjoyed showing me off to his friends. I guess he liked the way I looked. I didn't care much for his friends. They would say things like, 'My oh my, you sure got yourself one of them good-looking eye-ties. I'll bet she's a wild one in bed, eh,' and then they would all leer and laugh. Some would try to slap my behind. Real men don't need to act that way. His friends were crude and simple.

"I began to lose respect for Roger. Having such friends revealed a part of his character I didn't care for. I tolerated

Roger. He was a good provider. Our marriage became routine. He would drink more and more, not just on weekends now, but every night. I took in sewing. I made a little extra money, and it occupied my time. I stashed most of my money away, and some of Roger's too, every week. When he would come home and pass out drunk on payday, I would lift a few dollars from his wallet and put it with my savings. He never did notice it, or if he did, he never said anything. After the accident, I found out that he had a pretty good sum of money in the bank. I never really knew. He handled all the finances. I used the money from the bank along with my savings and was able to open this café. With Roger gone, and considering the way he had behaved in our marriage, I no longer wanted his name, and again I became Angelina Lombardi. And, there you have it, Mr. Nosy Florentine. Any more questions?"

"Just one," said Dom. "Why the sadness behind those beautiful eyes? Why the pensive preoccupied looks? I wasn't born yesterday," Dom said. "I can see there's something troubling you behind the mask you wear."

Angelina felt caught. She liked Dom and came to look forward to his visits to the café. She was surprised that he saw so much and how he came right to the point of the matter.

Smiling, she said lightly, "OK, Mr. Sees-all-things, maybe you've hit on something, but please, no more serious talk today. I've got work to do, can't you see? Maybe we talk some more another day."

Chapter 2

The group of tired Pomo Indians moved slowly down the dusty road. They had been walking and riding for two days since they left the rancheria, situated on the first ridge of hills east of the Pacific Ocean. Two men rode in the front seat of a wagon drawn by two healthy young horses. Three children and one gray-haired elder sat with their legs drawn up in the back. The group was headed for the small town of Healdsburg for supplies to bring back to the rancheria. Most of the group, fourteen in all, just came along for curiosity and excitement. It was good fun to stand or sit in the shade of the tree-lined plaza and watch the white man's world. That is, as long as the white man left them alone. The white man didn't always. That was a chance that one took for such pleasures.

The sun was going down in a cloudless September sky as the little group caught sight of the first of the white man's houses situated alongside the creek that ran through the narrow valley. The headwaters of the creek were within a half a day's walking distance from the rancheria. Each winter for thousands of years the tribe would camp along the creek to spear and trap the wild steelhead and salmon that migrated up the creek to spawn. The tasty flesh of the fish would be smoked and dried over alder wood and would be kept for many months.

All eyes turned towards the small white house. What curious things these settlers lived in. Square, perfectly square, with a peak on top like the crested jay. White, the color of clouds, with a red, square smokestack on the side near the top of the crest. Very few things in nature were square. What spirits could hide in all those corners? Who could live in such a thing? The people had a saying that only crazy people would live under the trees of the great redwood forest, yet these people cut down the redwood trees and made squares to live in. The sun wasn't square. We live under the sun. The cloud is not square. We live under the cloud. The tree and sky are not square, and these too we live under. Who could think to live inside a square?

The Pomos had white man's names given to them at the rancheria school. Fred was one of the little boys riding in the wagon. He looked at the house and thought of the first time he set foot in the rancheria school. School was out, and the door was open. He had seen the teacher in hot, stiff clothing walking towards the outhouse beneath the giant madrone in back of the school. Fred was too young for school then, and couldn't wait to get inside that square and see for himself. He ran barefoot from behind the tree where he had been hiding and charged through the doorway. He had seen the inside of the schoolhouse only through the window once, when his brother had held him up for a quick look. The older children sat in neat rows like lined-up quail, stopped while crossing the road. The view he had once glimpsed through the window had not prepared him for the quietness and vastness of the large square, which brought him to a halt as soon as he was inside. He immediately extended his left arm until his hand touched the horizontal siding of the wall. His finger touched the smooth brown wood, and he marched rapidly down to the first corner, where he stopped, stared above him at the high ceiling, then looked straight ahead at the corner and placed his pointing finger exactly where the two walls met.

The preciseness of the corner feeling told him all he needed to know about the white settlers. They were just too organized. They did everything like marching quail. The white man had to make a place for everything in his world. That teacher, who was out back moving his bowels, was doing it inside a small square box. The people did that under the nice sky with a breeze on their rear to blow away the offending odor. The teacher liked to trap the odor in the small wood box. The white man set traps for everything. The people only trapped what they needed to eat. Take the small, powdery, white sticks that the teacher used to write signs and directions on the black board behind his desk. These signs - directions and numbers, his older cousin had told him - explained many long stories. The elders told such stories at night around the fire or in the sweathouse. Here, all these stories were told with little white sticks. And where did the little white sticks go when they were finished telling the amazing stories? The teacher trapped them in a small square box where they could no longer get out to tell their tales.

As the group moved further down the road, closer to the little white house, they heard a door slam and saw two small children chasing a shorthaired dog that ran from the house. Fred, who was eight years old and about the same age as the children, reached out and tapped his uncle, who was driving the wagon, on the shoulder, and pointed at the house and the running children. Fred could see the fun of chasing that dog. There weren't many dogs on the rancheria to chase and play with. Dog meat was just too flavorful and was often needed during hard times.

The settler children chased the little dog around a thick valley oak tree until the dog suddenly stopped and started barking at the dusty group moving on down the road fifty yards away from them. The boy and girl froze in their tracks and immediately turned and ran into the house. Fred could vaguely catch the word "Indians" said in a small, shrill voice as the children slammed the door. Most of the Pomos looked at one another, some shook their heads, some laughed lightly, all kept moving slowly down the road.

The door of the white house opened again, and two men emerged, one old, one not so old, both with double-barreled shotguns in hand—one carried a box of shells, the other carried what looked like a cleaning kit. Both men took seats on the porch on either side of the door. The older one with the cleaning rod broke his gun open, attached a bit of white cloth to the end of the rod, and began cleaning the shotgun, not even bothering to look up at the Indians. Not the other one, though. He sat with the gun lying across his knees and stared straight at the group as they passed by.

The two men were Tom Fowler and his son, Dave. Tom was forty years old, worked in town three days a week for the blacksmith, and began homesteading in the valley four years ago in 1867. Tom was a reasonable man who enjoyed farming his plot of land and raising his livestock. His wife, Betty, was a God-fearing woman who worked just as hard as Tom at making a life in the lightly populated valley. One couldn't say much, though, for Tom's son Dave. Dave was twenty years old and just plain mean. Tom and Betty had done their best to raise Dave right, after all, he was their oldest and the pride of their dreams, but something had gone wrong. They both started noticing it when Dave was around ten.

In those days, Tom was a roving blacksmith, moving from one small gold rush town in the Sierra foothills to the next as work demand necessitated. While they were living in the town of Crooked Bar, along the Yuba River, they first noticed the change in Davy. Davy was what they called him then, and he had been such a quiet and solemn little boy, always so curious about any kind of animal life. There weren't many children in the foothill towns, not that many women either—mostly single miners, so Tom and Betty always had a dog or cat around, or both, for Davy to play with. One hot summer day while Davy's dad was shoeing horses and his ma was doing the wash at the little creek in the back of the house, Davy climbed up into the fir forest nearby with the curly-headed mongrel "Terry" following behind. As they moved through the forest, Davy began thinking about Hans, the fat German boy who had pushed him to the ground only a week ago, and had sat on him and farted. Then the large kid with the strange accent pulled down his pants and holding his member had rubbed it under Davy's nose while keeping his heavy, meaty hand on his chest, pinning him to the ground. Davy was thinking about the smell and the feel of that hot thing under his nose and decided that he had liked it. What he didn't like was being held down and bullied. One day Davy would grow bigger and stronger than the German boy and would rub his member under someone's nose.

As he and the dog walked, he wondered why he was always being picked on. Why, just last month he had found a small brown squirrel that couldn't walk good on the forest floor. It seemed to have a sore leg. Davy reached down to pick the little squirrel up, perhaps to help it, and what had the squirrel done? It had bit him. Bit him hard, leaving two red marks welling up with blood. And what about in that town of Downieville they had just left? The Mexican farm lady who owned a pretty tan and white cow had given Davy a pail and said he could have all the milk he could drink. He only had to milk the cow himself. Davy knew he could do that. He had seen cows being milked before, but being in his hurry to get at those large, swollen teats, thinking of the thick, warm milk, he charged straight for the cow from the rear instead of the side and began to squirt milk into the bucket. Davy figured the cow must have got excited because at that moment its bowels moved right there on Davy's head—the steaming loose cow patty running right down his face. The Mexican lady had been watching and laughed so loud that the whole town must have heard her. Davy's eyes filled with tears as he threw the bucket and ran down the road towards home, the laughter of the dark woman ringing in his ears.

The afternoon sun was hot now, and Davy's head began to ache a little as he and Terry came out upon a clearing near the top of a hill. A surprised jackrabbit stopped near some manzanita, saw their approach, and moved slowly into the bush. Davy knew something was wrong with the rabbit. Rabbits never moved that slowly. Terry acted like he had never even seen the rabbit. Davy walked quietly to the spot where the rabbit had disappeared. He immediately saw the animal breathing heavily, lying on its side with what looked like a little piece of its guts hanging out of a gash near its stomach. Davy wasn't about to do any good deeds for this animal. He figured its number was up, and he would get Terry to finish it off.

"Get him, Terry," he said.

Terry sniffed at the wide-eyed rabbit and wagged his tail franticly but made no aggressive move. Davy had figured the dog would pounce on the rabbit and rip its guts or its throat out—but nothing like that happened. The snarly-haired dog cocked his head looking at Davy and just stood there wagging his tail.

"I said get him, Terry," Davy commanded.

The dog just looked up again at Davy and then began to walk away. Davy couldn't take it. Nothing ever went his way. He ran up to Terry and kicked the undernourished dog as hard as he could. He could hear a "snap" near the area of the dog's hip as Terry rolled howling on the ground. Davy immediately panicked. He was afraid his mother would hear the howling and come to investigate. Then he would be in real trouble. A good-sized rock was lying nearby. He picked it up and raised it high over his head and brought it down on the dog's skull. Terry quit howling. Davy grabbed the dog by the legs and began to drag him towards some thick brush—suddenly he remembered the rabbit. The rabbit was still lying on its side, the little bit of guts sticking out of its side. "You started all this," Davy cried and kicked the rabbit in the guts, turned around and grabbed Terry and hid him under the thick brush. He would just tell his parents that the dog had vanished while running after a deer.

After that, it seemed like one incident led to the next. Like the time in Modesto a year or so later when Davy's mom had sent him to the little Chinese laundry to pick up the Sunday-go-to-meeting clothes. As Davy was coming out of the laundry with the freshly washed and ironed clothes, he saw a little Chinese girl tossing a small rubber ball against the side of the building and catching it in her fast little hands. Davy watched her in silence and marveled at her speed and dexterity. She never once missed catching the ball. He decided he wanted to try to throw and catch the little ball too, plus he wanted to get a better look at the delicate, nimble little girl. He had seen many Chinese before, but he couldn't remember ever seeing a little girl around his age, up close anyway.

Davy put the basket of fresh smelling clothes on the wooden walkway at the corner of the alley and walked up to the girl. She must have seen him out of the corner of her eye because she suddenly stopped playing ball and just stood there holding the ball behind her back.

"Hi," Davy said. "Can I throw your ball?"

The girl took a quick look at Davy in his ragged and dusty clothes and in a quiet voice said, "Yes," and held the red ball out to Davy.

All the while, Davy had been looking wonderingly at the girl. Her hair was so black and shiny; it reached the small of her back in two long braids. She was wearing a many-buttoned strange little dress—the last button reaching almost to the top of her throat. A dress, if you could call it that, unlike anything the American girls wore. *Why this girl isn't even an American*, Davy reasoned. Staring at her cute round face he realized the color wasn't even white or reddish-brown-white, like when the sun burned it. This color had a little pale yellow to it. He had heard his dad talk about the heathen yellow man, and now he was staring down at one, only it was a cute little girl. Davy suddenly got a little angry.

"Anyone can throw and catch a ball," he said and threw it at the side of the building.

The ball came back faster than he expected and hit him square on the nose, making his eyes water. The girl gave a little giggle and, bending down, picked the ball up and handed it back to Davy, whose face had turned red. This time he would not throw the ball so hard, and he would really keep an eye on it, he thought.

Davy's father barely made enough money for the family to squeak by, thus his shoes were usually worn, often with split soles flapping. He took no pride in his shoes and often neglected to tie them properly, as was this case. He let the ball fly at the wall with less force, but it hit where the siding was uneven and took a bad bounce to the left. Davy took a step and reached for it, but his foot landed on his shoelace, and he ended up falling hard on the packed dirt, scraping his hands and knees. This time the girl laughed right out loud. It immediately reminded Davy of the Mexican lady's laugh when the pretty tan and white cow had shit on him. Scrambling to his feet, he reached for the Chinese girl's braid and pulled it hard, straight back, her startled little face looking up at him. He looked into the shiny black eyes that seemed to register fear and pain, and he liked what he saw. Davy felt powerful, kind of like when he brought the rock down on Terry.

He knew he'd get in trouble if he hurt the girl, so he kissed her instead, hard on the mouth.

The girl was fast and much stronger than Davy thought. She suddenly spun around and, hitting his hand away from her braid, called out to him in clear English, "You smelly boy," and ran through the side door of the laundry.

Davy looked down at his dirty clothes then he lifted both arms and smelled under them. *Not a bad smell*, he thought. *Smells just like I always smell. Who cares what some China girl says? Chinese and Mexicans don't know good from bad no how.* Didn't he always hear his pa or some of his friends at the blacksmith's shop say that?

"Hey, hold on there," Dave shouted from the porch.

The wagon had already passed the house and the group on foot was just pulling even to it. The Pomos obediently stopped as Dave walked rapidly towards them carrying the 12-gauge.

"Where do you diggers think you're going?" Dave said as he came out on the road.

From behind the reins, Walter, who had been sitting on a fern-filled burlap cushion to ease the bumps, turned towards Dave as he approached and said, "Dave, why are you doing this again? Ever since you squatters have moved in, you've been coming out to greet us holding a shotgun."

"We're not squatters," Davy said. "We're homesteaders."

Walter had to smile to himself every time he heard Dave speak. His accent was so filled, as was his pa's, with the Ozark hills that at times he could barely understand him.

Tom Fowler had left his native Arkansas in 1855 when Dave was just a little boy. The Fowlers, originally from Ireland, were among some of the first settlers trying to carve out a living in the wild Ozarks. As soon as the announcement of gold in California made its way into the Ozarks, Tom had wanted to move the family west to make his fortune. Financial matters, the reluctance of his wife, and his inability to first make up his mind and go, had delayed the journey. He knew that there wasn't that much gold being found in California anymore, but he still wanted to move west along with many an American dreamer.

"Dave, why do you call us 'diggers'?" Walter said.

He had asked this before, but wanted to see if Dave would say something different. He didn't.

"Because 'diggers' rhymes with 'niggers,' and that's all you bunch of injuns are to me," Dave said knowingly, pulling up in a huff a few feet away from the wagon.

Exact same answer as last time, Walter thought. *Doesn't seem to be much original thinking going on in Dave's head.* Walter was quite good at original thinking. He had been the fastest natural learner that the rancheria teacher had ever seen. He had learned English so quickly it was amazing. Once he learned to read, he was insatiable. By the time he was twelve, he had read *Don Quixote*, both *The Odyssey* and *The Iliad*, and *The Last of the Mohicans* several times over. He was especially fascinated by Cooper's "Mohecians." He didn't think that the white man knew what he was talking about—most of the east coast Indians were sneaking around butchering people with tomahawks. Walter didn't even know what a tomahawk was until he learned to read. Sure, his people had stone axes, and a few had metal ones, but they used them to split redwood for their huts or to club a rabbit they had trapped. They had no intention of using them on settlers or on the Miwoks to the south of them.

The teacher was so impressed with Walter that he even gave him the key to the school. Walter would let himself in most Saturdays and Sundays and spend all day going over the books and practice writing with the chalk on the board. Chalk wasn't cheap, the teacher had told him, so he had to make one stick last a long time. He only used the chalk to write something special like, "Greetings friends, my name is Walter, and some day I am going to be the teacher or a great writer like Mr. Cervantes or Homer, but not like Mr. James Fenimore Cooper."

Walter would look at all the insects and such that the teacher kept in the jars. The big carpenter beetle and the baby rattlesnake fascinated him the most. They looked so perfect in death, floating in the clear liquid. The first time he saw them he didn't even think they were dead, but that the teacher had trapped them in the jar and had taught them to live in water. He didn't really agree with killing all these animals and putting them in jars. It would have been so much nicer just to walk outside and hunt for them going about their daily lives. A carpenter beetle rolling a little piece of dung up a small mound was much more entertaining and educational than one suspended dead in a jar.

The teacher knew what to do with a boy such as Walter. The governor, under pressure from certain groups, had created several institutes of higher learning throughout the state solely for the higher education of the native population. One of these schools was in San Francisco, and Walter had no hesitation saying yes when at sixteen the teacher told him that only a very few boys from the various tribes were being asked to attend. Walter's parents thought it odd that he would want to go off to a big city and live and study with various Indian boys when he could roam the beautiful hills hunting and fishing, or gather seaweed and mussels from the ocean, but they made no objections. They thought their son a little strange anyway since he first started taking such keen pleasure in the white man's education. They also knew that if they tried to stop a young man from doing what his heart was set upon, only resentment and turmoil would follow.

So one day in June, off to town went Walter and Mr. Hobson, the teacher who had sought out the position at the rancheria school, thinking that there he could actually do some good. He was a studious and caring young man who had felt for many years now that the American government and many of its citizens in general had treated the natives appallingly. Why, less than twenty years ago, some of the wealthier land owners in the county, a few of them even native Californios, had treated the Indians who worked the vast tracts of land like slaves—chaining them to walls at night and attaching cannonballs on chains to their ankles by day. This was no longer allowed, but other ill treatment remained. Perhaps the largest was just plain apathy. No one gave a damn about the natives, and many of them secretly just wished that the smallpox epidemic of 1837-38 had wiped them all out. Instead the epidemic left the people a shell of what they once were—much of the heart and soul of the tribes with their many customs and traditions were shattered and buried, along with their diseased bodies.

Mr. Hobson wanted to try to do good in the world, and saw teaching as one step. In turn, he too was being educated at the rancheria school. The students and their parents awakened new thoughts in him every day. Sitting next to Walter, waiting for the stage to San Francisco, he felt good that he was helping one student to go all the way. Walter had wonderful potential and, given the opportunity, could be a true standout in any society.

The rail line was not yet completed, so it took them three days to reach the large city. At the town of Sausalito they boarded a ferry that took them across San Francisco Bay to the city docks. Walter was speechless, taking everything in. He had truly never imagined that there could be so many people in one place. The ride on the ferry was beautiful and peaceful and highlighted the grandness of nature—but what greeted them at the docks was amazing: people of every size, color, and dress coming and going, running and laughing, talking and sitting. He heard so many strange languages, voices, and accents in two minutes, his head was confused. Wonderful-looking fishing vessels pulled up to the docks unloading crabs, oysters, and strange types of fish he had never seen. He felt a little less confused when he saw one boat unloading salmon. Those, he felt sorry for. It had been hard enough for them to elude the nets and spears of his people so that they could spawn and their young return to the ocean. And now, he could see where many of their young, now grown, had ended up—being tossed unceremoniously to leather-gloved hands that packed them away in crates full of ice.

He had little time for reflection, though, as they made their way to a buggy that proceeded away from the docks up a busy street. Mr. Hobson had told him that the school and dormitory were inside the Presidio grounds, originally an old Spanish military outpost built to keep an eye on San Francisco Bay. That was where Walter, so far, had spent the happiest two years of his life. The school was called "The Aboriginal Institute for Higher Learning," and most people thought of it as a joke, a waste of money and effort dreamed up by a group of bleeding hearts and do-gooders. After a month or so of classes, the teacher and dignitaries and officials who visited the school could see that this was no joke. These Indian boys were sharp. They were committed and dedicated to learning and had no intention of letting down their parents and their tribes. It didn't matter if they were Ohlone, Hupa, Miwok, or Pomo—they sucked up knowledge like a sponge because they wanted to. They needed to. For many of them it was simple. They wanted to be as good or better than the whites at their own game. Yes, they loved the amazing history of the wide world. And some especially excelled at math and science, but everyone there knew that they were given the opportunity to do one thing—become smarter and wiser than the average settler's son who threw rocks and made fun of them and called them "diggers" when they came to town.

The two years seemed to fly by for Walter. Of course there were a few bad days and an occasional fight—a bunch of boys from different areas and backgrounds thrown together will always fight. But none of these fights were very serious, and they never lasted long. No one wanted to get expelled. At the end of the two years, anyone that knew anything about the school thought them a grand success. Walter, along with most of the boys, was urged to go on to college. One scholarship to the newly opened University of California at Berkeley was awarded, and an overwhelmed Ohlone boy won the prize. But now, a year later, those golden days at the Presidio were gone, and Walter still hadn't decided if he wanted to go on to college. And where was he now? Staring at a filthy, smelly, jaundice tinged, sexually confused racist holding a Parker 12-gauge.

"David, you're not a homesteader. I've heard your father is arranging to buy the land you've settled on, but until the title is legally filled, you're what's referred to as a 'squatter.'"

Dave didn't like that term one bit. Every time he heard that word, he thought of what they did each day in the outhouse, and how his pa thought he should be responsible for the maintenance of that stinky place.

"Look, Mr. Know-it-all, my name's Dave, not David or Davy, and you ain't answered my question. Just where do you think you're going?"

"Well, Dave, it's like this. There's going to be a big dance in town tomorrow night, and we've been asked to perform."

Dave was astounded at this news. Why would anyone from town want to watch a bunch of heathens jump around?

"Well maybe I'd like to see a little advance performance right now. Why don't you just get down and show me some of that fancy footwork."

Before Walter could say anything, the quiet elder who had been sitting in the back covered in a red blanket suddenly stood up, the blanket falling away and revealing no clothing underneath. He shouted, "Go," pointing ahead while staring at Dave. Dave took a step back, amazed. Why, that old Indian's member was larger than his was. Dave had often taken a ruler to his own member and knew it to be approximately two and a half inches in the relaxed position. This old man's was probably four or five. When Dave thought about horses or cows mounting, or the frightened look in that pretty little Chinese girl's eyes, or even the fat German boy's smelly thing, his member had the capability to grow to exactly five and a half inches; who could know what that old Indian's could measure out at.

Walter suddenly gave a flick of the reins and moved slowly on.

"Bye, Dave," he said.

The elder sat back down and again covered himself with the red blanket. Dave just stood there on the side of the road holding the shotgun and waxing philosophical about members.

Chapter 3

Juan Rodrigo Fuentes, nickname El Zapo, the cripple, left Santiago Chile with the authorities hot on his trail. He had raped and strangled a young nun. This was the fourth time he had committed such atrocities throughout Chile. Juan only violated and killed nuns. He would have done the same to priests, but he would have only had half the satisfaction. Juan was a macho. He had dignity. It would be disgusting to violate another man. El Zapo murdered and raped nuns because he cursed God. He wanted to offend God for making him a cripple, and he came to think of himself as the devil incarnate.

He was born into a wealthy family. His parents couldn't wait for the day of his birth. They presented themselves to the world as pious Catholics, but secretly they consulted with an ancient *curandera*. The shamanistic witch had assured them they would have a healthy son to carry on the family name. There was a troubling sign though, the evening Consuela, the mother, went into labor. The hooting of an owl was heard outside the bedroom window, and the midwife had to dispose of a large black spider that had crawled up on the bed.

When the long painful labor was finally over, the baby, surely enough a boy, was born with one leg shriveled and shorter than the other, and immediately, the parents felt as though they were cursed. They neglected to place all their faith in God when they went to the *curandera*, and now they were being punished. It was hard for them to watch their little boy grow up. The other wealthy *hacendados* had strong boys who ran like the wind and learned to ride horses almost as soon as they could walk. Their son dragged his leg grotesquely when he moved. As soon as the boy was old enough to understand, they told him that he had been cursed by God. The condition of his leg was not an unfortunate act of nature, but was the direct result of God's hand squeezing his little leg inside the womb. Every time the other children teased him and called him cripple, a part of the sun would vanish from his sad eyes. Eventually Juan began to see the world as a dark place. If God could curse him, why couldn't he curse God? After all, didn't the devil curse God?

Juan told no one, but at a young age he decided to throw his cards in with the devil. He seldom went outside, so as to avoid the other children. His complexion became almost white and transparent from lack of sun. His parents brought in a tutor for him, and he studied and learned much. He became wickedly intelligent, and by the time he was sixteen, he had raped and killed his first victim. It was a young girl dressed in white who had just received her first communion. Juan had made a plan and had been watching these children for several weeks. He knew when the communion day was, and he wanted to nab a girl when she would leave the church after being close to Jesus. The church was on the outskirts of the village. Many of the girls would be walking ahead of their parents, talking and playing, heading towards the town square where there was to be a fiesta. The vegetation alongside the road was thick, almost impenetrable in places. Being alone so much, Juan had spent much time listening to birds and animals and had learned to perfectly mimic the sounds of many of them. He could easily mimic the cry of a baby; and that's what he did, hiding near an opening in the thick brush along the road.

"A baby, a baby," one of the girls cried, and vanished into the growth to investigate, another girl following shortly behind.

Juan moved fast. When he was out in public he always moved slowly, dragging his leg, but on his own, when no one was looking, he practiced running and could move with surprising speed. As soon as the girls entered the brush, he darted out and knocked both of them senseless with a club. He picked up what looked to be the lighter of the girls and ran to a horse-drawn wagon he had waiting. He threw the unconscious girl in the back and took off down a narrow winding road that climbed deep into the mountain. The road was overgrown and seldom used except for coca farmers who cultivated high on the side of the mountain. Juan knew exactly where he was going; he had traveled the road earlier and had removed any obstacles that might impede the speed of the wagon. He traveled for almost an hour, turning down several crossroads. He knew he had to operate fast. It wouldn't take long for the people to realize the girl was missing and come back on horses and search the area. He had been watching the girl often, keeping an eye if she awoke. He pulled off into a barely passable opening and proceeded until the jungle swallowed him up. He got out of the wagon and threw some water from a canteen on the girl's face. She had an ugly welt on the side of her head, oozing blood, but she soon came to. Juan had dressed himself totally in black and wore a black cape.

"I am the devil," he said, and ripped the girls communion dress off her.

He raped and strangled her. She was so weak from the blow she put up no resistance. No one was there to hear her piteous screams in the thick highland jungle. Juan left her body where it lay, got back on the main road, and wound his way down the other side of the mountain. He proceeded home and pulled the wagon into the hacienda barn and stalls. No one saw him until he approached his home. Now, truly Juan had become a devil, and he gloried in it.

Now, four years and five killings later, Juan was one step away from the law when he boarded a ship bound for Monterey in California. Among the clothes he had packed were the garments of a young seminary student, a priest in training. What more fitting way was there to enter California? Would not everyone trust a pious young man studying to become a priest?

During the long passage up the coastline from Santiago to Monterey, El Zapo heard the voice talking to him every night. It was Bael the devil who advised him.

"Be cautious," the voice said, "you must become a man of God who secretly worships evil. All the priests are that way anyway. They can't wait to stick it to a nun. Some even prefer little boys. Don't be in a hurry. Remember, the devil works in mysterious ways."

By the time the ship reached Monterey, Juan Fuentes had turned himself into a traveling seminary student who was headed for the Mission at Carmel to further his knowledge in the ways of God. He had some forged papers with him that he would present to the priests at the mission, introducing him as a traveling seminary student wishing to stay at Carmel and study how the word of God was being spread in this growing land. He thought it would be to his advantage if people heard that he was independently wealthy, so the papers announced that he was from a wealthy family and that he insisted upon paying his way for everything. After arriving at the mission and presenting himself, he inquired if they had received the letter from the bishop in Santiago requesting he be allowed to stay and study. No such letter had been received, but all agreed that the mail was slow and erratic and sometimes took forever to arrive. In the meantime, of course, he was welcome to stay. Such a fine and frail young man, so pious and humble, a pity about his deformity. Evidently, though, he was quite wealthy.

The Mission at Carmel was in shambles. It had been established one hundred years earlier by the Franciscan priest Junipero Serra to spread the word of God to the native population and to establish Spain's presence in Alta, California. The original adobe church was crumbling and in disrepair. New bright white wooden churches had been built in Carmel and four miles down the road in Monterey. Now mostly curiosity seekers visited the old mission. There was a newer rectory on the mission grounds where two priests lived. This was where Juan would stay and study.

El Zapo became quietly enraged when one of the doddering priests mentioned to him, "Did you know, my son, that the Holy Father Serra was also lame?"

So, he too had been cursed by God, and the weakling did nothing about it except ride around on a filthy mule, babbling about Jesus to a bunch of naked Indians. He could have been strong and lustful like me and sided in with the true ruler of the world. Juan soon found that though Father Serra had not died at Carmel, his remains had been buried under the floor of the old adobe mission. It would only be proper to show a fellow cripple a little respect, deemed Juan. On the third night of his arrival, after the old priests had retired, he entered the mission by candlelight. Near the altar, under the cracked concrete floor, rested the remains of Serra. Using a knife he had brought along, Juan pried up a section of the concrete, revealing the dirt underneath. Again using the knife, he quickly dug a hole over the remains of this man of God. Exposing himself, and thinking about all the nuns he would torture and rape, he ejaculated into the hole. After a pause to collect himself, he defecated into it.

Then, feeling thoroughly satisfied, he filled the hole back up and carefully reinstalled the concrete. *That should fix that son of a bitch,* he thought. *If he's somewhere with his inept little God, perhaps he's noticing an unpleasant odor.* Extinguishing the candle, he crept from the mission by moonlight.

The young theologian quickly grew bored with Carmel. Monterey was where the action was. The large Catholic church there had a building nearby that housed the nuns. It didn't take El Zapo long to pick out several ripe, juicy ones that would be suitable for sacrifice to the devil. His plan was simply to rape and murder his way up the California coast, perhaps even travel inland in search of prey. He thought his masquerade to be a stroke of genius and was looking forward to the first time he would see the look of shock and dismay on the face of some misguided nun when she realized a man of God was attacking her. He would be patient for now though, keeping an eye on his prey and learning their established routines.

One foggy day while sitting alone in the courtyard next to the old mission reading his favorite book, Dante's Inferno, he was startled by a sound. He looked up to see a beautiful young woman, dressed all in black with a large gold crucifix resting on her bosom, approach the door to the church and, crossing herself reverently, go inside.

The woman was Conchetta Lombardi, Angelina's sister, who had moved with her brother from San Francisco to Monterey. She had hired a man to drive her from Monterey to the holy mission church at Carmel so she could pray to the Madonna for a husband. She was twenty-five years old and looked a lot like Angelina. She was the youngest of the Lombardis; her mother had given birth to her late in life, and that act of giving birth had killed her. Conchetta's father had done his best to provide for the family. Life had been hard in Genoa. Mario, the brother, had started working at various jobs at a young age; so had Angelina.

Their father worked at two jobs, and that is what every-one said killed him. His heart failed at a young age, and now the Lombardis were alone. The only relatives they knew of were living in Rome, they had never seen them, they were on the mother's side, but there had been some type of squabble and their mother had seldom spoken of them.

At the time of their father's death, Angelina was already thought of as an old maid, but actually she was just like Dom; she simply couldn't make up her mind. It was Mario who suggested they all move to America. From the time he was a young boy he loved the sea, and he soon excelled at the skills and knowledge of a fisherman. He had heard stories of California, mainly San Francisco and Monterey. It was being said that off those waters the fish practically jumped into your boat. A man could become wealthy in no time. The three Lombardis really made an odd trio. Each was ten years of age apart. When they agreed to book passage for America, Conchetta was fif-teen, Mario twenty-five, and Angelina, a stunningly beau-tiful thirty-five-year-old maid.

When their mother had begun labor that third and final time, their father had said wonderingly, "Your mother is like clockwork, every ten years she gives birth. It is truly amazing."

A year after she was gone, he announced to his friends while drinking wine, "God took my wife because he needed more order and precision in heaven. No one has ever heard of a woman who gave birth so reliably three times every ten years. Such a marvelous creature obvi-ously was needed in heaven as an example," but then he reluctantly began to cry.

When the Lombardi's ship finally rounded the horn and the dream of California was really taking shape, the three Lombardis were convinced life would be glorious in America. Angelina would finally marry a handsome, kind, wealthy man. Mario would own his own fishing boat, perhaps a fleet of them, and become rich. And young Conchetta would continue her schooling and, since she loved to sing, study opera and one day perform on all the great stages throughout the world.

It didn't quite go that way. San Francisco was a confusing, ramshackle sort of place. Construction was constantly going on. The town seemed to lack planning and order. The Americans were brash and loud. Though most had only been in the city a short time themselves, they looked down on the horde of foreigners invading the golden shores. The Italians were "wops, dagos, eye-ties." They were greasy, oily, and stank of garlic. You couldn't trust them, and given the chance, the males would stick a knife between your ribs. The women didn't shave under their arms, most had mustaches, but all agreed they were wild in the sack. This was what the Lombardis soon learned to face in San Francisco, but they made the best of it. They soon found their biggest problem to be their lack of English. Mario was the only one who had picked up a few words in Genoa. He soon found companionship and a job with other Italian fishermen at the bay. Several of them spoke passable English, and Mario begged them to teach him. What he learned, he passed on to his sisters. All three of them lived at a boarding house, where the sisters shared a room, and Mario was close by in a small one of his own. Angelina found a job in a restaurant. Conchetta did attend sort of a finishing school run by a woman who had been a teacher in Palermo, and Mario worked on the boat.

Angelina felt the loneliness that goes with displacement the most, and shortly she married, though not the man of her dreams. For the first time in their lives, the three were split apart. Angelina had wanted Conchetta to come live with her and her husband. But it didn't take long to see that her husband wouldn't like that. Mario tried to keep an eye on Conchetta, but agreed when she suggested she move in with Mrs. DiBella, the teacher, who had a spare room, and who had come to enjoy Conchetta's wit and company. Conchetta had progressed very rapidly under the tutelage of Mrs. DiBella; by the time she was eighteen she excelled in both English and Spanish. The latter was simple for her to pick up, with its close proximity to Italian. Mrs. DiBella began to turn more and more of the teaching duties over to Conchetta. Soon, she was teaching full-time at the school and hiring herself out as a tutor on evenings and weekends. She had little time for a social life. Occasionally men pursued her, but she kept them at a distance. She was beginning to think she was turning into her sister. None of the men seemed good enough. She visited her sister and brother often, and on Sundays they got in the habit of meeting at one of the better restaurants for lunch. After a while, most of the men gave up trying to court Conchetta. They thought she was too pretty and stuck-up. Her beauty intimidated many of them. She carried herself in an aloof manner, as her sister did.

This was the pattern of her life until one day at lunch Mario announced to his sisters that he had finally saved up enough money to go into a partnership with a fellow Genovese immigrant on the purchase of a fishing boat. They would sail the boat down to Monterey and go after anchovies and sardines. They would make a mint. His friend had a sister living with his parents in Monterey. Mario was smitten with her and couldn't wait to make the move to Monterey.

Around this time, the accident that claimed Angelina's husband occurred. She suggested Conchetta move in with her. Conchetta considered the pros and cons. Yes, she would make her sister happy, and alleviate some of the loneliness, and she did enjoy daily bantering with her. She would not have to pay room and board, but could go on teaching and save most of her money. Against this were mainly two facts: Her nearly nonexistent social life would surely cease to exist, and Angelina would be grilling her any time she went out. But the worst of it was that she felt that by living with her sister she would complete her transition into an old maid. The two sisters dressed in black, both were attractive and aloof, one widowed, the other clinging to her virginity as if it were a rosary. It didn't take long for her to decide. Conchetta was much tougher than she looked. She had entered life with no mother. It had been hard growing up, being raised by only her father and neighborhood friends. True, Angelina had been like a mother to her, but nonetheless she learned at a young age that you needed to be strong to survive. Life had many disappointing and painful moments to throw at you. Only your will and determination could pull you through. She would feel freer and less trapped at the DiBella's. She would remain there for now, and who knew, life could turn on a dime. Mario had suddenly received a cupid's arrow to the heart. It would not be impossible for the same to happen to her.

Indeed, events did take a sudden though somewhat predictable turn. Only a month after Mario had left for Monterey, the sisters received a letter informing them that Mario and his sweetheart had suddenly eloped to Santa Cruz and had gotten married. It looked like the fishing business was going to be a great success, and Mario had gotten a loan enabling him to purchase a spacious, newer house in her parent's neighborhood. He mentioned that at the first chance he and his wife Lena would come to San Francisco for a visit. He also said that he knew Angelina had plans to open a café and couldn't be coaxed to move, but what about Conchetta? There were plenty of rooms in the new house, and Lena had said it would be nice to have company around when Mario was off at sea. Many people were moving to Monterey to pursue the sardines and anchovies. A tutor would have no trouble finding students.

The sisters were overjoyed at Mario's happiness and success. Conchetta's spirit and curiosity were awakened by Mario's suggestion. She had been in San Francisco for many years now, and what had happened? Mainly nothing. Sure, she had stayed healthy and had learned a trade, something of true value for a woman of these times.

But outside of that? Monterey sounded fresh and exciting, and perhaps there she could find the man of her dreams. With little hesitation, her mind made up, she decided to make the move.

Angelina was upset that her sister was moving, but knowing her to be headstrong and wishing her to be happy, waved with a smile on her face as the stage pulled out one day with Conchetta aboard, bound for Monterey.

Monterey indeed was a beautiful town, perched next to a bay filled with fishing boats. The surrounding coastline was rugged and haunting. Conchetta was enthusiastically welcomed into her brother's home and immediately hit it off with his wife, Lena. During the day, while Mario was fishing, the two of them would do the shopping or spend time at Lena's parents visiting over some sweets and coffee. Lena came from a large family. She had two sisters and two brothers. One brother was married, but the other one, eighteen-year-old Tony, soon became completely infatuated with Conchetta. At first she was flattered by his intentions, but after a while it became tedious. Tony was a nice boy and quite handsome, but that was it; he was only still a boy.

Mario had been right. Conchetta soon developed a clientele who employed her as tutor for their children. She would either go to their homes for the lessons, or often they would come over to the house to study in the large, sunny parlor where she conducted piano lessons with some of the girls. She noticed she was receiving favorable looks from some of the town's bachelors, but outside of Tony following her around at times like a puppy dog, no one had actually yet come by to call. Conchetta was happy enough. She did Miss her sister and wrote her often telling her all the interesting goings on at Monterey. Angelina wrote that she had found a place to rent and had actually opened up her own café. She promised to come soon for a visit.

Many of her students were Catholics, and she had heard it often said that if one really wanted to get their prayers answered they should go to the old mission church to pray. The Lombardis had been brought up devout Catholics, but as they grew older, all three of them spent less and less time at mass. Conchetta figured she could use all the help she could get. She had also heard that the mission grounds, though overgrown, were filled with old trees, shrubs, and flowers. Over the years, many varieties of roses had been planted, and the place was said to be a profusion of colors. It wouldn't take her long to get there by wagon, so one foggy Saturday morning away she went in a rented wagon. The June air was damp, but not very cold. Along the way Conchetta assured herself that she mostly was going to the old mission out of curiosity and to see the sights, and it couldn't hurt to say a little prayer or two while there. She would say a simple prayer to the Lord requesting health and happiness for her family and friends. And she would say one little prayer to the Madonna. A woman, she reasoned, would understand best. She would pray to the Madonna to allow her to meet a fine young man, her age or perhaps a little older.

Chapter 4

El Zapo's curiosity was immediately aroused upon spotting the woman. Not many people seemed to visit the old church, certainly not such a woman of beauty, unaccompanied by another soul. What could she possibly want? Why would one such as her have need of prayer and solitude? He noticed a side door was slightly ajar near where the altar of the church was situated. Rising and going to the door, he could barely see in. He spotted the woman kneeling at the altar, facing a large statue of the Madonna depicted in her white and pale blue robes. The woman's lips were moving. He could barely hear her, but soon realized she was requesting aid from the slut behind the altar in Italian. Juan had learned Italian at a young age, and had little trouble making out that she was asking for help in meeting a sweetheart. She was saying she was inwardly lonely, and was lacking a husband and children for her life to be complete. *Oh, what an opportunity,* Juan thought. *She has practically walked into my hands. So she wants a husband and child. Well, I can give her what a husband could, and maybe when I'm done she would indeed carry the seed of a child. Such a pity she won't live to find out.*

Conchetta wasn't prepared for the feeling that assailed her once she entered the church. Looking around, she mostly saw neglect. The sanctuary smelled like mice and mold, yet the essence of true spirituality hovered over the decrepitude of the place. Pale light filtered through the blue, red, and gold stained glass windows. The altar was beautiful, simply made, the savior hanging forlorn and alone on an intricately carved wooden cross. To his left was the Madonna, pure and resolute. On his right was Saint Francis holding a dove. She had never seen Saint Francis depicted on the front of an altar. In this wild land, evidently someone had thought the need of presenting a man who placed animals on a level with humans a necessary part of worship. That bold statement was what inspired her. She said her prayers, bleeding her heart out in honesty, and thinking that a place such as this, cold and damp as it was, surely was a house of God.

Disturbed from her reverences by the sound of an opening door, she turned to see the entrance of a priest. Her solitude lost, she crossed herself and headed towards the door. Juan spoke to her as she passed by.

"Excuse me, Miss, I am so sorry for having interrupted you."

Looking up, she met the dark eyes of a young priest. His Latin looks were set in a pale, almost transparent face.

He had addressed her in English, and in turn she responded, "I was just leaving, Father. Such a lovely church you have here."

"Oh, it is indeed a lovely church, Miss, but you honor me mistakenly by addressing me as Father. I am but a humble seminary student, hoping soon to take my final vows. I am on sabbatical from South America, studying under the local priests and learning the ways of the church in your beautiful California," Juan said.

For some reason, Conchetta felt a little awkward or uncomfortable talking alone in the dark isle of the church, and continued her progress towards the door, which the young theologian held open for her. Stepping out into the morning light, she briefly studied his face more clearly. He was about her age, she thought. His black hair was long, combed straight back. He had a thin mustache, too precisely trimmed for a man of God, she thought. The carefully groomed feature spoke to her of vanity. *Oh well, it's probably natural, he is young after all and not yet a priest.* His mouth, though, disturbed her. The corners of his thin lips seemed to turn slightly up and tighten into what looked like an arrogant, suppressed grin. He was very thin, slightly taller than average. He intently glared momentarily at her, then shifted his eyes away as if he had been caught, she thought.

"Do you come here to pray often?" he inquired. "I have only been here several weeks, and have seen very few visitors. Most go to the newer churches where mass is held."

He had spoken to Conchetta in perfect Italian and was openly smiling at her. What a strange bird, she thought. He had noticed her accent and boldly switched languages. She decided she definitely did not like this fellow. She had, of course, noticed that he limped and slightly dragged one foot after the other, and for some reason she concluded that it was an old affliction; possibly he was born with it. Perhaps this physical hindrance contributed to his odd manner, she thought.

She decided not to show surprise at anything he might say in any language, and answering him while looking away towards her wagon, in Italian said, "This is the first time I've visited this mission. Many people have told me about it and how beautiful the grounds are, so I decided to see for myself."

At this time, one of the old priests came towards them through the courtyard garden.

"Oh, Juan, my son, I see you're entertaining a visitor. We have so few these days; it is such a pleasure. How do you do, young lady? I am Father Donovan, and I see you've already met Juan. He is such a fine young man, and one day soon will be an exceptional priest."

I doubt that, thought Conchetta, but her focus now was turned towards this new arrival. Here now, was a man more befitting of wearing the robe. His wrinkled old face was beaming with a friendly smile. His pale blue eyes were watery and merry, reflecting an inner kindness and peace. He spoke with the thick Irish accent that Conchetta had always found charming upon hearing it.

"I only wish the sun was out," he was saying. "I do enjoy showing visitors the grounds on a bright, sunny day. The flowers practically dance in the light. Come, come, young lady, surely you will not begrudge an old man's pleasure and will allow me to show you these wonderful grounds. What might be your name now? And surely you have a moment to spare."

"I am Conchetta Lombardi, Father, and yes I would enjoy a tour of the grounds. I have heard nothing but praise for the beauty of this old mission."

"Well spoken," he said, and taking her lightly by the arm, began to escort her towards the garden. "Will you come with us, Juan?" he said.

"No, Father. I have to write some letters. You two enjoy yourselves. It was a pleasure to meet you, Miss Lombardi," he said, and excusing himself, he walked away.

Good, thought Conchetta, *but then again maybe I judge too harshly. First impressions can often be misleading.* Dismissing her thoughts, she turned her attention to the lovely surroundings.

"Father Serra founded this mission in seventeen seventy, originally in Monterey," the old priest was saying. "It was moved to Carmel shortly after for convenience in obtaining wood and water, we are told. So now, looking around you, you see the result of one hundred years of careful, loving planting. Do you not wonder and admire the beauty of nature, and the Lord's bounty, Conchetta?"

"Most certainly, Father. Oh, this is a special place," she said, looking around.

She saw large, twisted, silvery leafed olive trees, two thick-trunked fig trees, their broad leaves not yet attaining full dimension. All around were vibrant, colorful shrubs; azaleas she recognized, and rhododendrons, fuchsias, and both white and purple lilac. Bulbs of every type were blooming about. The air of the garden was intoxicatingly fragrant and full of butterflies. Wisteria was clinging to the old adobe walls of the mission.

The tour of the grounds seemed over before it started, she thought. Father Donovan, in his brogue, had been speaking almost nonstop, pointing out all the different varieties of plants and trees. He even knew the names of some of the priests of bygone days, who had planted a certain tree, or had designed some of the intricate cobble and brick paths that encircled the grounds.

"Conchetta Lombardi, you must come back in three weeks," he was saying. "All these wonderful roses you've been seeing will be beginning to bloom, and the rest of the garden should be in full color. Bring a companion, some friends. I enjoy seeing the smile this place brings to people's faces. We have so much fog here, but try to pick a day when the sun is out; then it is truly magnificent."

"I'll be back, Father," she said, arriving at the wagon. "I now understand the reverence for this church and grounds, and I do so want to see the roses in bloom. Thank you for such a wonderful tour."

Climbing aboard and taking the reins, she had almost forgotten about the strange seminary student. Looking around, she saw no sign of him and for an odd reason was glad. He had a disturbing effect upon her, and had given her the impression that he could not be trusted. *I'm turning too much into my sister*, she thought. Angelina was the one who was always talking about women's intuition. Where was her intuition concerning that drunkard she had married, huh? Oh well, she had said her prayers and had enjoyed herself. Pushing thoughts of the young man out of her mind, she turned her attention to the ride home.

Damn that old priest, El Zapo was thinking. *I would have loved to have ruined that pretty thing, and to have seen the light vanish from those large eyes.* He had been watching the tour of the grounds. It was easy to follow them with the many trees and foliage as cover. He had been so close that he heard most of their conversation. *That old sanctimonious priest,* he thought, *I think I'll put him out of his misery. Always talking about the beauty of life and God working in mysterious ways, the old fool's too blind to see that darkness and death are the only real winners. When he's begging for his last breath, covered in his own vomit and excrement, pain assailing him in uncontrollable waves, then let's hear him proclaim the beauty of life. And that Italian whore—she's no better. She was in there praying for a man to come between her legs. Imagine that, in there, praying to a virgin for a man to mount her. And they have the audacity to call this dump a holy place. Well, well, this is actually better than I hoped for in a way. If the old man hadn't come around, I would have taken my enjoyment out on her, and it would have been all over. Now I can have some fun planning it.*

Juan Fuentes had heard Conchetta mention that she lived in Monterey with her brother and his wife. She wouldn't be hard to locate there. Any young male in town surely would have spotted her. *How many arrogant Italian beauties could there be in that fish-stinking town,* he thought. Or, he reasoned, he could wait for her to come to him. She had said she would return when the roses were in bloom. *How fitting, maybe I'll put a rose on her grave, or more likely I'll shove one down her throat, thorns and all, before I strangle that delicate neck.* And away he limped, a twisted black gowned spider feeding off his own poison.

Three days later, Father Donavan, after having prayed in the chapel, took the path that led from the back of the mission towards the bluffs above the ocean. He thought he needed a good walk to clear his thoughts. After supper, the evening of the Lombardi girl's visit, Juan had seemed awfully interested in the young woman. Perhaps it was just the effects of the wine they had been drinking, but for a man about to take his vows and enter a life of celibacy, his interest in Conchetta was somewhat troubling. On a personal level, he liked Juan well enough, and he and Father Romero certainly appreciated the large donation he had made in the name of Saint Borromeo for mission repairs. Yet still, there was something that troubled the old priest. Over his seventy years he had seen many faces, and had come to believe that he could judge a man's character by reading his face. Juan was so pale and delicate looking. He was young and a hard one to read. It was the mouth though that was disturbing. Father Donovan thought he had seen elements of cruelty there. Juan's eyes always seemed to be darting about; he never held one's gaze for long. A bad trait for a priest, he thought. It was true that Juan had not been with them that long, but as yet no letter had arrived from Santiago introducing him. He also seemed to be lacking in certain aspects of church doctrine and religious history. One evening they had been discussing Saint Augustine, and Juan had been talking in a manner that indicated he thought Augustine had been born a Christian. Every seminary student should have known that Augustine, through long and agonizing study and soul searching, adopted Christianity at thirty years of age. This and other admittedly small discrepancies had aroused a hint of suspicion in Father Donovan. *I'm probably getting old, tired, and confused,* he thought. He had been forgetting many things of late. Maybe his mind had begun to compensate by inventing things instead.

Walking along the narrow path began to invigorate him, such a wonderful day. The fog could be truly beautiful at times and tended to create a sense of mystery. Today, a slight breeze was moving it about in thick damp swirls. Somewhere above he could hear seagulls crying.

"Say, Father, wait. I'll walk with you," he heard the voice of Juan call out.

Turning, Father Donovan paused and presently saw Juan emerge from the fog, coming rapidly towards him.

"I could use a good walk myself," he said. "How far are you going?"

"Oh, a half a mile, no more, my son. These old legs get wobbly after a while. I had been hoping the fog would break up. I do like to sit at times and stare out at the ocean and horizon. Spiritual reflection comes easy at such times."

"Spiritual reflection, Father? Tell me, where does our spirit reside? Does it live in this deformed leg of mine? Did the Lord single me out to go through life bearing such grotesqueness? Tell me, Father, why do you think I am choosing to enter the priesthood?"

"Juan, surely a young man of your age by this time would not question God in such manners. Those who choose to follow the call of our savior have no need of such reflection."

The path they were on was approaching the steep bluffs that dropped abruptly away to the beach below.

"Father, do you believe that God visits us in the womb? Did God place his hand inside my mother's belly and squeeze my leg with his all-judging hand and make me a cripple? Did God ordain that all the children of the town would call me El Zapo, the cripple, so that all the girls would giggle and shun me?"

Father Donovan was old, but no fool. This young man would never make it as a priest. Indeed, his tone of voice awakened a sense of fear.

He paused, put his hand on Juan's shoulder, and said, "Come, my son, let us go back to the chapel. We shall both pray for the Lord's guidance and forgiveness."

"Would the Lord forgive the devil, Father? Isn't he a vengeful Lord? Did he not punish the Egyptians with plague after plague? A plague on your confused God, dealing out forgiveness and punishment with the same hand. The devil acts with only one intent—destruction! Pray to your God as you hit the rocks, deceived priest!"

He suddenly turned, grabbed Father Donovan above the waist, and ran him towards the edge of the bluff. The old priest grabbed at his clothes. Juan shattered his grip with a blow and flung him over the edge. The priest hit once on the side of the cliff before landing amongst the rocks on the beach below. His body lay twisted and still. His face turned up towards Juan and the sky, his arms stretched out from his sides.

Juan began stomping on the soft dirt at the edge of the bluff with his good foot until a chunk broke loose. It had all been so easy, he thought, and well planned. The idiot liked to walk along the bluffs, the ground gave way. Such a tragic accident. No one was a witness. Night was approaching. In a day or two his body would be discovered. A terrible end for the life of a man of God. But after all, God does work in mysterious ways.

When Father Donovan did not return to the rectory that evening, Father Romero assumed he had left on a matter of religious importance. Perhaps he had been spirited away to aid the sick or dying. Usually though, he would leave a note. The next day, a man gathering mussels came upon Father Donovan's body. The town of Carmel mourned. A sheriff from Monterey came to investigate. The bluff gave way suddenly. He had probably approached the edge to look around. It was deemed an act of God. Father Romero and Juan were questioned; both were devastated and distraught. The old priest was buried at the Carmel cemetery. The Monterey paper would carry the news. Juan enjoyed thinking about the look of shock and sorrow that would come to the Italian slut's face.

It hadn't taken long for Conchetta to find out about the tragic passing of Father Donovan. What a nice priest, and she had just gotten to know him. She had been looking forward to seeing him again when the roses were in bloom. Now, without his cheerful presence, she didn't think she would be visiting the old mission for a while. She had not met the other priest, and perhaps he too was nice, but she could certainly do without running into the student, Juan, with his odd looks and disturbing demeanor. She went to the church in Monterey and lit a candle and said a prayer for Father Donovan. He had been warm and kind to her, but life goes on. Sometime later she would return to the mission with her brother and Lena. Maybe Angelina would soon arrive for a visit. Then all of them would go. Conchetta would show them around and think of Father Donovan.

Now that the old priest was gone, Juan Fuentes reasoned that Conchetta probably would not return when the stupid flowers were in bloom. And sure enough, when the mission grounds broke out in a riot of color, many people did come to visit, but not the one he was looking for. It made no difference. He had already formed a plan. For several weeks now, Juan had adopted a second disguise—that of a simple Mexican *campesino*, a farmworker, seeking employment wherever he could find it. Dressed in soiled work clothes and a straw sombrero pulled low over his face, he easily blended in with any of those who worked the thriving vegetable farms. It didn't take him long to locate Mario Lombardi's boat. From there, he simply followed Mario home, and he even saw Conchetta come out and sit on the porch. She was accompanied by a young girl of about twelve. The girl had a book, and he could see she was reading out of it aloud to Conchetta.

Ah, a young one and an old one, he thought. *Maybe I'll nab two. I could tie one up and let her watch what I do to the other one. Don't get greedy now. Everything needs to proceed smoothly.*

It wasn't unusual for traveling salesmen to arrive in Monterey. One day when Juan was in town he took special notice of a Gypsy-looking fellow and his wagon. The wagon was what actually caught his eye. It was so solid looking. It looked like a traveling fort pulled by two horses. The wood was thick, made of American oak; solid brass enclosed the seams. Someone with a whimsical nature had carved intricate designs deep into the wood. Cast iron pans and pots dangled securely from its sides. "Wares for Sale," painted on a red and white sign above the driver's seat, announced its intentions. Attached to the wagon, trailing behind from a shaft was an iron-barred cage on two wheels enclosing a lethargic black bear. El Zapo was astounded at the sight. He could use that wagon, he thought. A wagon such as that could traverse the length of California. To hell with the damn bear. His pockets were loaded with money. He had exchanged the currency he had left Santiago with for American dollars. Dusting off his clothes and tilting back his sombrero, he approached the driver.

"Excuse me, sir. I may appear to you as a humble campesino, but I am not without resources. I am wondering if your horses and wagon could be for sale."

Reaching into his pants pocket, he displayed a wad of bills to the driver.

"I am prepared to offer you a fair price for your rig, now and on the spot. I would have no need of the bear. I've recently arrived in Monterey on the urgings of a cousin, but the beauty of this land, and the tales that I've heard, has brought a wanderlust in me. If I were to own a wagon such as this, eking out a humble living as I travel, my dreams would surely be fulfilled. Might you consider a sale?"

The driver, dressed in colorful clothing, sporting a long, thick mustache curved upwards at the ends, hadn't taken his eyes off the money in Juan's hands.

"Actually, senor, I would consider a sale if the price was right. I have been thinking of settling down, and Monterey is as nice a town as I have seen. I do think you should reconsider your interest in the bear. His name is Oso, and he is a real moneymaker. I bought him several months ago from a man who had trained him since he was a cub. If I no longer owned the wagon, I would have no need of him. He is a responsibility. He eats almost anything, but he eats a lot."

Oh, why squabble, thought El Zapo. *I can always get rid of the bear later.*

"Will you accept an offer of eight hundred dollars for everything then?" said Juan.

"Nine hundred and you got a deal, sir."

"Eight-fifty and you have a deal, sir."

"Eight-fifty it is."

They made out a bill of sale. The Gypsy gave Juan some instructions concerning the caring and feeding of the bear, as well as a series of commands and motions the bear responded to as part of its performance.

"Take good care of Oso, senor," the salesman called out as Juan was pulling away. "The bear will bring you luck. He is a lucky bear."

Luck, what need I of luck? Juan thought. *Weaklings need luck. I make my own.* Waving to the man, now on foot, he drove back toward the mission—a traveling salesman.

The ride back had been rewarding. The horses pulled the wagon effortlessly; they seemed to be young and strong. The wagon felt like it could withstand anything. Arriving at the mission barn, he got out and began a closer examination of his purchase. The wagon was loaded with household goods. Various items of clothing, including men's work boots, were tucked away in boxes. But what interested him most was a separate sleeping compartment at the back of the wagon. A small, low door led to it. Inside was a thick mattress covered with blankets; a wooden hatch, easily opened and closed, was built into a wall to let in air.

He unhitched and fed the horses, gave the stupid bear a pan of water, and retired to his quarters, full of new ideas. By the morning he was ready to act. He rose early, dressed in casual clothes, and went to the barn to prepare the wagon for departure. Pulling out into the yard, he was met by Father Romero.

"Juan, is that you? Where did you get that wagon? What is this all about?"

"I'm leaving, Father. I bought this wagon to see California and to make a little money while doing so. Before returning to Santiago and taking my final vows, I must test myself in the everyday world, live as a normal man would. I must be certain that a life of a priest is what I truly desire. I'm sure you must understand. You were young once too, Father. You and Father Donovan, who I Miss so much, have treated me kindly here. Perhaps one day I shall return to this wonderful, holy place. Oh, by the way, I have left a small donation in an envelope under the crucifix in my room. I hope it will help out in the repairs. Bye, Father. Pray for me. When the letter arrives from Santiago, could you be so kind as to write back telling them of my plans?"

"I will write them, Juan. This is all happening so fast, and it's all so surprising, but again, thank you so much for the donation."

Juan was already heading towards the road to Monterey.

"Bye, Father. Bye," he called back.

Father Romero stood there and waved. *Yes, I was young once too and had my doubts, he thought. But*

there's something about that young man. He is too flam-
boyant. I doubt if he will ever become a priest. And turning, he headed towards Juan's room, curious to see how
much was in the envelope.

The doddering idiot, thought Juan. *He's probably hur-*
rying right now to my room for the money. He'll probably
use it to buy treats for his belly instead of wood for repairs.
Do what you want with it fool. It means nothing to me,
and I have plenty more. You were all so gullible, so trust-
ing. Your God has so blinded you that you never saw the
devil when he was standing right in front of you.

"The devil has work to do," he spoke out loud, and
towards Monterey and Conchetta Lombardi's he traveled, listening to the words of Bael, the devil in his head.

Bael had advised him a while back to purchase from
the druggist in Monterey some useful items: chloroform,
morphine, and cocaine. Dressed in his garb of a priest, he
had overpaid the druggist, who was only too glad to do
business, and said not a word of inquiry to Juan. Now he
was ready to act. He pulled the wagon off the road, and
climbing in the back, changed once again into the robe.
He was by now completely familiar with Conchetta's
routine. Today, at eleven o'clock, she would be walking
from her house to tutor a student who lived a mile or so
away in a clearing off the road. Several houses were situated nearby, but they were all located well back from the
road. Juan got out and waited amongst the trees by the
entrance to one of the houses. When Conchetta walked
by she would see him emerge, like he had been visiting
one of the houses. At a little after eleven, he soaked a rag
in chloroform, and sure enough, he saw Conchetta walking down the road.

When she drew almost even, he emerged from the
driveway and said, "Miss Lombardi, what a surprise. I was
paying a call to an ailing acquaintance. May I walk with
you a moment?"

Oh no, him, Conchetta thought. She paused only slightly and said, "I am in a hurry. I have a student to tutor, Mister? I don't think I learned your last name."

"Fuentes, Miss, Juan Fuentes."

He looked all around and saw no one. Hobbling up to Conchetta, he suddenly wrapped his left arm around her shoulders and clamped the chloroform-soaked rag with his right hand over her nose and mouth. She struggled longer than he thought she would, but he kept on walking with her tightly in his grasp towards the parked wagon. She suddenly went limp, and holding her up and dragging her, he once again looked all around. He reached the wagon, opened the door, and propelled her roughly in. He then tied her legs together and her arms around her back. He gagged her, so she wouldn't yell out when she came to. Then he lifted her into the sleeping compartment and secured her legs to an iron ring he had installed in the center of the compartment so that she couldn't kick and make noise. He secured the door and locked it.

Satisfied and pleased with himself, he got back behind the reins, turned the wagon around, and headed towards the road north out of Monterey. Shortly before dark, he decided to get rid of the bear. He had trouble freeing the rusty connections that secured the cage to the back of the wagon. He finally gave up and decided to just open the cage and let the bear loose. He removed the lock, undid the latch, and leaving the door slightly ajar, walked back to the front of the wagon, ready to jump aboard as soon as the bear made its way out. The bear seemed to know what to do. It pushed the cage door open with its head and jumped to the ground. Juan quickly got behind the reins and took off. After a little while, he looked back and saw the bear following awkwardly behind on all fours. The bear seemed to be favoring one side. Juan quickened the pace, then after a while, slowed the horses and turned to have a look.

The bear was still following at the same distance. He too had quickened the pace. Juan pulled the wagon to a halt. At that moment, the bear raised itself on its two hind legs and began to limp towards the wagon, its front paws stretched over its head. El Zapo couldn't believe his eyes. The bear was a cripple. Surely this was a sign from the devil. This bear was meant to be his. He hobbled rapidly to the back of the wagon and swung the cage door wide open. The bear had returned to all fours and obediently arrived at the cage and entered. Juan latched the cage and went inside the wagon and came back out with four ripe apples and some stale bread. He stuck the food inside the cage. The bear immediately began to eat. *I can't let this bear go now*, he thought. This was not planned for; he had to reconsider. But first he would think about what he was about to do to his prisoner, securely tucked away.

He kept traveling until full dark, then after fortifying himself with some beef jerky, crackers, and an apple, his thoughts turned to Conchetta.

Conchetta returned to consciousness with a blinding headache, and for one instant she thought she was blind. She then realized that she was bound and gagged, secured to the floor of a pitch-black compartment. She thought she must be in a wagon. She could feel it moving. It was that priest, that odd pretend-to-be priest. That was the last thing she had seen. She remembered struggling with him, as he held a sickening smelling rag to her face. She panicked—she was going to be killed. She couldn't breathe. A red and white whirl, a spiral pinwheel emerged from the darkness of her brain and blazed in front of her.

She had come to on her side. She struggled and flopped on her back. From this position she was able to sit up. She fought for control, forced herself to take deep breaths through her nose. Sitting there for a while in the dark, and doing nothing but concentrating on her breathing, she began to calm down a bit. The headache seemed to be subsiding. She was able to think a little. She had been kidnapped and trussed up, but was unharmed and alive. The sick madman had taken her for some reason; she ventured several guesses for what, and didn't like the picture. She began to concentrate on her surroundings. A slight bit of light came from around the cracks of what appeared to be some type of small door, or window, near the top of one of the sides. A musty smelling mattress took up most of the floor. The wagon was moving steady, and she could feel it hit a bump now and then.

She had to prepare her mind for the worst possibility, she was about to be raped and killed. Why would he have bothered with all this, she thought. He could have hit her over the head, had his way, and left her dead in the bushes off the road she had been walking. This animal fake priest was cruelly intelligent. He had enjoyed surprising her with his knowledge of Italian. She would have to be on her toes. Use her wits better than he did, be on the lookout for any opportunity. She would have to escape somehow, or kill him. She fought for the resolve to prepare her mind for anything. She decided that a man such as this would enjoy seeing fear and weakness. He wouldn't get that satisfaction out of her. She would have to try to remain as fearless and calm as possible, hiding her true emotions while looking for an avenue out of the situation. One minute she was involved with normally occupying her day, and in the blinking of an eye, she had been thrust into a life-or-death situation. She was too young to die and had struggled too hard, from difficult times in Italy to new hope in America. Whatever was to happen, she resolved not to let him touch her inner soul. No matter what the crazy man did, as long as she was alive, she had to find the strength in herself to say, "He did not touch me."

She had no idea how long she had been out, but she noticed that the light around the opening had practically vanished. It must be getting dark. People in Monterey, especially Mario, would be worried about her. Wait, not Mario, he was to be out fishing for another day, but Lena would worry and surely report her disappearance. The wagon suddenly stopped moving. She heard the sound of metal on metal hitting together. She turned her body as best she could to face the sounds. After what seemed like an eternity of silence, she suddenly heard the unmistakable sounds of footsteps and what was probably hands fumbling with a lock. A door suddenly was opened and there he was, no longer dressed like a priest, holding a small lantern in one hand, leering at her from inside of what was the front section of a wagon, the shelves of its sides lined with various wares.

"How do you do, Miss Lombardi. I hope you have enjoyed your ride. You must be hungry and cramped. Please allow me to assist you," he spoke in Italian.

Conchetta didn't say a thing. He set the lantern down and undid the knots that bound her to an iron ring and those that held her feet together.

He untied the gag around her mouth, saying, "If you even try to yell, I'll kill you."

Grabbing the lantern and stepping back he said, "I'm so sorry, you're on your own now. I'm afraid you'll have to crawl out of there if you care for some supper. You haven't fouled yourself yet, have you, slut? I suppose you'll need to use the bushes. Maybe I'll even have to clean you up before I take you. Indeed, I hardly find anything more offending than a smelly woman."

He was now speaking English. *He's even crazier than I imagined,* Conchetta thought, staring at the thin, pale, wild-eyed face. He hadn't untied her hands, yet she immediately crawled as best she could towards Juan and the open door at the back of the wagon. Keeping her head down, her eyes moved to the shelves along the walls. She noticed an open box that held kitchen utensils. She could see several knives. She had to get her hands free, even if the opportunity arose to run, she knew she couldn't get far with her hands bound in back of her. Running would be awkward. She'd probably just trip on her long dress.

"Hurry up, bitch! What's the matter? Do you feel crippled?"

He stepped down to the ground, laughing at her.

Conchetta reached the open door and looked out to see a bear sitting in a cage attached to the back of the wagon by a long shaft. In the darkness, with only the light of the small lantern held in Juan's hands, she could see the glow of the bear's eyes watching her.

Dio Bono, she said to herself. *If only I were dreaming.*

"Come on, get down from there. How do you like my bear?" he said. "That bear was personally sent to me by the devil. You should see him when he walks on his hind legs, he limps on the same foot, a cripple just like me—El Zapo, ma'am, at your service."

Conchetta was sitting on the edge of the wagon. She took her first steps on wobbly feet, and for the first time spoke.

"I have to use the bushes."

Juan came over to Conchetta and started sniffing around her lower half. At one point, she could have raised her knee straight into his jaw, but with her hands tied she was useless.

"Why, Miss Lombardi, it seems you have not soiled yourself. To the bushes, by all means."

"You'll have to untie my hands."

"In a fashion, yes, you may be correct."

Going to the wagon, he reached in and got a piece of rope. He tied one end to her wrist above where she was bound and, using a knife she had noticed he wore in a sheath about his waist, cut the lower bindings. For an instant, Conchetta had one arm free. She knew she was strong for a woman and thought of fighting him. He, though, was holding a knife, and the fight would probably not last long. He rapidly sheathed the knife and brought her arms in front of her, quickly tying them together, leaving about a foot of free space between them. Reaching under his coat, from his waist he produced a large revolver.

"A Colt forty-four, Miss. I have several for sale. Go over there and squat like a dog. If you make a move, I'll kill you. I couldn't Miss from this distance."

Conchetta really did have to use the bushes. She lost her temper at what was to be a lack of privacy.

"Leave me be, *animale*. I need to go off a bit. Where can I run, bound in the dark?"

The wagon was parked in a clearing surrounded by trees and shrubs. An opening led to what she assumed was the main road.

"Just stand in front of the bushes and go, or don't go. I don't have time for all this."

Conchetta gained control, walked the short distance away from the wagon, and squatted. Stepping away from the puddle, she had never felt so humiliated. *Perhaps this is only the beginning, she* reluctantly thought. Juan was just standing there smiling, holding the gun. She quickly took in more of the surroundings. Two horses were tied off at a short distance, munching on a flake of hay. A small fire was going near the front of the wagon. Even in the semi dark she was amazed at the wagon. It was as large as any she had ever seen, built out of thick wood with a roof that curved, covered with wood shingles. Pots, pans, harnesses, and other items dangled from the sides. She noticed a little sliding door with a lock on it along the front upper side. She knew that was where the light emanated from, that she saw from inside of what she realized was her cell. Juan motioned her over to one of two short stools arranged by the fire.

"Have a seat, Lombardi. Your dinner is about to be served."

From out of a nearby box he handed her a cup of water, which she immediately drank off. He next placed on her lap some crackers, a piece of jerky, and an apple.

"I regret offering you such a humble dinner, but you see I have other things on my mind than cooking."

Conchetta was eating fast. She needed to keep her strength. She could tell by the sneer, and twisted look in his eye, what he was probably thinking about.

In fact, El Zapo was thinking, *What a true beauty, the black hair so thick and all disheveled, and the figure that must hide under that thick dress. She's eating there, staring at me, trying to hide the hatred behind those lovely eyes. Well, be patient. It won't be long now.*

Conchetta had finished the food and asked for more water. Juan obliged and sat back down. No one said a word. Conchetta suddenly realized time seemed to be standing still. She began to feel relaxed and light-headed. She was having trouble thinking and concentrating on the terrible situation she was in. The pain had left from her cramped legs and arms. A red flag of realization suddenly went up. She knew what it was to be drunk. Occasionally, she had a little too much red wine and was familiar with the feeling. This wasn't it. The madman had drugged her.

"How are you feeling, slut? And slut you are about to be. I'm afraid I had to add a little medicine to your food; I certainly wouldn't want you to be in any kind of pain."

He rose from the stool and limped toward her. He jerked her to her feet and led her to the back of the wagon. By now Conchetta could barely move, but she reached inside her for some last remaining strength and suddenly she turned on Juan and tried to wrap the rope attached to her bound hands around his neck. She threw her momentum and weight on him, and he lost balance, both of them falling to the ground. She struggled to wrap the rope around his neck, but found it impossible with bound hands. She felt a sudden blow to the side of her face. He had maneuvered her under his control; her mouth filled with blood. She felt like she was going to pass out. He had forced her on her back and was pinning one of her bound hands to the ground above her head. With his free hand, he raised her dress and ripped away her linens. She struggled, but to no avail—before she knew it, he was inside her, grunting away like a wild animal.

She heard him say, "Look into the face of the devil, bitch, and learn to like what you see," before a wave of blackness enveloped her and carried her away.

Chapter 5

The little band of Pomos that were going to town couldn't stop laughing and talking about the crazy Davy. Surely he had been spending too much time sleeping under redwood trees, they all agreed. Anyone who would stare so intently at another man's nakedness, to the point that he forgot his intentions, was strange indeed. Of course, they were all glad he was distracted so easily. Crazy Davy holding a shotgun was a serious matter.

Pino, the elder, was proud of his performance. He had carried it off so straight and stately—just like his name, Pino, Pine. When everyone took white men's names, as a young man he had chosen the Spanish word for pine. He had first heard the word while working at the Russian settlement at Fort Ross on the coast. A Miwok, who was doing some trading there, had done much traveling and had picked the word up somewhere to the south. He had suddenly pointed to a tall tree and said, "Pino." Pino repeated the word immediately and liked the sound of it so much that he told everyone he saw that he was Pino. If a pine tree were nearby, he would use the tree as a linguistic instructional tool.

Too bad Davy was dangerous, he reflected. It would be fine to surprise him, disrobe, and run circles around him. Seeing the look on Dave's face would be priceless.

The slow journey into town certainly could be interesting, and usually was quite pleasant. Fred, sitting next to Pino, was thinking the same thing. He had seen this Dave once before, and he had also been carrying the long shotgun and had that mean, twisted look on his face.

Turning to Pino, he asked, "Why did you suddenly stand and take off your robe, elder?"

"Because both Thunder Man and The Old Man of the Mountain have told us that Dave is an odd duck."

Fred wasn't familiar with the term. "What is an odd duck?"

"An odd duck is one that can't make up its mind which way to fly. It can be very dangerous; the duck could drop right out of the sky."

"I don't think I understand, elder," Fred said.

"I will tell you more about this when you are older. I think we should think about the red onions we will buy when we get to town."

Pino was in love with red onions. He enjoyed the way they looked, smelled, and tasted. When he could get them, he often would eat them like apples, then go up to the women and blow in their faces. The red onions made him want to chase them and blow at them. His favorite way, though, of eating the onions was to slice them and fry them in his old skillet with bear grease. Someone in town was usually broiling venison. He would get some of the venison and eat it with his cooked red onions, keeping a sharp eye out for coyote. He was sure coyote could smell the red onions cooking from miles away, and he didn't wish to share. He hoped to trade the dried fish he had brought along for a nice sack of onions.

Walter tried to act unconcerned, but he didn't like these meetings with Dave one bit. So far nothing of consequences had happened, but Dave reminded him of a rattler, coiled and ready to strike. He had a feeling Dave wouldn't stay coiled forever. The chief of police in town was a pretty good fellow. Walter had mentioned Dave's behavior to him once. The chief just thought that Dave was a harmless no-good, but said that he would have a talk with him. If he had, nothing had changed. Dave still carried the shotgun.

"Walter," Pino suddenly asked, "What are you going to buy in town?"

Walter had been thinking about that. Besides the general supplies the whole tribe needed, Walter knew he should buy something for Melanie. Melanie was the Pomo girl, a few years younger than him, that he knew was sweet on him. He liked her well enough. She had the square build, flat breasts, and plump hands and feet that his people admired, and all thought that they would make a wonderful couple, but something was missing. He thought he knew what it was. He had just become too *cosmopolitan*. He knew he shouldn't like words only for the sound of them, like Pino did, but he couldn't help it. At the presidio school he had heard many people say that San Francisco was becoming a cosmopolitan city. He had lived in San Francisco, therefore he was cosmopolitan, and he had looked up the meaning of the word.

Walter couldn't help thinking of himself as a little worldly. Not every Indian had gone off to a school for higher learning in a big city, and in that big city he had seen many beautiful young ladies. European immigrants from every country on the continent: Chinese, Japanese, black-skinned ones, girls from the south of the border, blond girls from Norway—the list was endless, and thinking of them made Walter giddy.

Melanie enjoyed setting a fire circle to trap and roast grasshoppers. He knew there was nothing wrong with that, and he too enjoyed eating grasshoppers, but he couldn't picture any of the finely dressed girls walking the streets of San Francisco engaging in such activity. He figured he was just too cosmopolitan for Melanie.

"I probably should buy Melanie a gift," he answered Pino. "Gifts are good anytime between brother and sister."

"Melanie isn't your sister. Think carefully, Walter. You could find yourself in a trap. Owl Man could paralyze you and Melanie could slip a ring through your nose. How would you like that?" the elder said.

"Maybe I won't buy Melanie anything. Maybe I'll buy you some white onions."

"White onions have no power. The women run slower from me. I like to watch them run fast. Sometimes their skirts fly up," Pino stated. "Why don't you buy some of those sharp little hooks with the feathers on them that look like many colored flies. You don't like to use soaproot."

Centuries ago, Coyote had shown the people the ease of using soaproot to catch fish. All you did was wait until summer when the rainbow trout were trapped in pools, as the many little streams in places, before the first heavy rains. Soaproot was tossed into the pools poisoning the fish, and they were gathered when they went belly up. The fish were still perfectly edible on the spot or suitable for drying.

"Maybe I will buy some flies," Walter said.

He had purchased a fly rod and reel in San Francisco. It came apart in three sections and was the envy of all the young men on the rancheria. When Walter would go fishing with it and tie on one of those small flies to fish for trout, he always had a following.

"Walter, do you think my member is good looking?" Pino said out of nowhere.

Walter started laughing. Pino was so good at that, blurting out nonsense when least expected. In San Francisco he had attended several performances where men took the stage in funny dress and entertained the crowd by telling humorous stories. Comedians, they were called. If elders weren't in such need at the rancheria, he would have liked to take Pino to the big city and train him for the stage. He would have to learn better English though.

"Your member is quite good looking, elder. Dave certainly thinks it is."

"I don't care about Dave. I care about Betty Mae."

"Betty Mae is only sixteen," Walter said.

"I gave her a glimpse of my member once when I was doing the brush dance. She started squealing," Pino said.

"Let's go back and talk about fishing," Walter suggested.

"Walter, tell me again about Jose Pena," Pino said.

"You only like to hear about him because his name sounds a little like yours," Walter said, shaking his head. "We passed his house an hour ago. Why didn't you say something then?"

"Because I was thinking about red onions and Betty Mae. Thunder Man has only put so many thoughts into my head at one time. Tell me about Jose Pena."

For what seemed like the one-hundredth time, Walter repeated the story.

"Through powers granted by the Mexican government, Jose German Pena was granted a portion of land in eighteen forty-three called Dry Creek Valley. This land totaled fifteen thousand acres and was called the Tzabaco Rancho."

"Has the Mexican government ever been here, and does it know Dave?" Pino asked.

"No, to both questions," Walter answered.

"Why would they give Jose Pena something that they had never seen? Maybe if they had seen the valley, they wouldn't have given it away. The Great Spirit provided the valley for everyone. No one can own the valley like you own the three-piece fishing pole. Too bad Jose Pena is dead. I could explain all this to him myself. I guess it's for the best, though; he would be disappointed to find he didn't really own anything. Then he would be mad at the

Mexican government and might try to shoot them. Walter, how much is fifteen thousand acres?"

"It's all the land you can see and more," Walter said.

Pino looked around. He could see a long way.

"Someday I'm going to fall asleep and dream on Jose Pena's porch."

"Why would you want to do that?" Walter inquired, reluctantly drawn in.

Pino had never said before that he wanted to sleep on the Pena's adobe porch. He had also said dream, and Walter knew that word could have several meanings.

"Because once when we were going by the adobe, I saw a blackbird in that wisteria vine that grows over the porch and I wished I could dream my way into that blackbird. You know what good messengers blackbirds are. I then could enter the spirit world and look for Jose Pena. When I find him I could tell him that the government never really owned the land. Walter, do you think the government people are dead now too?" Pino asked.

The elder sometimes reminded Walter of a fly buzzing around his ears.

"Yes, I think that many of them are dead now."

"Good," Pino said. "In that case Jose Pena could punish them for lying to him."

"Makes perfect sense to me," was all Walter could think of to say.

Fred had been listening attentively to the whole conversation. He too had noticed a blackbird earlier today in that wisteria vine.

"Elder, some day would you teach me how to change into a blackbird?"

"Why would you like to learn such powerful medicine, Fred?" Pino said.

"Because I'm afraid to tell the teacher something myself. If I was a blackbird, I could whisper it into his ear."

"What do you want to tell him, Fred?" Walter interrupted.

"I would tell him that it's not healthful to move his bowels in that stinking box. I'm afraid his nose won't be able to smell anything good anymore, like red onions," Fred said, smiling up at the elder.

Walter and Pino laughed. Pino tousled Fred's thick, dark brown hair.

"I know what I'm going to buy when we get to town," Fred announced.

"What will you buy?" the elder inquired.

"Canned peaches and a dime magazine about cowboys."

"That's what you buy every time we go to town," Walter said.

"That's what I like best in town," Fred stated.

"Davy boy likes those stupid magazines too," Walter said. "He thinks he's turning into Pecos Bill."

"Pecos Bill is a good guy," Fred protested.

"What do you mean? He's always killing Indians, isn't he?"

"They're not like us," Fred argued. "They're sneaky and mean, and always trying to lift Bill's scalp."

"I think I'll lift Dave's scalp," Pino stated. "Then they will write about me, and I will become famous. Then Betty Mae will beg me to let her have a look at my member."

Fred and Walter laughed so hard they choked. Pino sat upright, straight as a pine and proud.

"Please, please," Walter said. "Let's talk about anything other than Dave, red onions, and members. I've decided what I'm going to buy when we get to town: two new baseballs!"

"You can kill rabbits with a well thrown rock. You waste your money on those hard white eggs with the red stitches," Pino said.

"Elder, you know I've been practicing to be a pitcher," Walter said.

"You should be pitching woo to Betty Mae, she's closer to your age," Pino said.

"If we can't carry on a normal conversation, then let's just not talk," Walter said, frustrated.

Pino looked at Walter and folded in his lips until his neck muscles strained and blinked both eyes in unison. He looked just like a lizard. He stretched out on his stomach in back of the wagon and began pushing himself up, using his arms, blinking, and keeping his mouth pursed tight. He looked just like a lizard doing push-ups on a hot summer's rock. All the Indians that could see him started laughing.

The sun was getting lower as they continued on. More and more farmhouses, orchards, and cultivated fields surround the road. They passed several wagons going the opposite way. The people were friendly and waved. Walter was thinking about baseball. He loved that game and he was trying to excel as a pitcher. He had always been accurate at throwing, and once he discovered the game, he was hooked. At the rancheria he had painted the strike zone on a giant redwood. He had measured the proper distance back and piled up dirt to create a pitcher's mound. He had four old balls and, whenever he got a chance, would practice throwing at the strike zone. He got so he never missed the tree, and most times he threw strikes.

Until he explained what he was doing and the basic elements of the game of baseball, many people thought he was angry and practicing to kill someone with one of the hard balls. A young Indian named Bob feared Walter was mad at him for sneaking up on Melanie and kissing her while she was grinding acorns. Walter explained the game to him and taught Bob how to catch the ball using a broken down leather glove that Walter had brought back from town.

Twice Walter had participated in a full-fledged baseball game at the new ballpark below the cemetery in town. Some of the other Pomos had come along to watch, but soon grew bored and spent their time trying to trap or spear the small fish that lined the creek next to the park. On the weekends it wasn't hard to find eighteen players to form two teams. At first it seemed that Walter wasn't wanted. The usual resentment that many of the young men had toward Indians was to blame. It didn't take long though, after seeing Walter pitching, for him to become a sought after team member. Accurate pitchers were hard to find. Some of the farm boys were exceptionally big and strong, especially one they called Harry the Swede. Harry could throw the ball with such velocity that it was frightening, but he was terribly inaccurate. The ball could go anywhere, and most were afraid they would be hit in the head. Walter couldn't throw nearly as fast, but at least people weren't afraid to stand in the batter's box and face him. Anytime Walter showed up, he was sure to be asked to play in the game. His hitting skills weren't bad either. He just didn't have the opportunity to practice them as much as he had throwing at the redwood tree.

Walter was sure that people would be playing ball at the new park. He hoped that tomorrow he could get involved in a game. He hoped that he could get a chance to pitch to Harry the Swede. Whenever Harry connected solidly with the ball, it usually was a home run. Walter looked forward to trying to strike him out.

"Walter?"

"Yes, elder."

"Tell me about the crabs you saw in San Francisco."

"The crab boats are painted many different colors. They go out of the bay and throw out traps with food in them that land at the bottom of the ocean. They wait a while, then pull up the traps on ropes. Many of the traps are filled with large, meaty crabs. They take them back to Fisherman's Wharf and throw them in huge pots of boiling water. People come by and buy them and take them home for dinner."

Pino liked to hear the story of the crabs. Most of the crabs he had seen were either dead or walking along on the beach with no place to go. He couldn't figure how they could allow themselves to be boiled up so easily. Salmon fought hard when you tried to trap them. The crabs walked carelessly into the traps and sacrificed themselves for someone's dinner. Until Walter told him this story, he had thought the crabs far superior in mentality than the mussels. The mussels let you pick them off the rocks and boil them up too. The crabs had eyes that seemed to look at you like the great salmon. He had never seen an eye on a mussel. It was disappointing to learn that the crab and the mussel were on the same level.

"Do the people who buy the crabs thank them for being so stupid, Walter?"

"No, elder, they're too busy eating them."

"That's a careless move on their part," Pino said. "Not taking time to thank an animal for providing you with its flesh is risky business. Someday they might find themselves in that place, Africa, you told me about, where they put people in pots and boil them. As they're being boiled, surely they would appreciate it if someone thanked them for allowing themselves to be boiled."

Walter admitted that there was a twisted element of logic to this, but he was tired and the thought of tasty crabs had made him a little hungry.

"Walter."

"Yes, elder."

"I've been thinking about that thunder god, Zeus, that you told me about. His daughter sprung from the top of his head when she was born, fully formed and ready to fight. Why was she ready to fight? Had coyote told her she had enemies?"

Walter regretted the day he went into the sweathouse and began to tell the stories he had read in books. Most of the people believed these stories to be facts. The white man's tales were so endless and varied that the Pomos had headaches. Many of them, when they left the sweathouse, had to go out and burn the dried excrement of the coyote and breath it in deeply just to get relief.

"Like you, Zeus' daughter, Athena, liked the owl. Maybe the owl had told her to be prepared for anything," Walter answered.

Pino knew that Walter liked to humor him, and he enjoyed every minute of it. Walter, more than anyone, had brought the white man's world to his people. Pino regretted it, but he saw its inevitability. It was better that Walter brought these new thoughts and experiences to the rancheria than for strangers to do so. The teacher at the school was understanding and had the best of intentions, so he thought, and he was even viewed as a welcomed friend. But he was not one of the people, and never could be. Someday everyone could walk together under the same sun, but Pino thought that day was far away.

"You sure weren't prepared the last time you met an owl, as I remember," Pino said.

Walter knew what he was talking about. Earlier in the year, as they were on their way to town, Walter had walked off the road to use the bushes. They were still in the hills above the valley in a thickly wooded section. Finishing his business, Walter noticed a large, rounded rock formation. It had two cave-like holes that resembled eyes. Below the caves and in between the two was a single cave that resembled a nose. Below the single cave was a line of short scrubby manzanita bushes that resembled a mouth. Walter went back and told the Pomos what he had seen. All of them wanted to go have a look, especially Pino. Pino liked to be called by his name, or by the title "elder."

Pino was also the Shaman of the tribe and looked after the tribe's spiritual well being. Pino was a "go between" the spirit world. No one had actually seen Pino do it, but most people thought that he was capable of flying and changing himself into other animals, such as a bear or an eagle. Sick people usually came to Pino for aid, and most times his cures were successful.

"I'm surprised I haven't noticed this rock before," Pino said. "This definitely sounds like a spirit rock and, as such, is sure to have great power."

They all climbed through the brush and there it was; a large rock formation the height of an average fir tree, and it looked just like a face.

"I'm going to climb it and look in those caves," Walter said.

The other Pomos looked at each other and shook their heads. All believed that a rock such as this should be left alone.

"I can see you want to do this, and I won't try to stop you," Pino said, "but be very careful. Anything might be in those caves. And I mean anything. Your great, great grandmother could come flying out of there for all you know."

Walter assured Pino he would be careful and took off. The climbing was pretty easy, there seemed to be a little curving trail that wound up the front of the formation. It didn't take Walter long to climb through the line of manzanita and reach the first cave. He positioned himself carefully, getting a good grip on an outcropping rock, peering inside. The rounded little cave only went back about four feet. There was nothing inside. It didn't even look like any animals had been using the cave for shelter. Strange, Walter thought.

He climbed further up and came to one of the eye like caves. Getting a grip on a manzanita that grew off to the side, he leaned his head out and peered into it.

Immediately, a huge white owl flew past him, its wing brushing his hair. Another white owl of similar size flew out of the other eye simultaneously.

They had startled Walter so thoroughly that he nearly lost his grip on the manzanita and fell. He noticed his heart was beating so fast that he had to close his eyes and take deep breaths. The sound of laughter reached his ears from down below.

"Hurry, come on down before those owls come back," he heard Pino yelling.

Walter scrambled back down, and all Pino said was, "I thought you might find one of your great, great grandmothers up there, but I didn't think you'd find both of them. Let's get out of here."

Thinking about the owls had produced a melancholy feeling in Walter. Looking around, he marveled at the strangeness of the world.

"Quit dwelling on your great, great grandmothers," he heard Pino say.

Chapter 6

Dom Londi was surprised to find that he was feeling the same way in his mind as when he left Florence. He was making good money, working at a fine restaurant in San Francisco. He had a comfortable place to live, and a few good friends, all this just as he did in Florence. Life was turning into the same old routine. Sure there were new sights to see around "The City" as it was starting to be called. He didn't care for the term "Frisco" as some were calling it. One should not be so unwise as to fool around with Saint Francis' name, he thought. But outside of the only challenge he had—that of learning English—life was pretty humdrum, and a sixty-year-old should not settle for humdrum, he reasoned.

One evening, after dinner, he was sipping a glass of red wine at Primo Nuti's house. Little Maria had just fin- ished reading aloud to them from a book of poetry, and the nanny had hustled her upstairs for bed. Pietro brought the bottle over and filled all of their glasses.

Dom took a sip, held up the wine to the light to check clarity, and remarked, "This is excellent zinfandel, but I see no label on the bottle. Where does it come from?"

"From the county to the north I have been telling you about, Sonoma. The grapes are grown, and the wine is made at a town called Healdsburg, that wild place where they're cutting down those giant redwoods you're always asking about, as fast as they can."

Dom was swishing the wine in the glass, awakening the aroma, holding it to his nose.

Again he muttered, "Excellent. Primo, tell me more about this Healdsburg. It sounds like quite the interesting place. Somewhat of a real Wild West town you say."

"The place is a dump of degradation," Pietro announced. "Trees falling down everywhere, the landscape looks like a Garden of Eden messed up by the hand of God in his confusion. Some of those redwoods have been standing since the time of Christ. Now, they're cutting them all down. The lumbermen are making a fortune. Most of the boards are being sent here. You've seen how this place is growing."

"We were just there two weeks ago," Primo added. "The train has just been pushed through to the town. I did some legal work for a fellow who's starting a winery there. In lieu of some of the money he owed me, I accepted several cases of his exceptional wine. The winery is not up and running yet, but for a few years he's been crushing and fermenting in his barn. He's been selling the wine mostly to restaurants and saloons in Santa Rosa and Petaluma. He can't keep up with the demand. He'll be rich once the winery is fully operational."

"Better to grow grapes than to cut down all those trees," Dom said.

"It's all part of the same picture. You've got to clear all those giant trees out before you can till a vineyard. There's work afoot to save many of them. Some of the larger property owners are preserving many of the trees. It's just that the soil is so damn good for grapes and the climate is just right. It's just like your Tuscany. You've been to Lucca, haven't you? Well, it looks and feels almost like Lucca. In fact most of the guys starting vineyards there are from the Lucca area. Giueseppe Massoni, the guy whose wine you're drinking, came from there."

"You bet I've been to Lucca," Dom said. "Such a beautiful walled city. I've been there several times on holiday. Vineyards everywhere, and some of the best olive oil you can get comes from there. I even recall meeting a Massoni fellow in a café there. He was pretty old. I wonder if he was a relative. Massoni's a pretty common name, though."

"You ought to take a ride up there some weekend on the train. Ask your sweetheart, Angelina, to go up there with you. It could be a romantic adventure, eh," said Primo, winking.

"She's not my sweetheart, and I'm too old for romance, and too old for her. We're just friends, that's all."

"Sure, that's why you go there almost every day for breakfast—just to see an old friend. Who do you think you're fooling, Paisano?"

"Enough, enough," Dom said. "You've placed a seed in my brain. I would like to see that area, falling down trees and all."

"Good for you," Pietro said, again filling the glasses.

"Let's make a toast. Here's to you, Angelina, and romance, and don't give me that 'too old' crap. Cupid's got his arrow in you, and you know it, and he doesn't give a damn how old you are. The slower you are, the easier a target."

"Yes, I agree," Primo said. "Just don't be slow when it comes to getting her in the sack. You're not getting any younger you know," he said straight-faced.

They laughed and tossed off the wine.

"Hey, before I go, tell me a little more about the area," Dom said.

"There's only one more thing a man like you needs to know," Pietro announced in a booming voice. "Mushrooms."

"Oh, say now," Dom said. "Now you've hit the ticket. What Italian doesn't like mushrooms? They got the good ones up there, huh?"

"Oh they got 'em all right. After the first rains in October they start popping up all over the place; big fat ones like the caucore and the servi, the finest I've ever eaten."

"And I know just what to do with them," Dom responded.

"I do too," Primo added. "Sauté 'em in olive oil and garlic and serve them over a fire broiled steak alongside a nice fresh vinaigrette salad."

"Hey, let's go eat," Pietro chimed in. "This wine is making me hungry."

"Yea, let's go to that little restaurant down the street, Rocas, the one that has all the pretty waitresses. You can't get the good mushrooms there this time of year, but they make those great spinach and cheese raviolis," Primo said.

"Why are we always talking about pretty waitresses?" Dom questioned. "Every time we get together, we end up talking about women like we're experts, and only one of us has even been married."

"You don't have to be married to know all about women," Pietro said. "A detailed examination of what's under the dress soon reveals the difference between man and woman. The great Leonardo Da Vinci said that," he deadpanned.

"But Leonardo liked boys," Primo added.

"Makes no difference," Pietro continued. "What do you think Mona Lisa was looking at to produce that smile? Another woman."

"Oh shut up," Dom said. "This conversation is going nowhere. Let's go get some ravioli. It's getting late."

Primo went up to have a look at Maria, who was sleeping, and told the nanny they were leaving to get a bite to eat. They grabbed their coats and hats and headed out the door. The night air invigorated them and the good

Massoni zinfandel and talk of mushrooms heightened their appetites. The prospect of being served by pretty waitresses propelled them jovially down the street. Dom, of course, was the true authority of food and restaurants, and he approved of Rocas. He had eaten there several times with the Nutis, and they had all tried various dishes, but all agreed the ravioli was the specialty of the house.

It was getting a little late by the time they took seats at the restaurant. There were not that many people inside. The lighting in the place was just right, Dom thought, dark enough to be soothing yet light enough to provoke avid conversation. Their solid wood table was covered with the traditional checked red and white oilcloth. A candle burning in a wax covered wine bottle illuminated the table. The walls of the restaurant were varnished wood, the ceiling was beamed, and some interesting paintings, mostly landscapes, hung here and there. Presently, what they were hoping for approached the table.

"Good evening, gentlemen. Here's our menu," a very pretty, probably Irish girl, with her red hair and accent, spoke.

"Thank you, Miss, but we won't need one. Raviolis, right?" Primo said, looking at Pietro and Dom.

"Of course," they announced as one.

"And we would also like a small green salad each and a bottle of—what?"

"More zinfandel," Dom said.

"Correct," the Nutis said.

"You fellas are easy to please," the waitress said, taking their order and leaving.

"See," Pietro said, "a pretty waitress to improve the scenery and lift the spirits. Just what the doctor ordered."

"The doctor should order you a head examination," Primo said.

"Don't start this again," Dom pleaded. "Continue telling me about Sonoma County and this Healdsburg."

"There's a beautiful river that runs right by the town. It's full of salmon and these giant trout called steelhead during the fall and winter. There's a pretty good-sized mountain that looms over the town called Fitch Mountain. This Fitch was a sea captain who married a Mexican noblewoman named Carrillo. By marrying her, he was able to get a huge grant of land. Have you heard of this fellow Kit Carson? No? Well, he was a famous explorer, one of the first whites to travel all over the west. I guess he fought a lot of Indians. Someone told me he got so pissed at the Navajo Indians that he burned down some peach trees they had planted."

"What?" said Pietro. "A man who would do such a thing has no heart. Even Napoleon, when he came through Italy, never burned someone's orchard. I don't like this Carson fellow."

"This Fitch hired Carson's brother to oversee and run the property, so I guess he was the first American to settle in Healdsburg. This was only a little over twenty years ago. Shortly after a fellow called Heald opened a store there to cater to travelers, and the town began to grow. There used to be a lot of squatters there—people who settled on the land without buying it. After the Mexican war, ownership of these land grants became confusing, and some took advantage of it. It's pretty much been sorted out in the courts now. But land is cheap there. If I weren't so busy here, I'd take advantage now while the price is right. That soil there is something; they're growing everything from prune trees to hops for beer, and the tomatoes," Primo said, "you should see the tomatoes. Better than the ones we had in Italy."

"Impossible," Dom stated. "Nothing is better than an Italian tomato, and we all know that."

"Primo, I've got to agree," Pietro said. "Next you'll be telling us that they grow figs better than in Italy."

"That too," Primo said, slamming his fist on the table.

"Dom, he's had way too much wine," Pietro announced solemnly.

Just then the waitress returned with the zinfandel and three glasses.

"No glass for him, he raves like a lunatic," Pietro smiled up at her while pointing a finger at Primo.

"Don't listen to him, Miss. My uncle wanted to be an actor, but I've always thought he'd make a better comedian."

"Pietro Nuti at your service, ma'am," he said, winking at her and twirling his long mustache.

"I think you've all been drinking a little too much wine," she said, mockingly reproachful. "I'll be back with your raviolis shortly, boys."

"See," Pietro said, "she calls us boys. That means she likes us. I told you I know women."

Dom filled the three glasses. They all swirled, checked for clarity against the candlelight, sniffed, and took a sip.

"Not bad," Primo said, "but nothing like that Massoni zinfandel."

They had almost completed their meal when three obviously drunk men brushed by their table, one staggering heavily against it. This knocked over the almost empty wine bottle.

"Whoops, sorry gentlemen," he said, struggling to focus on the diners.

"Say," one of them said, leaning against his buddy. "They ain't gentlemen. They look like dagos to me. I heard 'em talkin' some foreign gibberish. Look at the noses on 'em, and the mustaches. Dressed kinda fancy for wops, ain't you?" he said, reaching for the fallen wine bottle and upending the rest of the contents on Pietro's head.

"Animal," Pietro shouted, standing up, facing the three. "Do you know who I am? Do you?" he said in his heavily accented English.

"Yep," one of them said, belching. "You're one of them old greasy dagos, stinking of garlic."

"Wrong, sir. I am Pietro Nuti, former middleweight boxing champion of all of Sicily. And these are lethal weapons," he stated, displaying his fists.

"You're a funny old buzzard," the much younger man said and swung an awkward right at Pietro's wine-soaked head, missing him by at least a half a foot. Primo and Dom now stood up and faced the three.

"OK, OK, boys, you've had your fun. So far no one's hurt. My uncle probably would have spilled some wine on himself anyway before the night was over. Why don't you go sit up front at the bar, and I'll buy you all a beer."

The biggest of the three, and the one that seemed the least drunk, suddenly reached across the table and shoved Primo on the shoulder saying, "We don't drink beer paid for by foreigners, Mr. Macaroni."

Primo looked at Pietro and Dom, shaking his head and holding his hands up in frustration and said, "We have no choice."

In an instant, he was out from behind the table and had landed a kick that caught the tall man just below the heart, completely surprising him and taking his breath away. In a movement so fast Dom barely saw it, Primo hit the man on the side of the neck with the edge of his hand. At almost the same time he raised his knee hard into the man's groin. Pietro had not been still. As soon as Primo went into action he had grabbed the empty wine bottle and brought it down on the head of the drunk who had emptied its contents on him. The two men were now out cold on the floor. The third was running for the door. It was all over in what seemed like seconds. There had only been several other diners who had witnessed the events, and they were staring at the group, smiling. One of them even raised a glass and called out in a British accent, "Well done, chaps, bravo."

The waitress and a cook had been watching from a distance. Primo took a fifty-dollar bill and a twenty from his wallet.

"The large bill should take care of any damages, Miss. The smaller one should cover our dinner. By the way, the raviolis were excellent as usual. Well, gentlemen, shall we be off? Oh, let me suggest—I see those men on the floor are stirring, perhaps a pitcher of water emptied on their heads would aid in recovery."

The waitress agreed, and smiling, yelled out, "Pete, two pitchers of water."

The victorious Paisanos made their way out the door.

On the street, walking rapidly away, Dom said, "Primo, where did you learn to fight like that? It's not the traditional way."

"It can be traditional if you're Chinese," Primo said. "As I've told you, many of them are my clients. I saw some of the young men practicing this form of fighting. Kung Fu, they call it. I asked for some lessons. I guess they taught me pretty good, huh?"

Pietro butted in. "Bah," he said. "I could have used that wine bottle like Samson used the jaw bone of an ass, and annihilated them all! Now tell me, Mr. Londi, what was your contribution to the epic battle?"

"Uncle, you know Dom is a lover, not a fighter. He reflects only on the beauty of Angelina Lombardi and nothing else."

"Will you fools please shut up? I'm turning off here, good night, and may you always be victorious," and bowing a little drunkenly, he headed back to the Toscano Hotel.

Dom had now decided that without a doubt he wanted to ride the train to Sonoma County and stay a night or two in Healdsburg. He was even thinking of suggesting to Angelina that she accompany him. He would find them both clean rooms in a hotel, and they would enjoy seeing the sights and escaping the San Francisco fog. He thought asking Angelina might be a little bold, but he figured what the heck, he had nothing to lose. All she could do was say no.

One morning, shortly after the great fight, there was a lull in business, and he mentioned it to her during breakfast. Immediately, Angelina thought the idea would be fun. She would love to get away for a weekend, and she enjoyed Dom's company more than she cared to admit.

"I can't go," she responded to Dom.

"What do you mean you can't? Sure you can. You've got good help; they can handle the café for a weekend."

"I can't," she said, looking distant and troubled.

"Angelina, I think it's time you tell me what's been troubling you," Dom said in a kind, low voice.

Angelina's strength melted, and tears began to fill her eyes.

"It's my sister, Conchetta. No one's heard from her in almost two weeks. The authorities have been notified, but no one's seen her. It's like she has just vanished."

Dom was alarmed. He knew her sister was living with her brother and his wife in Monterey, and indeed this did sound odd. He tried to evoke a little lightness.

"Oh, there's probably nothing to worry about. Maybe she did like your brother and eloped. She's young, and the young do such things, and I remember you telling me she was very headstrong. She's probably on a honeymoon, maybe up at that Lake Tahoe everyone's always talking about. I'll bet you receive a letter any day announcing she's happily married."

"I admit it's a possibility, Dom. She is capable of such action, and I've heard her say she's afraid of becoming an old maid. She's always thought I waited way too long to marry and didn't want to follow in my shoes. But by now I think she would have written. Surely she would realize that everyone would be worried, and Mario and Lena said they didn't think she even had a boyfriend. No, I am afraid something terrible has happened."

Dom was upset. Upset at what Angelina had told him and upset that his plans for an enjoyable outing were tarnished.

"Angie, I'm going to tell my friend Primo Nuti about this. You know what a good lawyer he is. Perhaps in some way he can help."

Reaching across the counter and grabbing her hands in his he said, "Now I know what that sadness was behind your eyes. And now I know what you mean when you say you can't go. I have two train tickets for this coming Saturday. I was hoping one of them was to be yours. I'll return one, but I still need to go. Some of the outing could be business. Primo has arranged for a man to show me some wonderful properties for sale out there. They'll probably be snapped up fast. I'll be prepared to make an offer if I like what I see."

"Dom, you're thinking of moving?" Angelina asked, suddenly surprised.

"Who knows," Dom said, "buying property is usually a good investment. It's late. I've got to get to work. Try not to worry. Conchetta's probably not an old maid anymore, but I will mention it to Primo tonight. If I don't see you before I leave, I'll see you when I get back," and holding one of Angelina's hands to his lips, he kissed it and was gone.

It was a beautiful spring morning when Dom boarded the ferry bound for Sausalito and the train station. The ride across the bay was breathtaking. The fog was lifting in sections revealing patches of blue sea and sky and Angel and Alcatraz Islands. Gulls and pelicans were busy swooping down on fish. The pelicans would hover above a school, probably smelt, then abruptly fold their wings and crash into the water, coming up with a mouthful of fish. The sea gulls in a frenzy would fly darting in and out trying to grab a bite. Dom took pleasure at the sight. Nature indeed was an endless cycle.

Dom's spirits were a little low due to the absence of Angelina coupled with the news she had told him concerning her sister, but the freshness of the morning and the prospect of a train ride into new territory made him look forward to the unfolding of the day.

The ferry landed, and soon he was walking the short distance towards the waiting steam locomotive and passenger cars.

"Hey Joe, what's up?" he suddenly heard in a familiar voice.

Turning, he saw Angelina emerge from a crowd of people, dressed in her usual black and carrying a traveling bag, a slight smile lighting up her large, expressive eyes. She came walking towards Dom, her hips swaying slightly, the dress secured tightly at the waist, accentuating her trim figure. She wore large earrings and a small gold crucifix, her hair was pulled back stylishly in the bun, and Dom thought she looked like a million bucks.

"What's going on?" he said. "You've changed your mind?"

She stood even now with Dom, wearing her sturdy heeled shoes. The two were of about the same height.

"If you go out there alone, you'll probably get lost, or the Indians will get you. Who would pull you out if one of those redwood trees falls on your head?"

Dom started laughing, shaking his head.

"You don't know how happy I am to see you," he said. "This will make the weekend perfect."

Turning abruptly serious, Angelina asked, "You've told Primo about Conchetta?"

"Of course," Dom said.

"He was going to get hold of the sheriff in Monterey as quickly as possible. He was also going to notify some friends in Monterey and Carmel to be on the lookout."

"From what you've told me, I described Conchetta to him as best I could."

"Thank you so much, Dom. I decided that there's really not that much I can do about the situation. I can worry and be upset just as easily on the train, or in this wild place we're going to, as I could at the café. If good news arrives, everything will be fine. If bad news arrives, I'm in no hurry to hear it. This anxiety has been eating me up. Maybe getting away will keep me from going crazy. And you know there is nothing worse than a crazy Italian."

"Oh, heaven forbid," Dom said. "By the way, have you ever met Primo's uncle, Pietro? Now that's a crazy Italian."

"No," she said, "but by the smile you've got on your face, he might be crazy in a nice way, eh?"

"I've never seen anyone use a wine bottle better," Dom stated.

Angelina wrinkled her brows at him. "Actually, I'm quite excited. The weather is perfect. It's going to be a fine day to head north. And you know, I just realized I haven't seen a vineyard since leaving Italy. The young leaves should be freshly sprung, no?"

"Right," Dom said. "They should be that light green color and have that soft look. They tell me that zinfandels are what they're mostly growing up there."

Just then they heard the conductor announce, "All aboard!" and in spite of the shadow that clung to part of her, Angelina Lombardi and Dom Londi boarded the train together that soon rumbled on down the tracks, heading towards the wine and redwood country of Sonoma County.

Leaving the fishing village of Sausalito, the train soon entered an area of rolling green hills and oaks. A few farmhouses and barns dotted the landscape, and cows and horses grazed in the fields. Looking out the window, they hadn't gone far before they even spotted small herds of blacktail deer, browsing and cautiously stepping about. The two immigrants didn't talk much, content to let the train lull them and enjoy the scenery unfolding before them. The tracks ran through quite a lot of marshy areas loaded with ducks that took to flight as the train approached. It seemed like before they knew it, they were making their first stop. "San Rafael," a wooden sign above the station platform read. They could see what looked like the bell tower of an old church or probably a Spanish mission from their seats. The train paused only long enough to unload and receive new passengers, and they pulled out again under a belch of black steam and a fresh blowing of whistles.

"I think the next stop is going to be Petaluma," Dom said. "I looked at a map before we left. Lots of the chickens we buy in the city are raised around there. I think lots of those fresh eggs you have at the café come from there too."

The rolling hills and the oak and madrone trees continued, but more often now they were seeing large vistas of completely flat land, covered with a new crop of wild oats. There were very few houses on either side of the tracks.

"Dom, what's that?" Angelina pointed.

Out in the green field of oats they saw a furry black hump rising in regular intervals.

"I think it's a bear," Dom said, and sure enough the animal paused and raised its head to stare briefly at the passing train.

"That wasn't one of them," Dom said, "but I hear they have some of those giant grizzly bears around here that can rip a man apart. Primo told me that when the Spanish and Mexicans owned all this land, they used to capture grizzly and put one in an arena with their best fighting bull, have a fiesta and bet on who would win."

"I don't like that," Angelina promptly announced. "The bear is an undomesticated animal, while the bull is not. A wild creature of the forest should not be treated with such indignation."

"Well said, Angie. I concur. My, but you're an opinionated lady."

"A lady that has no opinion gets stepped on here, as well as in Italy. It doesn't pay to keep your mouth shut, Joe."

"OK, OK," Dom said chuckling. "Got any other opinions or observations?"

"Just one," she said, looking at him straight-faced. "Your pants have come undone."

Dom's face turned red, and he immediately looked down. Nothing was amiss.

"I see your sense of humor is coming back, Miss Lombardi. Even though it's at my expense, I'm happy for you," he said, patting her hand.

The train started a steady slow climb, and soon they were on a trestle spanning a sluggish, brown river. Some warehouses and various buildings came into view. A few small boats were plying up and down the river.

"We must be coming into Petaluma," Dom said. "And that must be the Petaluma River. At the restaurant, we get a lot of that delicious striped bass where this river empties into the bay."

"I don't like it; it's too muddy a river for me. It reminds me of sewer," Angelina said.

The train came to a halt in a cloud of steam. People left and entered. A conductor walked the car, announcing the stop would be a little longer than the last, and to feel free to stretch their legs or use the facilities. Dom and Angelina did both, and strolled along the street near the station, looking inside the shop windows. Dom spotted ladies' straw hats inside one of them.

"Quick, Angie," he said. "Go inside and choose one of those hats. I hear that sun gets hot around Healdsburg. The treat's on me," he said, handing her some bills.

"OK, big spender, if it makes you happy."

Dom waited outside, keeping an eye on the train. Angelina came out shortly, sporting a stylish huge hat tilted coyly to the side.

"You look like a Roman beauty," Dom announced.

"Thank you Julius," she said, and they hurried back to the train.

"Next major stop, Santa Rosa," the conductor called as the train again pulled out.

Angelina had taken off her hat, and again they became absorbed with looking out the window.

Leaving Petaluma, the tracks cut between low hills. Every flat area in between now held a house and small farm. They saw children tending to chores or playing. They occasionally spotted a farmer tilling his field. Each farm looked to have a good vegetable garden going. The hills on both sides swallowed the train up again, until after a slight climb, they came back out into the open again, and rounding a bend, were met by a flat plain of land, distant mountains encircling it, with one massive peak jutting off in the distance. It almost looked like a volcano, its peak covered with a little snow.

"I think that distant mountain is called Saint Helena," Dom said. "I saw it on the map. It's in another county, Napa or Lake, I forget which. Primo said there's a great little town near there, Calistoga, where people take mud baths and drink special waters. Some volcanic formed geyser shoots water and steam up into the air at precise intervals. It's really something to behold, I hear."

There were many tracts of land now that they could see were being farmed commercially. Dom recognized large plots of potatoes, fields of oats and alfalfa, sections devoted to young corn or strawberries. He saw varieties of beans and lettuces. Off in the distance, closer to the base of the hills, he saw the nice neat rows of fruit orchards.

"Wow," Angelina said. "Must be good soil around here. I didn't think this many people were living and farming around here. Where are all the wild Indians? And where are the vineyards and the giant redwoods?"

"I think the Indians might be in your head, Ang. And I think we've got a way to go before we see redwoods and grapes."

Angelina tapped Dom sharply on the shoulder.

"Don't call me Ang. You know as well as I that Ang is short for Angelo. Are you blind? Can't you see I'm not a man? You may continue to call me Angie as you have been on occasion, Mr. Londi."

Dom just hung his head and shook it. An instant later he was again looking out the window and pointing.

"Hey, look at that tree. I'll bet it's a redwood."

Near the tracks, off by itself, stood a very tall tree with long, dark green limbs sticking almost straight out, some circling upward, some downward near the ends. The trunk was covered with hairy-looking reddish bark. The side of the trunk facing the train must have been at least six feet before starting to curve in a circumference.

"Dio Bono! What a monster," uttered Angelina.

"I have a feeling there're even bigger ones," said Dom.

"Sir," he said, leaning forward, tapping and addressing a man sitting two rows ahead of them. No one was sitting directly in front of them. "Do you know if that is a redwood tree?"

"It sure is, Mac. You see more and more of them the further north you go."

Dom looked at Angelina and smiled. "He called me Mac. You said everyone calls everyone Joe. See, you don't know everything."

Angelina shook her head.

"He called you Mac after hearing your accent. Short for *macaroni*, you numbskull. Where were you born, under a rock?"

Dom pinched her hip. She slapped his hand. They both returned to looking out the window and saw much more activity. A well-used road ran parallel to the track with side roads at intervals leading to farms and houses. They spotted wagons carrying produce, people going by on horses or on foot, one fellow was even pumping away on a bicycle, that two-wheeled contraption they were starting to see more and more of these days. Shortly, the train was surrounded by buildings.

"Santa Rosa! Feel free to get out and stretch folks," the conductor announced.

As at all the stops, a few new passengers boarded, most left. Dom and Angelina got out. Santa Rosa was a pretty big town. Lots of people were milling around and passing by going about their business. Suddenly they heard rapid footsteps. A street urchin flashed by, grabbed Angelina's handbag, and ran off at full speed down the street.

"Hey!" Dom yelled. "Thief, stop him!" And he took off after the boy.

The dirty, ragged little fellow didn't get far. A Chinese man seemed to dart out of nowhere, and he grabbed and held the boy as he practically ran into his arms. Dom came up in a huff, Angelina following behind. The boy was struggling in the man's arms, but he held him fast.

"Thank you, sir," Dom said. "The little thief is fast, and I don't think these old legs could have caught him."

The boy quit struggling and went limp as Angelina came up and, staring him in the eyes, held out her hand for the purse. The boy thrust it at her. He was covered from head to toe with dirt, he wore rags for clothes, and he was unmistakably too thin. Angelina had seen many of this type wandering around San Francisco. She had also seen plenty of them back in the old country.

Kneeling in front of the boy, she said, "I know you're hungry, but that doesn't give you the right to steal. I'm going to give you a break, huh. No cops for you."

She reached into her handbag and pulled out a leather coin purse. She handed the boy several dollars.

"Go," she said. "And don't do anything like this again. And remember, don't be afraid to ask people for help. You'll find there are more good people in the world than bad. Now go."

The boy looked confused and just stood staring at the money in his hands.

Suddenly he looked up at Angelina with teary eyes and said in a low voice, "Thank you, ma'am," and he walked rapidly away.

"You sure came around at the right moment my friend," Dom said, facing the Chinese fellow. "This is Angelina Lombardi, and I am Dom Londi, and we are certainly grateful for your intervention."

"Oh, I am so happy I was to be of a little help. The boy ran right into me. It was not difficult to detain him. My name is Po Ling, and I hope to start a laundry business north of here in Healdsburg."

Po Ling was the father of the little girl that was throwing and catching the ball many years ago in the town of Modesto. That little girl whose braids were pulled by Davy, giving him his first feeling of real power and control over another.

Chapter 7

As did thousands of others, Po Ling arrived in California on a hunt for gold. He soon gave up on this quest after meeting a Chinese girl in Sacramento who worked with her parents and brother in the laundry business there. He had taken his few clothes in to have them cleaned when he laid eyes on the woman who was to be his wife. He was immediately smitten and put all his efforts into wooing instead of wading and grubbing about cold streams and creeks. He got a job in a livery stable cleaning stalls where he was also allowed to sleep, enabling him to stay in Sacramento. He bought some extra used clothing and blankets and would take them to the laundry just so he would have an excuse to see his heart's desire, Mai. Unfortunately, he usually had the odor of horse dung wafting about him, and upon seeing and smelling him, Mai would wrinkle her nose and wait on him as quickly as possible. One Saturday afternoon, after his chores were done, he took a bar of soap and stripping down to his shorts, jumped in one of the more secluded horse troughs to give himself a quick, but thorough, scrubbing. After filling the trough with fresh water, he dressed in his best clothes and proceeded to the laundry.

He found Mai alone, standing behind a table full of clothes, neatly folding and stacking them. She looked up to see Po amazingly clean and well dressed, even smelling quite good, though mostly of cheap lilac water. Po surprised her by asking if she might accompany him tomorrow afternoon to the downtown Fourth of July celebration, which included the traditional nighttime fireworks show. She told Po she had been planning to go too, though with her parents, and she didn't think they would mind if he accompanied them. She asked him if he knew that they would have to observe the celebration from a distance and not mingle much with the crowd. Often times, the presence of Chinese was not appreciated at such gatherings, she explained. He understood, but being a rational and thinking young man, found it hard to accept the fact that though the labor of his people was eagerly sought for the toughest and most dangerous of tasks, be it road or track building, or delving deep into mine shafts, they were meant to feel unwanted and unwelcome at any town function or celebration.

"The fireworks should be good from any distance," he told Mai.

The next day he arrived at the laundry at the agreed upon hour, and they all walked to the courthouse square where a barbecue was in full swing. Vendors were scattered about selling various items from candy and food to the latest mining gear. A beer garden had been set up and was dispensing beer at five cents a glass to thirsty patrons. Po couldn't help but notice that already a few drunks were stumbling about the crowd. The little group, which included Mai's grandparents, found a place to spread blankets and sit on a slight rise in a vacant lot between two buildings where other Chinese had gathered. Knowing they would be shunned at the barbecue and food booths, they unpacked the lunch they had brought and proceeded to eat and watch the crowd. The hot afternoon passed slowly, some of the people in the vacant lot even lay down and napped, wishing to linger until dark and the fireworks. Mai's grandmother, a small woman of a ripe and venerable age, was one of those napping. She carefully had lain down on her side on the blanket, and using the shawl as a pillow, soon fell asleep.

Po and Mai sat a short distance away, quietly talking, alone together for the first time. Most of the group had wandered off to watch some horse races going on over at one of the blocked off streets. Two rowdies, worse for wear from beer, lurched by and one, spotting the little silver Buddha that dangled from Mai's grandmother's neck, reached down and jerked the Buddha loose, breaking the thin chain.

"I know who this is, and it ain't Jesus," he slurred. "This fella ain't welcome in this country," and thrusting the little image into his pocket, stumbled on.

The grandmother had awoken and was patting at the soreness at her neck where the chain had snapped. Po and Mai had seen what happened, and instantly came to the grandmother.

"I will help," Po said, and he started to follow the men.

"No," Mai said. "They are big and probably have friends. Men like that usually even carry guns. My grandmother is safe, and the Buddha will find its own way."

"I'll be careful," Po said. "I'm only going to follow them for a way," and before she could stop him, he took off.

Po had his life's savings in his pocket, and it amounted to five dollars. He followed the men from a distance, with no plan in mind, only that of looking for any opportunity. Presently, the men stopped, and the one with the Buddha retrieved it from his pocket and began to drunkenly admire it. Po thought fast, and walking casually by the men, lingered upon seeing the carving.

"Lovely Buddha," he said in broken English. "I give four dollars."

The drunk looked to his partner, then at Po.

"Five dollars and it's yours, chink."

Po pretended to look pained and upset, shaking his head in a negative manner, then reached in his pants for the five one-dollar bills and extended them the money. Po thought the two of them could probably just take it from him, but they were amidst a group of people, and the men seemed like it was all that they could do just to remain standing.

"Same time," Po said, and reached his hand toward the Buddha.

"He don't trust us, Dick," the man said, but the transaction went off without a hitch. Po seemed to have a knack for retrieving things, and being in the right place at the right time.

Mai's parents were impressed with Po after this, and shortly after, when he asked for their daughter's hand in marriage, they did not object. They taught Po all he could learn about the laundry business, and with the money he saved along with Mai's dowry, the couple moved to Modesto several years later to open their own laundry.

Their laundry prospered, and after a time, Mai gave birth to a healthy baby girl they named Suen. Four years later a boy, Mat, was born. Life was good in Modesto, though the summer could get blazing hot. Both the children attended school and were quick learners. Suen dressed in a fairly traditional manner, but Mat wore his hair and clothes similar to that of all the other boys. The children tried to fit in the white society as best they could, and they both had several good non-Chinese friends, but often they still had to endure the catcalls of "slant eye" and "pigtail." One boy simply called Mat "rice bowl" every time he saw him. They did eat a lot of rice at Mat's house, but he preferred chicken, cooked any way he could get it, and he tried once to explain this to the other youth. The other boy just laughed and said, "Shut up, rice bowl," and walked away.

Suen grew into a beautiful young woman and pleaded with her mother to let her dress more and more like the

Anglo girls. She wore her hair in one long braid down her back, and in her teenage years, caught the eye of many a boy. Po and Mai were watchful of their children. They knew anti-Chinese sentiment could rear its head at any moment. Often, they felt the need to worry about their own safety as well as the children's. Any time a crime was committed and was unsolved, the sheriff, or some indignant leading citizens, would descend upon Chinatown looking for the culprit. In turn, if a crime or act of violence was directed upon a Chinese person, the law would often look away, or pursue the matter with the least amount of effort or in a negligent manner.

Suen seemed to have an easier time growing up than her brother. Outside of the usual "chink" or "pigtail," the worst memory she had was the time that smelly boy tried to play with her ball and got mad and pulled her hair. She never forgot the crazy look on his face, like he wanted to hurt or kill her. He had even kissed her roughly with his smelly mouth. She had realized that the kiss had been used as a tool to hurt, not loving as her parents kissed. Mat seemed to have it hard though. Dressing like all the other boys, and wearing his hair short, usually under a hat, and speaking good English just didn't seem quite good enough in the eyes of the other boys.

One afternoon when Mat was fourteen, several of the boys, with trouble on their minds, invited him to come over to their farm and help them work with the horses. One of the horses, a large solid brown one, was so skittish and violent that it had never been ridden. The father of one of the boys had obtained the horse for next to nothing from a passing stranger who said he had bought it from a man who evidently used to beat it. The horse had been covered with cuts and sores. The horse healed, but never would tame down. The boy's father bought the horse thinking that once in a secure, safe environment, and alongside the other horses, it would eventually settle down. It hadn't, and most people in town knew it. Many had tried to ride the horse. All had been thrown. It was next to impossible just to get a saddle on the monster. It tried to bite any hand that came near it. The farmer had tried to sell the horse. No one would buy it.

The boys were hoping to see a good show. They had turned the horse loose in the corral and couldn't wait for Mat to arrive. The sight of the slightly built Chinese boy running around with the horse chasing him, maybe biting his butt, would be a great laugh. Mat hurried to the farm, flattered and surprised that he was going to hang out with the others. When he got there, he found the other boys sitting on the corral fence, looking at the largest horse he had ever seen, standing in the middle of the corral, snorting and pawing the ground with its left front leg.

"Hey Mat," one of them called, "you're just in time. Tom's in the barn with a saddle. He's going to come out of the barn, after you've thrown a blanket on that horse, and saddle him. Here's the blanket, now do it fast."

The boys knew that to a farm-raised kid none of this would have made sense, but they figured that to a kid who grew up around a town laundry, it would seem just fine. Mat noticed that the horse didn't even have a bridle on it. *I guess that comes later*, he reasoned. Going alone into a ring with a horse like that terrified him, but not wishing to appear cowardly or hesitant, he grabbed the red blanket, hopped the fence, and walked towards the horse. The animal turned its head to watch the boy, but otherwise stood perfectly still. The closer Mat came to the horse, the more he marveled at its size. He would have to really stretch to arrange the blanket on the horse's back. Reaching the animal, he used a sideways motion to try to sling the blanket. The horse instantly turned and, raising itself on its hind legs came down with one hoof on the top of Mat's skull. He had been so startled, he had barely started to move.

One of the boys ran to a gate, allowing the running horse to go out into the field. The other two ran towards the fallen Chinese boy. Mat's little felt hat had been smashed flat on his head, a line of blood welling up through it. His eyes were wide open in a blank stare of surprise. He didn't move a muscle. The boys knew he was dead. He hadn't even run. The horse never chased him or bit his butt. No one even had laughed. All it was, was a hot afternoon filled with fear and regret as the smell of loosening bowels rose into the faces of the farm boys staring at the shattered head of the schoolmate they had loved to tease.

"I've got to get Pa," the boy whose father owned the horse said, and ran towards town where his parents had been shopping. One of the other boys removed the red blanket that Mat still held tightly in his hand, and covered his body with it, then went off to stand against the barn, feeling guilty as sin, and too much in shock to do or say much.

The other boy quickly located his parents at the dry goods store, and rapidly explained through tears what had happened. The father was livid, and had half a notion to beat his son right there and then. Instead, they all got in the wagon and rode straight to the Chinese laundry to inform the boy's parents. Po and his wife went hysterical. They thought maybe there was a mistake. Their son was only unconscious. They pleaded with the farmer to take them to the place as fast as possible. They reached the scene in minutes.

Po ran to the middle of the corral where Mat lay. He lifted the blanket, and a pathetic cry filled the air. One look told him his son was dead. Automatically, he put his fingers to Mat's throat, checking for a pulse. Nothing. His wife came up and threw herself on the ground sobbing, and raising her son in her arms to her chest. Several people from nearby farms had arrived along with a couple of hired hands. They must have noticed the wagon moving all out in a cloud of dust back to the farm.

As the Lings were leaning over their son, Po heard one person say, "Oh, it's only some Chinese boy, got himself killed playing around with that ornery horse."

They placed Mat's body in the wagon, and the farmer drove the Lings back into town. He had his son come along, who tried to explain that it all had been an accident. They were only trying to have a little fun, and no one forced Mat to enter the corral. Po and Mai knew exactly what had happened. If their son hadn't been Chinese, he would still be alive. They said nothing to the father or son as they removed Mat's body from the wagon and carried it to their living quarters. The farmer proceeded to the sheriff's office, where he explained the accident that had claimed the Chinese boy's life. Then, after returning home and taking the whip to his son, went out into the field and shot the horse. All had been done that could be done, he figured, and laid the matter to rest.

Suen came home from some friend's house to find her younger brother laid out on a cooling board in his small bedroom. Her mother was carefully cleansing his body, a white cloth had been wrapped around his broken head. Suen collapsed in a faint. When she came to, her parents explained what had happened. Suen knew those farm boys. Her first thought was that she'd like to kill them. Instead, she took her hatred into herself and vowed always to despise all white Americans from then on. Her parents were of somewhat the same vein, though Po insisted that he had been alive long enough to see that not all Americans were evil. Some were just ignorant; some were reasonable, kind, and caring. He tried to tell Suen that those boys would live the rest of their lives with guilt of that day on their shoulders. Suen didn't agree. She imagined them already laughing and joking over her brother's death. Why, he was too dumb to know anything about horses, she could hear them say.

It wasn't long after the funeral that Po decided it was best for his family to sell the laundry and leave Modesto. Seeing the boys who were responsible for Mat's death wandering about town or seeing their parents was just too upsetting for all of them. Po couldn't seem to get the comment, "It's only some China boy," out of his head, and thought that surely some other town in California would be more hospitable. Nothing would bring Mat back, and Po didn't think he was running away; he just felt it would be better not to see familiar faces that would constantly remind him and his wife and daughter of that terrible day. Through the grapevine, he had heard of a farming town to the north that was growing at a pretty fast rate. For some reason, many Italian immigrants were moving to the area to grow grapes. He had noticed that in his dealings with the Italians, he felt a lesser degree of hostility and superiority. The fact that they too were immigrants perhaps contributed to this. In any case, this town Healdsburg sounded as good as any. They would give it a try. Their hearts were filled with sadness and loss. Suen, also, was consumed with bitterness and hatred. A soft quality she had formerly had was gone, replaced with a guarded look of constant vigilance. She would be glad to get away from Modesto, but she doubted if things would ever change much for the better. The laundry had done good business. It didn't take long for them to find a buyer.

So in the spring, they bought a large wagon and two good, strong, gentle horses, and began their journey north and west. Most nights they slept outside near the wagon. At Stockton, they found rooms in the Chinese part of town to better clean up and rest. Traveling in such a manner seemed to lighten their spirits. Suen even attached hook and line to a long supple willow branch, and baiting it with worms, caught enough trout for a delicious meal from a small, cold clear stream near Lodi. Her parents were over- joyed to see her snap out of it a bit, and encouraged her to catch more fish as they traveled. Po said he would fish the next time too. He wasn't about to let his daughter out fish him.

When they reached Sacramento, they broke the news to Mai's parents. Her grandparents had passed away within months of each other. Her parents were devastated, yet supportive. Nothing could be worse than losing a son at such a young age, with his whole life yet ahead of him, they all agreed. Suen's grandparents had immediately noticed the change in her. They hadn't seen her in several years, but the young smiling girl seemed to be gone. They understood the reason, and agreed it was for the best to leave Modesto. They urged their son-in-law and daughter to stay in Sacramento and go back into the business with them; after all, they were getting old and could use the help. Some day the laundry would be theirs. Po and Mai stayed in Sacramento for a week, talking and thinking it over and having a good visit. In the end, they decided to push on to Healdsburg. They were still relatively young and eager for a brand new start.

Saying goodbye was very hard for Mai. She prom- ised they would be back for a visit, but she was so much more aware than ever before how life could vanish in the blinking of an eye. Amidst tears and good-byes, they left Sacramento heading west towards Napa. There were no towns of any size to speak of in between, and some of the days it rained, turning the road to mud. The terrain was mostly flat with gently rolling hills, and when the sun came out between showers, a rainbow often appeared deco- rating the sky with brilliance. It was hard to be sad at such times, and in spite of the weather, they made good time, and presently reached the town of Napa. This town had a thriving Chinese community, and they soon found rooms in a hotel, where they could clean up and spend the night. Over dinner in the small hotel restaurant, they met some people who had heard of Healdsburg, but suggested that Santa Rosa was a much better place to live and start a business. Many Chinese lived in Santa Rosa, and they weren't sure if there were even any in Healdsburg. Po took this information to heart. He knew there was more safety in numbers, and decided to investigate this Healdsburg thoroughly before he moved his family there.

From Napa they made their way to Sonoma, and from Sonoma to Santa Rosa. In between, they passed through some of the prettiest farmlands and forests that they had ever seen. The road between Sonoma and Santa Rosa wound through a narrow, picturesque valley, which they learned was appropriately called The Valley of the Moon. The Lings probably could have made it from Sonoma to Santa Rosa in one day, but they had gotten a late start and had lingered at interesting sights along the way. They pulled off the road in the late afternoon, to a spot where it was obvious other travelers had spent the night. They made a small fire and began to prepare the evening meal. They had bought several pieces of fresh chicken in a little town called Agua Caliente, and were cooking it in a single pot with rice, onion, and spices. They were sitting around the fire eating, when a huge full moon suddenly rose above the hills to the east, lighting up the little valley. Suen looked at her plate and, seeing the chicken, thought of Mat. That moon and the sight of her brother's favorite food pierced her to the heart, and she uncontrollably burst out in tears. Her mother glanced at the moon and started crying too. Po looked at the chicken in his plate, and suddenly scraped it into the fire. He grabbed the other plates and did the same.

He said, with watery eyes, directly to the moon, "Rice is good enough for us tonight. Thank you moon for bringing back Mat to us for a moment."

Taking solace in one another, and in the beauty of the moonlit valley, they finished their meal and slept peacefully under a sky filled with stars and the largest moon they had ever seen.

In the morning, they continued on, and in a short time they reached Santa Rosa. The main road cut right through the center of the town, which was bustling with activity. Po spotted a livery stable situated down a side street near the railway. He had come to the conclusion that the wisest thing to do was to board the horses and wagon for a day or two and journey on to Healdsburg by train. He had heard in Sonoma that the road to Healdsburg was often one long stretch of mud after recent rains. No use going through that, if they ended up not liking what they had seen and decided to return to Santa Rosa. Leaving their rig at the livery stable and carrying overnight bags, they walked the short distance to the train station. They bought tickets and lingered about the station waiting for the train to arrive.

It wasn't long before they heard a distant whistle blowing and presently the train came into view and pulled into the station. Many passengers got out, and the conductor announced that the train would be departing again shortly. They were making their way to the boarding platform, when Po noticed a young boy running, clutching a purse, with an older fellow chasing him yelling, "Stop him!" Po took a few steps out of the crowd and the boy ran right into his arms. Dom and Angelina came up at this point, and the three people introduced themselves to one another. Po liked the two Italians at once. Their accents and names identified them immediately. He liked the way they handled the situation with the little thief. Kindness often left a longer effect than punishment.

"Please, let me introduce my wife and daughter," Po said, turning and motioning to them. "This is my wife,

Mai, and my daughter, Suen. This is Mr. Londi and Miss Lombardi."

Pleasantries were barely exchanged when they heard the call to depart.

"Come," Dom said. "Sit by us on the train. We too are going to Healdsburg."

The Lings occupied the empty seats in front of Dom and Angelina, and shortly the train got moving again. Dom couldn't help but notice a few gawking stares the Lings received as they entered the compartment. There were not that many passengers left, most having departed in Santa Rosa, but Dom saw one lady traveling with a little girl actually give the Lings a haughty look, and abruptly turn her head away. *Italians don't really have it too bad around here*, he thought. *It's easier for us to blend in, at least until we open our mouths.* In San Francisco, most of the Chinese kept to their own section of town, unless to go off on labor details. He admired the Ling's courage at adventuring out on their own. An element of fear suddenly struck him, thinking about their safety. He knew this Healdsburg to be still a pretty wild place. How tolerant would it be of Chinese?

"Have you come here from San Francisco?" Dom asked, addressing Po.

"No, we have only recently arrived from Modesto. We have been traveling by wagon. We left it along with our belongings at the livery stables."

Dom and Angelina exchanged glances.

"Why, that's quite a journey," Dom said. "You have the spirit of an adventurer, huh?"

"Oh," Po said. "We needed to get away. The road helped in a small way to clear our minds."

"Speak for yourself, Father," Suen interjected.

"Suen, don't talk to your father that way," Mai admonished.

"Forgive us," Po said. "We have recently experienced great sadness, but that does not excuse impoliteness," he said, looking at Suen.

The travelers fell silent for a bit, staring out the window, reflecting on their own thoughts. They were passing through a lovely area of valley oaks, small farms, and orchards, and a field covered with vines growing up poles towards overhead trellises.

"What kinds of plants are those?" Angelina inquired.

"I'm not really sure," Dom said.

Po, overhearing, answered, "Those are hops. They use them mostly in the making of beer. Farmers around Modesto also grew them to furnish the local breweries. They are just starting up those trellises," he explained. "Eventually, they will fill in all that area overhead. People pick them from tall ladders."

"Interesting," Angelina said. "What trouble men will go through to drink beer."

"Primo was right. They do grow most anything around here," Dom said.

The train slowed to a stop. A rickety sign above a small platform said Poor Man's Flats. A new sign below it read West Windsor.

"This place must have two names," Dom observed, staring out and seeing only a few crude shacks scattered about a flat dusty area and several unbelievably dirty little children kicking a can down the road that went alongside the tracks.

"Well," Angelina noted, "I'd much rather live in a place called West Windsor than Poor Man's Flats. Someone probably got wise and suggested a name change."

No one got off there. One thin old fellow boarded, and going down the aisle announced to no one in particular, "Captain McCraken at your service, folks. Came out here in a covered wagon from Missouri going on twenty years ago," and abruptly sat down.

Angelina looked at Dom and shrugged. Po and Mai had smiles on their faces. The captain dug out a corncob pipe and commenced to smoking.

Leaving behind the dusty area of scrub oak, the tracks cut over towards what looked to be the main road between Santa Rosa and Healdsburg. Indeed it was muddy, and a wagon could be seen loaded with hay bales, making slow progress headed south. The terrain now became much more interesting. A range of densely forested hills came into view a few miles to the west. Rolling hills of green disappeared towards the east. They were traveling pretty much in the middle of a valley filled predominantly with fruit orchards and farms, cows grazing in the fields.

"Dom, look!" Angelina pointed.

Dom had seen it at the same time.

"A vineyard!" he exclaimed.

And sure enough, there, surrounded by mostly peach, and what looked like plum trees, were the gnarly, twisted trunks of grapevines neatly planted in rows, with fresh-looking, light green leaves all about them.

"Wow, it's been a long time," Angelina said.

"Longer for you than for me," Dom replied.

Po glanced over at Mai with a quizzical look on his face. Mai slightly shrugged her shoulders. *They sure seem to get excited by grapevines*, thought Po. *Must be some Italian trait.* Dom reached for Angelina's hand and gave it a squeeze. They were both thinking of the old country and the lives they had left behind.

"Say," Dom suddenly remarked, "this area's starting to look a little like parts of Tuscany. Primo said it did, and now I'm starting to believe him."

"I see what you mean," Angelina said. "I've only seen Tuscany in pictures and paintings, but this does look similar. No walled cities or large old cathedrals, though, eh?"

"Hey, give the place time," Dom said. "This is new land."

"Not to the Indians," Angelina announced.

"There you go again. You think some Indians are going to jump you and cut off all that nice hair of yours, don't you?"

The Lings suppressed laughter at their playful banter. Those grapes made them homesick, they reasoned.

"Anyone care for a drink?" Old Captain McCraken suddenly announced. "Missouri style moonshine," he said, producing a pint bottle of clear liquid. "The finest ambrosia Poor Man's Flats has to offer."

A boy of about sixteen jumped up and said, "I'd like some."

"Oh, sit down," his father said and tugged at his hat, pulling it down over the boy's eyes. *The boy's only a little older than Mat*, Po thought, and suddenly was a little homesick too. Not for a home, but for a son.

Dom was sitting fairly close to the Captain and said, "No, thank you, sir. It's a little early for me."

"Suit yourself," he said and, taking a sip, settled deep into his seat.

A symmetrical-shaped mountain came into view, smoothly round at the top, covered with trees and growth.

"That's probably Fitch Mountain," Dom mentioned. "It's named after some sea captain who used to own all the land we're looking at."

"What are you, a tour guide? Quiet, and let me look," Angelina said.

The train approached closer to the land at the base of the looming mountain, then rounded a bend and crossed a trestle bridge over a lively sparkling river.

"Russian River," Dom whispered in Angelina's ear.

The train had slowed and was proceeding through a developing residential area to the town depot.

"Healdsburg, end of line folks," the conductor announced.

Everyone got out, and Dom noticed that brand new tracks continued north.

"New track?" he commented to the conductor.

"Yes, sir, they're working on the line right now, pushing it on to Cloverdale. Chinese doing a lot of the work," he said, looking at the Lings exiting. Angelina looked around, a little confused.

"What's the train do now, Mr. Know-it-all?" she said, looking at Dom. The Lings had come up and were standing next to them. Dom nudged Po imperceptibly in the ribs.

"Well, Angie, it's like this. Hundreds of workers, mostly Chinese, pick the locomotive up and all the cars, one by one, and turn them around in the opposite direction. Yes, Miss, our people are very strong," Po deadpanned.

Suen couldn't help but giggle. Angelina slapped Dom on the shoulder.

"OK, OK," he protested. "The train's going to head for that area over there. It's called a roundhouse. The locomotive and all the cars enter that flat metal area where, one by one, they're disconnected, swiveled in the opposite direction, hooked up again until the whole train is back together pointing south."

"Makes sense," Angelina said. "I guess I never paid attention to how that was done."

"You're excused, Lombardi," Dom said smiling.

"How far to the main part of town?" he asked the conductor.

"It's just down there a bit," he said pointing to the west. "Just walk straight and turn right. Most of the businesses are down there around the town plaza."

"Will you join us?" Dom asked, inquiring of the Lings.

"Certainly, thank you," Po said, and off they walked with a small group of others, Captain McCraken included.

It didn't take them long to reach the center of the little town. Most of the establishments were built along the main road. There was a boot shop, furniture store, general merchandise store, a restaurant with a hotel above, a livery stable, and a beer garden. Most of the buildings were two-story, made of wood or brick. The road in front was wide and in pretty good shape. Across the road from the buildings was a lovely little plaza with benches and manicured paths and many young trees: redwoods, oranges, exotic-looking date palms, and some magnolias.

"Oh, oh Angie," Dom said motioning with his head. "Look over there at the plaza."

Sitting around one of the benches was unmistakably a group of Indians.

"You better put your hat on," he teased, "so they won't see your hair."

She just looked at him and rolled her eyes. Various people were walking through the plaza. They could see a few more businesses on the side streets surrounding the pretty little park.

"Shall we stroll the plaza?" Dom suggested.

The Lings agreed and the little group proceeded on.

"Ah, that's what I was looking for, just where Primo described," Dom said, pointing to a small building a short distance away with a sign that read, "Real Estate, Bought and Sold" in bold letters above a false front.

"Excuse me," he said. "I shall only be a moment," and he headed towards the building.

"Shall we sit down?" Po suggested, motioning to one of the plaza benches. "Perhaps we too will have use of those services later," he said, looking at Mai.

They all took seats on the long wrought iron bench and settled down to watch the town activity. It wasn't quite noon, and the day was bustling at a pretty good rate. Horses, buggies, and wagons were coming and going, and the shops appeared to be doing good business. Many people, some with children, were moving about on foot. They could see that some of the side streets leading east out of the plaza went off into tree-lined residential areas.

One of the Indians sitting on the bench a short distance away got up and approached the group.

"Greetings, my name's Walter. Excuse me for bothering you, but you people look new in town. I know pretty much everything about this place, and I would be happy to be of any kind of assistance."

Walter usually didn't do anything like this, but this group was a rarity in town.

The distinguished-looking man and woman, probably Italians he thought, or Greeks, traveling about in a happy, friendly manner with three Chinese people, one of them very beautiful and probably close to his age, certainly was a novelty. He hadn't seen such a sight since he left San Francisco.

Angelina looked at the dark-haired, handsome young man and thought, *Damn, he speaks better English than I do and with no accent.* She also immediately sensed a no-nonsense good nature. Po liked the Indian too. He genuinely seemed friendly and willing to help.

"How do you do," Po said, rising and shaking hands in the American fashion. "I am Po Ling. This is my wife, Mai, and my daughter, Suen. This is Miss Lombardi," he said, motioning to Angelina, who gave Walter a friendly smile saying, "Glad to meet you."

"Excuse me," Po said, "but are there many Chinese people living in town?"

"No, not full time," Walter answered. "I can only think of one other family. There are quite a few Chinese working on track building north of here, and some live in a little mountain town east of here called Pine Flats, where they work in a mercury mine. Are you thinking of settling here?" he said smiling, and glancing at Suen, who lowered her eyes.

"Perhaps," Po said. "Is there a laundry in town?"

"Not really. A few women take in washing on the side to earn a little extra, but most folks do their own wash.

Come to think of it, I'll bet a real laundry business would do well here. This place is beginning to grow pretty fast."

Angelina saw Dom coming back, a big grin on his face. Walter was facing away. Dom made a scissors movement with his two fingers to his hair. Angelina raised her eyes and shook her head.

Joining the group and introducing himself to Walter, he said, "Hey, lunch is on me. Let's all go over to that restaurant and get a bite to eat. I'm starving. Walter, go tell your friends to join us," he said motioning to the staring Indians.

"Oh, I think they're content to just sit there and enjoy the day, but I'd be happy to come along."

And across the plaza they went.

Chapter 8

A stage had pulled up in front of the hotel and restaurant in Healdsburg. Quite a few people were inside eating or ordering lunch when Dom and the group walked in. Immediately they received stares. Several people quit eating to gawk. A waitress, though, seemingly unperturbed, directed them to a large table near one of the walls. She had seen many different types of people, some quite unsavory, enter the restaurant and had been told by her boss that unless someone was an outright troublemaker, service was to be prompt and equal with everyone. The place needed as many customers as it could get to justify remaining open. Upon entering, Dom had noticed a chalkboard announcing the lunch special of the day, fried chicken, beans, and apple pie. Knowing that featured daily specials were usually pretty good, and were served promptly in most restaurants, he ordered the lunch special and suggested that the others might want to do the same. Everyone agreed. The Lings simply wanted to eat and get out as soon as possible. They had never been to a non-Chinese restaurant before or in any restaurant with such mixed company. They felt uneasy to say the least. Walter couldn't seem to stop smiling. He had sort of liked the commotion they had created, and was glad to be part of such a diverse table. Their lunches were promptly served. The chicken was fried to perfection, and the beans were quite flavorful. They ate mostly in silence, until the apple pie was served along with coffee for Dom and Angelina, and tea for the Lings and Walter.

"Well, we have the rest of the afternoon ahead of us. I won't be meeting with the realtor until tomorrow morning to look over several properties. You're the local expert, Walter. What do you suggest we do?"

Walter immediately thought of a plan, one that could be quite fun, in which he could play tour guide.

"Why don't we go to the livery station, rent a two-seat wagon, and I'll show you the sightsl, just like the tour guides in San Francisco do."

Earlier, during lunch, Angelina couldn't help but comment on Walter's good English, and had asked if all the Indian people in the area spoke so well. Walter had briefly explained his situation, and how he had attended the institute at the Presidio. All were impressed, and Suen couldn't help but think a little wonderingly of Walter. He must have great dedication and perseverance, she reasoned.

"Why, that sounds like a great idea, doesn't it Angie?" Dom said. "How about you, Po? Will you people come with us?"

All enthusiastically agreed. As they were leaving the restaurant, Walter suggested they book rooms for the night now. The hotel sometimes filled up fast. Dom thought that wise and turning to Po asked him his plans for the night. The Lings had little idea what Healdsburg was going to be like, but Po knew that the train departed from town in the late afternoon back to Santa Rosa. They had been having a unique, enjoyable day, and would love to spend the night at the hotel. They didn't think they would be allowed to, though. Po explained his sentiments to Dom. Walter had been listening, but could express only uncertainty.

"Well, let's go find out," Dom stated.

At the front of the restaurant was the hotel lobby. Dom inquired of the clerk if there were three rooms available, one for himself, one for his companion and one for the Lings. The clerk simply said, "Sure thing, folks," and related prices. They booked rooms and went back out on the street.

"Well, that was simple," Dom said.

"Life's meant to be simple," Angelina replied. "It's only people that complicate it."

"What are you now, a philosopher?" Dom teased.

"Just an observer," she smiled.

All were in great spirits now and headed eagerly for the livery stable. They had no trouble renting a rig, and off they went—Walter driving with Angelina and Dom up front, and the Lings sitting behind. Walter gave them a quick tour of the residential areas near town. There were many fine two-story houses, recently built, and also some simple, crude shacks. Small orchards seemed to be everywhere, many in between the houses. One street led to a tree-filled cemetery on a slight hill. Directly below, a ball field was under construction.

"Baseball," Walter said. "Everyone around here is going wild about that game."

"I know this game," Angelina said. "You hold a stick, and another man throws a hard ball at you. If it hits you in the head, you won't have far to go around here. That's a very pretty cemetery."

The Lings laughed. Mai really liked Angelina. She liked the way she joked and spoke up to Dom. She thought that they were probably sweethearts and wondered why they weren't married. They next headed east out of town and were suddenly surrounded by vineyards on either side of the road, along with more orchards and small farms.

"What pretty countryside," Angelina said.

"And look at that soil," Dom said. "So rich looking."

A farmer was tilling the soil between the rows, revealing large, rich chunks of dark brown earth. They crossed a wooden bridge over a lovely, rapidly flowing creek.

"If you follow that creek upstream many miles to its headwater, you will come close to where we Pomos live," Walter said.

They steered off in the direction the creek, headed east into the mountains, thickly covered with trees.

"Are those redwood trees growing along those slopes?" Dom inquired.

"Some are. Many are fir, pine, oak, and madrone. If we were to keep traveling along this road and take the turn to the south, then east into the hills, you would see where they are logging the redwoods. Huge, thousand years and older trees are coming down around a little stream called Mill Creek. There's a lumber mill up there that reduces them to a more manageable size. Quite a few people work there," Walter said.

After crossing the bridge and coming to where the road forked, going either south or north along a fertile valley, Walter turned the wagon around and headed back towards town. Pretty soon they took a side road between orchards and headed north. They came out on a road Walter said led into the Dry Creek Valley, a road that, if followed to its end, stopped at the Pacific ocean going past the Pomos rancheria. Looking into the valley from this point, Dom and Angelina were both reminded again of Italy, especially Tuscany, and especially the areas around Lucca, Dom thought. The noise of pounding hooves and the appearance of rising dust suddenly came to them, as they were paused on a small rise viewing the landscape.

Three riders came rapidly towards the wagon and a voice announced, "Whoa boys, let's stop. Oh my, is this a sight. What have we here? Why it's three chinks, an Injun, and what looks like a couple of fancy-dressed foreigners. You are a foreigner, ain't you, Mister?" Dave said, addressing Dom.

"I would imagine you could say that, young man."

Before Dom could say more, Angelina spoke up.

"You have no manners, cowboy. Your language is crude and impolite to strangers."

"Why, just listen to those accents! Foreigners, just like I said, boys. Say, what are you, Spanish?" Dave said glaring at Angelina. Suddenly he was reminded of the Mexican lady whose cow he tried to milk. Dave never forgot anything, especially when it came to embarrassing situations. Walter wearily responded to him.

"David, David, you always talk about accents, but yours is thicker than anyone's I've ever heard."

"How many times have I told you my name's Dave, not Davy or David, squaw man. No one's talking to you anyhow. I was talking to that uppity senorita."

Hoping that Dave was just a harmless fool, Angelina simply said, "My friend and I are Italians, and our friends behind us are Chinese, and I believe Walter is a Pomo Indian, and what are you, David?"

"Dave, Dave Fowler, a real American and proud to be it."

The other two young men had kept out of the conversation, listening halfheartedly. One of them couldn't seem to take his eyes off of Suen.

"Good for you, young fellow. It was a pleasure meeting you. Now we have to be off," Dom said patting Walter on the shoulder.

With his left hand Walter had been rubbing at his crotch in a distracted manner. Davy's eyes immediately were fixated and began to get that dreamy look, just what Walter expected. With his right hand he gave a flick of the reins saying, "Bye, Davy," and pulled away towards town.

Dave suddenly snapped out of it, and with his companions also took off towards town yelling, "Foreigners, go home," back at the wagon.

Dom and Angelina looked at one another and shook their heads. The Lings felt highly disappointed at the encounter. They had begun to like Healdsburg and were considering the prospects of a laundry. If the town held more people similar to the ones they had just met, it would probably not be safe for them to stay. Suen had the feeling that she had seen the one who only liked to be called Dave before, but couldn't be sure.

Walter could guess what his newfound friends were thinking.

"Dave's really a poor example of most of the people in town. There are probably a few others like him. Most just mind their own business, or keep their thoughts to themselves. We Pomos get ragged from time to time, and you never really get used to it, but it's usually the same ones each time, and we know what to expect. Dave's not really dangerous, I don't think. I mostly find him really pathetic and confused."

Dom had noticed Dave staring at Walter's crotch. Italy had its share of such types. "They don't know which way to fly," was a common saying to describe such people.

"At least that hothead didn't seem to have a gun," Angelina said.

"Oh, he probably had one in his saddlebag. I've seen him wear one in a holster slung down low on his hip. He was trying to draw it fast and shoot at cans near his house. He bought some magazines at the barbershop that show cowboys, gunslingers they call them, behaving in such a manner. In a way Dave's still a little boy in a man's body."

"Could be a girl in a man's body," Dom deadpanned.

Walter didn't say anything, but just looked at Dom and smiled.

"Hey, let's not let him ruin our day. There's one more area fairly close by I'd like to show you. It's called Alexander Valley. If we go now, we can have a look and still get back to town before dark."

They all agreed, and Walter reached the main road through town and turned north and then east. For a while the road paralleled the newly built railroad tracks. Between the road and the tracks, a large stone and cement building was under construction, surrounded by towering redwoods.

"Might they be building a winery?" Dom inquired.

"Right," Walter said. "It belongs to some of your fellow countrymen. Some of my people are working on it too. All those large rocks. It's going to be quite a structure, but it's slow building."

"That usually makes for a structure that lasts. In Italy things have been done in such a manner for thousands of years," Angelina chimed in.

The Lings too admired the building but were having trouble shaking off the encounter with Dave. "Chinks" was always a term they never had an easy time forgetting.

The wagon now was slowly climbing. They rounded a bend, and a large expanse of land opened up in front of them, ringed by hills, and one especially large peak, that jutted above the rest.

"Quite a little mountain," Dom said.

"It's called Geyser Peak," Walter said. "It's a strange place up there. Hot bubbling water steams out of the earth. People are going up there to bathe in it. There's even a hotel up there. The water is said to have curing properties."

"We have such places in Italy," Dom said. "They are quite popular."

"I've only been up there once," Walter said, "but things grow like crazy up there. Near one of the springs a wild grapevine is growing, that's got to be at least twelve inches in diameter, and a few years ago someone planted a fig tree nearby, and the leaves on it are twice the size of a normal leaf."

Po perked up at the announcement of such wonders.

"Now that would be a place worth visiting," he said.

"If you need a little excitement, the ride up there on the stage will give it to you," Walter assured. "The driver, usually Big Clark Foss, really knows the road, and often goes all out along the ridge line. Then it's best not to look down, just hold on and stare straight ahead. It's rugged up there. The last time anyone's seen a grizzly bear around was on that peak."

The valley they were gazing upon was bigger than any of the others they had seen. Nothing, of course, to compare to the Sacramento or San Joaquin Valleys the Lings were familiar with, but this compact expanse was far more picturesque. Again, fruit orchards and vineyards were everywhere, along with young fields of corn and wheat, farmhouses and cattle. Walter pointed out a distant line of trees, cottonwoods and willows that cut through the valley going north.

"Along that line of trees flows the Russian River. Most years it floods its bank and part of the land down there is covered in water. It seems to do more good for the soil than harm. Some of the best crops are grown alongside the river."

Dom was really impressed with what he had seen, and knew that one of the properties he was to look at tomorrow was down in that valley. One was also in the smaller Dry Creek Valley. He didn't see how anyone could go wrong purchasing such land.

"Well, folks, tour's over," Walter announced. "You've seen a little of most of the nearby area. Most of these roads just keep going through. This one branches off in three directions. One goes north into Geyserville and connects with the main northern road. Another heads straight east, into the mountains and the mining town of Pine Flats. If you turn south and then east, you cut through the Mayacamas Mountains, and come out at the town of Calistoga, and into the Napa Valley. They're really growing grapes there, Dom."

"Why not?" Dom said. "You could call this whole area Little Italy and not be incorrect."

"This definitely does not look like China," Po spoke out.

"You've been in California so long, that you wouldn't know China if it were in front of you!" Mai stated, in her best impersonation of Angelina.

Suen shot a surprised look at her saying, "Mother, you should show father more respect."

Po, smiling, said, "It's alright Suen, she's been hanging around Italians too long," tapping Dom on the shoulder. And with that, Walter turned the wagon around and headed back towards town under a cloudless sky with tints of red rising above the setting sun.

There was still light out when they returned the wagon to the livery stable. The nearby beer garden was doing a brisk business. Walter recognized Dave's horse tied up in front. Suddenly, one of the Pomos came flying out of the establishment with Dave hot on his heels, gun in hand.

"Whoa, squaw boy," Dave said, firing off a round near the Indian's feet, stopping him in his tracks. "Come back in here and finish your beer. I'm paying good money to see a drunk Injun, and you ain't finished drinking yet."

Dom, Angelina, and the Lings paused at the sound of the gunfire as they were proceeding towards the hotel. Walter started back towards the beer garden, but he didn't at all like the fact that Dave had actually fired a gun in town. Dom reached out and placed a hand lightly on Walter's shoulder.

"Let me talk to him," he said.

"Be careful," Walter said. "The police will have heard the shot; they should be here shortly."

"Well, hello there! If it isn't my friend Dave," Dom announced stepping forward. "Did I hear you say you were buying the beer? Come, let's go back in, I'm thirsty," he stated, motioning Dave towards the door.

Dave was startled by Dom's boldness and could only reply, "Oh, get out of here, you old wop. I'm having fun with this Injun."

Dave had recently been reading a scene in one of his dime magazines where one fellow had made another dance by shooting at his feet. Dave was eager to try it out on the Pomo.

"I'm going to make this sucker dance," he said, preparing to fire at the Indian's feet.

"Dance!" Dom suddenly exclaimed. "But of course!" And he grabbed Dave's arms, including the one holding the gun, about the wrists, and began twirling around with the drunken Dave in the street in front of the beer garden.

Dave, completely taken by surprise, stared into Dom's cheerful blue eyes, and momentarily began to enjoy the dance. Just then Captain McCraken came hurrying out of the beer garden, and approaching a smiling Dave from behind, slammed the butt of a heavy Navy Colt into the side of his head, knocking him senseless in the middle of a twirl.

"Hey, you ruined our dance," Dom said.

"Sorry, Mister, but I've seen Dave drunk before, and he can't be trusted. This is the first time I've seen him bring a gun out in public. No use in taking chances."

Several policemen now arrived, and after hearing the circumstances, dragged Dave off to the jail.

"Did you enjoy your dance, Mr. Londi?" Angelina said, hooking her arm in with Dom's.

"I think I'd rather be seen dancing with you, Angie. I don't think I've left a good impression with anyone who's witnessed this little scene."

"You'd probably be surprised, Dom," Walter said, his arm around the younger Pomo Indian.

"You thought pretty fast out there."

"I think his feet moved pretty fast too," Angelina added.

The Lings just looked at each other seriously, and shook their heads. They couldn't make up their minds if they were around crazy people, let alone if they wanted to stay in this town or not.

"Let's go eat," Dom said. "Dancing heightens the appetite."

Walter excused himself, saying he was off to camp for the night with his friends along a little trout filled creek that ran in back of the tracks. It was peaceful there, and a good spot to spend the night. He told them that he had had a wonderful time and hoped to see them all again. He hoped Dom would buy some property, and that the Lings would stay in town and open a laundry. Putting his hands together, as he had seen the Chinese in San Francisco do, he stood in front of Suen and bowed respectfully, saying, "I so hope to see you again, Suen." He returned to his friends, and they headed off towards the tracks and their camp by the creek.

The others returned to the hotel and went to their rooms to freshen up, agreeing to meet out on the second floor hallway at six o'clock. After encountering Dave, and remembering some of the stares the Lings got at lunch, Dom thought it best that they all go down to dinner together. Po had agreed. Safety in numbers did seem to be a good motto. Angelina and Dom came out of their rooms first. Angelina had changed into a black full skirt and a white frilly blouse, her hair still in the bun.

"Hey, Angie, you look great!" Dom said.

"You look great too!" she said. "Just like all professional dancers. Say, tell me, what were you going to do if that captain hadn't have come out and knocked that idiot senseless?"

"I just would have kept dancing with him, until he melted into my arms," Dom said wistfully.

Angelina gently shoved him as the Lings came out of their door, and they all headed towards the stairs and the restaurant down below. As at lunch, their entrance provoked stares, but again they were promptly seated and waited on in a timely fashion. Since the lunch choice had been so good, they all went with the dinner special: steak, smothered in onions, fried potatoes, and fresh green salad. Apple pie, again, was the dessert. Waiting for their dinners to arrive, Dom had noticed that the Lings were unusually quiet and pensive. He asked Po if there was anything amiss. Po expressed his misgivings about settling in Healdsburg. He told of his fears for his family's safety, and he had noticed how the one young man with Dave couldn't take his eyes off Suen. He couldn't bear it if anything terrible happened to her. As he spoke, a tear came to his eye. At the same time, Mai had to stifle a sob. Po couldn't hold back any longer. He didn't wish to upset Dom and Angelina, or spoil their dinner, but in a torrent of words he spilled out what had happened to their son Mat, and their reason for leaving Modesto. This was the first time he had spoken of the incident to anyone other than Chinese, but it seemed natural with these two Italians.

Dom and Angelina listened without commenting. Angelina's eyes filled with tears as she reached out and patted Mai's hand. Dom had a serious, stern look on his face. Looking at Po sitting across the table, eyes downcast, staring at nothing, he didn't see a Chinese immigrant. He simply saw a fellow man who had lost a son in a tragic, senseless manner. This was a beautiful country that promised freedom for all, but two words, bigotry and prejudice, cut right through the center of it, leaving a bloody red scar. Cruelty to fellow man could take many forms, but nothing could be more devastating than a careless act, designed to belittle and humiliate another, resulting in the death of a cherished son or daughter.

Words failed Dom. How did one reason with mindless acts? The Lings were dealing with their pain and loss as best they could. Time never really healed anything, but it did create distance between memories, and sometimes that had to be enough. Dom and Angelina expressed their humble sympathies, and empathized with their pain. They also expressed their abhorrence at the mindset, and ignorance that set in motion the end of a boy's life. Mechanically, they ate their dinner. The spark and wonder they had enjoyed on Walter's tour had died out. Attempts at optimistic conversation seemed to ring hollow.

Dom suggested that an after dinner stroll through the plaza might do them good. Stepping out under the star-filled sky into the clean brisk air lightened the mood a bit. Halfway around the plaza, near the courthouse, they saw two men dressed in business attire coming towards them. The men approached them smiling, took their hats off, and introduced themselves. One was the chief of police, the other the town mayor.

"You must be the Lings, and Dom and Angelina, correct?" said the chief.

"Right," said Dom. "But how did you know?"

"Walter told us. We checked on the Pomos where they usually camp. Wanted to make sure Davy's rowdy friends hadn't stopped by looking for trouble. We heard you're a pretty good dancer, Dom. That could have been dangerous. A drunk Davy holding a gun doesn't make for the best dancing partner."

"Actually, I felt fairly safe," Dom said. "I was holding the wrist of his gun hand. He was pretty drunk. I think I could have taken it away from him. Thanks to Captain McCraken, I didn't have to. Say, what was he captain of anyway?" Dom inquired.

The chief and the mayor exchanged smiles.

"Nothing that anybody knows of," the mayor said. "He usually just hangs around Poor Man's Flats, telling everyone he sees that he's the captain of the ship. I guess he's getting a little senile now, but in his younger days I hear he was a pretty tough hombre."

"He still knows how to use the butt of a pistol," Angelina added.

"All joking aside," the chief said, "that's the first time Davy's come to town displaying a gun. He seems to be getting a little nuttier than usual. He's not too happy about coming to behind bars, and that's quite a knot he's got on his head. Hope it learned him a lesson. He's a hard one to figure, and his parents are such nice people. I'm sorry he bothered you out there on the road."

"I guess most towns have a few bad eggs," Dom said. "Thanks for talking to us chief."

"Hold on," the mayor said. "Dom, I hear you're looking at some property around town. I wish you luck and want to extend you our welcome. Mr. and Mrs. Ling, I sincerely want to extend our welcome to you. Walter said you're considering opening a laundry in town. And that's exactly something that this town needs.

"I can almost guarantee you that you'd be doing good business in no time. I hope you won't let the behavior of that hothead influence your decision. Most people around here are good folks and would look forward to the services provided by a good laundry."

"I can vouch for that," the chief said. "My wife does not look forward to doing laundry. I'll bet she'd be your first customer."

The Lings simply listened in awe. Such a welcome had never been extended to them before. Po smiled and shook the two men's hands. He told them they hoped to arrive at a decision by morning. The mayor and chief wished them all a good evening and took their leave. Now the mood indeed had lightened up as they walked back towards the hotel. Fortune, for a change, seemed to smile a little on the Lings. Perhaps this wasn't such a bad town after all, Po thought.

Before returning to their rooms, they agreed to meet downstairs for breakfast. They were all pretty tired and in need of a good night's sleep. Saying goodnight to one another, they climbed the well-lit stairs to the hallway, and entered their rooms. Dom had experienced a full day with much food for thought, and he couldn't just sleep right away. Before going upstairs to the room, he had purchased from the restaurant a bottle of what the waitress assured him was the Massoni zinfandel. Angelina had looked askance at him and had shaken her finger.

"Only to help me sleep," he said. "I'm still a bit wound up."

He was sitting up in bed, sipping the wine and looking over some papers the realtor had given him, when he heard a quiet knock at the door.

"Dear God, let it be Angelina," he said, and rose in long johns to unlock the door.

Deeming it best to be cautious, he whispered, "Who is it?" before turning the key.

"Who do you think, you wine head?"

Dom was alarmed at how fast his heart suddenly started beating. *Calm down*, he told himself, *you're acting like a little kid.* He unlocked the door, and there stood Angelina in a dark green, thick, satiny robe, her luxuriant black hair tinted with gray, hanging loose and long down to the middle of her back. She had knocked Dom's breath away. He just stood at the door gawking. With her hair down like that, framing her large, perfectly chiseled face, the large, wide-set eyes, and the full lips that curved into a slight smile, she looked as wonderful and mysterious as anything he had ever seen. She reminded him of a woman he had seen once in an Etruscan fresco, holding a bunch of grapes with an owl sitting in a tree behind her.

"What's the matter?" Angelina said lowly. "Can't you talk? Do you want me to stand out here forever? I can't sleep, and thought maybe a glass of wine would help."

Dom returned to his wits saying, "Of course, Angie. I had been thinking about you. Come sit down. Have some wine."

She moved to the chair in her slippers like a large cat. Her hair seemed to have a life of its own as it lightly swayed to and fro, Dom thought, watching her from behind. He suddenly felt ill at ease and embarrassed, and hurried to the closet for his old flannel robe.

"Excuse me, Angelina. I was sitting in the bed looking at some papers," he managed to say.

Reading his mind she said, "Dom, don't be embarrassed. It's not the first time I've seen a man in long johns. I used to be married, remember?"

Dom was fumbling with the belt on his robe. He noticed his hands were slightly shaking, and he could still feel his heart pounding. *Good God, I hope I'm not having a stroke,* he thought. The presence of Angelina in his room, with her hair down, had completely unnerved him. Of course, he had been hoping all along for an event like this to happen, but now that she was sitting in a chair in his room smiling at him, it had reduced him to a quivering young man on his first date. *Wine, I need wine,* he reasoned. *And Angelina wants a glass of wine.* Struggling to gain control, he poured out two glasses. He hadn't even finished his first glass when he'd heard the knock on the door. The wine should calm his nerves, he hoped. Angelina sat straight up in her chair, legs crossed casually, and accepted the glass.

"It's that Massoni zinfandel I was telling you about, Angie. He lives somewhere around here and makes this wine. See what you think."

Dom had two candles lit: one near his bed, and one on a dresser near where Angelina was sitting. She held the glass up to the candle, and was impressed with its dark ruby clarity. As all knowledgeable Italians, she swirled, sniffed, and took a small sip, moving it around in her mouth before swallowing.

"That is excellent wine, Dom! Better than most we're getting at the restaurants in the city."

Dom was finally starting to calm down a little now. He took a chair opposite Angelina, and during lively conversation, mostly concerning the day's events, finished off his wine rather quickly. So had Angelina, he was surprised to note. He filled both their glasses, and they continued talking.

Angelina was thinking how natural it felt to be sitting in Dom's room, sharing conversation and a glass of wine. She was having a wonderful time on this outing, and had mostly succeeded in keeping thoughts of Conchetta at the back of her mind. She was glad she had accepted Dom's invitation, and though he was older than her, she still thought he cut quite a good figure, and certainly was distinguished looking. What she liked most, though, was his caring, sensitive nature. When she thought about it, she actually couldn't remember meeting a finer man. Dom was talking to her with those pale blue eyes boring into her. The old dog had been a bachelor for many years. She was sure that back in Florence he had many a fling. That sly smile he had on his face revealed a little of what he was thinking, she could guess.

The strong Massoni wine seemed to be going quickly to Dom's head. It was helping him to be more at ease with Angelina. What could a beautiful woman like that possibly see in an old codger like him? She was just too damn good looking and powerful, he thought. Why, if you put a crown of leaves and grasses in her hair, and dressed her in the finest of ancient gowns, she could pass for the alluring Circe in the Odyssey. But he knew he could never seal her away in a barrel, as the old wives' tales in Tuscany dealt with witches. The wine was certainly making his thoughts creative. Angelina was no witch. She was simply the perfect woman that he had been waiting for his whole life. And the fact of it left him devastated. He looked to his wine glass and found it empty, and looking at the bottle, found it empty too. With Angelina in the room, time had seemed to stand still. Why, it had seemed like she had just arrived, though he knew they had been sitting and talking for quite some time.

Angelina suddenly stood up. Dom stood up too, thinking she was about to leave. Staring at him with that slight smile, she quickly undid the buttons and the belt of her robe, and let it fall to the floor. She wore nothing underneath. Dom was astonished. It was like he had seen Aphrodite rising from the foam, the green robe like a wave about her feet. Dom moved automatically, knowing what to do, but it seemed like slow motion. He put his arms around Angelina and kissed her long and deep, and holding her in his arms, guided her to the bed. He fumbled as fast as he could with his robe and long johns, with the laughter of Angelina's sweet voice in his ears. He pulled the heavy blankets over them and, for the first time in his life, finally felt at home.

Dom awoke in the early morning light to find his arms around a warm Angelina snuggled up with her back to him, his head buried in that mass of hair spread about the pillow. *Oh my God, what have we done?* was his first thought. But he knew what had happened was what he was hoping and wishing for since the first time his eyes had rested upon Angelina. She awoke and turned towards him, looking at him with instantly wide-awake eyes.

"Get that smug look off your face, Mr. Londi. My head aches a little. I think we both had a little too much wine is all. We're both adults and free to do what we please. You don't need to go getting a swelled head, or big ideas. We'll have a good day today looking at some property and the local sites, and that's all. By the way, will you hand me my robe please?"

Dom reached for his robe, to go grab Angelina's. He couldn't stop smiling. *She's more like Athena, raising her shield, than Aphrodite*, he chuckled to himself. It was all right, though. He knew Angie was just trying to hide a little self-consciousness behind her words. He felt a bit awkward himself, but he also felt happier than ever. He felt sure his life from now on would be forever changed, and he was looking forward to it.

Chapter 9

Conchetta Lombardi regained her senses, only to find she was once again tied up in the back of the moving wagon. The nightmare she was in assailed her with such revulsion and horror that she felt if she had the means, she would not hesitate to end her own life, rather than go on another day. As quick as that thought entered her mind, it was gone. She wouldn't give up. She would find a way to escape. The morphine drops Juan Fuentes had placed in her water had pretty much worn off, but she was left in a heightened state of anxiety and desperation. A clear head was what she needed. She forced herself to focus on the events that had taken place. She had been drugged and raped. It must have been something in the water. It had tasted funny, but she was so thirsty at the time, she didn't hesitate. The animal had forced himself on her, but she would try to refuse the impact of it. If she hadn't been sore down there, it would have been easier to shove it to the back of her mind. She couldn't let herself be weakened by any of what had happened. Self-pity and feeling ashamed were two emotions she couldn't afford. She knew she had tried her best to fight him off, and forced herself to think back on the struggle. She had tried to wrap the rope around his neck, but she was far too weak. An image came to her. He wore that knife in a sheath around his waist. She should have focused her strength on going for the knife. What had happened to her before, she knew, could happen to her again. She would prepare herself as best she could for anything.

He hadn't gagged her this time, but she was still tied to the heavy iron ring in the center of the compartment. It was daylight again. She could tell by the square of light around the little door up on the wall. Her head slightly throbbed, and she was terribly thirsty. Desperation came to her in sickening waves. The best thing she could do was just to lie still and try to rest, hopefully to sleep.

She must have dozed off, because suddenly she came to at the sound of a voice, and a shaft of light entering the compartment. Juan was at the little door.

"Wake up, bitch. Need a little air? Perhaps some water."

Conchetta nodded her head. In a moment he had unlocked the back door and untied her from the ring. Stiffly she made her way out of the wagon to the ground. It was a sunny day. The wagon was somewhere off the main road, stopped in a clearing surrounded by forest. Adjusting her eyes to the light, she saw Juan standing about twenty feet away, facing the side of the wagon.

"Hey Lombardi, watch this. See that rose carved on the side of the wagon? Watch this."

In a rapid motion he pulled the knife from his sheath and flung it at the wagon. It landed with a thud right in the center of the rose.

"Been practicing that since I was a kid. Thought it might come in handy one day."

He retrieved the knife and came towards Conchetta. He cut away the rope that bound her wrists together.

"If you make a move to run, you'll find this knife in your back."

He then moved his coat aside and revealed the gun.

"I've made up my mind what to do with you. The devil has sent me a companion in the form of a bear. My companion will decide if you die or live for a while. If he doesn't maul you or devour you in five minutes, you live a while longer. I really have no need of your services. You're beautiful to look at, but you gave me no pleasure, and it would be dangerous to keep you around. Now walk over to the cage door," he said, pulling the gun. "My friend Oso has some decision making to do."

Conchetta had tried to prepare her mind for anything, but this was out of the question. She had no choice, and walked the few steps to the cage door. The bear looked huge. It stared at her with eyes she saw nothing familiar in. She couldn't detect curiosity, interest, or violence. The bear's small, dark eyes simply looked. It was poised on all fours in the middle of the cage. Juan, keeping the gun on Conchetta, pulled a key from his pocket and unlocked the door.

"Now get in, slut. Don't be afraid. What have you got to lose?"

Conchetta suddenly felt the wind ripple through her hair. She had heard the clear sounds of birds singing. She imagined the roses blooming at the old mission in Carmel, and Father Donovan's kind face. The bear wasn't going to harm her. She stooped, entered the cage, shoving the bear away with her head. The bear moved to the far back corner and curled up into a ball. It raised its head and opened its mouth, displaying a huge pink tongue, and sharp yellow-white teeth, and bellowed out a strange sounding growl. Conchetta crawled to the corner opposite the bear, and sat with her back to the cage, legs drawn up, her arms wrapped around them, staring at Juan. Conchetta had felt a surge of optimistic power; she just hoped it could last for five minutes. El Zapo had relocked the cage and pulled a pocket watch from his coat.

"So far so good for you. But five minutes can be a very long time, and bears, they say, are very temperamental animals."

Juan went to the front of the wagon and came back with an apple and sat on a nearby fallen log to watch the cage. He didn't like what was happening. He had hoped the bear would finish her off quickly, but he should have expected this. When he went to feed the bear and give it water, it had never made a violent move. If it didn't do anything soon, maybe he should just stick the knife in her and be done.

For some reason Conchetta was relatively at peace in the bear's cage. Instead of the five minutes seeming like eternity, before she knew it Juan was unlocking the cage saying, "All right, bitch, come on out. I guess you passed the test."

Suddenly deciding to take a different tact, Conchetta said in a normal voice, "Juan, I'm very thirsty and I could use a little something to eat. Maybe I could prepare us some food. I'm a very good cook you know."

She even forced a smile to her face. Juan was caught off guard by her tactic. Maybe, according to the devil's plan, it did mean something that the bear had rejected her. The talk of food made him hungry. Since leaving the mission he had been living on apples and jerky and a few stale crackers. In Santiago he always had the finest of foods.

"There's water in that barrel," he said, pointing at one sitting on a small shelf, lashed to the side of the wagon near the driver's seat. "Drink up."

Conchetta hurried to the barrel and lifted the lid, and finding a ladle inside, drank cautiously, then deeply. The water tasted fine.

"Look in that supply box in back of the wagon and see what you can fix. I'll light a fire. If anyone comes around, you're my wife. You say different, I kill them, then I kill you. Simple, huh?"

"Sure, Juan," she said, and began searching around in the box. She found quite a few various staples. She chose rice, a can of tomatoes, an onion, and a small container of chili powder. It was no trouble to find the proper pot. They were scattered all over the wagon, price tags dangling from the handles. Juan had moved close by and was watching her like a hawk. He saw her go to the utensil box and come back with a can opener. He knew there were knives in it. If he didn't kill her soon he would have to rearrange the wagon. Conchetta carried the pot to the barrel and poured some water in it. Juan went back to lighting a fire.

"Come over here with that pot so I can keep an eye on you," he said.

Conchetta considered smashing the pot over his head as he was bent over the wood. She instantly realized she had chosen the wrong pot. The one she held in her hand was much too light to do any damage. From now on, if there were a now on, she would constantly have to be more aware and plan ahead. An opportunity had been lost. It still would have been hard, though; he had constantly watched her from the corner of one eye. Juan got a small fire going, and arranged a grate over it. Conchetta set the pot down over the fire.

"Let's get your stuff, and this better be good. Who knows, your life could even depend on it."

Conchetta realized he wasn't going to give her a chance to get at one of the knives. They brought the items back to the fire. When the water boiled she poured in some rice and covered it. She opened the can of tomatoes and told Juan she needed to chop up the onion. He smiled at her, took out his knife, and chopped it up on a flat rock. After a while Conchetta lifted the lid and added the tomatoes, onions, and some chili powder along with a little salt and pepper. She replaced the lid and forced herself to smile up at Juan.

"It won't be long now," she said.

Juan kept an eye on her as he went to the wagon and came back with two metal bowls and spoons. He just stood there eyeing Conchetta. It was obvious she was up to something. In a way it was amusing to watch her put on this little charade. What was she thinking in that pathetic, simple mind? It came to him in a revelation from his guardian devil Bael. She was going to do something with the food: throw it in his face, and go for his gun or knife. He wouldn't take his eyes off her hands.

The rice was probably ready. Conchetta thought of throwing it in his face, but decided against it. She would have to go for the knife or gun, and use it successfully before he could recover. She decided the odds too thin. She took a spoon and tasted the rice.

"It's ready," she announced.

"Stand away," Juan commanded.

The cooking food had smelled delicious. He greedily went to the pot and emptied well over half the contents into his bowl.

"Help yourself to the rest, Miss Lombardi, and it better be good."

Conchetta didn't bother with a bowl, but began to immediately eat it out of the pot, squatting by the little fire. Juan had gone to eat leaning against the wagon. The rice really was delicious; he thought. It reminded him of a similar version of the Spanish rice he was used to in Santiago. The little whore was a good cook, and she had done it in a minimal amount of time. Maybe he would keep her around for a while after all. A man of his position shouldn't be traveling around the wilds of the west without proper nourishment prepared by a good cook. He would have to watch her constantly, though. She would be a constant threat. What if he kept her in a morphine stupor? No. She probably wouldn't care much about eating, and he'd lose a good cook. He'd just let things ride like they were for a while. Maybe the urge would come back to him to use her for sexual release. At least until he was able to find a nice timid nun. Sex was so much more rewarding when you were killing a sister of God, he believed.

Conchetta finished her food and asked if she could have more water. Juan just nodded.

"I need to use the bushes," she stated.

This was going to be a problem, he could see.

"And I'm going to need some paper," she added.

"I don't like this bushes talk," Juan said. "Come here."

He reached behind the wagon seat and grabbed a rope. He tied it tight in a complicated knot around Conchetta's neck. He walked with her towards the foliage.

"Do your stinking business. I don't care to see you. I'll be holding this rope. Go in there a ways, and I'll tell you when to stop. Stop," he said.

"The paper," Conchetta called.

"Use the damn leaves. You're just lucky you can cook bitch and that the bear left you alone."

Conchetta, humiliated but alive, took care of business as fast as she could. He pulled on the rope just as she was done. He untied her and at gunpoint told her to get back in her hole. She could see but no choice other than to obey. And again she was locked in, but unbound.

"I've got some house cleaning to do," she heard Juan say. He began going through the wagon and storing everything he figured she could use as a weapon or as a means of escape in a built in compartment he could lock. This compartment already held the several handguns and rifles he had for sale. He even threw in some boxes of nails and sewing needles. Who knew what she might try. He kept aside one of the chamber pots he had for sale and an old mail order catalogue. Looking about satisfied, he unlocked Conchetta's door. She had heard him rearranging things and wasn't surprised to fine the utensil box that held the knives missing, as well as other sharp objects. She noticed that the carpenter's hammers she had seen were gone.

"Here. Your new bushes," Juan said, pointing at the chamber pot and catalogue. "And you better keep it clean. I run a tight wagon," laughing a little crazily at what he had said.

Conchetta looked at him, keeping her fear hidden. She knew he was hopelessly insane, and it terrified her.

"A chamber pot, why thank you, Juan. How kind of you."

"Move towards the front of the wagon, Lombardi, and don't forget I've got a gun."

He closed up the back of the wagon, picked up the fire grate, and hung it from a hook on the side of the wagon.

"Get up front, you can ride with me for a while. If we meet anyone and you try anything, I'll kill whoever we meet, and then I'll kill you. Remember, you're my loving wife. Get up front now. I'll be right behind you."

Conchetta climbed aboard. Juan followed close behind. He took the reins and turned the wagon around and headed out of the clearing towards the main road. The day was still bright, and Conchetta sat up front, terrified, yet clinging to a glimmer of hope.

Juan hoped to reach Mission San Juan Bautista by nightfall. Like the mission at Carmel, it too was in a state of neglect and disrepair, but near this mission was a convent, and this convent held nuns. All this he had learned from that trusting fool Father Donovan. He urged the horses on at the optimum pace the road would allow. It hadn't rained recently, and the dirt was well packed by the many farmers that traveled it. So far, they had only met one farmer going the opposite direction. He had stared curiously at them and waved.

Conchetta hadn't spoken a word since she climbed up front. Her mind was bent on nothing but escape. When she saw the farmer approaching, her feelings of helplessness and frustration doubled. They were the only people on the road. No farmhouses were even in sight. If she screamed to the farmer for help or tried to jump from the wagon, Juan would pull the gun and shoot the farmer, then probably shoot her. Her actions would have resulted in the farmer's death. He appeared middle aged. Most likely he had a wife and children. She simply looked straight ahead as the man passed by in his small wagon.

Juan's knife and his gun were both on his left side. She would have to reach around him to get at them. She found herself struggling hard to control her anger. The means to kill this animal were so close by, yet she could do nothing, and it galled her. She had to talk, say something to distract her thoughts.

"It's a lovely day, isn't it?"

"I imagine that depends on your definition of lovely. And why are you suddenly speaking Italian, or speaking at all? Do you imagine me to be your friend?"

"You speak Italian so well, and I seldom get a chance to use it. That's all. You must have had good teachers somewhere. No?"

"My father paid for only the best. 'Cripples who must stay inside should always have their minds occupied in matters of an intellectual nature,' was his motto."

"Has your leg been bad all the time?" Conchetta inquired, forcing a note of sympathy in her voice.

"Ever since God squeezed it in the womb," he said matter-of-factly.

Conchetta could tell he wasn't joking. An image of a long-white-haired, thick bearded God reaching an invisible hand inside a mother's womb and sternly or gleefully squeezing the little leg of an unborn child was sickly comical. Or more likely, sickly insane.

Before she thought of what she was saying, Conchetta blurted out, "God doesn't do such things. Sometimes nature isn't perfect."

Juan suddenly reached out and backhanded her hard across the face.

"Shut up, you stupid whore. Who do you think controls nature? If that son of a bitch didn't want to make me perfect, that's his loss. The devil looks after those such as me quite nicely. Your holy Father Donovan could tell you that, before I made sure he found God while flying through the air, at least until he came to a halt upon some unusually hard rocks."

A little blood from the blow was trickling into Conchetta's mouth, but her pain hadn't diverted her attention from what Juan had said. He had killed Father Donovan. It hadn't been an accident like the Monterey paper had said. Juan had been there. He had pushed him. All this talk of the devil and God, his twisted view of his deformity, and now, the realization that he had killed a kind and caring priest, was almost too overwhelming for Conchetta. For an instant, she wanted to bolt from the wagon; not caring if a knife or a bullet struck her back. The pain in her jaw came to her aid and helped bring back her anger. She had a feeling now that this wasn't the first time Juan had killed. She knew that she could be next at any moment. Juan looked over at her and laughed.

"What's the matter, Lombardi? Cat got your tongue? I thought you wanted to talk. Use your Italian."

Flicking the reins, he urged the horses on to a greater speed.

Before dark, they came upon a few scattered houses, and suddenly the old mission was in sight. Juan turned the wagon around and went back about a mile to where he had seen a logging road that turned off into the forest. He could tell by the condition of the road that it currently wasn't being used, and figured it would be a good spot to stop for the night, feed and water the horses and the bear. Drawing his gun, he forced Conchetta to the back compartment, gagged her, and tied her securely to the center ring. Before locking the door, he smiled at her and threw the chamber pot in. He unhitched the horses, tied them off away with food and water, and took care of the bear. He went to the back of the wagon and changed into the black robe of those who followed the calling, and grabbing a bible, his knife secured under his robe, headed off towards the main road and the mission. He had eaten some jerky and an apple and was in fine spirits when he knocked on the door of the convent. An older fat nun answered the door, and Juan spoke quickly.

"Good evening, Sister. I am sorry to trouble you. My name is Jose Campos, and I am a traveling seminary student soon to take my vows in San Jose. My little wagon broke a wheel less than a mile down the road. I have a spare wheel and can raise the wagon by means of a lever, but I need another set of hands to assist me. It requires very little strength. Perhaps there is someone a bit younger here who could help me. I can see that the old mission here is in need of repair, and would be happy to help out with a small donation."

Reaching into a pocket, he pulled out two silver coins and handed them to the nun. She smiled gratefully at Juan, and expressed sorrow at his predicament, but assured him she would return momentarily with some help. In the meantime, wouldn't he care to refresh himself with some cool water from the well out front? By the time he had drawn a bucket of water she had returned with what he had been hoping for. He hadn't seen any houses near the convent, but thought there might be a caretaker living somewhere in the back and a man might come forth. Walking towards him, beside the fat nun, was a timid, pale, wide-eyed sister, quite tall though.

"This is Sister Jacqueline, Jose. She's quite strong and really quite ingenious. I know she would be glad to assist you. When you get your wagon fixed, there is a nice little room in the barn. You are welcome to stay there for the night. Since you are not yet a priest, I'm afraid I can't extend a spare room in the convent to you. I'm sure you understand."

"Oh indeed, Sister, and thank you, but once I'm on the road again, I'll be on my way. I was planning on spending the night under the stars. There will be a moon tonight, and I'm sure I'll have no problem continuing on for several more hours. Thank you, Sister, the sooner I change that wheel the sooner Sister Jacqueline will be back, and I'll be on my way."

That young man is going to make an excellent priest, the older nun thought to herself, returning to the convent and closing the door, having not an inkling of concern for the welfare of Sister Jacqueline.

Juan and the Sister walked back down the road. Once they were out of sight of the mission and the houses, Juan pulled out his knife and ordered Sister Jacqueline down a narrow trail into the forest. He loved the look of surprise in her eyes, and spinning her around, landed a fist along the side of her head.

"Don't even say a word," he growled and held up the knife.

"Keep going, Sister. You yell out, this knife goes in your back."

Sister Jacqueline was numb with fright. She had arrived in California with her Order from France only two years ago, and now she was at the mercy of a madman. She felt her life was soon to be over and couldn't believe that this was what God had in store for her. She looked for her faith to sustain her, but before she could gain strength, Juan had pushed her against a fallen log, lifted her robe, torn away her undergarments, and entered her, the knife held at her throat. Just as he was climaxing, Juan had a vision of Jesus rutting with Mother Mary, and he slid the knife across Sister Jacqueline's throat. She flailed for a moment, went limp, and then it was all over. Juan jerked her bloody robe off, dragged her body off a ways, and covered it with leaves and debris, throwing a large, fallen limb over it all to hold it down.

Once again on the main road, he followed it back to the wagon, keeping to the edge, not wishing to be seen. When he reached the wagon, he pulled off his robe and changed into the nun's. He unlocked the wagon and the compartment that held Conchetta. He had lit a lantern, and with unbelieving eyes, Conchetta stared out at Juan dressed in a nun's habit, the front part soaked with fresh blood. The maniacal look in his eyes brought her to the verge of insanity, and she struggled to breathe.

"Sister Jacqueline regrets that she couldn't come to your rescue. She had an unfortunate accident involving a sharp object, so she sent me here instead. My, but I do enjoy rutting with virgins, such good, clean fun to violate a bride of Jesus. Come out. Come out, Conchetta Lombardi. You must be hungry and thirsty. You will fix us some food, won't you? You're such a good cook. Oh, excuse me, I forgot we'll have to postpone dinner. I just remembered we must leave immediately. It just might not be safe to spend the night here. I trust you understand."

Slamming and locking the door, he quickly changed into his traveling salesman attire. Hitching the horses back up, within minutes he was once again heading north and east along the main road. When he came close to Mission San Juan Bautista, he saw the fat nun framed in front of the door holding a lantern. By the light of the moon, he waved to her and moved rapidly on. Traveling by moon he lost sense of time. The night was mild, and power surged through him. The cocaine he had taken earlier was wearing off, so he took some more. *Maybe I'll drive all night*, he said to himself. *Why put an end to a perfectly good evening?* For hours he met no one else on the road. Finally, sometime before dawn, he began to feel fatigued and pulled off the road to sleep. Before crawling to his bed in back of the wagon, he opened Conchetta's compartment and cut her gag away and tossed in a canteen of water.

"I'm a light sleeper," he said. "You know what will happen if you make any noise," and locked the door back up.

Conchetta managed to get the canteen to her lips and drink. She didn't want to think. She wanted to sleep. She knew she would be forced to think later, and her only hope was to stay strong and as alert as possible. The image of Juan in the bloody habit wouldn't leave her mind, but sleep came to her. The next thing she knew, Juan had unlocked the door, and daylight flooded the compartment. There stood Juan dressed like a Gypsy salesman or performer. He was wearing baggy white pants, a long blue shirt enclosed about his waist with a bright red sash, and a gold scarf tied round his neck. The most shocking thing of all, Conchetta found, was the large gold earring dangling from a freshly made hole in his left ear, blood still dripping from the puncture.

"I've got a matching outfit for you, young slut. I'm sure you'll be stunning in it. We have some eggs. I hope they're not broken. Won't you come out and fix us a bite to eat? I've got a nice little fire going."

This nightmare just never was going to end, and I feel I'm losing my mind, Conchetta thought. He untied her, and Conchetta, weak and cramped, walked stiffly to the fire to warm herself. It was a brisk morning, getting on towards noon she thought, glancing up at the sun. Juan was sitting down on a stool holding a rag to his ear.

"I didn't think ears had much blood. Oh well, maybe I made the hole too big," he said stupidly, nodding his head from side to side.

Conchetta found the eggs and some already sliced bacon set on a slab of wood near the fire. A frying pan was already hot on the grate. She was hungry and needed food. She didn't think about anything but cooking. She cooked the bacon first, then drained some of the grease and cracked six of the eggs into the pan and scrambled them together. When they were done, she dished it out on two plates Juan had set out. Juan ate his with a fork, she with the same spoon she had used to scramble the eggs.

"Hey, next time only five eggs. What do you think we are, rich?" he said laughing at his own words.

Conchetta finished every morsel and walked to the water barrel for a drink. Juan watched her every move. The barrel was almost full. He must have stopped during the night and replenished it from one of the many little streams that ran down from the hills, she reasoned. The water tasted fine, she thought. If he hadn't drugged the canteen he had given her, he probably wouldn't waste it on a whole barrel, she reasoned. Oh well, he'd probably kill her sometime today or tonight, she thought. Instantly, she pushed that thought out of her mind. She couldn't just meekly take things as they came. She had to use her wits and be ready to fight. Back in Genoa, her father had worked so hard to put food on the table and clothing on their backs that it had killed him. Conchetta would not dishonor him by giving up, no matter what happened. The cripple, El Zapo, she thought, watching him kick out the fire, and using his fork to hang the grate from the hook on the side of the wagon. He said El Zapo proudly once, like it was a title befitting him. She watched him move. He didn't even limp that badly. How could anyone let a little limp turn him into a sadistic monster? She could guess what had happened to that nun before he killed her. The sight of that bloody nun's robe had reminded her of the convent she knew to be at Mission San Juan Bautista. She had known that several of the nuns at Monterey had spent time there. *I'll bet he had dressed up as a priest,* she guessed.

"Hey, Lombardi, go try on your new clothes," he said, returning to the back of the wagon with the frying pan he had scrubbed out with dirt and rinsed with water.

Conchetta came to the back of the wagon, and watched him point to a stack of clothes on one of the shelves.

"Get in there and put them on. I'm tired of seeing you in that filthy black dress. And run a comb through that hair. Have you no pride?"

Conchetta didn't say a word and climbed into the back. She started to sob when she saw the first item on the stack, a pair of women's undergarments. She stifled the sob, and soon saw red when she thought about what had happened to hers. *Oh, I'll kill that bastard. Yes I will.* She put the garment on. Next she put on a frilly red skirt and a bright blue top, disgustingly the same color as Juan's. She tied it around her waist with a black sash. She saw a pair of shoes, but didn't put them on. Finding a brush on the shelf, she tried to get the tangles out of her hair. Stepping back out, she found Juan sitting on his stool close by.

He looked her over from head to toe and shouted, "Take those shoes off and put on the ones I set out. Don't you know how to look like a lady?"

Conchetta hadn't liked the shoes. They were low and flat with next to no support. Her shoes were sturdy, though somewhat clumsy, but still she felt they were better for running. These things would probably just fly off, and it would be easy to twist an ankle. Nonetheless, she put them on and found them to be a fairly decent fit.

"That's better," Juan declared. "Now twirl on one foot. All good gypsies know how to twirl."

Conchetta obediently twirled on one foot.

"Oh, I see what's missing. You need two large gold earrings. I only need to wear one, but you must have two."

He went to the back of the wagon and unlocked one of the utensil boxes. He took out an ice pick and, from a separate small box, removed two large earrings.

"I've already got pierced ears," Conchetta mentioned.

"Come over here and shut up, I want to make sure these fit. Don't try anything or you'll get this pick somewhere else."

He grabbed Conchetta's ear and, pulling the lobe, inserted the end of the pick clumsily into one of her holes and reamed it out. Standing back, he ordered her to place a ring in it. Conchetta's ear hurt like hell, and her fingers came away smeared with blood, but she didn't say a word. The same was done to the other ear. He stood back and admired his work.

"Now you look like a real Gypsy. Time for rehearsal," he announced. "Go take a seat on the stool."

"I don't want to get blood all over my clothes; I need a rag," Conchetta said.

He came back with a rag, and she tore it in two and held it to her ears.

"Now just sit there and enjoy the show," he said and pointed at the pistol tucked in his waist.

Conchetta had almost gone for that pistol when he punctured her ears, but she was afraid to do it, imagining him sticking the ice pick in her throat even as she got to the gun and shot him.

He grabbed a chain from under the front seat of the wagon, and unlocking the bear's cage, snapped the chain onto the iron collar around the bear's neck. He reached into his pocket, and holding something in the palm of his hand, extended it to the bear. The bear sniffed it and carefully licked it off his palm. Juan stood back and pulled steadily on the chain. The bear came slowly out of the cage.

"The secret is dried apricots. I've been told he'll do anything for dried apricots. Oso, up," Juan announced, in his best interpretation of a master of ceremonies, and raised his arms up in the air.

The bear obediently raised itself up on two legs.

"Twirl, Oso."

The bear turned around in a circle.

"Here's where you come in, Miss Lombardi. You come and stand a few feet away from Oso and start circling him, twirling as you go. Ladies and gentlemen, the traveling, twirling Gypsy show. We also have fine wares for sale. What do you think, slut? A true money maker, eh?"

Conchetta had obediently circled the bear, twirling as she moved. Under different circumstances, the whole thing was ludicrous enough to be funny. She felt like a puppet dancing beneath the strings of an insane puppeteer.

"I think that when we get to this town, Gilroy, we'll put on a show. Watch yourself, Lombardi. Don't get swell headed, thinking of yourself as star of the show. I've been thinking of throwing knives at you as part of the act. You wouldn't want me to get jealous and lose my concentration. Would you?"

Chapter 10

Angelina sneaked off to her room to dress and refresh herself for the coming day. She felt guilty for feeling so happy. The evening with Dom had felt like magic. But where was her sister? Where was Conchetta? She gazed out her window and saw three ducks flying south. She had to get back to San Francisco and wait for news, but she had a day with Dom in this wild place ahead of her. She felt helpless and confused. The thought of Dom's arms holding her close throughout the night momentarily comforted her and strengthened her resolve. She wouldn't give way to needless panic, yet she felt at the core of her being that something was terribly wrong. Dressing mechanically, she resolved that she would meet Dom and the Lings for breakfast as best she could. The Lings had gone through so much. Their son was taken from them in such a needless and cruel manner. Her plight paled in comparison to theirs. Conchetta could still be fine and experiencing nothing but happiness. Struggling to put her negative thoughts away, she finished dressing and went next door to Dom's room and knocked. He came to the door immediately, dressed in sturdy pants, a heavy brown flannel shirt, and ankle-high work boots.

"You look like you're going to work on a ranch," Angelina said.

"I just want to be able to check out these properties thoroughly. And I thought maybe later you and I could rent a wagon, look around some more, and go on a picnic. Sound OK, Angie?" Dom said.

"Sounds fine to me, Mr. Londi. My, you seem quite cheerful and vigorous."

"A certain beautiful woman rejuvenated me. Why, I feel like a young stallion."

Coming to Angelina, he wrapped his arms around her and buried his head in her hair, which was pulled back into the bun again. Angelina loved the sensation, but soon caught herself.

"Knock it off, Joe. I'm hungry. Behave yourself, stallion," she said, smiling up at Dom.

They went downstairs to the restaurant and immediately spotted the Lings seated at a large table, cups and a teapot in front of them.

"Good morning, Suen, Mai, Po," Dom said cheerfully. "Hope you all slept well."

Po was all smiles.

"Oh, we slept fine, Dom. Good morning, Angelina. We have talked things over, and we have decided to look for a building we could turn into a laundry here in Healdsburg. Perhaps, Dom, after you look at the properties with the realtor, we could arrange to meet with him?"

"Of course, Po. He seemed like a nice fellow. I'm sure he'd be glad to meet with you. Why don't you walk over to his office with me after breakfast and you can explain your plans."

"That would be excellent," Po said happily.

Over their ham and eggs breakfast, they all discussed their immediate plans. If Po could find a building they liked, they would return to Santa Rosa on the afternoon train and find lodging. They would return to Healdsburg as soon as they could arrange living accommodations. Who knew? Maybe that could all be arranged this afternoon.

The mayor and chief of police had so impressed them with their welcome that they couldn't wait to settle down in this pretty little town.

Dom explained that if he found some property he liked, he was prepared to make an offer. He too was impressed with what he had seen, and found the countryside to be as beautiful as any in Italy. That mountain that loomed over the town, Fitch Mountain, with its perfectly rounded top, lent a unique feeling to the town. He explained his plans to later rent a wagon, and he and Angelina explore a little on their own. They would head back for San Francisco on the following morning's train.

Breakfast finished, they all walked across the plaza to the real estate office. Dom introduced the Lings to the realtor, Tom Conroy. Sensing Po's shyness, Dom went ahead and explained briefly the Ling's plans. Mr. Conroy said he would be only too willing to help, and he knew of several vacant buildings that, with a little work, could probably serve quite well as a laundry. He arranged a twelve-thirty appointment with them.

The Lings returned to the hotel, and Dom and Angelina got in a coach with the realtor and headed out the road west of town. It was the road they had been on yesterday, but instead of continuing on to the bridge that spanned the creek, they turned down a narrow road through partially cleared farmland. They pulled into an open area where the two-by-four framing of a house stood.

"There's five acres here, Dom. The fellow who started this house died a half a year ago. His son's a policeman in Ukiah and is eager to sell. You can get a real good deal on this."

Angelina had been looking all around. The setting certainly was sublime, and it wasn't that far from town, but she couldn't picture Dom here at all. Too isolated. There were no other houses around. She had trouble with the fact that she had been picturing herself living there with

Dom. *What a preposterous notion*, she told herself. *It's been so long since I've been in bed with a man that now I'm thinking crazy.*

Dom saw the property and thought, *Too much work.* He was hoping to find something much more developed and more suitable, if need be, for immediate occupation. And for some reason he just couldn't see Angelina living here.

"Not bad," Dom said, "but a little too much for me. I was hoping to find something that I wouldn't have to work every day on."

"Then I think you'll like this next one," Tom Conroy said. "Let's go have a look."

They headed back the way they had come, then cut north on a road that came out on Dry Creek Road, the one they had met Dave on yesterday. They turned west, passing by a freshly built, white, one-room schoolhouse with the block letters spelling "Manzanita School" over the wide front door.

"What a pretty little school," Angelina commented.

"Yeah," Tom said. "It was needed around here. There're lots of farmers and ranchers around who have kids. Now they won't have to go all the way to town for school."

They continued on for about a half a mile until Tom pulled the buggy down a short road that stopped in front of a vacant house. The house looked small, but that was because in back of it and off to the side stood one of the biggest trees Dom had ever seen. It was a redwood, bigger probably even than the one he had seen from the window of the train. Out of the corner of his eye he saw Angelina staring up towards the top of the tree, her pretty mouth slightly open. Taking his eyes off the tree, Dom gazed about.

"Angie," Dom suddenly pointed. "Look."

Angelina looked in the direction he held his finger and saw the neat rows of a young vineyard. Tom Conroy saw what they were looking at.

"Sorry, Dom. That doesn't go with the property. That's the Massoni vineyard. That guy makes great wine. He'd be your closest neighbor. Their house is a little further down the road."

Both Dom and Angelina couldn't wait to get out of the buggy.

"Let's see the house!" Dom said.

"Sure, I've got the key here," Tom said, reaching into his coat pocket.

The house was small, but sturdily built. The front door led into a hardwood-floored living room. Light streamed in from windows on three sides. A kitchen was off a short hallway to the right, two bedrooms off a hall to the left. A small, enclosed porch or utility room was off a door at the back of the kitchen.

Dom and Angelina walked through all the rooms. They returned to the living room where they admired the fireplace, made with large rounded rocks instead of bricks. They looked at each other. Both their faces had turned a little red. Dom thought Angelina would look wonderful in this house. He could see her walking around in her robe. What was under her robe made him think of that cozy bedroom and Angelina's loose hair cascading over a pillow.

They walked to the partially screened in porch at the back of the house. Dom unlocked a screen door and walked off a few paces. Angelina stayed in the porch and watched him. She could see Dom working in a garden back there full of ripe tomatoes and onions and garlic, green beans and corn, some *basilico* plants for the sauce. She could be in the kitchen preparing a good soup for lunch. *Stop it,* she thought, and actually pinched herself.

She stepped out and joined Dom. The realtor had left them alone and was waiting out front by the buggy. The back of the property rose slightly, and to the west they could see quite a distance down the pretty narrow valley. They could see a line of trees and patches of sparkling water that marked the creek. A hundred yards away in the vineyard, they waved to a man who was looking in their direction, walking behind a plow pulled by a mule, disking the vineyard. The man took his hat off and waved back.

"What do *you* think of this place, Angie?" Dom said, trying to sound unemotional.

Angelina elbowed him in the ribs.

"What do you think, Mr. Big Shot? It's got a vineyard nearby. You can probably get all the zinfandel you want from the Massoni, and you've even got a giant redwood tree in your yard. What more could you ask for?"

Dom couldn't help himself.

"I could ask you to come here and live with me as my wife."

There, it was out. He had said it. A tension that had been building inside of him since he had first been struck by the thunderbolt when he laid eyes on Angelina flew from him as if on the wings of a dove. He took a deep breath of relief. Even if she said no and thought him an idiot, at least the cards were out on the table.

They had been standing close together, almost touching, looking into each other's eyes. Angelina's mouth broke into a smile, her eyes filled with tears. She put her arms around Dom, pressing herself into him. She felt that standing there on a beautiful spring morning overlooking that valley with her arms around Dom was all she had ever hoped for. She felt weak clinging to him, but she knew it was a good weakness. They broke apart, Dom looking at her expectantly.

"What took you so long to ask me, Mr. Londi? You had to sample the merchandise first, didn't you?"

"You will then?" Dom asked.

"Will what, old man?"

"Marry me."

Angelina could no longer be strong. Hearing the words "marry me" broke her down.

"Of course I will, Dom. There's nothing else on earth I could want more."

As soon as the last words were spoken, Angelina's bliss was momentarily shaken. Conchetta, where was Conchetta?

She threw her arms around Dom again, trying to use him to press the fear out of her. Women have intuition, she always believed. Usually it was right. Sometimes it was wrong. Holding Dom, she prayed that this time she was wrong.

Like at one point the night before, Dom felt that time was standing still. He could hold Angelina in his arms until the moon fell from the sky. His eyes were closed. He had buried his head in the softness where her shoulder joined her neck.

They suddenly heard Tom Conroy clear his throat.

"Excuse me, folks," he said laughing. "Don't mean to interrupt, but I've still got two more properties I could show you, and I promised to meet with the Lings this afternoon."

Dom looked at Angelina. She smiled at him and imperceptibly shook her head from side to side. Dom figured he knew what she meant.

"Mr. Convoy, I think I've found what I was looking for."

He realized that he was talking about the house and land, but found that he was thinking about Angelina.

"You like this place, eh," the realtor stated.

"Indeed I do sir. On this piece of property, in this place and time, I've proposed to this wonderful lady, and she accepted!"

Angelina turned scarlet.

"Dom, have some reserve!" she said, scolding, and slapped him lightly on the shoulder.

"I can't help it," Dom pleaded. "I'm happy." He shrugged his shoulders.

"Say folks, this is a pretty romantic spot if you ask me," Tom said. "Let me be the first to congratulate you," he said, walking to the couple and shaking their hands.

"Unless you want to stay a little longer, why don't we head back? We can talk a little business along the way."

On the way back, Dom was so ecstatic that he had trouble concentrating on business, but what he was hearing sounded just fine. The little house sat on three acres. It had a good well, and the soil was rich. Two established apple trees, a large cherry, and two pear trees were already on the property. One could always plant more. They could raise farm animals for food, and a large vegetable garden would probably provide enough excess that they could sell produce. Dom could even put in a small vineyard if he chose. Dom had enough money saved up, and more, to pay the asking price, but he knew he would be foolish if he didn't try to bargain. He made a lower offer, and the realtor said he would get in contact with the owner as soon as possible and present Dom's offer. No one else that he knew of was immediately interested in purchasing the property. Tom told Dom that he thought he had made a fair offer, and that a sale could be completed.

Dom and Angelina were blissfully excited and couldn't wait to get alone and talk about the future. When they reached the real estate office, they saw the Lings rise from a bench in the plaza and come towards them. Po immediately noticed a change in Dom and Angelina; so had Mai. Their faces looked radiant. Dom was squeezing Angelina's hand tightly.

"It looks like you two had very good luck," Po said.

"We sure did, Po. I found the perfect piece of property out in that Dry Creek Valley. But, more important, guess what?"

Mai had been studying Angelina. "I don't need to guess, I can see it in Angelina's face. You two are getting married," Mai said.

"See, Mr. Londi. That's women's intuition working. There's a clear cut example for you," Angelina pronounced.

"OK, OK, maybe you've got something there. Mai's right, we're going to get married."

Po came up and, bowing, shook Dom's hand. Mai and Suen congratulated and fussed around Angelina. Tom Conroy, an American who could trace his roots back to pre-Revolutionary War, marveled at the strangeness of the sight. Here was a group of people, all probably just "straight off the boat," two from Italy, the rest from China, best of friends, hugging and celebrating with one another in a growing little northern California town. *Probably no other country in the world like this,* Tom reflected.

Po broke away and came to Tom. "We are ready to look at some buildings, Mr. Conroy."

The realtor was eager to show them to him. The town could sure use a laundry. He knew that some folks were bound to resent the Lings simply because they were Chinese. He hoped there wouldn't be too many of them. After all, a town that had a good laundry could be a valuable selling point to a realtor.

Dom and Angelina wished the Lings good laundry hunting, and assured them that they hoped to be seeing them often in the future. Taking leave, they walked off across the plaza towards the stores. They came out of a little market with a small loaf of bread and some salami and cheese. Dom couldn't help himself and also purchased a bottle of Massoni zinfandel. After all, the day was a call for celebration.

At the livery stable they rented a cozy little black carriage that was pulled by a highly spirited dark brown horse. The man at the livery warned Dom to keep a tight rein on the horse. He was young and fast and at times could be a little hard to control. He said if they preferred he could hitch up an older, more experienced horse.

Dom looked at Angelina.

"I like this one just fine," she said. "Just don't run us over a cliff, Dom."

They got in and headed south out of town slowly, Dom getting the feeling of the horse and carriage. Dom knew just where he wanted to go. He wanted to have a nice picnic with his intended near that wooden bridge that crossed Dry Creek. After that he planned to continue on to that place, Mill Creek, where they were logging the redwoods. He wanted to see some of this logging for himself, before heading back to San Francisco.

Turning down the straightaway that lead to the creek, Dom picked up speed, letting the horse have a little fun. In no time they reached their destination. Dom pulled down a little side road before the bridge and stopped the carriage at a wide packed sandy area with room to turn around. They had stopped close enough to the creek that the horse was able to drink from the fast flowing water.

Getting out, and walking towards a nice little area where they could spread a blanket that was under the seat and eat, Angelina remarked, looking at the fast moving stream, "I wonder why they call this Dry Creek? Look at all the water."

"Walter told me. I think you were talking to Mai. By the end of the summer the creek dries up in places, leaving scattered pools. Sometimes you can go a quarter of a mile before finding the creek flowing again."

Angelina could see flashes of silver darting back and forth in the clear water. The creek seemed to be teaming with small fish, most no bigger than half a foot. Being a practical person, Angelina could see the advantage of living near such a creek. She would have to learn how to fish, she decided. Fresh trout fried golden brown, covered with fresh squeezed lemon would make a delicious meal to serve Dom. She suddenly remembered that Dom was a chef. He didn't like the term and preferred "cook." He would probably want to cook the trout she would catch. What a pleasure it would be not to have to do the cooking herself all the time, she reflected.

They spread the blanket and took out the food. Using his pocketknife Dom sliced up some salami and cheese, and pulled the bottle of zinfandel out of the sack.

"Hey, I should have bought a corkscrew," he realized.

"Oh, just use your knife and push it in," Angelina suggested. "Just don't cut your finger off."

With a little effort, he managed the task.

"I forgot to bring something to drink it out of, Angie. Do you mind drinking it out of the bottle?"

"I'd prefer not to, but I'm so happy I think we should have a little toast too," she said and snuggled herself up against Dom.

Dom felt like he was in heaven, but couldn't resist an opportunity.

"I'm afraid we're going to have to drink the whole bottle right here Angie. We have no way to re-cork it."

Angelina knew he was trying to be funny, but it was awfully early to be putting away a whole bottle of that strong zinfandel.

"Use your brains, Londi. Take your knife and whittle a cork from one of those willow branches. We might want a little wine later."

"By God, you're a practical woman, Angelina, but I think you're just trying to keep me from being a drunk."

Angelina turned serious. "I lived with a drunk. Remember, Dom? And it wasn't much fun. You're sixty and enjoy a little wine. What Italian doesn't?" she said, taking a sip from the bottle.

The food and wine tasted delicious, as it always did on a picnic. It would have been easy for Dom and Angelina to sit by the lively sparkling stream for hours and talk about the future. After a while, though, Dom did get up and break off a short piece of willow, and it didn't take him long to fashion a serviceable cork.

They brought everything back to the carriage, got in, and turned around and headed across the bridge, turning south towards Mill Creek. It was still early afternoon when they reached a road sign that said "Mill Creek Road." This road immediately started to climb heading west into the hills. At first they went through madrones, manzanitas, and large oaks, with large expanses of open field. Soon a forest of pine, fir, and small redwoods closed in on both sides of the narrow road. They went down a hill and rounded a bend and suddenly came upon what Dom had intended to see—a huge logging operation opened up right in front of them. The little road cut smack through the center of it, only the road wasn't little anymore. It had opened up into a wide, torn up terrain. Animals were moving about everywhere. Teams of oxen hauling giant logs, horses and mules doing the same with smaller ones. Trees had been cut down everywhere, and were lying about stacked every which way, many criss-crossed on one another. Huge piles of limbs and debris were burning everywhere, choking the canyon with smoke. Men were hustling about leading teams, chopping limbs, attaching heavy chains to redwoods so thick around that it was unbelievable. From the sides of the canyon reverberated the crack, split and boom of falling trees. Little children were playing, seemingly oblivious to the squalid, hastily thrown up shacks that surrounded them. Women were nearby hanging clothes on make shift lines. Some were doing wash in large iron pots over an open fire. Dogs were barking and chasing chickens. Dom half expected to see a devil chasing a running priest, trying to get at his rear with a pitchfork.

"Dom, look," Angelina said pointing.

Well ahead, and off to the side, they saw a huge wooden chute that stretched from the top of the canyon to the bottom. They could see men and teams working along the ridge. Somehow they had managed to get one of those huge logs into the chute, and it was sliding down at an unbelievable speed. The chute leveled out near the end, and the log went sailing off a distance and landed in the center of a muddy mess. Dom could see that the mess had once been a creek. It was the little creek they had been following for a ways. Mill Creek, Dom figured.

"I've seen enough, Angie. Let's get out of here," Dom said wearily. He turned the carriage around and they headed back the way they had come in silence for a while, and a little less exuberant. The devastating effect the logging operations had on the forest had dampened their spirits. Dom realized the necessity of extracting trees for lumber, and he knew that process provided employment for many, but he just wished there was a way to do this without making the area look like an avenging God had taken his hand and tried to rub out the beauty he had created. Perhaps if they went about their logging more selectively, leaving a few of the older trees around, and with more care and attention to preserving at least a semblance of a natural forest and surrounding, nature would have an easier time recovering. When the rains came to those bare hillsides riddled with stumps and debris, Dom could envision a sea of mud and erosion cascading down the slopes and choking what was left of the creek, leaving in its wake a wasteland that would take decades to recuperate.

"No one's going to come and chop down our redwood, Dom," Angelina suddenly said, breaking the silence. Dom was amazed at how easily Angelina seemed to read his thoughts and say something appropriate.

"That's right, Angie, plus we have enough room to plant two or three more of those beauties."

"Do you think the logging company is going to plant new trees when they're done?" Angelina said.

"I would hope so. I know they do in Italy. Of course, our old country is so ancient that all of the great forests have been cut down centuries ago, but they've always helped nature along by planting new trees. If they have any brains they should begin planting as soon as possible."

"The sooner the better," Angelina said. "Let's see now, why in the year three thousand eight hundred seventy, a tree planted now should be as big as some of those monsters they've chopped down. Didn't you say some of them were probably two thousand years old?"

"That's what Primo said. How come you're so quick with figures anyhow?"

"A woman who runs a café in San Francisco has to be quick at many things, including trying to snatch a handsome man," she stated matter-of-factly.

"I'll snatch you when we get back to the hotel," Dom said, putting his arm around her.

The terrain had turned idyllic again, and thoughts of logging were dwindling away. Dom and Angelina were too happy to stay morose for long. On the ride back, they talked mostly about their marriage plans and the house and property. Both of them thought at times how unfortunate it was that they hadn't met much earlier. Angelina realized that she would be lucky if she had twenty wonderful years with Dom. And Dom wished he were a younger man who could spend a lifetime with Angelina. Well, he would just have to fit a lifetime into twenty years, he resolved. He would have to stay as fit as possible, get plenty of exercise, eat well, and stay away from too much wine. Just being around Angelina made him feel younger, and he planned on being around her a lot from then on.

Before long they were again crossing the bridge by the picnic spot.

Looking down, Angelina said, "We've got to come here some other time, Dom, and I'm going to bring a pole and catch us some of those trout. You can cook them up for lunch over a little fire right down there by the creek."

"Can we bring a blanket and wrap ourselves up in it naked after lunch?" Dom said in a natural manner.

"Have you no shame, Londi? What if some kids came down here to fish?"

"Then we should go into the bushes with the blanket and no one would be the wiser," Dom announced.

Angelina just shook her head.

"You don't think I could catch a fish, do you?"

"I think you've already caught an old fish and probably should think twice about keeping it," Dom said, suddenly reflective.

"I know how to breathe life into an old fish, and I think I'll show you when we get back to the hotel," Angelina said alluringly, blinking her large eyes. Dom yelled out and flicked the reins. The spirited horse took off down the straightaway at a fast gallop that left them both laughing.

In a short while they were pulling up in front of the livery stable in the late afternoon. Dom settled up with the proprietor, and they walked back to the hotel. The sky was turning cloudy, and they both were a little tired from their excursion and the excitement of the day. Angelina went to her room to refresh, saying she would be knocking on Dom's door soon. Dom cleaned up, got undressed and into bed. Angelina soon knocked on the door and entered, wearing her green robe and her hair down. She locked the door behind her, disrobed, and crawled into the bed, and after a while had succeeded in eliminating all thoughts that Dom held in comparing himself to an old fish. With a contented smile on his face and the lines of age softened noticeably, he hugged Angelina as if she were his life force, and the two drifted off to sleep.

When they awoke, it was dark, time to go downstairs for dinner. Their meal was simple, yet delicious: roasted chicken, lima beans seasoned with salt pork and onions, and tossed green salad with vinaigrette dressing. They had a slice of cherry pie for dessert, and a bottle of the Massoni zinfandel to compliment the food.

They went back to Dom's room and sat up for a while talking and sipping a glass of wine from the bottle corked with a piece of willow. Their plans were to leave for San Francisco on the morning's train, and once they got there, to go about their business and wait to hear from the realtor. They planned on getting married in a month. That would give Angelina time to get the news to Mario, early enough so he and his wife could attend the wedding. Both were going to invite all their close friends, and Dom hoped that Pietro Nuti would sing. Pietro had a wonderful voice, and actually probably could have had a shot at the opera if he had pursued it.

Angelina prayed that by then she would have heard from Conchetta. If not, she knew that there would be a dark stone weighing on her heart. She didn't want to think about this. Perhaps, upon reaching San Francisco, she would receive news about her sister. Getting in bed with Dom, she tried to repress her negative thoughts and concentrate on her happiness. Thinking of the gurgling little creek, filled with silvery fish and Dom there by her side, she took comfort in his arms and let sleep wash over her.

Chapter 11

It was Saturday afternoon, and the sleepy little farming town of Gilroy had a little excitement for a change. A couple of gypsies were in town selling notions and pots and pans, and a little bit of everything from a massive intricately carved wooden wagon, parked under some trees down a side street. A large black bear was slowly pacing to and fro in a cage yoked to the back of the wagon. A group of onlookers, mostly children, had surrounded the cage and were staring and talking about the bear. El Zapo was having a wonderful time being a salesman, and business was brisk. He was selling things at a ridiculously low price. He still had plenty of money and was just having fun. A good large cast iron skillet sold for thirty cents, a wool shirt forty cents, a used pistol, five dollars. All the time he was selling, he was telling the people to come back at dark to watch the marvelous show that was to go on, featuring dancing and a trained bear.

In the small locked compartment at the front of the wagon, Conchetta Lombardi lay gagged and tied, off somewhere in a morphine-induced dream world. Somehow Juan had gotten it into her food or water. She didn't know how, and now she just didn't care. When the effects of the narcotic first started to hit her, she struggled for control, and the strength to not let herself be swept away, but the last thing she remembered was Juan leering at her as he tied her up in the wagon.

"Sweet dreams, bitch," he said as he locked the door, immersing her in total darkness. She soon felt the wagon moving, and sensations beyond her control assailed her. For a while she thought she could see in the dark, a wall of red came before her eyes. The wall of red was dotted with green-leafed plants with darker red flowers and a black center. A pale yellow sun cast a soothing light on the red wall. Conchetta had no thoughts of fear or impending doom. She heard a humming noise that seemed to emerge from the field of flowers, and listening to her heartbeat in rhythm with the hum, she lost herself in time.

Juan's plan was simple. He would rouse Conchetta at dark. She would still be in a semi-drugged state and therefore more easily controlled. Who knew? Maybe she would get to like the narcotic so much she would beg for more, he hoped. In any case, the effects of the morphine should have worn off enough by then to enable her to participate in the show. He would tell her that he himself did not care one thread if he lived or died, but that if she dared to open her mouth to anyone or scream for help, he would kill her on the spot and sacrifice himself in doing so. His demented brain, constantly advised by his guardian angel, Bael, believed that his plan would go off without a hitch.

The sun was starting to set as he hung a "Closed for Business" sign on both sides of the wagon. Juan sat at the back of the wagon eating some fresh boiled eggs he had taken in trade for some forks and spoons. The eggs were tasty, and in between mouthfuls he talked to Oso the bear.

"Oso, you have to put on a good show tonight and show the crowd how intelligent you are. You and I are spawn of the devil and therefore more cunning than normal. In fact, we're not normal at all. Are we my friend?"

El Zapo laughed, thinking that if the show was a success, he might get excited and decide to have some fun with the drugged Lombardi slut in the darkness of the wagon. He gave the bear a little food and water and then went about lighting torches and lanterns. The torches on poles he stuck in the ground to form a large circle where the performance was to take place. Next, he went to where Conchetta lay and untied her and removed the gag from her mouth.

"Come on out, Miss Lombardi. Let's have a look at you. We have to get you looking your best for the show now don't we?"

Conchetta was dressed in the red skirt and blue top—Juan's idea of a Gypsy costume. She still had scabs on her ear lobes where Juan had pierced her ears and hung large gold rings. Juan took a brush to Conchetta's long dark hair, and tried his best to brush the tangles out and arrange it.

"Your hair stinks, Lombardi," he said. "You should take better care of yourself. Why, a woman such as you should take great pride in herself, one would think," he said in a reproachful manner.

Conchetta's eyes looked glassy and a little out of focus. She hadn't spoken a word.

"Hope I didn't give her too much of a good thing," Juan said to himself. "Come now, Miss Lombardi, let's see you walk," he said, leading her to the side of the wagon that faced an empty field, and away from the street.

While still tied in the wagon, Conchetta's normal thoughts had started to come back to her, and along with them a pounding headache and a dry throat. She didn't know what was going to happen next, but she knew that sooner or later Juan was going to put on a show featuring her dancing around the bear. There would be people at the show and perhaps a chance for escape, and escape was the word she forced her mind to focus on. In an attempt to come out of her haze she began repeating the word "escape" over and over in her mind.

By the time Juan had opened the door and untied her, she had decided to act more drugged than what she really was. Possibly she could use this to her advantage, she reasoned. Sure enough, when she got out and saw the torches arranged in a circle and Juan dressed in a Gypsy outfit, she figured they were in Gilroy, and he was about to put on his pathetic little show. Obeying his orders and walking mechanically, she moved to the side of the wagon. Once shielded from any onlookers, Juan grabbed her by the throat and pinned her against the wagon. With his other hand he held the point of the knife directly under one eye, barely touching the skin.

"Listen, weakling. Are you hearing me?" Juan exhaled into her face.

Conchetta nodded affirmatively.

"You remember that little act we rehearsed with you and the bear? Well, we're going to do it tonight."

Juan explained that he cared nothing for his own welfare, and would sacrifice everything to kill her if she tried to seek help or escape in any form. Conchetta knew him to be crazy enough to do just that, but had a tough time hiding the spark of hope she felt at the fact that there were to be people around, and she would be in their presence.

"I need some water," she said. "I understand."

"Good," Juan said. "You can go get your water and you had better act natural. People should begin arriving any minute. After the show I'm going to open up the wagon for business again, and you can help me take in the money. After that you can have some food, and maybe a little more of that drug I think you're beginning to enjoy. Just remember, I don't give a damn what happens to me or you, and if anything goes wrong, I might just kill a few women and children before I meet my devil. So be good, Lombardi."

He pushed back the black coat he wore over his blue satin shirt and revealed the pistol stuck in his waistband.

Conchetta was suspiciously drinking water from the barrel when people started arriving, a few at first, then actually quite a few. Many women and children were among the crowd, Conchetta noticed with disappointment. The water tasted good, though she had her doubts, but she was so thirsty that she rapidly drank two full cups. She wished her head would clear faster. She wasn't able to think of any definite course of action. She felt weak from the drug and was having trouble concentrating. She started repeating "escape, escape" to herself silently, but she knew that escape could lead to death for others as well as herself. Conchetta had no idea what to do, and felt as helpless as a moth trapped in a web.

She moved to the back of the wagon and gazed with eyes that still had trouble focusing on the crowd that arranged themselves in a circle around the torches.

Juan came over to her and whispered in her ear, "OK, let's begin the show. Now just do what I tell you and you'll get through this alive. Put a smile on your face. Look happy. You're about to become a star," he pronounced dramatically.

Conchetta remembered the stupid little act. It would take several minutes to perform and that would be it. People would be disappointed. Surely they would expect more. Only a crazy person could think that something so brief would be viewed as entertainment.

Juan left her and limped to the center of the circle. His eyes were beaming with excitement. Conchetta noticed that his right eye even had a slight twitch. His thinness and pale complexion were even more noticeable in the gaudy colored clothes. He wore a wide-brimmed black hat, tilted back and off to the side. He had sewn a button on his coat, hiding the pistol. Conchetta could see the people quiet down as he moved to the center, dragging his foot. She even heard the word "cripple" float out of the crowd. Normally such insensitiveness would upset her. But in this case she just looked about transfixed by the insanity of her predicament.

"Ladies and gentlemen, boys and girls, for your evening's entertainment, the king and queen of the Gypsies are going to put on a magnificent performance for you tonight, featuring Oso, king of the forest. After the show, the wagon will be open with many fine goods and wares for sale. Now, let us begin the show!"

Conchetta was amazed that everyone was actually listening. The crowd was silent, all eyes riveted on Juan. Now would be a time to make a dash into the crowd and beg for help, but she could imagine Juan spotting her, and cutting her down with a bullet before she got far. He would probably then turn the gun on the crowd, or try to make a run for it. Either way, death seemed to be the result of such an attempt.

Juan, limping to the cage with as much dignity as he could muster, grabbed a coiled chain, and reaching the bear, snapped it onto Oso's collar. He quickly gave the bear an apricot and opened the door announcing, "Come, Oso, come and greet your admirers."

He led the obliging bear to the center of the circle, Oso wagging his head lazily from side to side. Juan shot Conchetta a look as she moved to the side of the wagon, facing the crowd. She was surprised and disgusted that some men applauded, and one or two even let out a yell as she became more visible in the torchlight.

"Ladies and Gentlemen, Boys and Girls, I now present to you the beautiful Conchetta, queen of the Gypsies, and Oso, king of the forest."

Juan beckoned Conchetta forward with a slight nod of his head. The moment she stepped into the circle he boomed, "Up, Oso, up!" and gave a slight flick of the chain. The crowd gasped as the bear stood up on its hind legs, paws raised up to the stars. Conchetta advanced as gracefully as she was able, and began circling the bear, twirling on the tips of her toes as she moved. Oso began turning around and around on his hind legs, seemingly following Conchetta with his eyes as he turned. The crowd broke out in applause. Children stood with their mouths agape. Some of the younger men didn't give a damn about the bear, but were mesmerized by Conchetta's appearance and delicate twirling. Conchetta had a hard time staying on her feet. Her head was still pounding, and moving in circles had made her dizzy. For a moment she felt as if she was going to pass out or vomit.

Juan was basking in the applause. He congratulated himself on his decision to keep Conchetta and the bear around. No one had ever clapped for him before, and he reveled in his role as master showman. When the applause died down, he doffed his hat to the crowd and began to lead Oso back to the cage.

Someone in the crowd yelled out, "More, more, we want more," and suddenly the applause was replaced by catcalls and boos.

Conchetta had made her way back to the wagon, and had trouble keeping a hint of glee off her face. What had that crazy man thought? His whole act had taken around three minutes. Juan's joy quickly turned to utter disillusionment. The noise of disappointment rising from the crowd stung him worse than his father's whip when he failed to perform satisfactorily at his studies. Always quick to think his way out of a situation, it didn't take him long to come up with an idea.

"My dear people, attention please, dear people. The show is not over. The king of the Gypsies has but just begun to perform," Juan announced pausing with the bear. "The king of the forest has done his work for the evening. Once he is secure in his cage, a daring exhibition of skill and courage will follow. One moment, my friends, only give me one moment."

Conchetta immediately became alarmed. What could he possibly do next? After locking Oso up, Juan went to the back of the wagon, and unlocking one of the boxes, chose six hunting knives of approximately the same weight and length. Walking towards Conchetta with a demented smile on his face, he went up to her and whispered, "Just stand against the wagon with your arms outstretched, queen. I'll throw a few knives near you, and that ought to shut them up. The show's going to be over then, whether they like it or not. Those idiots don't know good entertainment when they see it."

Conchetta wasn't that surprised that he had come up with this. She had seen his skill throwing knives. Her partially numb brain was ready to accept anything. She was starting to tremble and was feeling a powerful calling to sleep.

"Remember," Juan whispered. "Don't try anything funny. The show is almost over."

Conchetta remained standing against the wagon, as Juan walked off towards the center of the ring of torches.

"Ladies and gentlemen, boys and girls, for the final performance of the evening you will see knife throwing at its finest. My skill, coupled with the queen of the Gypsies courage, will leave you breathless and forever remembering this evening."

The crowd had grown attentive and silent again. El Zapo had spoken with confidence and enthusiasm, and all eyes moved back and forth between Juan and Conchetta. He took a couple of steps forward to shorten the distance a bit and said, "Are you ready, my queen?"

Conchetta extended her arms at chest level until they rested against the solid wood of the wagon and nodded her head affirmatively.

"Speak up, O queen. The crowd yearns to hear thy melodious voice."

"Oh shut up, blow-hard," someone mumbled at the back of the crowd.

Juan didn't even hear. He was caught up in the power he was feeling. The knives felt good in his hands. Seeing Conchetta vulnerable and pinned against the wagon, made him want to launch a knife straight at her heart. Wouldn't they all be surprised then, he laughed inwardly.

Conchetta brought him back to reality as she called out in a rather weak and shaky voice, "Yes, I am ready, O king."

Juan transferred all the knives except one to his left hand, and raising his right arm rapidly, he took aim and threw the knife. It landed with a thud, sticking in the thick side of the wagon a few inches from Conchetta's head.

The sound the knife made going into the wood suddenly brought an image of Angelina to Conchetta's mind. She thought of Angelina, doing the job she hated the most back in Genoa; killing chickens for dinner. Angelina would grab the chicken and hold it down on a stump in the yard and cut its head off with a large knife. She would let go, and the headless chicken would flap around for a while on the ground. Angelina, in disgust, would fling the bloody knife into the stump, and go pick up the chicken.

Juan was already poised to throw another knife. Conchetta began to feel faint, and began to cry, thinking about her sister and brother. Juan threw the knife just as Conchetta began to lower her arms and slide to the ground. The knife whizzed past her arm, slicing into it and leaving a deep gash before it stuck into the wagon. Conchetta didn't even feel it. She had passed out before touching the ground.

Juan ran to her in an instant, thinking as he ran. He bent over her, and shielding his movements from the crowd, pulled the bottle of morphine from an inner coat pocket and squeezed a dropper full down Conchetta's throat.

Many in the crowd had screamed when Conchetta collapsed. Quite a few had come forward and were hovering over Juan. Blood was flowing freely from Conchetta's wound.

"We'll get her to Doc Taylor's, Mister. It's not far from here," a man said.

Another man produced a handkerchief and tied it around Conchetta's cut. The two of them picked her up and started carrying her away. The crowd didn't seem to want to disperse. They stood there talking amongst each other and staring at Juan.

"Excuse me folks, as you can see my wife has had an accident. She must be sick. No more business tonight. I'm heading for the doctor's office. I'm sure you all understand."

The crowd began to disperse, some offered their condolences; one even shouted out, "Hope the queen will be OK, king."

Juan locked up the wagon and followed after the men that were carrying Conchetta. He soon caught up with them as they were turning down a street.

"That's Doc Taylor's office there," one of the men said, nodding at a nearby building with a Dry Goods and Pharmacy sign out front.

"The Doc's office is on the second story up those stairs. His light's on; that usually means he's in."

Juan followed as they ascended the steps on the side of the building. They knocked on the door, and an old man in spectacles answered immediately.

"This little lady passed out, Doc. She's with a Gypsy show, just pulled into town. Her husband there, the king, accidentally hit her with a throwing knife as she collapsed," the man who was carrying Conchetta from underneath the shoulders said.

"That's right, Doctor. I don't think her cut is that bad, but I don't know why she suddenly fainted," Juan said.

"Let's get her on that bed, and I'll have a look," Doc Taylor said.

The men who had carried Conchetta excused themselves, wishing Juan the best of health regarding his wife. Juan thanked them, then stood at the doctor's side. The doctor was taking Conchetta's pulse with one hand, and lifting her eyelids with the other. He undid the handkerchief and looked at the cut.

"Pretty deep wound," he said. "She's going to need a few stitches."

"But what's wrong with her, Doctor?" Juan said, his voice full of concern.

"Don't know yet, son. Her pulse is steady, and she's breathing normally. Just as well she fainted in a way. She shouldn't feel a thing when I put in those stitches. If you got something to do, why don't you come back in about an hour or so? By then I should have her all stitched up and bandaged, and I can try to find out what made her faint. I didn't like the way those eyes looked. She could be coming down with something. Has she been sick before this?"

"No, Doctor. Up to now she's been very healthy," Juan assured. "My wagon is down the road. I should get back and tend to it. I'll be back shortly as you said. I hope you can figure out what is wrong with her, Doctor. I'm so worried I can't think straight," Juan said in a distraught manner.

"Calm down, son. Go do what you've got to do. Your little lady's in good hands here."

Juan thanked him profusely and headed out the door and down the stairs. Conchetta would come to and tell the doctor everything, he was convinced. He hurried back to the wagon, striving to plan a course of action. He had to get Conchetta out of that doctor's office, and he had to get out of this town. He was getting way too sloppy and carried away. Before he knew what he was saying, he had introduced the bitch as "Conchetta." By now, people might be looking for "Conchetta." At least he had done the right thing by slipping her the morphine; she might be out for a long time.

The wagon had been fun, but had outlived its usefulness. It moved too slowly, and now could be correlated with a woman named Conchetta. All he knew was that he had to move, and he had to move fast. Juan had two strong horses. All he needed was a fast wagon. Surely in this dirty farming town he could find a place to quickly steal a wagon.

The thought of leaving town without Conchetta never even entered Juan's mind. He just wasn't finished with her. Sure it would be much faster and easier to leave by himself on a horse, but what enjoyment could he get out of that? The look of fear and surprise on Conchetta's face, when once again she found herself at his mercy, would be worth the risk. Besides, she hadn't done enough cooking for him, and he hadn't had his fill of making use of her well-proportioned body. It just wouldn't be right to leave her behind without slitting her throat, he gleefully reasoned.

At the wagon he lit a candle and quickly packed two suitcases with clothing and blankets. In a large canvas bag he placed cooking items, some food, a canteen of water, an extra pistol and ammunition, and a long coil of rope.

A voice suddenly startled him, and turning and rising, he hit his head on the top of the wagon.

"Hey, Mister! How's the queen?" a pimply teenage boy said, standing in the dark outside the wagon. Some good Samaritan had extinguished all the torches and lanterns while Juan was gone. Rubbing his head, Juan forced a smile to his face.

"Looks like the queen's going to be all right, son. The doctor's tending to her now. I may have to leave the wagon here overnight. Do you think that would be all right? I'm going back to the doctor's office. I may spend the night there."

"Sure, Mister. Nobody will bother it. I live just down the street and get up at five every morning to milk the cows. I'll check on it for you. Say, does the king of the forest like milk? I could bring him some."

"Why yes, Oso would like that, thank you, son. You'd better go now. I've got to pack some of the queen's things. In the morning she's going to want to look her best."

"Night, Mister. Sure was a good show," the boy said and walked off.

Juan waited until he vanished, then unhitched the horses and threw a saddle he had for sale on one of them. He secured the suitcases and bag to the horse, mounted it, and leading the other one, headed quietly out of town the way he had come. He avoided the town's main street and saw no one. It was pretty late now, and everyone seemed to be asleep. Only a few houses he passed were lit.

A quarter of a mile or so before he came to town, he had noticed a wagon sitting abandoned in a field of what looked like garlic or onions. He headed straight for it, hoping it wasn't broken. There were no houses within sight, and the moon, if there was one, was hidden in clouds. He reached the wagon by going down a narrow road between the crops, which indeed were garlic. The horse had strayed momentarily off the road and had stepped on some of the young plants, whose aroma instantly dispersed, identifying them to Juan. The wagon seemed to be fine. It was full of hoes and shovels and caked with dried manure. The wagon reeked, but Juan had no time for being picky. He trusted that the devil Bael was guiding him and immediately began to hitch the horses to the wagon. He tossed out the hoes and shovels and threw in the saddle and his possessions and headed back towards town.

Conchetta opened her eyes to find herself in totally unfamiliar surroundings. By the supplies around her, she could see she was in a doctor's office. Her arm was bandaged, and an old man, probably the doctor, was sitting in a chair by the bed she was lying on, staring at her. She felt drugged, more drugged than she had ever been. She tried to move her arms and legs, but couldn't seem to do it. It didn't matter, she felt fine just laying right there. The image of Juan flashed across her mind.

"He's going to kill me. He's a killer," she managed to say in a slow slurred voice to the doctor.

The doctor had a stern, disappointing look on his face. He came over to Conchetta, and raising her eyelids, peered into them with a small magnifying glass. He noticed the silly grin on her face, and a slight stream of drool leaking from the corner of her mouth.

"Hey, what are you doing?" Conchetta said and started giggling and wagging her head from side to side.

"A dope fiend," the doctor pronounced silently to himself. He had seen Conchetta's type before, and could even guess that the drug was morphine. It was used widely by some, and often many of them were gypsies. Unfortunate a girl so young and pretty was already addicted to the vice.

Conchetta repeated with a glazed faraway look, "He's a killer. He's a killer."

"Be calm, little lady, be calm. You just rest easy. I've stitched up your cut. You're going to be fine. Just rest and sleep it off. Morphine isn't it? You like morphine, right?"

"Drugged me, drugged me," Conchetta managed to say.

They try to blame everyone but themselves for their weaknesses. This stuff about a killer was nothing but hallucinations and dreams. She probably even saw lions and tigers at times, he figured. Nothing he could do for her but let it wear off. *That poor nice husband of hers. He*

*sureseemed a caring but odd type. Must be a patient sort
to put up with this stuff*, he thought. It was getting a little
cold, so the doctor covered Conchetta with another blanket. Conchetta's eyes were fluttering between open and
closed; he could see she wasn't really looking at anything.
He went to the back room and lay down. If he fell asleep,
he figured that the husband would wake him when he
came back.

Juan had changed into his workers clothing and a wide-
brimmed straw hat. He drove the side streets slowly until
he came near the doctor's office. He parked the wagon
behind an abandoned building and walked towards the
office. Only a dim light shone from the window. Maybe
everyone was sleeping, Juan thought hopefully.

On the way there he had stopped and partaken of
a large amount of cocaine. Speed and boldness was
his plan of action. He had no time for second-guessing,
and the drug gave him the confidence he would need to
carry out his plans. He looked around, and seeing no one,
listened quietly at the door. Hearing nothing, he knocked
lightly at the door. The doctor didn't answer. He tried the
door, but it was locked. Using his knife, it took him only seconds to pry the bolt back from the strike and open the
door. Conchetta was lying still on the bed. He entered
soundlessly and immediately saw the doctor asleep in the
back room. He took some bills from his pocket and left
the doctor more than an ample payment on a cluttered
table. From a small can he carried in his coat pocket, he
took out a rag soaked in ether and covered Conchetta's
nose and mouth with it. She hadn't even moved. *I guess
she was already asleep*, he noted. *Well, she won't wake
up for a while now.* He easily picked Conchetta up and
carefully left the room, closing the door silently behind him.

It was difficult carrying her down the stairs; his deformity
hampered him, but he made it, and soon had Conchetta
tied securely on her back in the wagon. He pillowed her

head with blankets and made his way to the main road. There was no avoiding a saloon that was still open on the outskirts of town. Juan, with his head lowered down, moved slowly by. A man came out of the saloon and started to get on his horse that was tethered out front. Juan passed by him, giving a short wave. The man nodded, and mounting his horse, rode off in the opposite direction. Juan continued on until there were no more buildings in sight, then flicking the reins he urged the horses on, and moved quickly yet cautiously down the dark road. He was headed down El Camino Real, the King's Highway, north towards San Jose. He was exuberant and felt the devil leading him. North he must push. Always north. Why? He did not know.

Chapter 12

Walter knew it wasn't good to think too long about owls, even if they were your grandmothers. He had studied and learned many amazing things at the presidio school, but he had also learned at the rancheria never to sell Pino short. Too often he had seen him predict the future or display an uncanny knowledge of his natural surroundings.

Too bad they hadn't started from the rancheria earlier; now it was getting late. Everyone was tired. The wagon was full, to capacity now, of Pomos. Only a few remained walking, trailing way behind the wagon, where the dust could not reach them. They passed the Massoni vineyards and turned down a side road that led to a small, well-built house with a giant redwood out back. Several of the Massoni children had seen the Indians turn down the Londi's driveway, and followed after them, keeping hidden and darting in and out of the bushes. In their minds they had invented a massacre. What could those Indians want with Dom and Angelina Londi, other than to lift their scalps? By the time they snuck down the driveway, there were no Indians to be seen. In the semi-dark, they made their way to a window and peered in. What they saw astounded them. The little house was full of Indians, and there were Dom Londi and Angelina, safe and laughing. Dom was heating up tortillas on a slab of iron over a small fire in the fireplace. As soon as the tortillas were warm, he handed them to patiently waiting Indians, who took them and went to a big pot of tomato sauce, where they dipped the rolled up tortillas in and took a bite. Everyone was talking and laughing. Angelina was scolding the Indians if they dripped tomato sauce on the floor, and was urging them to use their hand as a cup to catch the drips. Many of the Indians were speaking amongst themselves in their own language, but several of them were speaking to Dom in very good English. They saw a boy about their own age speaking to Angelina in better English than hers. He was asking her if she had been catching any trout. An older Indian was asking Dom how his red onion plants were doing. The kids were amazed at what they were seeing, and couldn't wait to get home and tell their parents.

Dom and Angelina had been living in Dry Creek Valley for almost a month now. Their wedding had been a joyous event. Pietro Nuti was in perfect voice, and along with a few musicians, had entertained them all with old Italian folk ballads. Mario, his wife, and her family, arrived a day early from Monterey. The only news they brought concerning Conchetta was the same information that Primo Nuti had passed on to them. Someone in Gilroy had seen a beautiful young woman named Conchetta traveling with a Gypsy and a bear. They had sold some wares, put on a show, and had vanished. They had left their wagon and all their goods, along with the bear, off a side street in Gilroy. Primo had investigated further and had learned that this "Conchetta" had been wounded in a knife-throwing performance. The doctor who had stitched her up felt certain that she was a morphine addict, and that sometime during the night, while she was semi-comatose in his office, her husband had come for her, and the two had mysteriously left. The next day a wagon had been reported stolen. Possibly it could have been the gypsies who took it.

Angelina was very suspicious of this story. She had had an easy time convincing Dom that Monterey would be the perfect place for a honeymoon. They could pass through Gilroy, and she could talk to the doctor and get a good description of this Conchetta. Dom could see the sense in this, and was happy to do anything that might ease Angelina's mind.

Arriving in Gilroy, they had no trouble locating the doctor. He was the only one in town. The description he gave Angelina matched Conchetta perfectly, but Angelina knew it also could match many young and pretty dark-haired girls. The doctor's opinion that this Conchetta was a dope fiend certainly confused the whole issue. Angelina found it hard to believe that, even if Conchetta had run off with some Gypsy, she would also become addicted to a drug. None of this behavior seemed like Conchetta, but still there was an element of doubt.

Dom wanted to know where the wagon was that they had been traveling in. The doctor explained that the sheriff had auctioned it off, and a local farmer had bought it, intending to convert it to a produce wagon for his son. Dom and Angelina located the farmer, who took them out to the barn where the wagon was. Angelina explained the reason for their interest in the wagon, and the farmer was only too glad to help in any way. He explained that the wagon was pretty much in the same state as when he bought it. It would be another year before his son was old enough to take the wagon out on his own and sell produce, so he was in no hurry to sell all the contents the wagon held.

It was dark in the barn, so he lit a lantern and handed it to Angelina, who looked inside hoping to find anything that would remind her of Conchetta. She found it right away. Conchetta's sturdy black shoes were amidst a pile of clutter, off to the side on the wagon floor. Angelina examined them closely. They looked identical to the

pair that Conchetta had bought in San Francisco, shortly
before leaving for Monterey. They were also her size. This
was all the proof Angelina needed. Conchetta was alive,
and evidently had run off with some young Gypsy—but
this didn't fit Conchetta at all. Even if she had done this, by
now, surely she would have contacted her brother and sister. They were all too close not to keep in touch and share
life's changes. The only possible reason that Angelina
could think of for Conchetta to behave in such a way
was if, as the doctor said, she had become a dope fiend,
and that her mind had been altered from the drug—confused and uncaring. Angelina was familiar with the stories
about people hooked on a drug. All they cared about
after a while was the drug, and how to obtain it. Could
Conchetta possibly have sunk to this? Angelina couldn't
believe it. Her intuition told her that something terrible was
going on. She just didn't know what.

Angelina kept the shoes, and they were getting
ready to board their rented carriage for Monterey, when
Angelina suddenly remembered something about a bear.
Conchetta had always liked animals, any animal, since
she was a little girl. Traveling with a bear was something
that she could actually imagine Conchetta doing. She
asked the farmer about it, who said that the sheriff, after
failing to find anyone who could take the bear, had hauled
the cage out to the woods and opened the door. The
bear walked out, urinated, and then walked back and
entered the cage. The bear just wasn't wild anymore, and
the sheriff figured it would either starve or make its way to
town and cause trouble, so he shot it, and gave the meat
to a couple of poor families, who certainly appreciated it.

Everything that Dom and Angelina had seen and heard
since they reached Gilroy was astonishing. Angelina was
so confused on the road to Monterey that she started crying. She didn't know what to think about her sister, and it
was driving her crazy. Dom hugged her and kissed her,

and tried to assure her that everything would probably turn out all right. Conchetta might come to her senses and quite this drug. She and this Gypsy fellow, her husband, the doctor had called him, were young, wild, and foolish. Hopefully they would realize the danger of their behavior before it was too late. A damper had been thrown on their honeymoon, but in a way Angelina breathed a little freer. At least she had learned something, as disturbing as it was, about Conchetta.

When they reached Monterey, she showed the shoes to Mario, who agreed that they looked exactly like Conchetta's. They took the shoes to the sheriff's office, and explained what they had learned. The sheriff listened patiently, but said that there was nothing he could do. Her sister was of legal age, and had married a Gypsy and went off somewhere. This was no crime. No one could help it if she hadn't told her brother and sister. Case closed, as far as the law was concerned.

Mario and Angelina left the office feeling frustrated and confused. Evidently, there was nothing they could do but wait for Conchetta to contact them. Angelina tried to take pleasure in spending time with Mario, his wife and her family, and was overjoyed to hear that Lena was pregnant, and soon she would be an aunt. Determined to try to make the best of their honeymoon, Dom and Angelina stayed in Monterey four nights in a nice cottage overlooking the bay. They took long walks together and talked deep into the night by a fire in the cozy little cottage.

The sale of the Dry Creek property had gone through, and as soon as Angelina found a buyer for her café they would make the move to Healdsburg. This didn't take long, and soon the Londis found themselves back on the train headed north. The first thing they did when they arrived in town was to inquire if a new laundry had opened up. They found the Ling's new business off a side street near the plaza. Mai, Suen, and Po were delighted to see them and were looking forward to visiting them at their new house in the valley. The laundry had been doing good business, and the Lings had found a suitable house to rent nearby. Most people in town had treated them well and were glad to do business. They were only troubled once by an unfortunate incident, and that involved Dave and some of his friends. Suen had made some purchases at the Dry Goods store and was leaving when Dave and his cronies, Butch and Wesley, approached her in front of the store.

"Well, well, if it isn't Ball Thrower all growed up," Dave said to her, bowing and removing his hat. "Bet you remember me from Modesto. I'm all growed up to, but at least I'm no stinking Chinese," he said displaying his bucktoothed smile to Suen.

Once Dave had found out that the new Chinese laundry was run by a family who had operated one in Modesto, he had observed Suen several times unseen, and had decided that she was the little Chinese girl who had laughed at him and called him "smelly boy." Dave remembered pulling her braids and kissing her. This girl, Suen, looked just like her, only older and more alluring. He figured that he and the boys would have a little fun with her, maybe get to see that look of fear in her eyes he remembered so well.

The instant Dave mentioned ball throwing, Suen recognized him. She thought he looked vaguely familiar when they had met on the road that day with her parents, Dom and Angelina, and the nice Indian boy, Walter. He hadn't changed at all. He was still filthy—she could smell him from a distance—and he was staring at her with a mean, sadistic look. She couldn't help glancing at his shoes and noticed that one of them was untied. The two other men he was with just stood there gawking and looking her up and down.

Suen noticed that the nearest people were quite a distance away, and aside from the lady who waited on her, there was no one else in the Dry Goods store. She decided it was best not to show any recognition of Dave.

"Say, Dave, aren't you going to introduce us to your friend?" one of his pals said, stepping forward and coming close to Suen.

This one she remembered also seeing on the road that day. Every time she had glanced at him, she saw his eyes appraising her.

"My name's Butch Baylow, ma'am. What's yours? China Doll?"

"I am Suen Ling, and I must be going. Excuse me please."

"Woah, woah there, Suen. It's too soon for you to go," Dave said, thinking that he had made a great joke. "You haven't said how glad you are to see me again. You remember me now, don't you? I'll bet you remember the kiss I gave you, huh?" he said, opening his small, jaundiced eyes as bug-eyed as he could.

"Hey, I didn't know you kissed her," Butch said. "My turn now," and he quickly grabbed Suen and pressed his lips into hers.

The others started laughing, as Suen struggled to get out of Butch's grasp. The clerk in the Dry Goods store heard the commotion, and looking out the window saw what was happening. She was the sister of the owner, and her name was Maddie Knight. Her husband, Tom, had recently died suddenly, and she was more bitter than lonely, and easily roused. She grabbed a broom, went out the door, and smacked Butch Baylow on the back of the legs as hard as she could, breaking the handle.

"Let go of that girl this instant," she said at the same time, in a voice heavy with authority. "You no goods get out of here before I scream for the police, or go get my gun. Davy Fowler and his little gang of thugs, why don't you all find some man to bully, instead of a young gal? I hear old Captain McCraken knows how to take care of you, Davy. Coldcocked you with one blow is what I heard." Maddie derided them.

Butch had immediately let go of Suen. He didn't want any trouble with the police. Sometimes he didn't even know why he hung around with Dave. Dave usually got him into trouble, and every once in a while he caught Dave staring at his crotch.

"We're leaving, Mrs. Knight. We was only having a little fun."

"Yea," Dave spoke up. "She's only some damn foreigner. Celestials, I hear they're called," he said proudly, using a term he had discovered in one of his dime magazines.

"Davy Fowler, you don't know a Celestial from a centipede. Now get! And the next time your mother comes in, I'm going to tell her what you've been up to."

Maddie walked up to Suen, and taking her hand, led her back into the store. Dave forced out a laugh, and walked off with his pals towards the beer garden. Suen thanked Maddie for helping her, and assuring her that she was all right, Suen excused herself and hurried towards home. She told her parents what had happened, and how she had met Dave many years before in Modesto. They decided that it would be for the best if Suen didn't walk about town unaccompanied, and Po was going to report the incident to the police. Perhaps they would have a talk with these young men's parents. Though in the past, he had always found that the law didn't exactly move swiftly when it came to dealing with the complaints of the Chinese.

Dom and Angelina didn't like this Dave one bit. Everyone just seemed to think he was harmless. Shortly after they were settled in their new home Dom purchased a shotgun. He told Angelina that he was sure he could bag some nice ducks down by the creek now and then, and there were many valley quail amongst the brush. The main reason he had purchased the gun though was for protection. He didn't trust Dave one bit, and it didn't take him long to find out that there were a few other hotheads in town like Dave. They all seemed to have one thing in common: their dislike for anyone other than a native-born, white American, and he and Angelina didn't fit in that pot.

Now, with their house full of Indians, thoughts of Dave were far from Dom's mind. He enjoyed being around the Pomos, especially Walter, Pino, and the young boy Fred. He ran into Walter a couple of weeks after arriving in town and sat with him on a bench in the plaza for a long talk. He told Walter that he and his people were welcome to spend the night at his place anytime they were on their way to town. Angelina was picky about her living room, but they were welcome to sleep on the back porch, or in the yard. This was the first time that so many had arrived at once. Pino, Walter, and Fred had spent the night once before, and Angelina even allowed them to sleep in the living room by the fire, it being a cold night.

Dom had especially come to enjoy talking with Pino. The man's knowledge of his surroundings was astounding, and he came up with the most hysterical observations. Pino could watch a bird fly and predict the next day's weather based on his observance associated with the bird. So far he was right every time. Dom had gone walking in the hills with Pino alone once. It was an unsettling experience. Every rock formation, unusually shaped tree, or pool of water they came across was either given a name by Pino, or assigned an identity of good or evil, as well as its special power and influence over a person. Walking with Pino, Dom began to look at everything suspiciously. He knew that the ancient Etruscan priests had viewed the world in a similar manner, and especially were successful at predicting the future by also observing birds in flight, and dissecting them to read their entrails. Dom even began to speculate if it was possible that long ago some of the Etruscans had made their way to North America, and that somehow Pino's people were descended from them. Dom liked that idea. He too felt that he was descended from the Etruscans. No wonder he got along with Pino so easily, he reasoned.

In the kitchen Angelina had boiled up a big pot of spaghetti. She enjoyed being around these Indians too. They always treated her with respect, and were more than willing to help Dom with any chores whenever they came around. It seemed like usually only the men made the journey into town. Only once had she met any of the women. One was named Melanie, who seemed to follow Walter around everywhere. The other was a little younger and named Betty Mae. Both girls were rather short and squat with shiny black hair that glistened in the light. Angelina had remarked once to Walter about the unusual shine the girls had to their hair.

"Oh, the bear grease does that," he mentioned matter-of-factly.

Angelina frowned. *Their hair must stink*, she said to herself. *Oh well, who am I to judge tradition*, she thought. *Obviously the men don't mind it.* She had noticed how many of the young men were competing for Betty Mae's attention. But Betty Mae, she noticed, always seemed to be staring at old Pino.

Angelina rounded up all the plates and bowls she could find along with her forks. She dished spaghetti into each container and covered it with the good sauce she had made out of fresh tomatoes, garlic, onions, and herbs. She had even added some dried local mushrooms that Dom had purchased at the general store. She told Walter that everybody had to eat outside, that spaghetti could be messy. All the Indians except Walter looked at their bowls and plates in bewilderment. They looked at Angelina in confusion. They all liked this strange lady who was quite pretty in the white man's way, but why was she trying to make them sick by serving them long worms with the sweet tangy tomato sauce over them?

Pino was the first to speak. He told Angelina in his broken English that it was true they often ate the big red ants and the tasty grasshoppers, but never had they eaten long white worms. They had seen many of these worms before, and usually they had broken off and were hanging from the anus of some sickly dog. Why was Angelina serving then such disgusting food?

Walter, Dom, and Angelina burst out laughing. Dom began to choke, he was laughing so hard, looking at Pino's disappointed face. Walter explained that these were no worms. He himself had eaten this food in San Francisco. It was only made from flour, thinly sliced he explained, and twirling some on his fork, took a big bite. Dom and Angelina did the same and rubbed their stomach in contentment and smacked their lips. Several of the Indians dropped their bowls in fear and ran behind the redwood tree to hide. The rest of them cautiously tasted the food; all eyes were turned on Pino. Pino had trouble getting the spaghetti to stay on the fork, but managed to get some into his mouth and swallow. It was delicious, he thought, and indeed these were no worms. Immediately the thought he could improve this eating experience by chopping red onions into his bowl, and asked Dom if he could please have one of his red onions.

Everyone now began to eat heartily, and soon all the spaghetti was gone. The Pomos were tired, and retrieving blankets from the wagon, most of them ended up sleeping under the stars on a grassy area in the back yard.

Dom got out a bottle of the Massoni zinfandel and poured out glasses for himself, Angelina and Walter. Pino did not trust wine and refused the glass he was offered, preferring to drink the cold lemonade Angelina had made.

It hadn't taken Dom long to make friends with his neighbor, Guisepe Massoni. Dom mentioned that he had met a Massoni in Lucca many years ago. He couldn't remember the man's first name but he described him to Guisepe. The description fit his father perfectly, and the two had a wonderful time talking about Lucca and Tuscany. Dom had told Guisepe that he would like to plant a small vineyard on part of his property for the sole purpose of making a little wine for Angelina and himself. Guisepe had assured him that he would love to help him get started. He explained to Dom that an insect called phylloxera was destroying many of the vines at the root. Guisepe and some of the other growers had found out that the problem could be avoided by planting only native American vines and grafting imported varieties on to the mature roots. When it came time to prune the zinfandel in the fall, Guisepe assured Dom he could have all the cuttings he wanted, and he would help him secure and plant the native vines. Dom had never made wine before, but liked the idea of drinking something you made all by yourself, with nature's help, of course.

Dom and Angelina already had a good vegetable garden going. Primo had been right; it seemed like all you had to do was throw out the seed and stand back and let things grow. The many fruit trees he had planted were also doing amazingly well, especially the French plum trees. In a couple of years, when they would begin to bear fruit, Angelina looked forward to drying them on wood trays in the hot sun. The plums then would be prunes and they could enjoy them all winter. As for livestock, they had pigs, two steer, a milk cow, and a large flock of chickens. Neither Dom nor Angelina really knew much about farming, but they were fast learners, and many people they had met were happy to give them advice. Looking at his pigs, Dom could tell he would have a hard time when it came to butchering them. He even thought that, when that day came, he might have to pay someone to do it for him. Those silly pigs were coming to be too much like funny little friends. Angelina hated killing chickens, and every time she had to, she thought of Conchetta standing by her side in Genoa, watching her doing the butchering in childlike fascination. If Dom wasn't busy, she always sought him, to go out and round up and butcher a chicken for dinner.

With the money Angelina had received from the sale of her café, along with Dom's savings, the Londis looked like they were going to do all right making a life in the picturesque valley. Sitting in their living room, talking comfortably with Walter and Pino, the Londis truly felt that lady luck had smiled on them when she had brought them together.

"Are you going to play baseball tomorrow, Walter?" Dom asked.

"I hope to," he said. "It will be nice weather. I'm almost sure enough people will show up so we can have a good game."

"Maybe Angelina and I will stop by. We were planning on going to town anyway. I'm starting to enjoy this baseball. If I was younger I would give it a shot myself," Dom said.

"I can make you younger, Dom," Pino said.

"Now, how would you do that?" Dom inquired.

"I would feed you young, tender cat tails for stamina, and then I would place you alone in a cave with Betty Mae."

Angelina got a reproachful look on her face, rose, and slapped Pino fairly hard on the shoulder.

"He doesn't need to get young that way, Pino. He's doing just fine like he is. That baseball's dangerous anyway. Just standing there and letting someone throw a hard ball at your head, it's lucky someone's not killed every time that game is played."

"Maybe the Lings would like to come with us and watch the game," Dom suggested. "The last time we were in town we saw Suen, Walter, and she asked if we had seen you lately. I think that girl might be a little interested in you, huh?" he said, raising his eyebrows.

Before Walter could answer, Pino butted in, saying, "I have seen that Chinese girl. She reminds me of the dark-winged hummingbird with the white chest. I think she could be good for Walter, but he moves kind of slow and would have trouble keeping up with her. Also, there is this to consider; Melanie likes Walter and enjoys feeding him grasshoppers. The Chinese girl would feed him the white mealy bugs—rice. Why is it that so many people lately enjoy eating food that looks disgusting? Walter, I think you should go to that large rock where your grandmothers live, and pose this question to them."

Everyone except Pino just shook their heads and looked at one another.

"So you met our friend, Davy, on the road?" Dom said, addressing Walter.

"Yes, he greeted us as is his custom—holding a shotgun. He seems to be losing control; he's worse every time I see him."

"How did you get away from him this time?" Dom inquired.

"The usual. Pino took his shirt and pants off and covered himself with his robe before we got to Davy's. When Davy stopped us, holding the gun, Pino stood up and let the robe drop. Davy lowered the gun and just stood there staring, and off we went."

"Davy finds my member good looking," Pino announced.

"Pino, stop talking that way," Angelina scolded, doing her best to hide a smile. "You'd think that the police or sheriff would do something once and for all about Davy," Angelina said in a frustrated manner.

"Yea, what's he got to do, kill someone before he's taken seriously?" Dom said. "I've seen his type in Italy. One day they just snap and do something terrible, and by then it's too late," he added.

The hour was getting late, and presently Dom and Angelina retired to the bedroom. Pino and Walter got their blankets and joined the others out in the yard.

Chapter 13

Dave Fowler was lying in bed thinking about Suen Ling. He had the window open in his little bedroom, but it did little to alleviate the heat. Dave's room was a mess. His mother had given up on getting Dave to clean it, and he was way too old and capable for her to have to clean the cluttered room herself. Besides, it smelled in there. Betty Fowler just never could get her son to bathe enough. Dave insisted that every time he soaked his body in water it made him sick. He told no one that the real reason he didn't like soaking in water is that it made his member all shriveled and shrunk. Dave was afraid that the day might come after water immersion that his old friend would fail to restore itself, and Dave would be left on the short end of a stick.

His room was cluttered with dime western magazines, stale licorice, shotgun shells, and revolver bullets. Dirty clothes were strewn everywhere—only one area of the room was orderly, and that was the closet. He had put a lock on his closet, telling his parents that the reason was to keep any neighbor children that might come over for a visit from getting hurt. He kept his shotgun and rifle along with his prized possession—a 36-caliber Navy Colt revolver in a soft leather holster—securely locked away. Also in the closet were articles of clothing that his parents had never seen: a black ten-gallon hat, white frilly shirt, black trousers and black coat, and painted boots with fancy leather stitching and inlay. The outfit was almost an exact replica worn by a character in one of the desperado magazines, complete with a 41-caliber Philadelphia Derringer neatly hidden in an inner coat pocket.

When his parents were gone, Dave would dress in his fancy clothes and strap on the revolver. He would look at himself in the large mirror in his parents' bedroom and practice drawing the Navy Colt from its holster as fast as possible. He liked the way he looked and would experiment with tilting the large hat at rakish angles coupled with various expressions on his face until he appeared, he thought, as an avenging force that would strike fear into the hearts of his enemies.

Now, laying on his back thinking about Suen Ling, he had trouble falling asleep. He felt that the time for him to act was soon at hand. All his life Dave had felt he hadn't been dealt a fair hand. He wasn't handsome and strong as some. Quick wittedness escaped him, and for some reason, he had little interest in chasing after girls. His lack of interest in females even upset his parents. Often his mother would say, "David, when are you going to find a nice girl and marry and raise a family of your own?" Or his Pa would say, upon spying a pretty young lady in town, "Hey, Dave, there's one for you, look at the hips on her, fine breeding stock, hey son." Dave's jaundiced, pimply face would turn red, and he would stutter out an, "Aw shucks Pa, quit joshing me," and would struggle to find another subject to switch to. Dave wanted to find a woman to cozy up to but just couldn't bring himself to speak up when the opportunity arose. Some of his friends would ride into Santa Rosa on the weekends and pay a visit to one of the town's brothels. They would urge Dave to come along, but every time he would make up some excuse as to why he couldn't go. No one even bothered to ask him anymore.

Dave spent most weekends alone, often going off to the remote hills to practice drawing and shooting his revolver. In this area, he excelled—he could hit even the smallest target dead on at fifty feet. He could throw a can up in the air and hit it twice before it touched the ground. No one knew Dave was this accurate. This secret he kept to himself. Why? He didn't know.

Now, lying on his soiled bed thinking about the wide-eyed Chinese girl, his mind soared to new heights. Why had those Chinese suddenly showed up in town? And why, of all the Chinese in California, did one of them have to be a girl out of his past, a girl who had laughed at him and called him smelly? Every female he had encountered had laughed at him at one time or another, even his own mother. Oh, wouldn't it be nice to get back at all the females who had laughed at him. This he knew would be impossible. But it wouldn't be impossible to get back at one of them. One of them could be made to quiver in fear and beg Dave for mercy. One of them he could throw to the ground, strip of her clothes, and mount like an avenging stud. Suen Ling would come to know Dave for what he was—a man to be feared and not laughed at. A man of bold courage and action, handsome and resplendent in his suit of black clothes, the revolver slung low on his hip.

"By God, I'm going to do it!" Dave said aloud. "I'm going to get me that Chinese girl and for once I'm going to have my way, and if I hear so much as a whisper of laughter, I've got a bullet that can silence anything."

Dave sat up in his bed. He knew what he was going to do. Chinese, Mexicans, Indians, and Darkies were fair game. So were those garlic-eating Italians. The law didn't care much what happened to low life and foreigners, but just the same, plans had to be made, thought Dave. Jail wasn't a nice place. He would have his way with Suen and, who knew, when he was done with her, maybe she would want to marry him. She had better want to marry him, he thought. If she didn't, he would have to silence her for good. Kidnap and rape could get him jail time, even if she was Chinese. Sure, they'd go light on him, and he'd probably be out in no time, but Dave didn't like life behind bars, and there wouldn't have to be any bars. All he had to do was plan well.

He got up out of bed, and taking a key from under an oil lamp that sat on a box he used for a nightstand, he walked over to his closet. He unlocked the door, and lighting the lamp, gazed admiringly at his attire and weaponry. He saw himself dressed in his finery, riding down on Suen and scooping her up in full gallop, as he headed east out of town to the high mountains that were dotted with abandoned quicksilver mining shacks, and hastily thrown up shelters that once housed various squatters. One of the shacks would be a perfect place to have a long talk with Suen, and maybe even convince her to marry him. He gazed at this costume until his mind was filled with visions of a bold, handsome Dave staring down at a helpless, naked Suen Ling. Dave had never seen a naked woman before. Once his Ma had bent over on a hot day doing the wash and he had caught a glimpse of white breast. It looked soft and smooth just like a cow's teat, but cow's teat looked a little like a male member, and the thought of a male member seemed to arouse Dave's interest more than a woman's breast did. Dave had to admit to himself that he was just plain confused when it came to matters of a sexual nature. Maybe once he got Suen undressed, everything would fall into place. He got back in bed with his head full of plans. In the morning he would ride into town and spy on the Lings, watch their movements, especially Suen's. Maybe he'd even ride into the hills and look at abandoned shacks. One of them was bound to be a good destination for a honeymoon or a killing.

Early the next morning, Dave ran into Butch Baylow on his way into town.

"Hey," Dave said. "Want to have some fun spying on some Chinese?"

"Sure," Butch said. "I could look at that Suen from hell to breakfast. Why, I could even look at her until I turned blind."

Dave looked sharply at Butch whose face had turned red and lively just thinking about Suen Ling.

"Hey," Dave said. "That girl may be my wife one day. I may take pity on her and make her a real American. Why, if she was to marry a Fowler and quit dressing as a Celestial, and if she fixed biscuits and bacon, I do believe that would be a step in the right direction, away from the path of a heathen."

"What's a heathen?" Butch said, a dull, quizzical look on his face.

"A foreigner who ain't an American," Dave answered patiently and knowingly. "I'm surprised at you, Butch. Didn't they learn you nothing in school?"

"I can count, and I can spell my name. You know I only went to the fourth grade. Pa needed me on the farm. Someone had to help him trap wild pigs. You know all that, Dave," Butch said, looking a little offended.

They soon reached the plaza, and tying their horses to a rail, walked off in the direction of the Ling's laundry. Hiding behind a fence along an alley they sat in the dirt and peered between some broken boards at the establishment. Dave reached into his pocket and brought out a small leather pouch filled with marbles. The boys were a little old for such a pastime, but if someone saw them sitting in the dusty alley, their presences there could more or less be explained. The laundry was already doing a brisk business for an early morning. Dave could see Suen's parents chatting amicably with customers dropping off or picking up clothing and bedding. Dave was mainly curious to see if both the Lings stayed in the laundry most of the day, and what part Suen played in the operation. Dave and Butch had drawn a circle on the ground in front of them and had spread a few marbles in it. They were both leaning forward with their heads a few inches from the fence staring intently and didn't even notice when a small scruffy-looking dog half bald with mange trotted over, and after sniffing Dave briefly, lifted its leg and peed all over his lower back. Dave jumped at the sudden warm feel of liquid and swung his arm at the little dog as it ran off, its mission accomplished.

"Damn it!" Dave said. "Now what am I going to do?"

"That's easy," Butch said. "Take that stinking shirt off and walk over to the laundry."

"Oh, yea, Butch. The girl I'm going to marry is probably in there, and you expect me to stroll on over stinking of dog piss. She already called me smelly once. Don't you think once is enough, for Christ's sake?"

"You never told me she called you smelly," Butch said.

"Well she did. It was many years ago when we first kissed, and none of that's any of your business by the way, Mr. Baylow. It's a nice morning; I believe I'll just go shirtless."

Dave stared down at his narrow, caved in chest. He was mostly hairless and was beginning to feel a bit self-conscious. Just then Suen Ling entered the alley. She came from an opening between two houses and was carrying a large straw basket loaded with laundry. She stopped dead in her tracks when she realized who it was sitting cross-legged in the dirt playing marbles. She found it odd to find these two bullies hanging out in the alley so near to her house. That smelly one, Dave, didn't even have a shirt on.

Dave and Butch sprang to their feet. Both were amazed to find Suen standing so close, staring at them wide-eyed.

Dave knew he had to say something, so he walked a little closer and began talking just as Suen was turning away in the same direction she had come from.

"Wait, Miss Ling. It's me, Dave Fowler, and Butch. We were just having a little game of marbles, but since you're here we'd like to apologize for joshing you around a while back. We've learned our lesson, and nothing like that's ever going to happen again."

Dave spoke so humbly that it took Suen by surprise. She still didn't trust him one bit and figured he was up to something. And why wasn't he wearing a shirt? As soon as he had taken a couple of steps closer to her she detected the strong odor of dog urine. She glanced down at Dave's shoes and noticed them to be untied. Did nothing change with this jaundiced-looking young man? *Now he even smells worse than ever*, she thought, *and does he think that pimply-looking scrawny chest is something to show off?*

All she could think of to say was, "Good-bye now, I must be going," and hurried out of the alley in the direction of the laundry.

Butch started laughing, and punched Dave in the shoulder.

"Didn't look like she was too anxious to come over and kiss you big boy. Could be that perfume you're wearing scared her off some."

"Oh shut up," Dave said. "This day isn't going at all like I had planned, and now I suppose I should go home and take a bath. Let's just get out of here, Butch."

Dave parted with Butch at the hitching post and rode home thinking about his name. He had been pissed upon by a mangy dog and began to wonder who the hell he really was. When he was little, they all called him Davy. When he had got a little older everyone used to call him by his Christened name, David, after the fool in the bible who threw a rock in a leather sling at some large man.

He didn't like Davy because it reminded him of being a kid, and he didn't like David because it reminded him of a fool, so he just liked being plain Dave, safe and sound, bread and butter, guns and bullets. Dave was safe—short and to the point.

He started thinking about September. September was a cooler month. September was full of fruit, and Suen Ling was just ripe for picking.

The following day, Dave rose earlier, saddled his horse, and rode east towards town. His plan was to ride up the Geysers Road and scout out abandoned squatters' or miners' shacks. He didn't really know how or even why he was going to do it, but he could envision himself alone with Suen in one of those shacks.

Before long he was passing by the Londi's property, and sure enough there was that foreigner and his haughty wife pulling weeds and tending a flowerbed along the drive that led to their house. Dave couldn't believe how fast those wops had transformed that run down property into some high-faluting-looking place. New fences, gardens, trees, even a little vineyard seemed to spring up almost overnight. What Dave despised the most was all those fancy colored flowers that were growing all over in neat little beds. His ma and pa had never planted flowers. What a waste of time. You couldn't eat them. What was their use? Only high society and foreigners seemed to like flowers, Dave reasoned. He wondered where this Londi fellow had gotten all this money to spend on fixing up his place. Probably by using his foreign ways to swindle good hard working Americans out of their earnings. He had heard that those two used to live in San Francisco, and everyone knew that town was rife with swindlers and con men.

The Londis looked up from their work upon hearing an approaching horse.

I wonder if them eye-ties are going to wave at me, Dave thought. For some reason he had suddenly hoped that they would wave at him. The man looked briefly at Dave and threw his hand up in a brief salutation. The dark-haired, pretty woman just stood with one hand on her hip and a bunch of flowers in the other, staring expressionless at Dave.

They should have recognized me with more respect, he reasoned, and urged his horse on faster. *One of these nights I'm going to ride right through those flowerbeds*, he told himself. But soon he had forgotten about the Londis, and arriving at the main road that ran through town, turned northeast toward Alexander Valley and the lowlands that led to Geysers Road. Before long Dave reached the Russian River where he paused for a while to water his horse and eat a couple of two-day-old biscuits. By noon he was climbing the dusty stagecoach road that led to The Geysers. It had been a year or so since Dave had been up the road with Butch Baylow hunting for deer. Dave had spotted quite a few empty shacks set back from the road, but at the time had thought little about them. Now, with a purpose in mind, he was eager to find one that would suit his needs. The building had to be unseen from the main road, and he wanted one that was still fairly clean and in good repair.

Not quite halfway to The Geysers, he stumbled upon what he was looking for. He had turned down an old overgrown trail, and tucked back amidst the oaks, manzanitas, and madrones, stood the perfect honeymoon cottage—an old squatter's or hunter's shack complete with a small front porch and a hitching rail. Dave dismounted, and tying his horse, walked up the rickety, crudely made steps. The door appeared tightly closed, maybe even locked, Dave thought, and reached for the doorknob, but then suddenly and rapidly drew his hand back. It was the doorknob that had startled him. It was a round polished knob, shiny and black. It looked so out of place on the run down abandoned building that Dave felt a chill run through him.

That damn doorknob looks just like someone polished it yesterday, he thought to himself. He suddenly felt very alone and somewhat uncomfortable. He backed off the porch and decided to circle the shack before again trying the door. A warm breeze was blowing, shaking all the drying leaves clinging to the trees. The only other noise he heard was the sound of his feet crunching the brittle grass laid down flat around the building. *This grass is all trampled,* Dave thought, *like someone's been walking around here.* He found himself circling the shack cautiously and half expecting to see someone suddenly emerge from behind the trees.

It's nerves is all, Dave told himself, but his mind was running away with itself. Something bad must have happened here, or maybe an Indian used to live here, he suddenly became convinced. The shack had two windows; one on each side, both boarded up from the inside, and no back door. A rusty stovepipe protruded through the roof that was covered over with wooden shingles, half of them blown off. Dave noticed some of them lying amongst the grass. Just to be safe, he returned to his horse and removed his revolver from the saddlebag, and again climbed the steps towards the door. He reached his hand out for the black knob, but couldn't bring himself to touch it. He just stood there, gun in hand, the other outstretched and shaking several inches from the knob. His heart was beating fast, and he couldn't take his eyes off the black doorknob that seemed to look shinier than ever. Suddenly his horse snorted, and that seemed to bring him back to his senses. He shook his head and took hold of the knob and turned it. The door wasn't locked, and Dave slowly pushed it open on creaking hinges and peered inside. At the same instant he heard a rattle and saw a huge coiled snake smack dab in the middle of the doorway, as if guarding the entrance. From a safe distance, Dave stood staring at the snake. It was easily the largest rattler he'd ever seen. Its color seemed to blend in with the floor, and its coiled body appeared in the dim light to be thicker than Dave's arm. The snake had its mouth open displaying two unbelievably long fangs.

Dave had been around rattlesnakes his whole life, and after the initial shock wore off, he carefully took aim and blew the snake's head off with one shot. Cautiously, he entered the shack, looking and listening for more snakes. Except for the dead snake, the place seemed empty. A rusty old wood stove was against the far end, and a few empty shelves lined one wall. It was dusty, full of spider webs and smelled like mice.

Doesn't look too promising, Dave thought, but then he noticed the bed. Leaned up against the wall, and partially hidden by the open door, was a rusty set of bedsprings. Dave kicked the dead rattler out the door and walked over to the springs and laid them flat on the floor. No springs were broken. With some padding this would make a comfortable bed, he reasoned. For an instant he saw a vision of himself and Suen lying on the bed—her delicate head resting on his arm, and he dressed in his white frilly shirt, creased black pants and fancy boots, his hair neatly combed back and shiny with fragrant pomade.

The vision didn't last long, and the smell of mice jolted Dave back to reality. What he saw now was a rundown, lonely shack with a bloodstained floor where the snake had lain, and yet, still, it just might do. Why, he could fix it up! Make it real cozy. After all, it was in a pretty little setting, surrounded by trees. Suen just might like this place. *Why, I could even find out who actually owned this place and maybe buy a hundred acres or so and run cattle! Dave and Suen Fowler—cattle ranchers up on Geysers Road. I'd have me an orchard and a big garden. Suen could sell fruits and vegetables to tourists on their way up to The Geysers.*

Making big plans had made Dave hungry. He cheerfully went outside, picked up the huge rattler, and went to his saddlebags for his knife. He expertly gutted and skinned the fat snake, and soon had a nice little fire of oak going. When the coals died down, he carefully laid meaty chunks of the snake directly on them. Dave had once seen a Mexican cook meat this style, but the Mexican had had a lemon, and used the cut lemon to brush away the ashes and flavor the meat at the same time. Dave turned the meat over with his knife, then walked over to a large fern and cut several fronds. When the meat was done he laid it out on one of the ferns and used the other one to brush off most of the ashes. *Doesn't work as good as lemon*, he thought, but except for a little grit, the fat snake tasted delicious.

As he ate, he became more resolved to deck the shack out as a honeymoon cottage. He'd gather up items in town, and make as many trips as necessary, until he turned the shack into a regular romantic getaway. In one of his desperado magazines he had read that term "Romantic Getaway," and that's just what he would create, and Suen would love it—and love him too, he was now convinced.

He kept on cooking and eating snake until he felt that his belly was going to burst. Walking over to a shiny red barked madrone he sat with his back against it and stared at the shack. *Why, there's nothing strange about this place*, he now thought. Some feller just happened to have a shiny black doorknob lying around. The trampled grass was probably just deer or some hunters snooping around. And it certainly wasn't odd to find a big old fat rattler hiding out inside. *Got so damn big eating mice around the shack, that's all.*

All the thinking, the riding, and the meat made Dave sleepy. He decided to take a little snooze before he made the ride back to town. The breeze had picked up a bit, and just before he dozed off he thought he heard what sounded like someone whistling. Suddenly Dave was dreaming. An old Indian woman with long gray hair was staring him straight in the eyes. Her eyes were shiny and mesmerizing like a snake. He broke away from her stare and realized that her body was that of a coiled rattlesnake. She had two short arms that resembled rat's claws. In one of the claws she clutched the black doorknob. In the other she held a knife. She moved rapidly and brought the knifepoint up to Dave's throat. With the other claw-like hand she reached out with the doorknob towards Dave's gaping mouth. The old woman loomed in front of him with a crazy grin on her face, and he could hear her tail rattle, preparing to strike. Then he was awake, sweating and breathing hard. Nausea flooded over him, and he leaned to the side and threw up. Weak and sick he stumbled to his horse and rode away from the shack as fast as he could manage. Shortly the nausea passed away and his head began to clear.

What a nightmare, Dave thought. *Must have eaten too much snake, and it didn't agree with me.* He couldn't believe how real the dream seemed. On the way back, he kept reliving it. He began to think that he had actually seen an old Indian woman around town who looked just like the one in the dream. *Didn't have a snake's body, though.* He began to feel stupid and silly. *I'm never going to eat rattlesnake again*, he vowed, and decided to dismiss the whole episode from his mind. *That's a nice little shack up in those hills, and I'm not going to let some silly dream scare me off*, he reasoned.

The next day, Dave began to gather up the necessary items he'd need to transform the shack into a romantic getaway. He went to the livery stable where his dad was shoeing horses and asked if he could borrow a horse to use for packing in goods to fix up a hunting cabin. He got the horse and rode back home with it in tow. He went to the barn and began packing saddlebags and tote sacks with all the various items he thought would dress that old shack up just fine. He couldn't do it all in one trip, but he'd get a good start on it, he figured.

When both horses were all loaded up, he headed back down Dry Creek Road a satisfied man on a mission. As he turned northeast towards Alexander Valley and the hills he ran into Butch Baylow coming in towards town.

"Hey, Dave, where you heading all geared up like that?" Butch said, riding up to him.

"Oh I found some old shack up Geysers Road. I figured I'd turn it into a hunting cabin. We're low on venison, and I've even seen bear tracks up there."

"Hey, sounds like fun," Butch said. "I'll come with you, huh?"

"Why sure, Butch. After I fix the place up, you and I will spend some time up there drinking and shooting deer."

"You bet, pardner, sounds like a plan. Well, I gotta go. They're having baseball practice in town. Guess there's going to be a game tomorrow. That show off Indian Walter's supposed to pitch for the other team, and I can't wait to get a hit off of him. Hey, what's that sticking out of your tote sack? Looks like some type of fancy cloth or curtain. You ain't going to hang curtains in a hunting shack are you?

"Hell no," Dave said. "It's just some old rag I'm going to use to wipe off the place is all. See you Butch," he said and rode off.

Dave got to the shack as fast as he could, and after opening the door cautiously and checking for snakes, he began to clean the place up and begin the transformation. When he was done he was amazed at how good the place looked. Sure, before the rains he'd have to fix the roof, and much more work was needed to be done, what with painting and all, but by golly the old shack was already looking pretty damn fancy, he thought.

It was early afternoon when he decided to close the door on the honeymoon cottage and return to town. On the way back, Dave thought about nothing but Suen, and how impressed she would be when he carried her through the door.

When he got home, he forced himself to clean up. He took a cake of soap and walked down to Dry Creek and scrubbed himself, being very careful not to get too much cold water on his member lest it shrink up. He was tempted to dress in his fancy gunslinger outfit, but decided against it. Instead he put on his best clean clothes, pomaded his hair, and rode off in the early evening towards town with the intent of running into Suen Ling. Riding by the Londi's place he spied the colorful flowers that Angelina had carefully planted and tended. Looking around and seeing no one, he came to the flowers, and reached down from his horse to pick a handful of colorful ones, but came up with the whole plant instead.

"Hey, what are you doing?" he heard a woman's voice yell out, and guessing it to be that haughty Italian, set heel to his horse and galloped fast towards town. He rode straight towards the Ling's laundry, and after tying off his horse, he began to separate the flowers from the plant, and arrange them into a bouquet. Watching the laundry from a distance, he didn't have too long to wait until Suen emerged carrying a large basket full of neatly folded clothes.

Dave walked towards her boldly and decisively, and coming up to her said, "Good evening, Miss Ling. Those clothes look heavy," and putting the bouquet of flowers on top of them he took the basket from Suen's hands saying, "I picked those flowers especially for you. I do hope you like them."

Suen was bewildered. She picked the bouquet off the clean clothes. The flowers had dirt clinging to their stems and leaves. The freshly washed and pressed white shirt on the top of the pile was now soiled and stained. She looked up and down the street. No one was in sight. Dave didn't seem dangerous at the moment, but she felt that this could change at any time. What in the world was he doing? He was all clean and dressed up. Some smelly grease was all over his thinning hair, and he was smiling like an idiot, revealing two yellow-stained buckteeth. Immediately the truth of the situation became apparent to her. The flowers and his manner of dress explained everything. Dave had come to court her, and she would have to watch her step. The last time she had seen him he smelled like dog urine, but even that smell was not much worse than the odor of that grease wafting off his hair.

"Thank you for carrying the clothes, David. The flowers are pretty. Where did you get them?" Suen asked, forcing herself to be civil.

"Just call me Dave," he said. "Oh, I bought them off some wops. Where were you heading with the clothes?"

"To the hotel," Suen answered.

"Why that's fine," Dave said. "I'll carry them there for you and we can talk along the way."

Dave thought everything was going fine. Suen was being polite to him. Maybe she even liked him a little.

He was feeling so giddy he became bold and blurted out, "If I was to rent a buckboard, er...carriage—would you go riding with me some Sunday to see a romantic getaway?"

Suen was dumbfounded. Why would that idiot think she would go off riding alone with him? And what in the world was a "romantic getaway"? Luckily they were coming close to the hotel. She wished she had a stick so she could hit Dave in the face and knock those yellow teeth out.

Thinking quickly, she answered him saying, "I'm sorry, my father doesn't permit me to ride alone with young men."

She reached out and quickly took the basket from Dave, placing the flowers on the soiled shirt.

Lying, she said, "I have work to do inside the hotel, David. Good-bye, and thank you for the help and the flowers," and she vanished off inside.

Dave felt like he had been walking on water. Suen smelled good. He could even smell her over his pomade hair oil. Why, of course her father wouldn't let her go riding alone. That didn't mean she didn't want to. Well, there was only one thing to do—kidnap her by moonlight and carry her off to the honeymoon cottage.

Chapter 14

Conchetta Lombardi had trouble remembering her name. The sun came up and went down. She drank water and emptied her bladder and bowels. She recognized the feeling of movement and the breeze on her face. Cold and warmth were easy to define from time to time. She felt unclean and cared little about it. The smell of manure was constantly in the air. It came mostly from the wagon she was tied down in, she thought. Time seemed to crawl by, just like the shiny black beetles that she saw crawling over her body as the wagon rolled and bumped down the road. She thought about little, noting mostly the arrival of the dark and the stars or the sun and the light, and the shiny black beetles crawling all over her. When she was a young girl in Genoa she would turn over a piece of wood that was to be carried to the house for the fire, and see many black beetles scurrying off the wood, dropping on the soft ground. Now she saw those same beetles crawling over her filthy dress and she was too weak to brush them off. She had been tied down on her back in a manner that left her arms free. One arm was sore and bandaged, but she just couldn't make them move to brush off beetles. Besides, her arms too were covered in beetles, so what did it all matter?

She thought of how her brother and sister would laugh at her for being too weak to shake off bugs. What bugs? She raised her head to look at her prone body and in one moment of clarity saw absolutely no bugs. She saw the sun filtering through trees, and the familiar wood of a wagon caked with manure and littered with the paper-thin skins of garlic. The wagon was moving somewhere, she reasoned, as she threw her head back on a scratchy pillow of burlap sacks. She closed her eyes to the light and saw nothing but a red ground covered with thousands of small, shiny black beetles.

Drifting in and out of an opiate haze, several days passed by. Conchetta could recall only drinking water and not partaking of any solid food. Of course, the drug was in the water she reasoned, but she was thirsty and no longer cared. She could remember Juan's pale, almost translucent face looming over her from time to time.

"My, my, but aren't you getting ripe, Miss Lombardi," he said once, holding his nose. "Guess it's going to be my duty to get you cleaned up once again shortly. Won't be long now until we reach San Jose."

Juan was dressed in his normal clothing of a day laborer. Now that it was daylight he had tied Conchetta's arms to her sides and had thrown a blanket over her colorful Gypsy outfit.

"You know the routine by now, my little dope lover. I doubt if you care to do too much talking if we should meet someone, but if you do try any such nonsense I shall kill you and anyone you utter a word to. You are my sick wife who I am rushing to the doctor, then on to relatives in San Jose. If all goes well, by early this evening you will be in a comfortable hotel, and I shall personally clean you up and put you away wet, as they say. Now, doesn't that sound a lot more pleasant than lying in the back of a stinking wagon, my queen?"

In a way, Conchetta registered what he was saying, but only looked at him and blinked her eyes.

"What? Cat got your tongue? Oh, I can see you're pondering deep thoughts. Well, I'll leave you to your dreams," he said, turning his attention back to the road ahead and flicking the reins.

It was morning, and the sun was beginning to warm the California earth.

Well, there are all things that can end well, thought Juan. Even though the Conchetta bitch was thoroughly drugged, there was something about the look that emanated somewhere from the depth of her eyes that struck a sense of uneasiness in Juan. *When we get to a hotel, I should take one last pleasure with her and then rid myself once and for all,* he reasoned. *That silly woman has begun to remind me of the poem by that Coleridge hombre. The one with the bad luck albatross draped around the neck. Why am I having trouble just dropping this woman like a dead weight? I can't believe that slip up I made in front of an audience, calling her Conchetta. A man could get his neck stretched for such carelessness. The devil has always brought me luck, but he has also furnished me with this dark-eyed Italian. Maybe it's all a sign telling me I should move further down life's endless road with her at my side.* No, that's senseless, he thought. *The woman's going to get me killed. That's all, and the road will end.*

His musings were interrupted by the appearance of a sign along the road in front of what seemed a prosperous dairy that read, "SAN JOSE 2 MILES."

For the last hour or so, Juan had been traveling with grazing land or orchards alongside the road. He had only met several people that day, either on horse or wagon, and none had paid any attention to him other than the slight nod of a head. Now, coming towards him was a cloud of dust that shortly turned into two riders dressed in the garb of ranch hands with broad-brimmed hats and rifles in scabbards strapped to their saddles.

Juan didn't like the looks of this. Just when he was thinking about luck, a dead albatross, and his destiny, men with guns were approaching. He felt beneath the wagon's seat where his revolver lay under a folded blanket, loaded and within easy reach. Quickly, he looked at Conchetta, who lay still, her eyes closed as if sleeping. At the same time, he felt for the handle of his knife, resting in the inner pocket of his worker's jacket.

The riders had slowed down as they approached the wagon; Juan could see that, unlike others he had passed that day, these men were looking straight at him, and pulling up as if preparing to speak. The men looked about Juan's age, one maybe slightly older, both had slight grins on their faces.

"Hey there, Mex, we could smell you coming for quite some time. What you got back there, a pile of raw manure?" the older man said, riding a little closer and peering into the back of the wagon.

What he saw stopped him in his tracks. He was gazing into the face of the most beautiful woman he had ever seen, lying flat on her back in the wagon, a mass of matted black hair spread over a filthy burlap pillow. Her eyes were wide open and held his with a fierce look that he could not fathom. The back of the wagon reeked of manure and another smell—the smell that could only be identified with human excrement.

"Hey, what's going on here? Take a look at this, Bob," the man said, motioning his partner over.

The younger man rode up and looking in the wagon saw the wide-eyed woman lying flat on her back, motionless and covered with a dirty blanket.

"Say amigo, what's going on here? Who's the lady back there? She don't look too well," the older rider said.

In the meantime, the younger one, Bob, had been staring closely at Conchetta and had noticed two ropes going from the sideboards of the wagon over the top of the woman, the blanket hid them, but knots on either side were clearly visible. One rope seemed to go over her chest, while the other crossed over her legs.

Bob, wanting to confirm his suspicions, reached down and pulled back the blanket and saw what he suspected. The woman was dressed in a gaudy colored outfit and tightly bound to the bottom of the wagon.

"Larry, look," he said. "This woman's tied down, and boy does she smell."

Larry, who had been eyeing Juan suspiciously, turned in his saddle to look back in the wagon and at that moment Juan reached rapidly under the seat, and grabbing the loaded revolver, put a bullet at that short distance straight into the chest of the older rider, Larry. He immediately took aim at Bob, but Larry's body falling sideways off his horse caused him to hesitate for an instant, and in a flash Bob had launched himself off his horse straight at Juan. Both men tumbled off the wagon and hit the dirt hard, Juan hitting the ground first, Bob's hand on the revolver, and his knee jamming at the impact hard into Juan's groin. Bob recovered fast and ripped the gun from Juan's hand. He kicked him viciously in the ribs with the toe of his work boot. Juan doubled up groaning, and Bob, holding the gun on him, lurched over to his partner who lay twitching on the ground, a massive pool of blood soaking his shirt and the earth around him. Taking his attention from Juan, he stared down into Larry's fluttering eyes. That was the only break Juan needed. In an instant he had reached inside his coat, and pushing aside his nausea and mustering up all his remaining strength, grabbed for the haft of his knife and threw it straight at the kneeling Bob, where it imbedded itself deep into his neck. Bob's hands flew to his throat, a look of terrified surprise in his eyes. The last thing he saw was Juan coming towards him, jerking the knife from his throat, and driving it viciously into his chest.

After looking about him and discerning no one in sight, Juan withdrew his knife from the still body, and though in much pain, managed to drag it off the road and over the other side of a slight berm. He did the same with the other body and kicked and scooped dirt over the dark stains of blood that were soaking into the dusty road.

Through his pain he began cursing his luck. He had no time or strength to conceal the bodies better. Shortly, lying so close to the road, they would be found. Again he looked around and saw not a soul. With no witnesses, how could anyone link the death of those two men to him, he reasoned. Maybe he was lucky after all. Only moments had passed. He was sore and injured, but felt confident he would heal. And, oh what a look of surprise on the younger one's face when the knife entered his neck! What a perfect throw it had been, and from a kneeling, off balance position! The drama and excitement of the incident was worth the pain he was suffering, he decided.

Limping to the wagon he looked in back at Conchetta. Her eyes were closed. Surely the sound of the gun discharging must have roused her. From her position she couldn't have seen much, if anything, he thought. What a shame she had missed his performance. A thin humble campesino dispatching two strapping vaqueros with such speed and efficiency surely would be a marvel, he reasoned. But what was she doing now with her eyes closed so tight and lying so still? Playing possum perhaps?

Dismissing her from his mind, he painfully climbed back into the wagon and moved on down the road towards San Jose. It hurt every time he breathed in. He wondered if he had broken ribs. The pain in his groin had not subsided either. He put the idea of seeing a doctor from his mind. Too many questions and he was in no mood for talking. He would be his own doctor, he decided. All he needed was to find a hotel to rest up in, which should be no problem in a growing prosperous town like San Jose. He stopped the wagon suddenly and untied the ropes that were holding down Conchetta. He slapped her sharply in the face and her eyes snapped open. Pulling the still bloody knife from his coat he held it under her throat.

"Oh, my queen, what a performance you missed. Your loving husband, king of the Gypsies, single handedly fought off the attack of two rowdies who had the audacity to look upon your lovely face. I taught them a lesson they'll never forget, or is it ever remember? For I left their bodies mutilated and lifeless off the road behind us."

Juan thought he detected a look of surprise, or possibly fear in Conchetta's eyes, but he could not be sure and quickly continued.

"Look, Lombardi. You had better understand what I'm saying, if you want to cling to your precious life for another day. We're coming into a town and we're going to find a hotel to put us up, but first I've got to get you cleaned up and out of those stinking clothes. We've been paralleling a creek for some time and at the first point of easy access you're going to get a little bath. Understand?"

Conchetta nodded her head affirmatively, though her eyes now had a glazed over look, Juan thought. She's still so doped up she'd probably nod at anything. *Oh well, I guess she's way too weak to try any tricks*, he reasoned, climbing painfully back into the wagon.

Two hundred yards ahead he found a pull-off that led straight to the little creek. The water was low this time of year, but he could see a fairly deep pool a short distance away. Getting down from the wagon, he grabbed a spare blanket and Conchetta's clean clothes from under the seat. He went to the back of the wagon, removed the backboard and, gritting through the pain, reached for Conchetta's arm and roughly pulled her up to a sitting position. He saw she had a hard time keeping her head straight. It seemed to want to wobble and tilt listlessly towards her shoulder.

He set the clothes and blanket down and helped Conchetta to stand upright. It was the first time she had tried to stand on her own two feet for quite some time, and her legs started to crumple, but she caught herself somehow and took a step or two towards the water.

"That's it, my lovely, just walk on down to that pool and throw yourself in and wash that stink off of you, I'll be right behind you."

Conchetta stumbled off slowly, then more rapidly and did exactly what Juan said. She came to the deep little pool and stumbled into the cold clean water. Juan followed behind carrying the blanket and her clothes. The coldness of the water awoke a dim light of clarity that had remained burning somewhere in the recesses of her mind. They were going to a town, a hotel. Some riders had approached the wagon and Juan somehow had managed to kill both of them. She remembered seeing a man's surprised face staring down at her, and part of her wanting to shout out to him, but feeling incapable of making her mouth move. She had heard a gunshot, and what sounded like a fight, and then nothing. Only Juan's face twisted into a painful sneer, burning his eyes into hers and holding a knife to her throat.

She sat in the water and automatically started scrubbing herself. She had no soap but grabbed handfuls of soft sand at the bottom of the pool and began to rub it all over her body. She looked at her Gypsy outfit and hated it. She pulled the clothing off and watched as it drifted slowly away until snagging a little way off on a branch jutting out of the water.

Behind her she heard a laugh and Juan saying, "What's wrong, my queen? Tired of your royal regalia?"

Conchetta was staring at the snagged clothing. The bright red and blue cloth looked so silly fluttering up and down in the water, she thought.

Suddenly she began to get very chilled and began shivering uncontrollably, a wave of nausea assailed her, and she vomited up a little fluid into the creek. Juan came to the edge of the water and stepping in a little ways reached an arm out for Conchetta, who took it and managed to climb out of the pool. Juan, looking over her nakedness, realized how thin she had become. No longer was she the healthy vibrant young woman he had first seen at the mission. She was now pale and gaunt, her eyes were sunken, and there were dark, almost yellowish circles under them.

Guess I should have fed her more and not given her so much dope, he thought. And at the same instant, he questioned himself as to why a thought of care for her should even enter his head. He dropped the blanket over her, and found himself rubbing her shoulders and back, to awaken some circulation in her. She just stood there shaking with her head down staring at the ground.

"Come on now, we've got to move fast. Get into your clothes and pretty soon we'll be in a nice warm hotel, and I'll get you some good food."

Bael, the devil, whispered in his ear, "Why are you being nice to her, fool? Slit her throat here and now and be done with it. You know what you have to do. Why do you hesitate?"

Juan started to reach for the knife in his coat, then for some undefinable reason, stayed his hand, and after Conchetta was dressed, helped her to walk back to the wagon. She immediately crawled into the back and lay shivering in a fetal position, a trickle of drool seeping out the corner of her mouth. Juan looked at her and shook his head.

"Listen carefully, Conchetta. When we get to town you don't say a word. You've been sick, but are recuperating. If things go smooth, shortly you'll be resting in a comfortable bed, and after you eat maybe I'll give you some more of that drug you've become accustomed to. Or maybe I won't. Perhaps we'll have to talk about it, no?"

For the first time in days Conchetta uttered two words, "Yes. Food."

"Good," Juan said. "Seems you're coming around some. Just remember, don't try anything. I can kill you so quick and move so fast that I could even escape. And if I didn't, well the ride has been worth it."

Trying to get back in the wagon, he lost his footing and doubled up in pain. His groin hurt so much it took his breath away. *No wonder the sight of her naked didn't arouse me,* he thought to himself. *I imagine I'm going to be out of action for some time. Unfortunate for the Italian slut. I imagine in her current state, she'd even enjoy it. Well, plenty of time for that later. If I let there be a later for her,* he pondered, feeling the supreme commander, dealer of life and death.

Once back in the wagon and out on the main road, it wasn't long before the first building marking the entry into San Jose appeared. Traffic on the road had increased, most of it seemed to be farmers heading out of town, probably back to their homes. One of the wagons he met going the opposite direction had a large dog trailing behind. *I'll lay odds that dog finds those bodies,* Juan thought. *Oh well, had nothing to do with me,* he laughed.

He was sure a town of this size had to have a Mexican section, and sure enough, presently he met a campesino leading a donkey loaded with sacks coming his way.

"Hey, hombre," he said, speaking in Spanish. "Where can I find lodging for myself and my wife, perhaps a good hotel that serves good Mexican food, eh? I'm new to this town."

The man gave Juan directions and soon he pulled up to a two-story wood building called "Hotel Valencia." Occasionally, going through town, he had looked back at Conchetta. She hadn't moved much, just curled up lying on her side. She didn't seem to be shaking as much, he noticed.

Seeing a vacancy sign above the door, he dismounted the wagon trying his best to show no signs of pain, and tied off the horses. Helping Conchetta out of the wagon and on her feet, and putting his arm around her waist, he helped the sick woman enter the hotel. The old man behind the counter looked at them wide-eyed, but said nothing until Juan spoke. Using less than pure Castellian Spanish he explained that they were new in town and that his wife had been sick, but was recuperating—could they possibly get lodging for two or three nights until she was more rested, and ready to push on north to relatives? The clerk looked sympathetic and assured Juan they had a nice clean room at two dollars a night. Juan gave the man five dollars for two nights, requesting that they be as undisturbed as possible, his wife badly in need of rest and quiet.

Before helping Conchetta up the stairs to the room, he inquired as to the location of the nearest livery stable, then proceeded to slowly mount the stairs. With Conchetta barely able to walk, he leaned on the handrail as much as possible, the pain in his ribs and groin shooting into him. Locating the room and unlocking the door, they entered, and Conchetta immediately stumbled to one of the two single beds and threw herself down on it, back again into a fetal position. Finding himself apologizing to her, he took some coils of short rope from his pocket and tied her hands and feet to the bed and gagged her mouth. Telling her he would be back in no time, he locked the door behind him and left to go sell the wagon and the horses.

Once at the livery stable he pretended to be interested in negotiating with the proprietor over price, but soon settled on what he knew was a poor deal for him. The smug look on the proprietor's face told him little would be thought of the transaction.

On the way back he stopped at a Mexican bakery and purchased some flour tortillas and a large wedge of hard goat's cheese. Hurrying back to the hotel, he untied Conchetta, who had awakened from a deep sleep, and making her sit up, sliced her some cheese and wrapped it up in one of the tortillas.

"Eat, Lombardi. You've got to get your strength back. In a few days we're going to go on a little train ride, so you've got to get in good shape. Perhaps after your snack, you would like a little morphine for dessert, or have you had enough of that for a while? You're not that far hooked on that stuff that we can't wean you off it in a couple of days, but if that's to be the case, you've got to cooperate and be the perfect little wife. Got it?"

Conchetta was forcing herself to eat every bite of the food, though her stomach was cramping and her hands were shaking.

"No morphine," she said weakly between bites.

"OK," Juan said. "If that's your decision, but it's going to be rough. I can't think clearly myself right now. I've got to get some sleep so I'm going to have to tie and gag you. You may start convulsing and seeing things for all I know. At least you won't hurt yourself tied down. No?"

Conchetta felt agitated and confused, but lay cooperatively on her side and soon was again bound and gagged. Juan collapsed on the other bed and immediately fell asleep. Six hours later he awoke. It was dark out. He found a lantern and some candles and lit them. He was in terrible pain, and reaching for his traveling bag took out the vile of morphine and allowed himself a few drops. He went over to look at Conchetta and found her with eyes closed tight, sweating profusely and twitching sporadically. *Guess I'd better not take too much of this stuff,* he thought, sure wouldn't want to end up like that.

He went downstairs and nodding to a different clerk walked out into the street. He saw a little cantina a ways off with a "*comida*" sign in the window. He asked the woman who came to wait on him how the *frijoles* were. She assured him they were delicious, freshly made with lots of peppers. He asked for two large bowls full, explaining he was staying at the hotel, and would pay extra if she would let him take the food with him and return the bowls later. She saw no problem with this, and he ordered a small beer before she went off to prepare the food.

She shortly emerged from the kitchen with two steaming bowls of fragrant beans on a wide, thin board that served as a tray. Half a dozen corn tortillas and two jalapeno peppers were also on the tray wrapped in cloth. Juan thanked her profusely and carefully carried the food out the door and back to the hotel. The morphine had helped him some, but it was all he could do to limp up the stairs without clutching the handrail, but somehow he made it, and unlocking the door he entered, placing the tray on a little table that stood against one wall. Once her hands were freed, Conchetta reached for the pitcher of water by the bed and drank frantically from it, not bothering to pour it into a glass.

"My, my but aren't we the thirsty one," Juan cackled while sitting on his bed eating beans and tortillas. "Come and get your bowl of beans, queen. Eat them while they're hot, and I think you'll find these tortillas surprisingly light and fresh. I doubt if you can stomach this jalapeno in your condition, so I'll eat it for you," he said, biting into the large green pepper.

Conchetta walked hesitatingly to the little table, and pulling up one of the two wooden chairs, sat and began methodically to spoon the pungent beans into her mouth.

Her stomach was still queasy, but she thought the food tasted delicious. After asking Juan for a thick slice of the cheese, and after finishing off every morsel, she went back to the bed and sat back against the headboard with her knees drawn up and her arms clasped around them. She sat there staring at Juan, trying not to shake, while searching for clarity in her head. Juan had finished his food, and was ripping in half lengthwise one of his shirts, tying the ends together. He removed the shirt he was wearing and began to wrap the cloth tightly around his ribs.

There was one window in the room. It was closed, but for an instant Conchetta thought of the possibility of making a dash for it and throwing herself through it, and end this torture once and for all on the street below. *You're a weakling*, she told herself. *Instead, you should be trying to kill that son of a bitch who's binding his ribs.* As long as she was alive she knew there could be hope. Her mind would get clearer as the drug wore off. She had eaten her first good food in days, and now she must get healing sleep, she told herself.

She stretched out on the bed and said to Juan, "Go ahead and tie me now. I'm sleepy, and I know you won't feel free to rest until I'm bound, so go ahead and get it over with."

Juan had finished tying off the bandage and began chuckling upon hearing Conchetta.

"Well, well, my pretty wife. I can see you're seeing reality much clearer. Good for you. Why I shall oblige you immediately, and if that stupid gringo had not wounded my maleness, perhaps I would have tied you to that bed in a different manner, and we could have had a little fun, huh?"

Conchetta didn't say a word. Juan came over smiling and tied her, and brought out the handkerchief he used as a gag.

"It makes it hard to breathe. I promise I won't yell out."

Juan paused. "I'm getting too soft with you Lombardi, but OK. Just remember, I'm a light sleeper, and I'll hear any sound that comes from your mouth. And if one does, other than a snore, I suppose I'll create another mouth for you across your throat—a nice blood-red opening. How's that sound?"

Conchetta nodded and closed her eyes. Such nice images that bastard liked to create, she thought. *If I could only get my hands on his knife, I would know where to put it.*

In that thought, Conchetta knew that she wasn't defeated yet—that she still had the strength and resolve to get out of this. In the morning things would be clearer. Somehow she would search for a way.

Chapter 15

Primo and Pietro Nuti were sipping zinfandel in the dark-paneled, comfortable study, the distant sound of Maria practicing piano upstairs filling their ears.

"Maria gets better every day," Pietro said.

Primo didn't seem to hear. He just sat there in his leather chair staring into his glass.

"Huh," he said, raising his head.

"Hey, nephew, where were you?" Pietro queried. "That's only your third glass. What are you thinking about?"

"Dom and Angelina, and mostly Angelina's sister, Conchetta, the one that's missing. It was wonderful to see Dom so happy at their wedding, Angelina too, but there's that veil of sadness about her—that surely won't be removed until she knows more about her sister's whereabouts and safety. Those two deserve an untroubled, happy life, free from such worries. Imagine two such as that meeting and falling in love, thousands of miles from their native land. There's got to be some way I can find out more about Conchetta," Primo said.

Pietro sat reflective for a while. He too felt bad for Dom and Angie, and this whole story of Conchetta running off with a Gypsy smelled fishy to him.

"Say," Pietro said. "Why don't you send young Augustino down to Gilroy to snoop around and ask some more questions? You said he's been real good at coming up with information on some of your tougher cases. You said he's got intelligence and perseverance, two necessary qualities that would help him to be a good lawyer one day himself, if he really wanted to be."

"That's true," Primo said. "If I could just convince him to slow down chasing after women and going off hunting and fishing at the drop of a hat, he'd do fine in law school. We could even help him out a little financially, if he'd only show more interest."

"Why, I'll bet he'd want to get on the road immediately once you show him that picture they gave you of Conchetta," Pietro said, going over to a book case where a small picture of Conchetta sat propped in a corner against a book. "I wondered why you kept this picture out. She's certainly, what do they say, a looker? But a little too young for you I would imagine. You've become too proper and respectable to chase after young women. A socialite of fine standing is your type now, eh?"

"Oh, be serious," Primo said. "Maria put the picture there. She says she wants to look just like that when she grows up. She's been coming in at least once a day to look at it. But say, I think you've got a good idea there. Frank Augustino probably would be the perfect fellow to send out on such an assignment."

"I'm telling you," Pietro said. "Once he sees the picture, he's going to want to do this for free."

"Nonsense," said Primo. "I'm going to give him expenses and a small wage. And when next you see Dom and Angelina, don't say a word about this, capisce?"

"Of course," Pietro said. "Philanthropists such as you are always doing good deeds unrewarded," and patted Primo on the shoulder.

Primo playfully batted his hand away saying, "Go pour us some more wine. I'll have Frank come to my office tomorrow, and I'll explain everything to him."

"Don't forget to bring the picture," Pietro said. "That face is similar to the one that launched a thousand ships. You just watch Augustino tear out of your office for Gilroy."

The following day the dark blonde, blue-eyed Frank Augustino knocked on the door of Primo Nuti's office. Frank got the blonde hair from his mother, who was of all things, Finnish. Frank's father had met his mother, Annikki Niemi, while in the Finnish city of Turku. He was a minor performer and set builder touring with an Italian opera company playing there. After the show he and a friend, still in costume, were smoking a cigar outside the opera house and marveling at the cold clean air, when two lovely blondes passed by after exiting the building. The taller one, Frank's mom, had looked at his dad, Arturo, and giggled at his costume. As in many of these cases, that was all it took, and the following day when the ship pulled away from Turku, Arturo stayed behind after escorting Annikki home the previous evening. Love knows no ethnic boundaries, and before long, though they could communicate at first with one another only in a smattering of English each had picked up, they were married. With the help of Annikki's reluctant father, after all she had not married a Finn, Arturo got a job in the shipyards of Turku, and less than a year later little Franchesco was born.

When Franchesco, or Frank, was ten, his parents left Finland for America, and after a perilous rounding of the horn landed in San Francisco, where Frank's father had been promised a job building sets for the lively opera house. He had kept in touch with his cigar-smoking friend he had last seen in Turku, who was now working there, and felt sure he could get him a job. Arturo and Annikki took to San Francisco immediately, as did their handsome son.

The only regret they both had was that their son did not act like a Finn or an Italian. The way he behaved and insisted upon being called Frank left them little doubt that their son was an American. His flaw was that he was too footloose. At twenty-five he already had dabbled at many jobs from carpenter to fisherman, utility city worker to store clerk. He hadn't stayed at one job very long, either having gotten fired for failing to show up or quitting to ride off into the Sierra foothills for extended camping, hunting, and fishing. He no longer lived at home, but rented a room near the racetrack where he stabled his horse, Tuli, Finnish for fire. The horse had a reddish coat and was extremely fast with exceptional endurance.

In school Frank had been an excellent student, especially enjoying reading. He spoke both a little Finnish and a little Italian. His good looks and athletic ability had made him a pretty popular fellow, and his teachers thought he had the potential to go far if he chose. The problem was, he couldn't choose. He got bored easily. All who knew and cared for him felt that if he didn't buckle down and apply himself to one goal, he would turn into one of the many young rakes in the city, squandering their time in pool halls and saloons, drifting from job to job. His parents hadn't given up on him, though. His mother insisted that if only he'd find a good woman and marry, everything would change for the better.

Frank's father had introduced him to Primo Nuti. He used to tell him, "Now look at Primo. There's a successful man who knows how to use his head. You should study law like he did. The guy makes money hand over fist. I showed you that mansion where he lives. You could be just like him some day if you'd apply yourself for Christ's sake." Frank had to agree. Primo certainly was successful and extremely popular in the Italian community. More and more he had been considering law school.

Now, getting ready to enter Primo's office, Frank was excited. Primo almost had him convinced to try law school. He had dropped out of college a year short of graduation, but Primo felt that if Frank were truly dedicated and applied himself, it would be possible to finish his college courses and attend law school at the same time. Primo had given Frank a taste of the legal world, hiring him several times to do research work for him, that included talking to people or witnesses that may have a bearing on a case. Frank had enjoyed the work, and liked the idea that he might be aiding in helping someone. Primo had a reputation as a lawyer who didn't mind representing the "little guy," and this impressed Frank heavily.

Usually Primo's secretary answered, but this time Primo opened the door himself.

"Hey, Frank. *Como asti?* Good to see you. How's the parents?" Primo said, shaking Frank's hand firmly and motioning to a seat opposite his desk.

Upon exchanging pleasantries Primo quickly got down to the matter at hand.

"Take a look at this picture, Frank."

Frank took one look at the photograph and immediately felt struck by the thunderbolt. It had been taken at a studio in Monterey. Mario and his wife had insisted that they all pose for photographs, now that a new studio had opened. Conchetta was sitting in a chair near a large potted palm. She was wearing a dress with a frilly front. Her hair curled and mostly piled up with some of it dangling loosely and long on the sides. Her eyes were staring straight into the camera, and a slight Mona Lisa smile adorned her full lips.

To Primo, Frank had seemed to turn a little pale and was breathing fast. *Oh no, it's the thunderbolt,* he thought to himself. He wondered how long Frank would just sit there holding the picture and staring at it.

"Have you ever seen that woman around the city, Frank?" Primo asked.

Primo's voice appeared to startle Frank, who struggled for composure.

"Definitely not, Primo. I can assure you I would have remembered that woman if I had seen her around town."

"Well, she used to live around here before moving to Monterey a while back. Her name is Conchetta Lombardi. She's the sister of Angelina Lombardi, who married a good friend of mine, Dom Londi. And she's missing. No one seems to know exactly what has become of her. She hasn't made contact with her family, and all anyone has heard about her are sketchy tales that don't seem to make a lot of sense. Would you be interested in helping her family and me find out as much as possible about what's become of her?"

Frank was ready to burst out the door and blindly go looking for the young woman in the photo. Primo could see this, and smiled to himself, thinking how right his uncle had been, talking about Frank's reaction to Conchetta's picture.

It didn't take long for Primo to fill Frank in on all the facts, and armed with all the information that was pertinent to the mystery surrounding Conchetta, Frank left for home to pack his gear. He was far too impatient to inquire about rail or stage transportation to Gilroy, and after leaving off a note to be delivered to his parents as to what he was up to, he headed straight for the racetrack. As usual, he thought, Tuli was glad to see him, and he immediately saddled and packed the horse for travel.

Several days later, after some hard riding, he arrived at Doctor Taylor's office in Gilroy. He waited in a corner chair while the doctor bandaged up a boy's arm, and soon was explaining the purpose of his visit. The doctor agreed that the young woman in the photo was the same one whose cut he had bandaged, but he had already been through this all before with the woman's sister and others. He had told them all he knew. She was a morphine addict who traveled around with a Gypsy and put on an act that had included a trained bear.

"Doctor, please think back," Frank said. "Did this woman say anything to you at all?"

"Well, yes. I didn't think much of it at the time, her being under the influence and practically delirious—but I must admit, I thought about it some later. She said she had been drugged, and that he was a killer, he was going to kill her. I suppose she was referring to her husband, but I've seen drug cases babble on about anything, most of it purely fabrication. Her husband seemed the nicest, most concerned young fellow—a far cry from any killers I've seen or heard of. I was a little surprised when the two of them suddenly vanished during the night. Left me a good payment, though."

Frank asked several more questions, had the doctor describe Juan to him as best he could, thanked him, and left. He was convinced that Conchetta wasn't with this Gypsy willingly. He found the whole situation to be pretty simple. The fellow had abducted her, and was probably keeping her under his will through the use of drugs and the threat of violence. The woman in the picture, who had driven straight into his soul, couldn't possibly have run off and married a man such as the doctor had described. Nor would she suddenly turn into a sideshow performer and drug addict. He believed that when she had told the doctor that "he's a killer, he's going to kill me," and that "he's drugged me," she was being deadly serious.

Frank felt that he had found further evidence that Conchetta had been kept against her will, when he paid a visit to the farmer who had bought the Gypsy's traveling wagon. The farmer found it curious that once again someone was interested in looking over the wagon, but didn't hesitate to escort Frank to the barn and even provided a lantern for him. The wagon was empty now and in the process of being turned into a produce wagon, extra shelves and storage bins were in various stages of completion and sawdust littered the sturdy oak floor. Frank peered in with the lantern and noticed a door at the far end.

"What's behind that door?" he inquired.

"A small compartment, maybe a sleeping space," the farmer answered.

"Mind if I look inside?" Frank said.

"Go ahead, nothing in there though."

Frank climbed inside and opened the door.

The first thing that caught his eye was a solid brass ring bolted to the center of the floor. Leaning down and taking a closer look, he noticed that in places the brass was shiny, as if something hard had been rubbing in contact with it. Looking carefully all over the floor and walls, he found several strands of long black hair caught on a small splinter of wood off to a corner. He next noticed a tiny little door near the top of one of the outside walls. The door opened from the outside, as if placed there for someone out to be able to look in. He instantly formed a mental image of Conchetta chained to that ring in the floor, and the Gypsy looking in on her from time to time. For some reason he reached for the strands of hair, coiled them around his finger, and placed them in his shirt pocket.

Once back on his horse, he rode to the house of the garlic farmer whose wagon had been stolen the same day the Gypsy and Conchetta had vanished. The man told him that he had discovered the wagon missing the morning after he had left it in the field, once done unloading a pile of manure. He had noticed that the tracks the wagon left were headed north, on the road that led to San Jose.

Frank headed north out of town and came to a saloon, the last commercial building on the outskirts. Dismounting and going inside, he ordered a beer. Five or six people were scattered about either at the bar drinking, or sitting at tables playing cards. Frank explained to the bartender that he was working for a lawyer out of San Francisco and was in town doing some research work. On a whim, he showed the man the picture of Conchetta, and asked if he had ever seen her.

"Why sure," he said. "That's the queen of the Gypsies, Conchetta. Came through town a while back and put on a show featuring knife throwing and a trained bear. She and the Gypsy fellow, her husband I heard, suddenly left their fancy wagon here and vanished. One of the strangest things that's ever happened in this town. A manure wagon vanished about the same time they did. Most folks around think they stole it. They don't call Gypsies 'thieving' for nothing, if you get my drift."

One of the drinkers at the bar had been listening and abruptly chimed in.

"Yeah, and come to think of it, I think I saw that Gypsy fellow in that wagon heading out of town late the night of the show. This bar was getting ready to close, and when I came out a wagon passed me headed up the road towards San Jose. It was pretty dark, and he was dressed in farm hand's clothes, but after we all found out about the abandoned show wagon, and the stolen manure wagon, I put two and two together and figured out it was probably the Gypsy I saw heading out of town. I was at the show and saw him throwing his fancy knives. He had one of the thinnest, palest faces I've ever seen. The fellow heading out of town that night had a whitish-yellow face. A white Mexican, that's what we call 'em around here. Didn't see a woman with him though. Say, Mister, I bet I helped you out some, huh? How's about buying me a beer, OK?"

"Sure friend," Frank said. "Maybe you did help me out," and after paying for an extra beer, he left the saloon.

He couldn't help but chuckle to himself thinking about "thieving Gypsies" and "white Mexicans." *I wonder what they'd call a Finn-Italian. A flat-head dago? That sounds about right*, he reasoned. Smiling to himself, he mounted Tuli and headed north. He kept an eye out for game along the way, and before long shot a jackrabbit for his night's dinner. At dark he camped by the same little stream that

Juan and Conchetta had stopped at weeks earlier, and prepared the stringy rabbit for cooking, keeping only the hindquarters for roasting over the fire. The rabbit, some hard tack, and a handful of raisins he grabbed out of a small sack provided a good enough meal. Using his saddle for a pillow, soon he was asleep under a cloudless sky.

In the morning he pushed on towards San Jose. Along the way he kept thinking about what he would do when he got there. He could check in with the town authorities and show them Conchetta's picture and describe the Gypsy. He could go to the livery stable where one could sell a wagon and a couple of horses. Visiting saloons and showing the picture was a possibility. Going to lodging establishments was probably where he thought he should begin. If indeed it was the Gypsy driving that wagon out of town that night, and Conchetta was tied down or possibly drugged or knocked unconscious in the back, rest and lodging would surely be a priority on the wagon driver's mind.

He knew he was proceeding on pure conjecture and intuition, but every time he got Conchetta's picture out and looked at it, or felt in his pocket for the strands of hair—something seemed to whisper to him that he was doing what made the most sense. All he could do was go with his hunches, and hope luck was on his side.

He paused at a sign in front of a dairy that read, "SAN JOSE 2 MILES." He noticed a sharp breeze had picked up, and he felt a slight chill at the back of his neck. Unconsciously, he took Conchetta's picture out for the umpteenth time and was glancing at it as he went along, when Tuli let out a nicker and made an abrupt move to the left towards a little pull off that led to the creek.

"OK, I get the idea, you're thirsty," Frank thought.

Reaching the creek, he dismounted while the horse proceeded to drink. Something fluttering in the water suddenly caught Frank's eye. He walked on over and saw it was a pile of red and blue cloth, snagged on a partially submerged stick. Red and blue! An alarm immediately went off in his head. Conchetta was described as wearing a red and blue outfit when she was putting on the show in Gilroy! He waded into the water and grabbed for the cloth. One piece was a dress, the other was a blouse. He rung them out as best he could and walked back to his horse.

"Tuli, were you trying to tell me you were thirsty, or are you trying to help me find this woman too?" he said, stuffing the clothing in his saddlebag.

Strange coincidences, he kept thinking once back on the road, *even eerie. I feel a chill, take out the picture, and my horse heads straight for a spot where I find what seemingly was her outfit. Everyday gals certainly don't wear such gaudy colored clothes*, he reasoned. *If fate's helping me out, I hope it doesn't desert me now. The odds on my finding her are getting slimmer each day. Sure I've got hunches, and what you might even call evidence, but I'm coming to a pretty big town with side roads that go off in many directions. Why, I suppose it's possible they could be in Sacramento or beyond by now—could even have taken a train back east.*

Shrugging his doubts off as best he could, and trying to focus on the day ahead, Frank entered San Jose about midafternoon. *Concentrate now*, he thought to himself. *Go on the hunch that you've been following the cold trail of the Gypsy in the stolen wagon, with Conchetta lying down or tied in the back. He's been telling people she's his wife. Maybe she's been sick. They need lodging and rest. He's dressed like a farmworker and looks like he's originally someone from south of the border. A "white Mexican" so to speak*, he thought shaking his head. *Conchetta is somewhat Latin looking. I suppose the safest bet to look for lodging would be the Mexican part of town.* Before long he was tying his horse up in front of a large building called Hotel Valencia.

"*Hola, amigo*," he said, addressing the man behind the front counter.

Operating on the old adage that money talks, he held out Conchetta's picture along with two dollars in front of the man's face.

"I need some help, amigo. Have you ever seen this woman?"

Carefully plucking the bills from Frank's hand, the clerk shook his head affirmatively, and said in broken English, "*Si, senor*, the woman and her husband stopped here for two nights. She was very sick, and he walked with much pain."

"How long ago was that?" Frank said.

"Over a month ago. I remember this because he paid well, and even a little extra, when I told him where to go to inquire about a little house or cabin to rent. My cousin helps run a service that finds housing for our people. Most are humble shacks on the big ranches and farms, suitable for campesinos, but also he knows of some that are a little better, tucked away in the foothills and arroyos. The man, Juan, said he needed a quiet place where his wife could rest and recuperate, before moving on to a town where they had relatives."

Frank couldn't believe what he had been hearing! Fate or Lady Luck indeed seemed to be guiding him. So many of his hunches had turned out to be correct that it almost felt scary. *Maybe I would make a good lawyer after all, or more likely a police detective*, he thought.

"Well, you've certainly been a help, friend. Appreciate it. Now, where can I find this cousin of yours?"

The man lowered his head and fingered the bills in his hand. Frank got the message, and digging into his pocket came up with two more bills that he slid over the counter to the clerk. The clerk smiled and told him where his cousin lived. Frank got back on Tuli and headed off to find the place. Half an hour later, he rode up to a whitewashed, low-roofed adobe dwelling. Chickens were in the yard, and two small children played in some mud near a water trough. A small dog began to bark, and soon a man emerged from the house and gave a slight wave to Frank. Dismounting his horse and holding it by the reins, Frank walked up to him as chickens scattered, and the little dog barked at Tuli's hoofs.

"*Buenos dias, senor.* My, what a fine horse you have. I am Ramon Diaz. May I be of some service?" the man said.

Frank quickly noticed that he spoke much better English than his cousin at the hotel. He also saw that the man was staring him straight in the eye with an open smile on his face. His house was modest but neat in appearance, and the children looked well fed and content, pausing in their mud playing to gaze at the stranger who had entered their yard.

Frank decided to be open and honest with him, and told him the purpose of his visit. The man's face seemed to light up when he showed him the photograph of Conchetta.

"Oh, *si senor*, the pretty lady. *Muy inferma*," he said, slipping into Spanish and informing Frank that she was very sick.

Frank nodded in comprehension.

"Yes, I hear she was sick. Your cousin told me that you might know where these people are."

"Yes, senor. They rented a cabin near Penetencia Creek. The man, Juan, paid my boss two months in advance. I don't know if they are still there though, I saw them about a week ago in line at the train depot. The other day, the boss told me to ride out there when I get the chance, to see if perhaps they have left without notifying him. He is not too concerned though. Rent is not due again for some weeks. If you wish, we could ride out there now and see.

"Great, Ramon, that would be just great," Frank said, and reaching again into his pocket came up with three dollar bills, and pushed them into Ramon's hand saying, "Buy something for the kids. I really appreciate your helping me."

Ramon looked surprised, thanked him, and went back inside to tell his wife he would be gone for a little while. Going to a shed in back of the house, he soon had his horse saddled, and the two men headed off in an easterly direction.

It was late afternoon when they pulled up to an isolated cabin situated near a creek. The place looked deserted, no horses or wagon. There was a bit of a chill in the air, and no smoke issued from the rusty pipe protruding from the roof. They dismounted and walked to the front door. Ramon knocked, but no one answered. He tried the latch and found the door unlocked. He pushed it open and both men looked inside. The place was empty. Cupboard doors were open with nothing inside. The shelves along one wall also were empty. There was a bed in each of the two rooms, both neatly made. No clothes hung on pegs or were in a small closet. Frank walked over to a dresser and began opening drawers. Each one was empty.

"They are gone, senor. They probably left the day I saw them at the train station."

"It was about a week ago you say?" Frank said.

"Si, senor, a week, no more."

The cabin had been left in a fairly neat manner. There was nothing to lead one to think that it was hastily abandoned. Looking about Frank noticed some folded newspapers in an empty wood box near the cast iron wood stove. Going over he picked the stack up, and saw the date on the top one was indeed a little over a week ago. Ramon looked quizzically at him, when he sat in the one wood chair near the stove and began looking through the papers. Suddenly, Frank paused. On a page devoted to religious happenings, someone had underlined in ink news concerning the opening of a new Catholic church in the town of Healdsburg, many miles to the north. The new parish was to be called St. Johns, an order of newly arrived nuns were to be on hand to start a parochial school for the education of the town's young Catholic children. In the margin next to the article a heart had been drawn with an arrow running through it. Frank wasn't sure what to make of this, but after going through the rest of the papers and finding nothing, folded the page that had the heart and the underlining, and put it in his pocket.

"You have found something that may help you on your quest, senor?" Ramon said.

"I'm not sure," Frank said, "but I'm glad we came out here. Guess I go to the train depot next," he said. And leaving, they mounted their horses and headed back towards town.

By the time they got back it was dark, and Ramon had told Frank the depot would be closed until morning. He extended him an invitation to spend the night at his house if he so chose. His wife Rosa was an excellent cook, he assured him, and though the food would be simple, there would be plenty of it. Frank was pleased with this. He was tired and had much to think on, and finding food and lodging in a strange town could be time consuming and an effort. He gladly took Ramon up on his offer.

Rosa didn't seem to think it strange that there would be a total stranger staying for dinner and the night. She went about preparing and warming up food over a home-made brick stove and oven situated out the back door. The cooking area was open on three sides, and covered over with a roof of tin.

"How do you like my patio roof, Senor Frank?" Ramon said, handing him a cup of tequila. "Better than thatch, no? We had to save quite a bit of money to purchase that tin, but only the best will do for my Rosa when it comes to her cooking space. Wait until you taste the enchiladas we'll be having along with our beans. People come to our house just to buy her enchiladas and tamales. Most of the money for the roof came from her earnings."

Frank was impressed, and the smell of the food made him eager to eat. When all was ready, they sat at a large table in the center of the main room, the two children looking up from their food often to stare at the guest. Frank wondered how good beans could be for a dog, when he noticed the older child, a boy, giving small piles of beans he held in his palm to the little black and white dog hovering under the table. Indeed the enchiladas were delicious, stuffed with chicken, rice, and cheese, and covered with a rich, spicy red sauce made with plenty of peppers. Frank praised Rosa's cooking profusely, and after dinner he and Ramon sat out on the front veranda, each with another cup of tequila.

Frank was disgusted when Ramon began talking about the sad situation the farmworkers were in around San Jose and the Sacramento Valley area. Most of them lived in hovels barely fit for a dog; many camped out in the open near rivers and creeks. Often the children were sick and undernourished. The large landowners were making money at a phenomenal rate selling the produce to a growing population, and now that the railroad was completed, much of it was being sent back east, where people marveled at the fruits and vegetables that California was producing. And what of the hard working people that picked the crops? Were they too sharing in this wealth? No. They were paid next to nothing for providing backbreaking labor from sun up to sun down. Ramon had often heard the excuse, "Oh well, they're only Mexicans, they're used to working and living like that—hell, they don't mind it."

But they did mind it. Especially when they saw a young mother give birth and die in the middle of a strawberry field where she had been working in hundred-degree sun until the moment her baby was due. Then, collapsing amongst the green plants, covering them with her blood, as an emaciated baby came crying into the world. The mother, so undernourished and exhausted from overwork, could do nothing but die after using all her strength to push out another life into the often cruel world.

And the foreman, the landowners son, upon seeing the disturbance and interruption of work, yelled, "Get that woman off those strawberries dammit. She's bled all over them. Move her to the end of the row and get back to work."

Frank wasn't all that surprised to hear such stories, but he had no idea that it could get that bad. The law should step in somehow and strive for better working conditions, he reasoned. Here he noticed yet another reason for becoming involved in legal work.

Ramon was staring into his empty cup. Frank rose and, grabbing the man's shoulder, gave it what he hoped would be a reassuring squeeze.

"Things can only get better, Ramon. Sure sounds like they can't get much worse. I know a few people I'm going to tell about all this. Don't give up, better rights and conditions have to come for the farmworker—hell, without them what would people eat? Just pig, chicken, and steer?"

"Possibly, Francisco," Ramon said reflectively. "As long as they have Mexicans to do all the butchering and cleanup."

Both men shared a quiet sarcastic chuckle in the dark night.

Frank went inside and retired to the blankets he had spread near a wall. Ramon, following, headed for the bedroom where his wife and children were already sleeping.

"Francisco, I wish you luck in locating the senorita in the picture. I know that you say this is all business, but perhaps you wish to make that woman your *novia*, no?

Frank was taken aback. Were his feelings that obvious?

"Ramon, I can tell you this. If I were to meet up with a woman like that, I wouldn't want her just for my sweetheart. I'd want her for my wife."

"Wise thinking, my friend. *Buena suerte y buenos noches*," and carrying the candle he held in his hand, Ramon passed on into the room and closed the door.

Frank rose at first light, found a scrap of paper and a pencil and quickly scribbled "*Gracias Ramon y familia*," and left it on the kitchen table along with a five-dollar bill. Picking up his belongings he quietly left the silent house, saddled Tuli, and headed towards the center of town. He figured it was probably too early for the depot to open, and stopped at a small café for a cup of coffee and a couple of eggs and bread. After breakfast he arrived at the depot just as it was opening. He sat at a bench on the elevated platform alongside the tracks watching workers enter the depot office. When everything seemed to be ready for full operation, he walked up to the ticket office, introduced himself, and after explaining his purpose, showed the ticket master Conchetta's picture.

The man's eyebrows rose. Yes, he had seen the woman about a week ago; she and her husband had purchased a ticket. Frank was afraid to ask the next question. If the man said east towards Sacramento, by now Conchetta could be anywhere.

"Do you recall what destination they bought tickets for, sir?"

"Why sure, a woman who looks like that sticks in a guy's memory. Too bad she was limping though, and looked a little morose. Both of them limped, come to think of it. Kind of strange. Bought tickets to San Francisco, they did."

Frank exhaled the breath he had been holding. There was hope yet. His mind traveled to the folded newspaper in his pocket and the underlined words concerning a new church in the town of Healdsburg, fifty or sixty miles north of San Francisco. Could they be heading there?

Chapter 16

"Penitencia Creek. What a fitting place for me to heal up at and do my penance. For I have sinned greatly, it is true," thought a smiling El Zapo, as he left the shack that served as a realtor's office.

The pain in his ribs and his groin had grown so acute that in spite of his reservations, he had sought the attention of a doctor. The diagnosis was two broken ribs and a ruptured groin. He would need to be still and move as little as possible for at least a month. Total bed rest was even more preferable. This was what had led Juan to hunt for a place to hole up, an isolated place, far from curious minds.

After hearing the description of the cabin up on Penitencia Creek, he thought it perfect. The name alone had convinced him. Why, a good Catholic such as himself would heal up perfectly after saying his penance along the cleansing banks of Penitencia Creek.

He had paid the realtor for two months rent, plus a tidy extra amount if the man would arrange for someone to stop by once a week to see if they would need anything from town. After finalizing the agreement, he rented a horse and wagon and loaded it with food and supplies purchased at a general store. On his way back to the Hotel Valencia, he took pleasure in the thought of the expression that would come to Conchetta's face when she heard that they would be moving to a wonderful lover's cottage, perched alongside a picturesque, bubbling creek, a mile or so away from their nearest neighbor. Just two young lovers, the king and queen of the Gypsies, alone together with many hours ahead for quiet conversation and connubial bliss, perhaps a little penance afterwards. *Too bad that damn bear isn't still with us. I kind of miss him,* Juan thought, turning serious.

"Oh, it would be good to get off these feet," he lamented, painfully limping up the stairs to the room. Unlocking the door, he smiled broadly at Conchetta who lay bound and gagged on the bed.

"Well, well, Miss Lombardi, cooperate with me once again and in a short time you will be queen of your own domicile. No more gags for you. You could scream your lungs out, and no one would hear you where we're going, though I wouldn't recommend your straining your vocal cords in that manner. Your screaming might be off key, and offensive to my sensitive hearing, thus forcing me to strangle that pretty white throat. Now, we wouldn't want that would we, my queen?"

Once again, Conchetta had a terrible headache. Several days had passed, she knew, and during that time she had eaten a little food, drank lots of water, and mostly slept. This extended nightmare she had been living was momentarily blotted away the easiest with sleep. At times she had violent cramps and several times had vomited into the bedpan, but as the hours passed by, slowly her head began to clear and emerge from the morphine fog.

Now Juan was grinning the grin of a madman, and obviously had made some type of plan. What torture had he conceived of now? Whom would he kill next, and why in the world was he keeping her alive? All these thoughts assailed her splitting head, as she stared up into his cold, goat-like eyes. *There's absolutely no soul behind those eyes,* she thought. *Listen to him talking about going off somewhere. Somewhere isolated. What makes him feel the need to take me with him? At times he's even been acting somewhat concerned about me. Yeah, acting,* she thought. *He obviously finds pleasure in torturing me and mainly that's what's keeping me alive,* she reasoned.

The grin suddenly vanished from Juan's face. Going over to Conchetta he released her from the bindings, telling her to get up and make herself presentable. They would be leaving as soon as possible. He had horse and wagon waiting out front.

After issuing the usual threats, Juan grabbed Conchetta by the arm and they proceeded down the stairs. He informed the clerk that they were leaving, and thanked him for the good rest and quiet that they had received.

Oh, he's so polite, Conchetta thought. *Everyone thinks he's the perfect gentleman.* She asked herself why God just didn't step in and trip this sick animal up somehow. All she could console herself with, though, was the bible verse that said something about the Lord helps those who help themselves, and she was certainly going to have to help herself if she hoped to stay alive.

She had been having a difficult time walking, and was surprised at how weak she still was. She was happy to note that Juan looked even weaker. He was limping worse than she had ever seen him, and had his hand pushed against his ribs. Outside in the bright morning sun, he led her to a wagon that was loaded with supplies. If he kept her alive, or if she decided to stay alive, she thought darkly, at least it appeared there would be no lack of food. The wagon held a large sack of flour, several sacks of dried beans and rice, canned goods, potatoes, a large smoked ham and a couple of slabs of bacon. Blankets, cooking supplies and other household items filled the rest of the wagon.

"So, *mi esposa,* off we go to the house of your dreams," he said to Conchetta, smiling and in Spanish.

She answered him with one word in Spanish, "*Bastardo*."

Juan's smile grew broader, and he started nodding his head up and down like a gleeful grinning idiot. Conchetta embraced her nightmare and climbed aboard the wagon. The sun was bright and hurt her eyes.

No sun is going to set on me, at least for a while, she said to herself. *That son of a bitch doesn't deserve to live under the sun. One of these days I'm going to watch those goat eyes stare into it for the last time. I can wait for that day, even if it takes my last drop of patience.*

As the wagon pulled out, for some reason she started thinking about a blue swan. One of the Scandinavian students she had tutored in Monterey had written a short poem that mentioned a blue swan. The swan was on its way to Tuonela. She had asked the youth what was Tuonela. He had answered that it was where people went after they had died.

"You mean heaven," she had said.

"Yes, like heaven, or the other place," the youth had answered. The blue swan went to Tuonela on the waves of a dark river.

She couldn't remember if the boy had said his parents were from Sweden or Finland, but she was sure it was one of those two countries.

The color of the sky certainly is a vibrant blue this morn-ing. I suppose that's what reminded me of the blue swan. There's no such thing as a blue swan, is there? She found herself thinking. *That drug must still want me to drift back into dreaming,* she thought, and pinched herself to gain more alertness.

They were moving out of town towards the foothills to the east. Before long they crossed a bridge spanning a narrow creek. The gravel bed of the creek was quite wide, but the water that flowed in it was confined to one side and was very shallow.

The road followed the creek and a mile or so past the bridge Juan, who up until this time had not spoken a word, said, "Yes, there's the turnoff."

A giant valley oak towered above a field of wild oats, which had a narrow rutted wagon trail running through it, towards a tree line that marked the creek. Proceeding on into the trees, they traveled on a short distance until a sturdy-looking little cabin came into sight.

Conchetta's heart dropped. The place was so isolated. It had been impossible to even see the cabin from the main road, and the last house she had seen was at least a mile back. She turned her head towards Juan and found him staring straight at her, minus the sardonic smile he often wore on his thin lips.

He stopped the wagon and said, "I'm sure you're wondering what's going on, Lombardi. Well, I'm going to tell you. The other day while you were sleeping it off, I went to see a doctor. Seems that *pendejo* cowboy broke two of my ribs and ruptured my groin. I need to remain as still as possible in order to heal up. He thinks that the one rib has come close to puncturing my lung. I want to heal, and I want to heal fast. I have many important things to do, and I hate wasting time. But as they say, some things can't be rushed. Now this is where you come in. You are to cook and wait on me, and keep our little house warm and cozy. I've brought along several books, and I expect you to read to me upon request. Of course I won't be too incapacitated to shoot or knife you should you try to escape. So see, it's simple. If you cooperate and follow my demands, you shall live on. If you don't, and I am forced to eliminate you, well, I suppose, in that case I'd be forced to cook for myself. I would so hate for this to happen. I regret I have never found the time to acquire competent cooking skills. In Santiago, my parents employed only the finest of chefs, but Lombardi, I am pleased to tell you that after sampling your food I find you're worthy of being my cook. What do you say? I'm tired of talking. Will you rise to the challenge or do I kill you now?" he said, reaching rapidly inside his coat and producing a knife that he held to Conchetta's chest.

She simply nodded her head affirmatively. There was no choice, and in spite of the bleakness of the situation, hope of escape would keep her going.

"Oh by the way, do you know the name of this creek?" he said, pointing to the stream that ran less than fifty yards from the cabin.

"Of course. It's called insane asshole creek," she blurted out, in spite of the fact that he was still holding the knife to her chest.

Juan broke out laughing and put the knife away.

"Well done, my queen, I see your spirits are up, and you shall provide me with fine entertainment. But please don't make me laugh too much. It hurts my ribs. I do like your name for the creek, but actually it has a much more serious name. It is called Penitencia Creek, and here I shall do my penance, and ask God's forgiveness, for some may say that I have sinned mightily. Don't you think?"

"Oh yes, my king, you are a mighty sinner and crazy as the cuckoo and certainly more fiendish," she answered.

Juan struck out and backhanded her sharply across the face.

"I told you don't make me laugh. Not for a while anyway. We can play games later. My only regret is that there is one game that I would enjoy playing with you, and it involves you minus your clothes. Unfortunately, my condition prevents me from playing that game—but fear not, lovely Conchetta! One day I shall heal and share your bed as a loving husband should."

Conchetta's face stung. She must remember not to go too far with this rabid dog.

"Well, you say you want a cook, and I am hungry myself. Move on now, please."

"Why, that's better," Juan said. "I like that."

He flicked the reins and moved on to the cabin. Reaching under the seat, he came up with his revolver, and told Conchetta to get down and to never think of running. The 44 would leave a very large hole in her back. Juan stiffly got down, and taking a key from his pocket, walked up to the front door with Conchetta a step ahead of him and unlocked the door. Peering in, Conchetta saw two rooms, two beds, and two chairs. A cast iron stove was in the first room. She could see that someone had built a sturdy little place. It was actually fairly clean inside and didn't even smell too dank or musty. How could she exist here though? Day after day with a madman, a killer, a rapist. A wave of revulsion assailed her, and for a moment she felt like she was going to faint. Juan's voice jolted her senses.

"Lombardi, I'm going to rest on this chair near the window and watch you unload the wagon. Now, there's no hurry, rest when you wish, just remember I have this gun in my lap. The sooner you unload, the sooner you may begin cooking. Didn't you mention you were hungry? Ah, I see the previous tenant has left us with a little wood for the stove. My, it has a nice flat top. One may fit two pots at once on there I believe. Perhaps later you could cook us that rice dish you made for me once. I'm sure I remembered to pick up all the ingredients. You'll come upon them as you unload. Now off you go, look lively my dear."

In spite of all this insanity, Conchetta found herself having to refrain from busting out laughing. *I've been drugged, violated, posed as an entertainer, had knives thrown at me. I've been tied up more than I've been loose, thrown in a cage with a bear, and now, at least for the immediate future, I'm to be chief cook, slave, and caregiver for an insane murderer who has posed as a priest, killed a priest and a nun, and talks to the devil. Why would I want to laugh at all this?* she thought. *Nothing is funny here.*

Could I be going insane? Best to keep busy and not think, she decided.

Methodically she began to unload the wagon, while Juan sat by the window, gun in hand. She lost count of how many trips back and forth she made, but eventually the wagon was empty, and most of the supplies put on shelves or in cupboards. Blankets she laid on the beds. The back bed was actually a bunk bed, a narrow one below and one above. They were built against a wall attached to outer posts that protruded through the wood ceiling. She noticed that the posts looked unmovable, and the beds were strongly built.

He'll probably tie me to that post at night, she thought. *No way would he let me sleep freely. He knows I'd do my best to kill him if I got the chance.*

"What are you doing back there, queen? Looking at your bed?" Juan said from his chair, as if reading her mind. "Looks to me that you should be quite comfortable on that lower one. Of course you'll have to be chained to one of those posts at night, but I'm sure by now you realize that I have no choice."

Conchetta shook her head in disgust and frustration, then walked towards the wood stove, intending to build a cooking fire.

"Hey, Lombardi, I know you're hungry, but you must help me move this bed to a different location. The doctor prescribed as much bed rest as possible, and I intend to strictly follow his orders."

The two moved the bed until it was exactly where Juan wanted it. The headboard was set against one wall where he could look out the front window while either lying down or sitting up. From that position he had a clear view of the well, with its rusty pump where Conchetta would be drawing water. From the beds new position he could also keep a direct eye on the opening that led to the other room. This accomplished, he took his boots off and got in the bed and stretched out with his head propped on the pillow.

"Nurse!" he shouted out to Conchetta, who once again was trying to build a fire. "Get me one of those spare blankets; I need to fold it up under this pillow. My head is too low, throwing me off balance should I take the notion to shoot you."

She did as she was told and started back to the stove when Juan said, "Oh, one more thing. Well, actually two. Bring me one of the books. The bible will do for now. I feel the need of brushing up on the description of Sodom and Gomorrah.

She went to the shelf where she had lined up the books and got it for him.

"I watched you when you put that screwdriver away with the forks and spoons. Will you get it please? Good. Now go over to that door that separates our rooms and take out the screws that secure the hinges. A door shouldn't separate such good friends as us, correct?"

Conchetta did as she was told, struggling over two of the screws that didn't want to budge, but with persever-ance she finally got the door down and leaned it against a wall.

"Well done, nurse. I see you've got some carpentry skills, just like that cry baby Jesus. Trying to forgive people from that cross. What a weakling. He should have been cursing his good Lord, his Father who let him be nailed up on a stick stuck in a hill. Stick stuck in a hill, stick stuck in a hill," he began singing the line, and moving his arms and fingers like a band conductor.

He had taken his hand off the gun, but Conchetta knew that she was too far away to lunge for it. She still held the screwdriver and thought of throwing it at him and then going for the gun. No, just too risky, she decided.

"Carpenter!" he abruptly shouted. "You keep giving me ideas and creating work for yourself. Go over and get that cigar box you placed near the book and bring it over to me."

Juan picked up the gun as Conchetta came near with the box. She set it near him on the bed. Reaching inside he came out with a latch and hasp set-up, and a few screws.

"For some reason I just don't feel you should have access to sharp objects such as knives and screwdrivers. I'm afraid you might cut yourself, you see. I think we should keep them safely locked away in that drawer under the counter," he said, pointing. "You're a smart little carpenter, I'm sure you can figure out how to install this set up. Here's a little tip you may not have learned," he said, handing her a nail. "Grab a piece of wood over there that you can use as a hammer. I'd let you use the butt of this revolver but I'm afraid it might go off and hurt you. Now, when you're ready to start those screws, use the nail to create what is called a pilot hole. Those screws should go in much easier. Pilot hole, must have something to do with Pontius Pilot. The fellow certainly saw that the Savior had some holes in his hands and feet," he mused out loud.

Conchetta rolled her eyes and felt like screaming, but she did as she was told. She had it all figured out pretty quickly, but as she was using the stick and the nail to create the last screw hole, the nail twisted as she hit it, and the stick smacked hard on her thumb. She let out an involuntary "Ow!" and immediately put her thumb up to her mouth.

"Carpenter, carpenter. What have you done? Come over here and let me have a look," Juan said from the bed.

The last thing Conchetta wanted was any sympathy or attention from the murderer, and she knew he just enjoyed playing a role. *Playing a role. That's all he's ever done since this nightmare began. There's no real Juan in there,* she thought, *just El Zapo playing one role after another.*

"Come, I say, let's have a look. Carpenters, nurses and cooks must be well looked after," he said authoritatively. "Wait, wait, drop that stick," Juan said as she started to walk over.

She obeyed, walked over to the bed, and held out her thumb. It had turned red and was throbbing, but it wasn't the first time that she had suffered a smashed thumb, and she knew the pain would subside shortly.

"Well, well, a red thumb," Juan said, gently rubbing the top of the nail and the area below. "Let's see you wiggle that thumb," he said. "Good, not broken. Let's see it again," and reaching out he took hold of her hand, being careful not to touch the thumb. "Conchetta, Conchetta, what am I doing to you? You must wonder why I put you through this torture," he said, reaching for the revolver and laying his hand on the grip, after noticing Conchetta's eyes imperceptibly travel to it.

A look of momentary sadness seemed to come over Juan's pale face, and he began stroking the back of Conchetta's hand. Suddenly he looked like a lost little boy lying helpless in a bed, she thought, as tears began to well up in his eyes.

"Good acting, huh," he spat out, a sneer back on his face. "Fooled you, didn't I, Lombardi?"

No, Conchetta thought to herself. I wasn't fooled, but for one instant when he was touching my hand and I saw his lip quiver, for one split second there may have been a real human trying to come out. She would need to remember this. Somewhere buried deep inside, a trace of decency may still be living in Juan. Or, maybe he was right. Every bit of it may have been an act. *I'm tired and hungry*, she thought. *I'm inventing notions is all.*

"Now, back to business. One more task, and then you can start cooking. Try your best to secure that last screw, then gather up all the knives, forks and, yes, even spoons, along with the screwdriver and deposit them in the drawer.

Oh, keep what you need out to prepare and serve the meal. Good. Now come over here and take this lock and secure the drawer. Very good, carpenter. Now you may turn into a cook. Go about your business and leave me to my reading please."

He made sure Conchetta was watching as he laid the gun on his lap, tapped it, and picked up the bible.

Thus began the first day of what was to become the darkest, longest month in Conchetta's life.

The following day two men rode up to the cabin and picked up the rented horse and wagon, and once a week an older Mexican man rode out to check on their supply needs. When the man arrived the following day with Juan's order, he always brought the local San Jose paper, as well as the San Francisco one, at Juan's request. Upon his arrival, Juan never took his eyes off Conchetta and kept the gun cocked and ready under his blankets.

On the third day after their arrival, Conchetta acted upon what seemed like a real opportunity for escape. It was beginning to get dark, and she had been reading out of *Don Quixote* to Juan. During the passage that Sancho drinks a strong potion at the inn, and begins to "discharge the mixture from both ends," Juan began to softly chuckle, and shortly after his eyes seemed to get heavy, flutter and then close. Conchetta kept quietly reading. *He's pulling a trick*, she thought, but was further amazed when he began to snore, and his hand relaxed its grip on the gun he had under the blanket.

Ever since she had removed the door and had stood it against the wall near the bed, she had imagined the possibility of flinging the heavy door down on a prone Juan and bolting out the front door. Now seemed the perfect time. The front door was open, letting in a cooling breeze, as the day had been very warm. No doubt Juan was acting, but even if he was, with his eyes closed and his hand relaxed and seemingly fallen away from the gun, she just might have time to fling the door and run for the trees.

Deciding not to think anymore but just to act, and ignore the fact that a bullet would probably come crashing into her back any second, she sprang from her chair, grabbed the door, pivoted it on one bottom corner and brought it down hard on the upper part of Juan's body, covering him completely.

She ran from the cabin and was close to the trees, when two bullets landed in rapid succession in the dirt at either side of her feet and a voice yelled out, "Next one's in your back."

She froze. The trees were so close. But she knew she'd never make it. She turned and walked automatically towards the cabin. The moment she entered the door she felt a blinding pain as Juan, standing off to the side, came down with a large piece of stove wood right across her ankle. She thought she heard the cracking of bone and rolled on the floor in pain, grabbing at her foot.

She hadn't even realized she had been screaming when she heard Juan say, "Cut the howling, Lombardi, you sound like an old bear with its foot caught in a trap. At least you're alive and not lying out there with a bullet in your back. The door trick of yours took me completely off guard, I must admit, but you didn't really think I was sleeping did you? I was testing you, setting a trap for you one may even say, and you jumped right into it, didn't you? And what did you get for it? A broken ankle. I had been thinking about ways to slow you down, and now you just gave me the perfect excuse. Accept it. I'm not going to let you get away. You'll be moving a lot slower from now on. Isn't this romantic? We can recuperate together, huh."

Conchetta's ankle was throbbing like hell, and every time she tried to move it, the pain increased. She was sure it was broken. Until it healed, her running days were over, and chances for escape much slimmer.

Juan found one of the thinner blankets, and using the throwing knife he always kept somewhere near him, cut narrow bandaging strips from it.

"Stay put, queen, looks like that sage plant out front's going to have some use other than flavoring," he said, going out and breaking off a few branches.

Conchetta was still sitting on the floor gritting her teeth and trying to get a handle on her pain when Juan came back in, grabbed the bandages, and after a brief look at her swollen ankle, began tearing off sage leaves, moistened them with his mouth, and placed them on her ankle. He placed more leaves on the cloth, then began to wrap it tightly around the ankle. Conchetta didn't say a word and forced her eyes to just gaze off out the window.

"I'm no doctor, but I don't think you've got that bad of a break. Stay off it as much as possible and you'll heal up. We wouldn't want you walking forever with a limp like some people we know, now would we?" he said in a concerned voice. "Oh, by the way. Would you like a little morphine to ease the pain? I'm sure that could be arranged."

Conchetta immediately shook her head negatively. Juan began to laugh.

"What's the matter? Now when you could really use the stuff you don't want it. Oh well, who knows? Maybe it will find a way to get inside you on its own. A powerful drug, that morphine. Seems to have a mind of its own. Here try some of this instead," and going over to a shelf, removed a bottle of whiskey and handed it to Conchetta, after drinking from it himself. "See, no drug in it. You don't think I'd risk confusing my well-ordered mind with that stuff, do you? Now a little whiskey, that's OK, taken in moderation. Go ahead, drink."

Hoping it would ease the pain, Conchetta drank deeply.

Juan helped her to the back bedroom, chained her to the post, and told her to get some sleep.

In the morning when she awoke she found a crudely fashioned crutch, and a sturdy cane fashioned from madrone leaning against the bed. The pain in her ankle had subsided some, but she figured it would probably worsen as the day went on, and she went about her chores. Her chores. Waiting on El Zapo. Now she was La Zapa. *Oh, what a cruel joke,* she thought, as tears began to fill her eyes. *My, he's so thoughtful. A crutch and a cane. Why, I'll have absolutely no trouble drawing water, getting wood, making fires and cooking and cleaning while he lies in bed watching. He must have planned this all along. He knew I'd try to run. How was I so foolish?* she thought, second-guessing herself, when Juan entered the room.

"I trust you're feeling healthy and joyful this morning, Lombardi, and I'm sure that the sight of the wonderful presents I made for you cheered you up immensely. Say, I don't know about you, but I'm hungry. Why don't you slice us some of that ham for breakfast along with the eggs," he said cheerfully, coming over and unlocking the chain. "Take your time, there's no hurry. I even helped you out some by starting a fire, but I believe I may have overtaxed myself. I'm going to go back and lie down and read the papers. I must keep up on local events, you understand."

The pattern was now established that would last for over a month. Conchetta waiting on Juan while both nursed their wounds. Time seemed to crawl by for Conchetta, but each day her ankle felt a little better, and slowly the swelling went down. Juan seemed to be enjoying himself, she thought. Most days he lay in bed and read, usually from the bible, *Don Quixote,* or *Moby Dick*, along with the newspapers. When he wasn't reading, he would simply stare at Conchetta with the sardonic sneer masking his face, but once or twice she had caught him gazing at her with a look of sadness and moist eyes. Each time he followed up this look by saying something threatening or cruel to her. Near the end of a month he began to get up and move around a little more. He even helped Conchetta gather wood, instead of sitting on the porch with a gun and watching her move about the trees.

One day while reading the paper, he let out an involuntary, "Ahah! Why, I think the day is drawing near, my dear, when we shall be leaving our little home and seek out greener pastures, so to speak. You seem to be moving about much better, as am I. I think the time is coming when once again we will venture out into the mysterious world and see what fate has in store. What say, my queen, would a change of scenery suit you?"

Conchetta simply nodded yes, and continued putting away cooking utensils. Indeed her ankle was feeling better, as long as she didn't put a lot of weight on it. She struggled to contain her excitement at the prospect of leaving the lonely cabin. Her sanity had been pushed to the limits, and she didn't think she could remain there much longer without breaking.

The following week, when the old man came by to check with Juan, he talked long and enthusiastically with him. Conchetta watched them from the window as they stood in the front yard. The following day they began to load up what supplies that remained on a wagon the old man had brought back to the cabin. Most of the food was gone, but Juan had Conchetta carefully load all the cooking supplies and most of the blankets back in the wagon. He wanted to leave the little cabin just like they found it, or better, he said.

Before they left, Conchetta had the opportunity to glance at the paper Juan had been reading when he uttered his exclamation, and started talking about leaving. She saw that he had underlined a few sentences about the opening of a new Catholic church in the town of Healdsburg. In the margin next to the article he had drawn a crude heart with an arrow going through it. Fear and revulsion ran through her as she read on and came to a part that talked about the arrival of some nuns that were to teach school. She thought about the nun Juan had raped and killed near the Mission San Juan Bautista, and how he had come back to the wagon dressed in her bloody habit. He probably wanted to go to Healdsburg, she reasoned. She had heard of the place. They grew grapes there and fruit trees, prunes mostly, she remembered.

While Juan had his back turned, she neatly folded the paper and placed it along with others in the empty wood box by the stove. The fact that he had underlined some words concerning another town gave her a brief flutter of optimism. She knew this was stupid to think, but for some reason she couldn't help but hope that Juan had grown careless and had slipped up. If in actuality they were going to Healdsburg, that paper fairly pointed the way. But who, if anyone, would see it, and how could it possibly aid her? Dismissing it all as foolishness, she contented herself with the fact that she was still alive, alive and heading out once more into the world. When all was loaded, Juan, dressed in his good clothes, and Conchetta, wearing a clean black dress, boarded the wagon and pulled away from the cabin heading out towards the main road and back to the town of San Jose.

Chapter 17

Angelina Londi was busy catching trout for dinner from the cold clear waters of Dry Creek. The creek had dried up in spots, but she was fishing in a deep shady hole where many trout were trapped, waiting for the fall rains to swell the creek, enabling them to reach the Russian River and continue downstream to the ocean. Baiting her hook with a worm, she flung it out, her line attached to a long bamboo pole. Almost immediately, the tip of the pole dipped down, and Angelina pulled up and back landing another silvery, ten-inch, ocean-going rainbow trout. She unhooked the fish and placed it in a fern-lined basket alongside ten others, all about the same length. A part of her regretted that these fish weren't destined to live to reach the ocean and one day return to these waters as adult steelhead to spawn. But there seemed to be an endless abundance of them in this stream, as well as all the streams of the area, she had learned. These fish certainly provided a tasty meal, and everyone around town agreed that they would be thriving and reproducing in local waters for hundreds of years to come.

Deciding that she now had plenty of fish for her and Dom's dinner, she was getting ready to leave when she heard the quacking sound of mallard ducks coming towards her. Dropping the pole, she swiveled and grabbed the shotgun that had lain loaded behind her. She knew the flight pattern of these ducks. Shortly, they would come into view, rounding the downstream bend, flying relatively low, heading up the creek. She stood poised and ready, and when four fast flying mallards came into view she lead the point bird at what she figured, from Dom's tutoring, was an appropriate distance, and swinging through, squeezed the trigger and saw feathers explode as the lead duck fluttered and fell to the ground. Good, she thought, no need now to go into town for anything. Trout tonight, duck tomorrow night. More money now to spend on rose bushes, she reasoned, pleased with herself. The duck had landed in a shallow pool of water. Angelina walked over, took her shoes off and hiking up her dress waded in and retrieved it.

"Wow, nice legs," she heard, turning to see Dom making his way down the bank towards her.

Damn, she looks good down there. What a lucky man I am, Dom thought to himself. *A woman who catches our dinner, knocks down fast flying ducks and just happens to look like a million bucks. My old friends back in Florence wouldn't believe all this if I were standing in front of them right now.* "Keep dreaming, Londi," *or,* "Have some more brandy, Londi," *is what they would all say.*

He walked to the basket and peered inside as Angelina arrived holding the duck. He put his arms around her and began pumping against her suggestively.

"There's nothing more stimulating than holding a pretty woman who is holding a dead duck," he proclaimed decisively.

Angelina shook her head and gave him a quick kiss on the lips.

"Look at those trout. Almost every one of them the same size, and look how plump they are!"

Dom appraised the fish with a cook's eye.

"Three for me and three for you. Six will fit nicely in our largest skillet. The rest will make a nice lunch," Dom said. "How will you cook them, Mrs. Londi?"

"No, no. You are the master chef, Mr. Londi. I caught 'em, you cook 'em!"

"How many times do I have to tell you, the term 'chef' reeks of pretentiousness. I am a humble man, yet a competent cook, who just happens to have the most beautiful and accomplished woman in the county for a wife. That said, the menu for tonight will be pan-fried trout, breaded and cooked in bacon drippings, tossed green salad with homegrown tomatoes and scallions, covered with a light balsamic vinaigrette, and small delicate red potatoes sautéed in butter and garlic. The chilled Massoni Riesling will be featured as this evening's wine of choice."

Angelina dropped the duck and gave him a big hug while rubbing her body against his.

"Why, Mr. Londi, all this talk of food is exciting me. I think we should go back to the house as soon as possible and get in bed. Why, you know we got up way too early, and it's been an awfully warm day. I can't wait to get out of these clothes."

Dom began shaking his head up and down, and extending his tongue, imitated a panting and excited dog.

"Knock it off," Angelina said, playfully slapping him on the shoulder. "You're starting to act just like Pino. That's something he would do after talking about Betty Mae. Why that old dog, he should be ashamed of himself. He's old enough to be her grandfather."

"Oh, don't be hard on Pino; he's all talk and no action. That's all," Dom said.

"Don't be so sure of that," Angelina retorted. "I've seen the way Betty Mae looks at him, and it's not granddaughterly."

"She's just showing him some respect. He is the shaman of the tribe after all."

"Yeah, well I think she's been showing him something else besides respect, you naïve goat."

"It's hot," Dom said. "Let's go to bed and I'll take your clothes off for you."

"OK," Angelina said, "my arms are too tired from shooting ducks and hauling in fish. You carry the shotgun and the basket. I carry the pole and the duck."

"Whatever you say, dear," Dom said politely, as the two turned their backs on the creek and walked on towards the house.

After a relaxing interlude in bed, Angelina went about her chores while Dom plucked and cleaned the duck. Evening was approaching, and Dom went inside and started to prepare the meal. He was always surprised that even after all those years spent cooking in restaurants, he still enjoyed preparing a good dinner. He took a bottle of brandy down from the cupboard and poured out a small glass. Looking out the back window he saw Angelina pause in the hoeing she was doing around some roses and cock her head and stare off at an oak tree a short distance away. He was surprised to see her drop the hoe, and her body suddenly convulsed in a deep sob. Dom watched her wipe tears from her eyes, and immediately he walked out the back door towards her.

Angelina saw him coming, and held a finger up to her lips suggesting quiet. Dom came up and stood by her, as she pointed off in the direction of the tree. He saw a large gray squirrel moving amongst the branches. It paused still and let out a shrill cry that sounded exactly like "Chetta." Again it repeated it, "Chetta, Chetta."

Dom reached his arms around his wife.

"It's OK, Angie. I see why you're crying. That silly squirrel is almost saying 'Conchetta' isn't it? Damn it, I wish we'd hear something more about her. I can't stand seeing you torn apart this way."

Angelina pulled herself together.

"Good. I'm glad you heard it too, Dom. I thought I was going crazy for a moment. A squirrel almost saying my sister's name. It's a sign though, Dom. I know that's some type of sign. The odds of that little squirrel coming so close and chirping out 'Chetta' are just too strange. I feel something's happening concerning my sister, but I just don't know what. I may go crazy if I don't hear something soon."

"Don't talk that way, Angie. It won't do any good. I believe a little in signs like that too. I think that's a good sign. That certainly was a healthy, fat squirrel. Spoke pretty good too for an American squirrel trying to pronounce an Italian name," he said reflectively.

Angelina couldn't help but give a slight laugh. The couple just stood there amongst the roses staring off at the oak tree, but the squirrel had vanished, and they never saw it again.

The following day a wagon pulled into the yard filled with Pomo Indians. Walter was driving with Pino and Fred sitting up front. Betty Mae and Melanie were in back along with two other young men. The Londis went out to greet them.

"Hey, Walter," Dom said. "You must be going into town for the baseball, huh? Hello Pino, Fred. Hi girls. Hi guys," he said.

"Oh, Dom that's Ronald and Lloyd. They're the only other ones on the rancheria that are interested in baseball. They've never seen a real game and are curious. Are you and Angelina going to come into town and watch? I hear they've erected some seats, bleachers they're called, where you can sit and watch the game."

Dom looked over at Angelina.

"Well, we weren't planning on going to town. We've got plenty of food around. Angie shot a plump duck yesterday and also caught a basketful of trout. I hope she's not going wild on me," he said, elbowing her.

"Shut up, Londi. You cook them. I catch and shoot. That's the way you like it you said."

"That's the way it should be," Pino chimed in. "A woman should provide for her man, isn't that right Betty Mae?" he said, turning and smiling at her.

"Yes, Pino. You enjoyed that acorn mush I brought to you this morning, didn't you," she said, rolling her eyes.

"Why, of course, Betty Mae. It did taste better though after I shaved some red onions in it," he said seriously.

"Come on, Angelina," Fred spoke up. "Let's all go to the game. Walter's going to strike out Butch and the giant Swede."

Angelina couldn't resist, and walked over and rubbed her hand over Fred's little head. His hair was cut fairly short and stood straight up.

"So, porcupine. You want everyone to go to the game, huh? Oh, OK. What woman could resist a cute fellow like you," she said, watching Fred's light brown complexion take on a shade of red.

"There's been a loose agreement that anyone who wants to play is to meet at the park around three," Walter said. "I just hope enough people show up so we can have a real game. Nine players to a team," he added.

"Great," Dom said. "That will give us time to stop by the Lings and see if they want to come along. I also want to stop by the store and buy a large bag of peanuts in the shell. I read in the San Francisco paper that back east, mostly in New York, eating peanuts and watching baseball is starting to become a regular tradition."

"I thought you liked to drink beer while you ate your peanuts," Angelina spoke out.

"Good idea, Angie, we'll buy some bottles of beer and bring them to the game too. Now, why didn't I think of that?"

"Look what I'm bringing," Pino shouted out and reached under the seat for a cloth sack from which he proudly withdrew a large slab of venison jerky and a huge red onion.

Walter shook his head saying, "No one's going to want to sit next to you, Pino."

"I will," Betty Mae shyly volunteered.

"Look what I'm bringing, Walter," Melanie spoke from the back, holding out a handful of toasted grasshoppers she had pulled from a bag.

"Why great, Melanie, maybe you'll start a new tradition," Walter said seriously, amidst everyone's laughter.

"OK then," Dom said. "We'll see you all later this afternoon at the new ball park," and started to turn back for the house while reaching out for Angelina's hand.

"Hold on, peanut eater. I want to ask Walter one thing before he leaves."

"What's that, Angelina?" Walter queried.

"Why in the world did they build the ballpark below the cemetery? Who can enjoy a game while at the same time watch a coffin being pulled up to its final resting? Couldn't they have put that park somewhere more cheerful?"

Before Walter could answer, Pino spoke, "Angelina, that coffin you speak of is only a box holding some meat that used to be a living spirit. The spirit is free now to rove amongst the winds, hide in caves or pine trees, or to enter some animal or even another human. I have even seen spirits hiding in rocks and streams. If that spirit was following the wagon holding the coffin, it would be doing so because it hadn't yet got used to freedom, and still felt attached to that rotting meat inside the wood box. I can assure you that once the spirit passed by the baseball game and saw the freedom and reckless abandon that people were enjoying by playing or watching a game, that the spirit would curse itself for being so stupid and self indulgent, and fly on eagle's wings to the nearest mountain top to reassess its predicament. Spirits don't like to be dumb, you know."

Angelina felt a bit chastised yet illuminated. She hadn't been expecting such an answer. Part of her knew all along what Pino was talking about, and he was right. She definitely liked the way he reasoned, and his answer had made her feel lighter and more at ease.

"Pino, once in a while I have to admit you make good sense. I guess I wouldn't mind sitting beside you at the game also. You would have to give me some of your red onion though. I too have a certain fondness for them, especially sliced over fresh tomatoes and drenched in a little olive oil, salt, and pepper."

"Fred, do you hear this," Pino spoke in wonderment. "I may have a good-looking woman sitting on both sides of me. See, I've been telling you that becoming a shaman has its high points. Number one being that it impresses the girls."

Fred just looked at him wide eyed and nodded his head.

In the early afternoon the Londis boarded their wagonette and drove into town. Dom had purchased the wagonette, nothing more than a wagon with side rails and a sturdy flat top, to keep goods dry, as well as to provide shade from the sun, and with its two facing side seats the wagonette could also carry six or more with ease. With its black canvas top and short fringe dangling down the side, the Londis, dressed in Sunday clothes, cut quite the dapper figure moving down the main street.

They stopped at the general store, and Dom bought a big bag of peanuts and two bottles of beer. The beer was made locally, in fact at a small brewery off of First Street, not far from the ballpark. The next stop was the Ling's laundry, where after talking to Po and Mai, they convinced them to come with them out to the ballpark. The Lings had reservations, though. It wasn't that they didn't feel comfortable going away for a few hours and leaving Suen in charge. Sundays were usually slow, and often they closed up early. What troubled them was what they perceived would be the reaction of many of the Anglo-Americans to them and the diverse group they would be sitting with. Dom had enthusiastically explained that Pino and some of the other Pomos would also be there, and that they could all sit together on the new bleachers.

Po could just hear some of the town's people snickering and commenting on the bunch. "Why would you look at that...My, if that isn't quite the sight...Greasy Italians, digger Injuns and pig tails all just sitting together as happy as clams...This has got to change, boys...Why this town's going to the dogs..."

Po had heard it all before, and tried always to stay away from controversy. As long as they kept mostly to themselves, and concentrated on nothing but providing a cleaning service, their presence in town had been tolerated. Going out in public to social functions by themselves, let alone with such a diverse group, was sure to set tongues wagging. Why it would even be bad for business, Po reasoned.

It was Dom and Angelina's faces that made Po put aside his reservations. Both of them were beaming with good humor and enthusiasm, and saying how eager they were to watch Walter pitch, and maybe strike out that bully Butch and some of his rowdy pals. They begged them to come and bring some food along too. Eating while watching the baseball was the latest thing, Dom seriously explained.

Po did have a nice bottle of rice wine he had purchased a while back in Santa Rosa, and Mai had made a fresh batch of egg rolls just that morning, and it was a glorious afternoon. And yes, they did like Pino, Walter, little Fred, and most of the Pomos they had met. How could they possibly say no to their best friends in this at times unfriendly town? Po looked over at his wife, who wall all smiles listening to Angelina talk about how she wasn't going to let the sight of a hearse going up to the cemetery ruin her enjoyment of the game. He knew that she would love to sit next to Angelina and trade gossip and talk about gardening and such.

Dismissing his fears, Po agreed to go, and after quickly changing clothes and packing the food and wine in a small basket, the Lings climbed aboard the wagonette, told Suen to close up early, and left for the ballpark.

They turned down Piper Street, a straight, dusty road lined with a few houses, many open lots and small orchards. The street ran east towards Fitch Mountain, but after crossing a small creek abruptly ended and turned into a narrow lane that led to Oak Mound Cemetery, where the town's founder was buried, as well as members of the pioneering Fitch family.

As they neared the ballpark, they began to see more people walking or riding bicycles, or in wagons proceeding in the same direction.

"Seems like there's lots of interest in the game," Dom noted.

"I think people want to try sitting in those new bleachers," Po said, as they parked and tied the horses alongside several other wagons.

Dom gave the horse a flake of hay he had brought along, and soon they were walking amongst some newly planted sycamores towards the ball field. They were amazed to see the town's mayor there, selling tickets for admission. "Five cents a ticket" the sign behind him said, "Proceeds go towards the purchasing of uniforms for next year."

"Wow, they're taking this baseball pretty serious," Angelina commented.

"Angie, look over there," Dom said. "Now, that's something really amazing."

They all looked in the direction he was pointing and saw a Mexican family near the back of the bleachers selling fresh tamales also at five cents each. They had made a small fire and had suspended an iron box with a hinged lid on the front by a tripod set up. The aroma wafting from the box told them it was stuffed with tasty tamales.

"Why, we didn't even need to bring food," Dom said. "I'm going to buy one of those tamales right now. Anyone else? The treat's on me."

Everyone wanted a tamale, and shortly they were making their way up the bleacher seats. They sat in the row where Pino, Fred, Melanie, and Betty Mae were already sitting.

"Dominico," Pino said. "You're just in time, the games going to start pretty soon. Two full teams just like Walter hoped. Angelina, don't forget you said you'd sit by me," and Pino held up the sack of jerky and red onion.

"Of course, I haven't forgotten Pino, but Dom's got to sit on the other side of me. I want to be the only woman at the game who is surrounded by dashing gentlemen."

"If I sit on your lap, Angelina, you'll really be surrounded," Fred spoke up, grinning.

"That's true, Fred, but you're a little big for my lap. Next time though, it would be an honor if you were to sit by me," Angelina said, giving him one of her ravishing smiles.

The bleachers began to fill, prompting Dom to look closer at the construction. Not long after moving to redwood country, he had learned the way that boards were measured. These bleachers were mostly constructed of 2" by 8" boards, bolted and nailed together with 4" by 6" timber supports running to the ground that rested on wide slabs of redwood.

"I hope these seats can support everyone," he casually mentioned to Po, who was hunkered down, hat pulled low on head.

"Have you noticed people have been staring at us, Dom?" Po remarked.

"Yes, Po. Looks like we represent one of the most diverse groups anyone in this town has seen."

Fred had been listening closely, and leaned towards the men and said, "Walter told me that in San Francisco everyone sits together at big events, and they don't even hit one another with sticks or clubs. They all just get excited together and cheer."

"Sounds good to me, Fred," Mai spoke up. "But you'll have to tell me when to cheer because I have no idea what is going on."

"When the game starts, just watch Walter, and when he strikes out a batter, just start yelling like me," he said seriously.

"What is 'strike out'?" Mai asked.

"It's when the batter swings at the ball and misses, that's a strike. Or if the batter doesn't swing at the ball, but the ball is over the plate, that too is a strike if the umpire says so. When a batter gets three strikes, he is out. It's simple," Fred declared.

"Oh yes, simple," Mai repeated, looking over at Po, who shrugged his shoulders and raised his eyebrows.

"Look the games going to start," Melanie announced. "Walter's walking out to the mound."

The players had been standing together in a group under a large valley oak. Nine of them came forward and took their positions in the outfield and infield. The players who were to bat sat on boxes lined up along the third base side.

Dom started laughing, "Those players could really use uniforms. Look how they're all dressed."

Each player indeed was dressed a little different from the others. Some looked like they had come straight from the ranch or farm in dusty denim coveralls, work boots, and straw hats. Others wore their Sunday best and round derbies. A few lumberjacks were there in high-laced boots and thick plaid shirts and knit caps. Two off duty trainmen were playing, one in his conductor's uniform, the other in his engineer's clothes. A couple of mechanics who worked at the livery stable were there in grease-and-soot-stained shirts and pants. The person who looked oddly the most out of place was the young farmer, the one everyone called "Big Swede." When his father had heard he was going to play baseball, he had decided his son should only have the best. The Sears Roebuck catalog at the General Store showed a picture of a real baseball uniform, so he sent away for it. The first player coming to bat was about six foot four, two hundred and fifty pounds, had long blonde hair, and was wearing a uniform he could barely fit into, with a large number on the back, and the word "Giants" on the front.

A round of laughter from the bleachers greeted the "Big Swede," who took off his round cap with a long bill, and laughing himself, waved at the crowd.

He took his stance at the plate and menacingly waved his bat. Walter went into his wind up and threw the ball as fast as he could straight over the plate. Big Swede had barely seen the ball, let alone had time to swing at it.

"Strike one," the empire yelled out.

Fred and Mai immediately started clapping. Mai nudged Po, who began clapping too, as did the others sitting on the row.

"Dom, this might be kind of fun after all," Angelina said, reaching for some of the peanuts.

"It's making me hungry already," Pino added, reaching for an onion.

"Me too," Melanie said, munching on a toasted grasshopper.

Betty Mae, who had been sitting on the other side of Pino announced, "It's making me excited," and dropped her small well-shaped hand on Pino's knee.

In a matter of seconds the first batter was gone. Walter had struck him out on four pitches. Big Swede had only made one clumsy attempt at swinging the bat. The next two batters didn't fare much better, and soon the first half of the inning was over.

Now that there was a break in the game, Dom had more of an opportunity to look around. He gazed off towards the narrow road that led to the cemetery and was glad to note, for Angelina's sake, that no dark travelers were ascending. Looking off to the side and back of the bleachers, he noticed that the tamale vendors were doing a brisk business, and that the mayor was still selling tickets. For a moment he couldn't believe his eyes when there buying tickets were his old friends the Nutis.

"Angelina, the Nutis are here! Look!" He said, pointing.

Angelina was amazed. She hadn't seen Primo and Pietro since the wedding. They seemed to be in the company of a good-looking younger fellow who was talking to them, as they proceeded on towards the bleachers.

"Excuse me, Angie, I'm going to go down and meet them. I wonder what's brought them to Healdsburg. Wine buying possibly," he mused.

The Nutis immediately waved at Dom when they saw him walking rapidly towards them.

"Primo, Pietro! What are you guys doing here? And what a pleasant surprise! And who's your young friend here? He's got the look of a paisano about him," Dom said, shaking hands all around.

"This is Frank Augustino, Dom. You guessed it. His dad's a Tuscano. Frank's sharp eye and good work is what's brought us here," Primo said. "Angelina's here, right?"

Dom nodded, smiling.

"Well, you better go get her. She's going to want to hear all this. But first I'll tell you briefly. Frank's got news about Conchetta. She's definitely alive. He's even caught a glimpse of her. But we think that Gypsy fellow she's been traveling with has been keeping her against her wishes. Kidnapped, it would seem," Primo added.

Dom noted the seriousness in the men's faces. *This sounds like both good news and bad news,* he thought.

"I'll get Angelina right now, Primo. This is astounding news," and turning, he walked rapidly back towards the ball field and the cheering crowd.

Chapter 18

Frank Augustino was tired. He was in a quandary, dealing with the fact that he hadn't been getting enough sleep lately. He knew his mind was a little confused, so he began to think of the words that his mother had told him.

"In Finland, when men get confused, they get drunk. And after they get drunk, they get to work."

Well, it was way too early to get drunk, so without thinking too much, he bought a ticket that would take him in the quickest manner from San Jose to San Francisco. He paid extra to have Tuli loaded into a boxcar where there were several other horses. Then he boarded the train, found a comfortable seat, and tried to get some sleep.

Since he was a young boy his mother, Annikki, had told him stories of growing up in Finland. Finland was a land where superstitious beliefs died hard, she explained. Though Christianity had spread to Finland around the early Middle Ages, many of the people still clung to notions that originated in the pagan past. Shamans, sorcerers, and conjurors still moved around mysteriously in this cold country, especially in the north, she had said.

One of these traveling conjurors had stayed once at their house at her father's invitation. He told stories around the fire late into the night. One of the tales had stuck in Annikki's mind, and she in turn had passed the tale on to her son. It was actually more of a technique than a tale; a way of looking into the future using sleep and dreaming, and it had to be practiced often to assure success. Right when you're beginning to feel yourself falling asleep, doors that lead to the future are opened, the old man had explained. All one had to do was find one of these doors, enter it, and begin dreaming. The trick was to wake up, remember the dream, and notice if elements of the dream eventually came to pass. Annikki had found the thought of this actually working truly amazing, and many nights had tried the technique with mixed results. A few times she was convinced that what she had dreamt indeed had come true several days later.

Stretching his legs out in front of him and pulling his hat down over his eyes, Frank concentrated on the sound of the train wheels passing on down the tracks. His intention was to let the train lull him to sleep. He needed to find a door. A door that would lead him to Conchetta, who had left on this same train a week earlier. He was tired, and it wasn't long before he felt himself falling asleep. A reddish hue appeared before his closed eyes, and a blue door briefly came into view. Frank felt himself walking towards the door, then fell deep into sleep.

An hour or so later, when he awoke, he remembered part of a dream. In the dream he saw himself swimming in cold water staring up into the face of Conchetta, who was slowly moving away. *Swimming in cold water*, he mused. *That would be all right if I had just come out of a good hot sauna. Why do I still try this hocus-pocus? Ma sure enjoyed filling me with stories.*

Part of him, though, was excited, for within himself he knew, just as his mother, that several times such dreams had come true. The little nap actually had refreshed him, and gazing out the window at the golden rolling hills passing by, he planned out his next moves. When the train arrived in San Francisco, he led Tuli down the gangplank to solid ground, saddled, and mounted the horse, and rode off to Primo Nuti's office. Primo was astounded upon hearing all the information Frank had uncovered and pieced together concerning Conchetta. Together the two men planned out a course of action that they hoped would lead them to her.

Primo would begin by explaining all they knew to the police. He doubted though that they would be much help. San Francisco was the largest city in California, a city rife with crime and much of it violent. Searching for a woman who may or may not be traveling with someone against her will would be low priority. The fact that the man claimed to be her husband certainly didn't help matters either.

Their best hope in the search for Conchetta seemed to be putting the word out on the streets. Primo knew lots of people who would be more than willing to help. Using the picture of Conchetta, he had an artist friend draw up many copies depicting her. They were astonishingly accurate, and looked exactly like the photograph. These he distributed to people he knew in various sections of the city. If anyone saw a woman who fit the drawing, they were to immediately notify Primo's office or the police. Two officers, who were good acquaintances of his, agreed to aid in any way they could, and had believed him when he had expressed his suspicions and fears for Conchetta's safety.

Frank went to the livery stables and the waterfront, where boats could be rented or chartered, and where the ferries departed. He also went to the train stations, showing Conchetta's picture and leaving off one of the artist's copies at each place, suggesting they tack it up on the wall. No one, so far, had seen a woman who they thought was Conchetta.

Both Primo and Frank were highly suspicious concerning the page of newspaper with the town of Healdsburg and its new church underlined, with the heart and arrow drawn alongside. The little farming town to the north certainly could be a possible destination. One either had to cross the bay or go around it to get there. If Juan and Conchetta had headed directly for the town they would already be there.

Primo wired the local police describing the two and briefly explained the situation. He even sent a friend off on the train with a drawing of Conchetta. The man was to show the drawing at all the train stops in the hopes that someone at a ticket office may have seen her. The irony of the fact that Conchetta could be destined to arrive in, of all places, the same town where her sister lived hadn't escaped him. Frank too had commented on this, wondering if fate indeed was drawing Conchetta to her sister.

Frank Augustino was so deeply involved in the search for Conchetta that he could think of nothing else. Shortly after arriving back in San Francisco, he had visited his parents and explained to them what he had been doing, and his fears for the beautiful woman whose picture he had showed them. Immediately, both could tell from the passion in their son's voice and the fierce look in his eyes that he was smitten—smitten by the picture of a woman he hadn't even met. What if this Conchetta was legally married and all the suspicion and fear concerning her was simply a mistake? They hoped their son wasn't in for a big disappointment. Frank usually behaved, for the most part, in a rational, intelligent manner. How could he be acting like some star-struck schoolboy who had fallen head-over-heels with a picture of, say, Lilly Langtree for instance.

They mentioned this to him in somewhat of a casual manner, simply saying, "Frank, aren't you getting a little personally involved in all this?"

They watched their son's face turn a little red. He assured them in a defensive manner that this was all strictly business and reminded them that this was a job. Primo had been paying him rather well for his services. Well, he was a big boy and they knew that there really wasn't much they could say or do. At least he was working, so to speak, and had mentioned a renewed interest in finishing college and attending law school.

For two days Frank roamed the city looking for and inquiring about Conchetta. He could tell that some people he spoke to thought him a fool, some type of obsessive possibly looking for his runaway wife. Moving about the sprawling city began to depress him. There were too many small, ragged children working in deplorable conditions. Working when they should be in school. Many of them were laboring along the docks, cleaning or moving fish, their filthy clothing covered with gut and scales and reeking of rotten flesh. He saw other young boys working in lumberyards trying to carry boards too heavy for them, or raking or gathering bark into large piles, their wood-oil-stained fingers riddled with splinters from the great redwoods. Boys, prematurely bent with dull eyes, were working alongside men old enough to be their grandfathers, unloading iron rails for the trolley system from boxcar after boxcar. He saw one boy fall under the weight of the load, hitting his knees hard on the shale-lined earth.

"Get up, you lazy little curr," he heard a dapper dressed man in a stovepipe hat yell out.

This was in a part of the city where factories were belching out coal smoke so thick, that when it mingled with the fog, it covered your face and body with a damp grime. Frank thought of the conditions the farmworkers in the valley were working under. Some of these young boys he had seen certainly weren't fairing much better.

All this, mingled with the futile feeling that he was spending his time looking for a needle in a haystack, had put him in a pretty black mood. By the late afternoon he found himself walking along the embarcadero sipping on a half pint of whiskey he had purchased in the hopes of shrugging off the spell of melancholia he was under. Hearing the barking of sea lions, he walked closer to the water to have a look. A small boat was pulling away from the dock. Two people occupied seats near the aft with their backs to him. One was a thin man, his hand extended, holding the wrist of a woman with long black hair. The woman suddenly turned her head and looked in back of her. Conchetta Lombardi's eyes bore straight into Frank Augustino's.

Frank reacted automatically. He dropped the whiskey bottle he was holding and dove headfirst into the cold waters of San Francisco Bay. At the sound of the splash, Juan turned to see a man swimming strongly towards the boat.

"Conchetta," the man yelled out.

"Yes," Conchetta cried, as Juan clamped his hand over her mouth, his other hand drew out the heavy revolver from under his jacket.

He shoved it in her ribs saying, "Utter one word, Lombardi, and whomever that is swimming towards you gets a bullet in the head. I'll shoot that pilot too if I have to. I can get this boat across the bay."

So far the pilot hadn't seemed to hear a thing. His back was to them, his hands upon the wheel. Through flailing arms and spray, Frank had seen what happened to Conchetta and swam with all his might. In seconds he had caught up with the boat and reached out and grabbed the gunnel. Juan was waiting. He lashed out with the revolver, bringing it down hard on Frank's head. Frank saw a blinding light and his hand relaxed its grip on the boat. He treaded water for a second, blood running down into his eyes. He began to feel himself losing consciousness and knew he was about to drown. His body began to sink under the water. For some reason, the thought of a blue swan moving down a dark river filled his mind. Then all went black. His mouth involuntarily opened, and he began to swallow cold seawater. The sensation must have brought him to his senses. In the next instant he was struggling to regain the surface. He felt he was going to pass out again just as he broke water, gasping for air and choking. He forced himself to stay afloat, consciously treading water and staring at the boat moving across the bay. If he wanted to stay alive, he had to get back to shore as fast as possible. He was dizzy, and the possibility of passing out again was too real. Weakly, but steadily, he swam back to the dock. A hand reached down and helped him out of the water and on to the dock.

"Say, Mister, you're lucky to be alive. I saw the whole thing. That fellow hit you something fierce."

Frank tried to focus on the man. He was old, toothless, with a long gray beard. Frank tried to stand, but his legs gave out from under him and he sat back down.

"Thanks for helping me out of the water, friend. Could you do me another favor and help me to that warehouse? I think if I could sit over there with my back against the wall I might be all right in a while. If I do happen to pass out could you see I get some help?"

Frank reached into his pocket and came up with a wet one-dollar bill. The man's eyes opened wide.

"Why sure, son. You bet," he said, and helped him to his feet and over to the warehouse.

Frank sat down heavily, his back against the wall. His eyes caught sight of the whiskey bottle lying unbroken on the ground. He could see some of the brown liquid still inside.

"Could you get me that bottle over there, friend? I dropped it a while back."

The man retrieved the bottle. There was still about an inch of whiskey in it. Frank sipped it slowly.

"Could you stay with me for a while until I get my bearing friend? I'd offer you a drink, but right now I'm afraid I probably need it more than you."

"Why, of course, young fella. I see a little color coming back to you. Let me take a look at that gash on your head."

Frank reached into his back pocket and brought out a handkerchief and handed it to the man.

"What's your name, friend?"

"Bob," the man answered, folding the handkerchief and placing it on Frank's head. "Better keep your hand on it until the bleeding stops. The cut doesn't look that bad, but you're going to have a hell of a goose egg up there."

Frank sat against the building, choking up a little water from time to time. The dizziness was starting to leave him. Soon he got up and tested his legs. He felt strong enough to walk. He thanked Bob, who never asked him what all this had been about, and walked off to find a ride that would take him to Primo's office. He was just too weak to try to go after Conchetta on his own. He could tell he wasn't thinking straight. The streets didn't even seem familiar to him. The term concussion came to his mind. Primo would know what to do. He had to get to Primo's office. On wobbly legs he moved away from the waterfront. He wasn't even sure how many minutes had passed. Turning around, he looked out on the bay. Many boats were moving, but the one with Conchetta aboard was nowhere in sight.

Juan Fuentes arrived in San Francisco wide-eyed. Santiago Chile had been an old, venerable city teaming with people. A sophisticated city compared to what he saw before him. San Francisco was alive with noise and activity. Building was going on everywhere.

Upon arrival from San Jose, he and Conchetta had boarded one of the many horse-drawn cabs lined up at the depot. Juan had simply told the driver to take them to the main part of the city. He immediately was enthralled with the excitement of the place, and he looked about with a sense of wonderment. The city seemed to be a series of hills, up and down, up and down, and each street filled with the sound of hammers and saws. Before they had traveled more than a few blocks, he lost track of how many different languages he had heard. People of all nationalities walked the streets and passed by on wagons.

Conchetta was excited too. Though her ankle still bothered her some and kept her from moving at full speed, she felt like making a dash for it, and would have bolted from the cab when it slowed if Juan hadn't been sitting so close to her, with a derringer he had bought in San Jose pressed against her side. The reality that here she was, back in the city she knew so well, with people about that she may even have known, that had known her, galled her to the marrow. Freedom was just within her grasp, but the cold steel of the derringer that rubbed against her every time the little cab hit a bump forced her to continue biding time and avoid a futile attempt at escape.

They were approaching the side street where Angelina's little café was. Conchetta's heart beat faster thinking about her sister. By now, Angelina must think she was dead, having mysteriously vanished from Monterey without a trace. There was still a dim ray of hope though. Angelina and Mario were not quitters. They would be doing all that was within their powers to locate her, or seek news concerning her.

Why, Angelina would probably be at her café right now! She had to get Juan to proceed down that side street. What if her sister was out front sweeping off the wood sidewalk and saw her! Instantly, she realized what the consequences could be. She could get her sister shot. Angelina would rush out to the cab, and Juan could shoot her. Shoot the driver for that matter. Take over the reins and try for a desperate escape. So many times he had said to her that he had nothing to lose, and didn't give a damn about his own death. She wanted desperately, though, to just see the café. She could sit way back in the cab and avert her head at the last second.

"Juan, where are you going? I know this city well, probably better than this driver," Conchetta said.

"I just want to see the center of this Sodom and Gomorrah of the west. That's what I've heard it called in print."

"Well, have the driver turn down the next street. You can get there much quicker. I'm starting to get hungry," Conchetta said, feigning a pout.

"You Italian slut. That's all you think about is food. Very well, I've noticed less traffic on these side streets. I suppose we would make better time."

Juan had the driver turn down the street where Angelina's café stood. Shortly, the small redwood building with the bark still clinging to it came into view. Conchetta's eyes began to fill with tears at the sight of it, but something had changed. A new sign was out front that read "Café Clementine, B. Sayer Prop." As the cab pulled even, she casually looked straight at the place. It looked dirtier than she had ever seen it. Globs of mud were splattered against the siding, and several of the boards had come loose. The reality that her sister no longer owned the place jolted her into alertness. Quickly and discreetly, she rubbed away the tears that had fallen down her cheeks.

"The driver should take a right at the next corner. That street leads right to the center of the city," she casually told Juan.

As they neared their destination, the buildings around them changed from wood to brick. Multi-storied buildings, many of them even pleasing to the eye, loomed above the little cab.

"Market and Van Ness," Conchetta said. "I guess you could call this the center of town. A city this size can have many centers," she added.

"Certainly are plenty of hotels and restaurants," Juan said. "I'll buy you a good dinner, Lombardi. Just remember, if you want to continue to feed that stomach of yours, don't try a thing."

Juan had the cab pull up at an elegant-looking little restaurant called Valentino's, and soon they were ordering food.

"Let's splurge, Gypsy queen. How about pheasant under glass, saffron rice, and a fine French champagne," Juan announced, putting away the menu.

Conchetta was more sick than hungry. She just nodded at Juan and pretended to be interested in the decorations appointing the restaurant. Where was Angelina? What had transpired since the last time she had heard from her? A great depression and sadness assailed her. A sense of utter hopelessness seemed to unfold before her. She almost wished she was under the influence of the drug, at least then life didn't appear so real.

Juan hadn't tried to rape her lately. She knew it was because of his injuries.

"I think we should begin with some oysters," Juan quietly said, looking straight at Conchetta with a gleam in his eyes. "We are going to have to find a hotel later, and I do believe my injuries have healed to the point where I may be able to enjoy you for dessert. Certainly would be cheaper than ordering something here. The pricing in this place is really quite extravagant," he said nonchalantly.

Conchetta glared at Juan and snapped. She grabbed a fork, leaned forward, and jabbed it straight at Juan's eye. In a flash he had grabbed her wrist.

"Oh, temper, temper, Conchetta. Just sit back down. Now!" he commanded. I came close just now to letting the derringer under the table send a bullet between those pretty legs. Now, don't get excited. What would you rather have, a bullet up there or me?"

Juan looked around. It was early, few people were in the restaurant, and no one seemed to be paying any attention to them. Conchetta was sitting back normally in her seat, she reached out and picked up the fork she had dropped on the table. *He keeps threatening to kill me, but he's had plenty of opportunities. He's afraid of getting caught. That slimy weasel doesn't want to die. Everything he says and does is an act,* she reminded herself again.

When the meal arrived, she forced herself to eat. She drank one glass of champagne. Juan drank the rest and became in turns both jovial and sarcastic. He would brag about the quality of the food, and what pleasure he was going to have later in the hotel, and the next instant hurl insults at Conchetta, criticizing her sunken cheeks, and her lack of appreciation for fine champagne and delicate saffron.

From time to time, out of the corner of her eye, Conchetta glanced at Juan daintily eating pheasant, carving it carefully into small pieces. He was dressed in the new suit he had bought in San Jose; black coat and pants, white shirt and black, pinstriped vest with gold brocade and shiny red buttons down the front, a silk tie was nattily tied around his neck. With his long fingers, bony hands, and pointed elbows, sitting in a hunched position over his food, he reminded her of a thin black widow spider who had reluctantly ventured out to feed.

The dinner over, he paid and left a big tip. Out in the street, a cab was nearby. They got in, and Juan told the driver to take them to a hotel, a good hotel, but one away from the hustle and bustle of Market and Van Ness.

A while later the cab pulled up to an imposing brick structure at the end of a street, near the waterfront. Paying the driver and grabbing their bags Juan and Conchetta entered the hotel; he signing the register "Mr. and Mrs. Carlos Rivera, Los Angeles, Ca." Once inside the room, Juan unpacked his bag, setting aside some chain and a lock, short pieces of rope, and a cloth he could use as a gag. Conchetta sat in a chair, not speaking a word, just watching him as he took sips from a bottle of brandy he had withdrawn from the bag. He preened in front of a large mirror above the dresser. Removing a comb from his pocket, he began running it through his thin hair, which he wore straight back. Thinking he looked his finest, he turned and addressed Conchetta in a low voice.

"Well, slut, I'm going to take you now, and I'm going to do it by knife point. If you cooperate, maybe I won't slide the blade across your throat when I'm done, as I did to that useless nun in San Juan Bautista."

Conchetta bolted from the chair. In an instant she had a pitcher of water from a nightstand in her hands and sought to bring it down on Juan. He sprang nimbly off to the side and the pitcher shattered harmlessly on the floor. He hit her hard alongside the head, stunning her. Grabbing the rope from the dresser, he quickly tied her hands then gagged her. He pushed her over the bed and using his knife ripped away her dress and undergarments. But something was going wrong. By this point, he should have been enlarged. This time, nothing at all was happening. Conchetta, struggling on the bed, the smooth skin on her well-shaped rear before him, was having no affect.

"I curse that gringo who's ruined me," he spoke out, sitting heavily on the bed, and beginning to cry.

Conchetta had rolled onto her side and stared in revulsion and fear at Juan. His back was to her and his narrow shoulders heaved in tune with the quiet sobs that were coming from him. *Now, surely he's going to kill me,* she reasoned. *What use could he have of me now? Sex seems to be out of the question.*

Juan stopped sobbing. He sat still for a moment, then took a deep breath. He walked around to Conchetta's side of the bed and arranged her shredded dress more neatly about her. She glared up at him and saw eyes that were completely vacant, and lips molded in a pout, tears were still running down his cheeks. Suddenly and roughly, he bound her feet to the bedpost, and ran a rope from her tied hands to the upper post. He took the piece of cloth and gagged her.

His eyes grew alive as he snarled out, "Evidently the lingering pain in my groin is still having an effect. I must need more resting time is all. After tonight we'll do nothing but rest and eat for say five or six days, then we shall proceed on. Perhaps after five or six days we can practice this little scene all over again. Sounds good, eh, Conchetta?" he said, lowering his face to hers, and blowing in her ear. "Right now, I feel the need of alcohol and conviviality. You just lie quietly there and get your beauty rest. Why, if you've been a good girl while I'm gone, tomorrow I'll buy you a nice new dress. Something cheerful. I think solid dark blue would suit you fine. I know you'll miss me while I'm out. Luckily there are two beds in this room, or else I'd have to move you to the floor when I return. A soft mattress and perhaps hot compresses is what I need. Yes, tomorrow I'll arrange for plenty of hot water to be brought up. A drug store might even have something that could aid in my recovery. Why, yes, I think I feel better already. A few stiff drinks right now would probably be just what the doctor ordered," he announced happily and walked out the door, locking it behind him.

Conchetta lay still on the bed. The throbbing in her head matching the beating of her heart. For a while she tried to reason why he was keeping her alive, then realized the futility of this. He was crazy. Crazy people didn't have logical reasons for their behavior. When he came back to the room, her life could end right then and there. Just as easily, the madness could continue, and on it would go—the madman and his wife. She dwelled on what had just transpired. In her young life she never had a real lover. A few discreet kisses by suitors, who for one reason or another had amounted to nothing, had been the extent of it. She had just now come close to being raped for a second time. If she survived all this and got away, would life ever be normal for her? She wondered. What if one day she did fall in love and met a kind, wonderful man? Could, or should, she tell him what had transpired during her time kept captive by an insane murderer? With these thoughts in mind, she finally drifted into a troubled sleep.

El Zapo roamed the early evening on foot until he came to the first saloon he saw. Entering, he was greeted by walls lined with paintings. Many of them were large and in ornate frames. Each one had a candle burning beneath it, illuminating the figures and scenes in an otherwise dark saloon. The place was pretty lively; there were few empty stools at the bar. Juan sat at one in between a woman, that he figured by her dress and state of intoxication was a prostitute, and an older fellow, dressed impeccably. Probably a businessman or even a lawyer, he imagined. Neither recognized his presence. He ordered a double brandy, drank it off quickly, and ordered another one. The alcohol felt nice and warm going down. After his second drink, he ordered a third, then a fourth. His gaze became transfixed on two paintings directly in back of the bar. One was of Jesus whimsically drawn in white robes, a serene look on his face, ascending arms outstretched up to heaven, an adoring multitude beneath him. The other painting was of a naked, voluptuous woman reclining sideways on a large white bull, her heavy breasts resting on the back of the animal. Juan, staring at the two diverse paintings, wondered what it could all mean. The fraud, Jesus, with all the gullible fools at his feet, alongside a naked woman, who resembled the Madonna in facial appearance, at ease on a bull, an ancient pagan symbol of fertility and dominance. Finishing off one more drink, it all became clear to him. The woman in the painting with the long dark hair, large, soulful eyes, and sunken cheeks looked just like Conchetta. The bull was Juan, and that coward Jesus was running away to hide behind his unjust father!

He couldn't wait to get back to the hotel and explain to Conchetta his revelation. He purchased a half pint of brandy and left the saloon. After walking several blocks, drinking along the way, he realized he was much drunker than he should be. He was proceeding down a street he had no recollection of. He was lost. He turned down a short alley, lurching into some stacked crates and upturned barrels, and staggered to the ground. At daylight he awoke, his head pounding and the dull pain in his groin reminding him of his foolishness.

Wearily, he got up and moved off to find the hotel. Shortly, he found a familiar street. He passed by a grocery and bought some food. Upon reaching the hotel he dusted off his clothes as best he could, and trying to look dignified, nodded to the clerk and proceeded up the stairs. He unlocked the door and found Conchetta still asleep. He threw himself on the other bed and within seconds was fast asleep.

Several hours later he awoke. Conchetta was lying on the bed, eyes wide open. He looked at her and felt that he needed to tell her something, but he couldn't remember what it was. Why this morning did she remind him so much of the Madonna, he ruminated. He untied her and removed the gag, telling her to help herself to the food in a sack on the table.

So began another four or five days of rest and recuperation for El Zapo. He had food brought to the room, relaxed in hot baths, even ventured out briefly to buy Conchetta two new dresses and some books for himself. Always, he had his revolver or knife at hand, and showed them during the day to Conchetta from time to time. Every night she was bound and gagged. During the day he encouraged her to read. She would love Dante's *Inferno*, or could finish up *Don Quixote*, which she had started reading up on Penitencia Creek. He had the papers brought up daily. Finally he felt better and was surely well enough to travel, he decided. Healdsburg and a nunnery are beckoning, he said to himself.

One afternoon, bags in hand, Juan and Conchetta left the hotel and boarded a cab for the waterfront. Juan's intention was to board a ferry, cross the bay, and continue on by train to Healdsburg. They arrived at the point of departure to see the ferry, loaded with passengers pulling away.

"Damn it," Juan uttered out loud.

A man in dirty sailors clothes standing nearby overheard.

"Hey, Mister, looks like you've missed your boat. I'll take you and the pretty lady across the bay, for a slight fee, of course."

Juan immediately agreed and paid the man. They pulled away from the dock and hadn't gone far when Juan heard a loud splash behind him. He turned to look and saw a man swimming hard towards the boat.

"Conchetta," the swimmer yelled out.

"Yes," she answered.

He reacted instantly. He clamped his hand over her mouth, grabbed his revolver, held it on her, and threatened to shoot everyone. When the swimmer reached out and caught the boat, he came down with the gun on the man's head. For a moment he thought the man was going to drown, and then was disappointed and angered when he saw him surface and swim weakly to the docks.

Who was the man? For the first time since he had taken Conchetta, he felt true fear. The man spoke her name so forcefully, and dove in the cold waters heedlessly to try and reach her. He began to feel like he might be hunted. He would have to make new plans and think fast upon crossing the bay.

Still holding the gun, and pressing the barrel into Conchetta, Juan said, "Seems you may have an admirer, perhaps a hero coming to your rescue, Gypsy queen. Sit straight now and look lively. Soon we'll be across this bay. Just keep cooperating, Lombardi, if you want to live, and don't say a word. Something is amiss, and I've got to think."

Chapter 19

Dave Fowler carefully packed two horses. He told his parents he was going to spend a week or so fixing up an abandoned shack and deer hunting.

"Who knows," he said. "I might even come back loaded with bear meat, and you could have a nice rug, Ma," he bragged confidently.

He rode off slowly down Dry Creek Road towards town. Turning on a trail that led off into oaks and madrones, he dismounted and began to change his clothes. When he emerged back on the road, he was in the dress of a dime magazine gunslinger; black trousers and coat, frilly white shirt, fancy leather boots, and black ten-gallon hat. A 36-caliber navy Colt was slung low on his hip and a 41-caliber Philadelphia derringer rested snugly in his inner coat pocket. He would have preferred to sweep Suen Ling off her feet by the light of the moon, but figured now would be the perfect time. Most of the town would probably be at that stupid baseball game. Why a thinking man like Butch Baylow would even want to set foot in the same field as that stinking smart-alecky Injun Walter was beyond reasoning. *Must be that stupid little ball and bat, and running around them bases that's got everyone addled*, he concluded.

Riding at an even, steady pace into town gave him time to think. He began to question what he was doing. There was really no need for any of this. What he was planning on doing could get him thrown in jail, maybe even shot. He should just turn around and go home. Hell, if he wanted a woman that bad, he should go see the whores in Santa Rosa. But what if he went to see the whore and nothing happened? What if his member would just sit there shrunken? Why, the woman would laugh at him of course. Now the thought of sweeping a struggling Suen off her feet, and throwing her on the bed of a honeymoon shack, began to excite him a little right then and there. Even if something went wrong, alone up in that desolate place, no one would know. If Suen didn't want to marry him or had laughed at him, he would just have to kill her and hide the body. *It's all really pretty simple,* he decided, and with a new resolve and a tightened jaw, he urged his horse on at a quicker pace towards the Ling's laundry.

Reaching town, it looked just like he figured. The place was pretty dead. Even the beer garden only had one horse tied up out front. A cool beer sure would taste good about now, he decided. Passing by the beer garden without stopping in for at least one, was a habit that was hard to break. Thinking about Suen and his plans, Dave had momentarily forgotten how he was dressed. He caught himself, just as he was ready to dismount and tie up the horses.

"I can't go in there dressed like this," he suddenly realized and started to turn away. Just then Al, the bartender, came out, broom in hand, intending to sweep off the plank sidewalk.

"Whew-wee, is that you, Dave? Where you heading off to dressed up so fancy? Why, you're even wearing your gun. What are you up to boy?"

Dave wasn't used to having to think fast. Thinking fast sometimes even made him stutter.

He did his best, and trying to act casual said, "I'm going into Poor Man's Flats as soon as I deliver this horse. They're having a shooting contest over there, so I hear. First prize is a new shotgun."

"Why, I haven't heard of no shooting contest over in the Flats," Al said. "Where'd you hear of something like that?"

"Why, one of them sheep ranchers out there told me about it. Supposed to be some type of fancy private fiesta going on out there, and I've been invited."

"David, someone's been pulling your leg. A saloon keeper would have heard of something like that, and I ain't heard a thing."

"Well, Al, I guess you just don't know as much as you think you know. Good-bye now, Mr. Know-it-all," and off Dave rode.

Traveling down the main street he cursed himself. *How could I have been so stupid? I had planned on being seen by as few people as possible. And who do I run into? The town's biggest blabbermouth. I should just turn around and go home right now if I've got a lick of sense,* he thought.

He needed time to think. Moving south out of town, he turned off onto a narrow little lane that ended abruptly at a small creek. Foss Creek, people were starting to call it, after Clark Foss, who took tourists up to the Geysers Resort with his six-horse team.

Dave paused at the little creek and began thinking about Geysers Road and the "romantic getaway." *All those people going up the mountain to take the cure at the Geyser's Resort, and me and my celestial bride, Suen, selling figs, grapes, dried fruit and cold lemonade. Why, I'll bet I could convince old Foss to make our place a regular rest stop. "Our Place," sure like the sound of that,* he mused. *Well, I've come this far. No use turning back now. Strike while the iron's hot, as Pa often says.*

Turning back the way he came, he proceeded in a roundabout way towards Ling's Laundry. The town indeed looked deserted, except for several old folks sitting on porches, Dave saw no one coming in from the back way. He tied the horses to a fencepost at the head of the alley that ran alongside the laundry. On foot he proceeded, after seeing no one, down the alley where the broken fence boards provided a clear view of the laundry. He looked around sharply for the scruffy little dog that had pissed on him a day earlier.

I wish he'd come around, thought Dave. *I'd kick his little teeth in.*

Through the laundry window he could see movement inside. It was Suen! He watched her for a long time. She seemed to be the only one there.

I wonder if even her parents are at that stupid ball game. No, Chinese wouldn't be allowed at a baseball game. Americans invented it. No Chinaman ever invented a thing, except fireworks, he recollected proudly.

Dave kept looking about him, making sure that no one was around. It sure would seem odd if someone spotted him all dressed up and sporting a revolver hung low from a fancy belt and holster. He didn't look around for too long though. He had a hard time taking his eyes off of Suen. *She sure looks pretty there, folding clothes*, he thought, and leaned closer to the fence for a better view.

Suddenly he smelled something. He heard a noise and turned around to see the small scruffy dog running fast down the alley. He noticed a puddle seeping into the dirt near the back of his fancy boots! That damn mangy mutt had done it again. Pissed on the back of his leg, and he hadn't even felt it. His boots had shielded his legs from the warm moisture. Dave drew the revolver in anger and was ready to squeeze off a shot at the retreating dog, then caught himself. *Not the right time to go shooting a dog*, he thought. *I'll just wash that pant leg later is all*, he concluded in an offended manner. He reflected for a moment, think-ing about his pants. This was the first time that he had worn them out in public. And what had happened? They had gotten pissed on. The dream of swooping down on Suen and carrying her off her feet in a romantic manner had just been tainted. Tainted by a scruffy, mangy little dog's hot piss. Standing there in the dusty alley he could smell his pant leg. He decided to do something about it right then and there. All he needed was a bucket of water or a water trough. Probably be one at the end of the alley, he reasoned. He started to move off when he heard a door slam, and saw Suen emerge from the laundry carrying a basket of clothes.

No time for cleanliness now, he thought, and dashed back down the alley to the horses. Now's my moment. It's now or never, Dave said to himself, mounting his horse, leaving the other one tied to the fence post.

Charging down the alley and turning the corner onto the street, he immediately spotted Suen only a few feet ahead. She turned, hearing the sound of the pounding hoofs. Before she had time to react, Dave was upon her. He reached down and scooped Suen off her feet. The basket of clothes went flying from her hands. He bent her over in front of him on the horse and raced around the block. Dave had never felt so strong and powerful in all his life. Barely slowing his horse's stride, he had successfully swooped down on the beautiful girl and carried her away on the back of his mighty steed.

They should write about me in a magazine for this, he concluded, coming to the end of the alley where the other horse was tied.

Suen was so taken aback, she hadn't had much time to think. What was that smelly Davy doing? Kidnapping her? It had all happened so fast that it took her a moment to realize that indeed it was that idiot boy. Leaning over the horse, her head near his leg, she detected a strong odor of dog urine reeking off his pants. She could even see that his pant leg was wet.

"David Fowler, what are you doing? Put me down this instant," she yelled at him.

"Miss Ling, I know your pa won't let you go riding with me. This is the only way I can show you a romantic get-away," Dave said.

Suen's anger reached a crescendo and she started screaming, "Help! Help! Help!"

She was in the midst of another scream when Dave let her have it. He had been holding Suen down with his left arm, his hand entwined in her hair. With his right fist he struck down hard on Suen's head near the temple. Immediately she went limp and was out cold. He slid down off his horse and transferred Suen to the other one. He laid her across the middle, took a blanket from his side pack, and in seconds had her wrapped in it, trussed and tied securely to the horse and saddle. So far he hadn't seen a soul. He knew he had to move fast, carefully and boldly. Now wasn't the time for second-guessing and hesitating.

Getting back on his horse, he headed north out of town, Suen in tote. Taking back roads and narrow trails, he finally came out on the main road going northeast towards Alexander Valley. Along the way several people had seen him, but all from a distance. He knew that on the main road north out of town, as well as Alexander Valley Road, he was bound to meet up with people. He just hoped it wouldn't be anyone he knew. His plan was to ride at a steady comfortable pace directly through the valley, and up Geysers Road to the honeymoon shack. If he met people along the way, he was just going to keep his hat pulled low and ride on without saying a word.

Suen hadn't moved a muscle. He hoped he hadn't hit her too hard, but what choice had she given him? Her screaming like a panicky goat. He reached his hand under the blanket to where Suen's mouth was. He could feel warm air on his skin.

Hell, she'll be just fine, he figured. *Wait until she comes to and finds herself all nice and tucked away in a romantic getaway. So far things have been turning out just fine,* he concluded.

He didn't see a soul until he turned off the main road going north on to Alexander Valley Road. Off in the distance he could see two riders approaching at a gallop. Dave crossed his fingers, hoping that it wasn't someone that knew him. Hopefully they would just keep on moving. By the dust they were kicking up they seemed to be in a big hurry. The riders slowed as they approached Dave, putting their hands up and waving.

"Say, Mister," one of them yelled, still a few feet off. "Do you know if that baseball game has already started? We've been riding all the way from Knights Valley."

The riders were two boys, late teens Dave figured, neither one had he ever seen. Dave felt highly uncomfortable, but he thought it would seem odd if he didn't slow down and answer them.

"I know there's a game in town this afternoon, boys, but I don't know what time it was supposed to start."

The two young riders were staring at the body strapped down over the horse. One of the boys was cocking his head off to the side, looking at a mass of long black hair that had escaped the blanket and hung down the horse's flank.

The boy looked up quizzically at Dave, but before he could speak, Dave said, "Bringing my sister home for burial. She drowned in one of the deep pools around Fitch Mountain. Ma wants her buried near the oak tree she used to swing on. Pa died last year. Our family's all torn up."

Dave put his fist up to his eye as if trying to push back a tear. The boys took off their hats and shook their heads with downcast eyes.

"Real sad to hear it, Mister. Drowned around Fitch Mountain you say?"

Dave shook his head affirmatively, "Ma used to call her a little heathen. She was visiting a friend, and they climbed out on a rock to try and spear fish. Sally slipped and went under. Couldn't swim a lick. Sheer luck I suppose we even recovered the body. Can't dally anymore, boys. So long," Dave said, and rode off head hung low.

Why, that was fun, Dave said to himself. *I ought to consider moving to San Francisco and taking up acting. Dave Fowler, Lesbian, or is it Thespian? Oh hell, I can't remember which.*

On down the road he proceeded, anticipating the delight that awaited him at the honeymoon shack. After a while he came to the bridge that spanned the Russian River. The water was so low this time of year that normally he'd by pass the bridge and just wade across. But he figured it would be smoother on Suen if he used the bridge. The horse's hooves echoed loudly off the wooden planks.

Right before the end of the bridge, a ragged-looking man popped out from underneath it and said, "Say pal, could you spare a dime for an old veteran down on his luck? I been eating nothing but fish for three days. Sure would like to eat a biscuit once I get to town."

The man was filthy, even by Dave's standards. His clothes were ripped, he stank of rotten fish, and a couple of thistles were even clinging to his matted beard.

"You wouldn't know it to look at me, but I fought under General Winfield Scott. We took Vera Cruz and drove on straight to Mexico City. You ever hear about them kids at Chapultepec? Los Ninos Heroes, they came to be called. Fought us hard, they did. Threw themselves off a tower rather than be captured. One of them jumped and landed straight on my waiting bayonet. Skewered him like a sausage, I did. A sight I'll never forget. In fact, I think that's what made me addled. Folks say I'm addled, you know. Shouldn't be no wars. There'd be less addled folk wandering around, I can guarantee you. Say, what are you doing running around with a dead China Mary? A woman ain't no good for practicing on once she's dead. Even I know that," the ragged man stated matter-of-factly.

Dave reached in his pocket and came up with a dime, which he flipped at the man.

"Say, what makes you think my poor dead sister's a China Mary? And none of it's any of your business anyhow, you old fish head."

"No, it ain't my business, Sonny, but that ain't your sister. I know Chinese hair when I see it, and I know the perfume of the Celestial. Special oils those folks are fond of. I was familiar with that smell, intimately once," he said, a distant look in his eye.

"Why, all you smell is rotten fish, you dirty bugger. Stand aside before I ride you down." Dave said.

The man suddenly ran at Dave and sunk his teeth into his leg above the boot and wouldn't let go. Dave grabbed his revolver and brought it down on the man's head. The man let go and moved away, but the blow hardly seemed to even faze him.

"Your leg smells like dog piss, boy. What have you been up to, you yellow jacksnipe?" the man said, a wild look in his eye.

Dave holstered the gun and urged his horse forward abruptly. He rode on a short distance, then paused to turn and look back towards the bridge. The ragged man hadn't moved. He was still standing on the bridge, shaking his fist at Dave.

Dave lifted his pant leg and looked at the bite. Sure enough, it was bleeding in several spots. The crazy man had left his mark on Dave.

He sure was acting crazy, Dave thought. *I wonder if he could have had rabies?*

Dave rode on a little further, thinking about nothing but rabies. He remembered the bottle of whiskey he had in his saddlebag, and got it out and doused some of it on the bite. Worried, he took a swig himself, hoping it would calm his nerves. Things had been starting to go wrong. The good luck he had been having seemed to be running out. He still had a ways to go to get to the "Romantic Getaway." What could possibly happen next, he mused.

Suen's hair had been getting Dave in trouble. He did his best to tuck it under the blanket, and arrange it in a manner so it wouldn't keep falling out. Satisfied, he urged the horses on at a faster pace.

The lush valley he was passing through was mostly orchards and grazing land, and oat and wheat fields. Most of the farmhouses were set back from the road, and the few people he had seen had only given him a momentary glance. Finally, he came to the end of the flat land, and at the bottom of the hills that climbed steadily to over three thousand feet.

Proceeding up Geysers Road, he hadn't gone far, when he saw a mountain lion racing down a side hill straight towards him and the horses. Dave took off at a full gallop, but the big cat came out on the road and chased after him. The animal was unbelievably fast, and before Dave could get at his revolver, the cat had sprung up on the horse's rump that was carrying Suen. Dave had his hands full just trying to maintain a grip on the terrified horse's reins. The cougar's big paw lashed out and took a swipe at Suen, but its claws got caught in the blanket. Struggling to free itself, it ripped much of the blanket away, and somehow was still able to remain perched on the moving horse, its claws dug in deeply. The animal let out a high-pitched screech, as Dave finally freed his revolver and fired a bullet into it. The mountain lion tumbled off the horse, but wasn't dead, and ran off slowly back down the road.

Dave stopped, still holding the gun, and jumped from his horse and took a look at Suen. The cat hadn't seemed to have left a mark on her. He tucked the blanket back around her and checked her breathing. Other than still being out cold, she seemed fine, he decided.

He got back on his horse and continued on, shaken and amazed. He couldn't help but think about the dream he had about that half Indian, half snake woman, and the shiny black doorknob she had tried to place with her rat's arms into his mouth. Never in his life had he seen or heard of a mountain lion acting like that—charging and leaping upon a moving horse. What was going on? Then and there, he just realized that he shouldn't be doing what he was doing. He should just turn around right now and take Suen back and face the consequences. Aside from a lump on the head, why, she'd be all right. If he just brought her back right now, he'd probably only have to do a little jail time is all. Why, it wouldn't be the end of the world. When he got out, he'd have a hell of a tale to tell to the boys in the beer garden.

That's what I'm going to do. I'm just going to turn around right now.

Dave turned the horses and noticed that the blanket had already slipped off, revealing Suen's legs and rear.

That's a pretty nice-looking rear, Dave said to himself. Since I'm going to take her back, I might as well lift that skirt a bit and take a look at her bloomers.

He dismounted and lifted her skirt. The outline of her well-shaped rear was before him. Dave froze, transfixed. Now, he really was in a quandary. He wanted to have Suen naked on the bed, now more than ever. And, what if everything went smooth and Suen agreed to marry him? The honeymoon cottage, Mr. and Mrs. Fowler, and barons up on Geysers Road.

Nope, I'm going on with it, he decided. *No overgrown pussycat is going to claw up my dreams. Time's a wasting,* he said to himself. *I just hope I don't die of rabies is all.* And back up the road he proceeded.

He was almost at the turn off that lead to the shack when he saw the stage from The Geysers Hotel heading back down the road towards town. Dave pulled to the side of the road as far off as possible and moved slowly on, his head down and hat pulled low. Luckily, the grade was steep and the driver barely slowed down upon sight of Dave and the horses. When the stage passed, Dave was surprised to see that the driver turned his head to look back at him.

Must wonder what I've got lashed to the spare horse, Dave thought. *Thank God I'm almost there. I don't think I could go on much further. I guess I'm just lucky that stage didn't run me down,* he mused.

Finally, he reached the overgrown trail that led to the old squatter's shack. There it was—the honeymoon cottage.

Why, it seemed to just naturally belong there, along with the oaks, manzanitas, and madrones, he thought to himself.

The little shack looked pretty much the same as when Dave first stumbled upon it. A few loose boards now had been renailed, and curtains could be seen hanging from the two windows. Dave tied off the horses, and taking a key from his pocket, walked up to the front door and unlocked the sturdy lock he had installed. Grabbing the shiny black doorknob, he pushed the door open slowly, half expecting to see a huge rattler waiting to greet him. But there was no snake this time; the place looked just like he had left it. The narrow spring bed, barely big enough for two, was neatly made. Canned foods, beans, flour, and lard were neatly arranged on a shelf. There were no cobwebs in sight, and the place looked freshly swept and dusted. The wood stove was in functioning order, some wood stacked neatly next to it. A few pots and pans occupied another shelf, and a barrel of water and a dipper stood against one wall. Dave had found a couple of planks half buried in weeds in the back of the shack. These he had scraped clean and placed them on some old oak logs someone had cut years ago. Now stood a table of sorts, near the center of the shack. On this sat a rusty can filled with dried weeds, ferns, and manzanita branches.

Wait until Suen sees all this, he thought. *Then she'll know the true meaning of a "Romantic Getaway."*

He went back to Suen's horse, which was still oozing blood from the claw marks the mountain lion had left. Have to tend to that later, he thought.

Untying Suen, he carried her in and laid her on the bed. Dave stood back and stared at her. She was breathing evenly, but the side of her pale face was turning color where he had hit her. *She sure is pretty*, he thought. *Looks like a China doll, not a China Mary. Wonder why they call them "China Marys,"* he mused.

Turning his mind to the horses, he got a dipper full of water and went back outside. He unsaddled both horses, bringing packs and saddles in, and arranged them in a corner.

There was lots of clay in the soil near the shack and he scooped up a handful and placed it into the dipper, working it until he had thick mud. He put a layer over the wounded horse's bleeding claw marks, and took some oats from a sack and fed both animals. After they finished the oats, he led them to a broken-down corral in back that he had crudely repaired with fallen limbs. He had previously filled a rusty tin tub, that miraculously didn't leak, with water, and the horses immediately went over and began drinking. Satisfied that they'd be secure overnight, he went back to the honeymoon shack. Suen hadn't budged. Dave figured that she'd be hungry when she woke up so he went to the wood stove and built a fire. He opened up two cans of beans, and taking a slab of salt pork from one of his packs, diced up some along with part of an onion and put all of it into a pot on the stove.

A pleasant aroma began to fill the little shack. Dave set out two metal bowls and two spoons on the make shift table. Two metal cups he filled with water.

Suen might wake with a headache, maybe I should pour a little whiskey into her cup, he reasoned, and did so, along with a little for himself.

Dave walked over to stare at Suen. Her nose seemed to be twitching. I knew that food cooking would bring her to, he said to himself.

Suen let out a low moan, then suddenly opened her eyes. She had trouble clearing her head, and was startled to see who was staring down at her. Then it all came back to her. David Fowler had kidnapped her. The smelly little boy she had met many years ago in Modesto had swooped down on her and carried her away. The last thing she remembered was screaming for help, and then all went black. She had a terrible pain on the side of her head. *That idiot must have hit me*, she concluded.

Dave was so surprised to see Suen's eyes snap open that suddenly he became scared, and he couldn't think of the proper words to say. He looked about the "romantic getaway" and saw only a rundown squatter's shack with some dirty curtains hanging from the windows. What had he been thinking of when he decided to bring Suen to such a place?

Suen glared at Dave, not saying a word, and sat up in the bed and looked around. She was in a one room shack with a stupid little table, not even level, with some weeds in a rusty can sitting on top, along with two bowls and a couple of spoons and cups. A fire was going in a stove, and something, beans and pork she figured, was cooking in a pot on top. Filthy curtains were hung, again not even level, from two windows. Then she noticed how Dave was dressed. Why, he looked just like those gunslingers she saw on the cover of the dime magazines they sold at the general store. At least his clothes were clean for a change, she noted, but a smell was wafting off him, in the closed-up shack, that reminded her of dog urine.

"David Fowler, what have you done, and where are we? You hit me, didn't you? You filthy man."

Dave wasn't expecting such a warm greeting, and it made him a little angry.

Recovering himself he said, "Suen Ling, this is the romantic getaway I told you about. Your pa wouldn't let you go out riding, so I brought you here anyway. I'd like this also to be our honeymoon cottage. Miss Ling, will you marry me?"

Suen was dumbfounded. She desperately wanted to laugh, but her head hurt too much, and Dave was wearing a gun strapped low on his waist. She realized the danger of her position. She had no idea where she was, but she was alone with a dangerous idiot wearing a gun. The thin, jaundiced-looking young man, with the pimply, buck-toothed face, had done nothing but bully and frighten her since she was a little girl throwing a ball against a building. Now, years later, he had kidnapped her, hit her on the head, and had proposed to her all in the same day. She had been brought up to believe that destiny and fate played an important part in the meaning of one's life, but what whim of God had placed her here and brought her to such a hard destiny?

The Fowler boy was confused. She knew that. One minute he behaved like she was heathen Chinese and unwanted. Other times he acted like he was sweet on her, and wanted to court her. Now, he had actually proposed to her! She knew she should measure her words carefully; her life could depend on it. In spite of everything, she realized she was hungry and that her stomach was growling.

"David Fowler, I don't even know what to say to you, just that my head aches and that I'm hungry. Is that beans you have on that stove?"

A smile came to Dave's face. Suen was talking to him! Even kind of friendly!

"Why, yes it is, Miss Ling. Beans with salt pork and onion. Come sit at the table and have a bowl. I'm afraid the chairs are too tall for the table so we'll have to use the floor, but it's clean. I just swept it the other day," Dave said enthusiastically.

Suen got up a little dizzily and sat on the floor in front of the crooked table, as Dave ladled beans into her bowl. He did the same for himself and sat opposite her.

"I figured you'd be thirsty," he said. "I poured a little whiskey in your water in case your head hurt. Your head doesn't hurt too much, does it Suen?" he said in a soft manner.

Suen tasted a spoonful of beans—they weren't bad, and she figured she had better eat up. Who knew what type of strength she might need to get out of this predicament.

"Yes, David, my head hurts bad. What did you hit me with, that large gun you're wearing?"

"No, Miss Ling, it was just my fist. I had to do it. You started screaming 'help' loud enough to wake the dead. I had no choice."

Suen's temper began to soar wildly out of control. What did that bonehead mean "had no choice"? Of course he'd had a choice. He could have chosen not to do any of this, and just left her alone. She took a sip of water. Yes, it had whiskey in it. Once, at Dom and Angelina's, she had tasted some, and wondered how people could drink it. The sip did warm her inside though, so she took another larger one. She tried to force herself to remain calm, and she steadily spooned beans into her mouth until the bowl was empty. Dave had been eating and drinking too. Suddenly, he began to cry.

"I'm sorry I hit you, Suen. I didn't really want to hurt you. Why would I want to hurt someone I want to marry?"

Suen wanted to strangle Davy. When Mat died, her father taught her some self-defense moves he felt she should know. One was the use of thumb and finger placed precisely on an area of the throat. Done correctly, with the appropriate pressure, a person could be made to pass out. The other move was catching a person unaware, while placing both hands on either side of the head and twisting sharply with all your might, snapping the person's neck. Suen was eager to try either move on Dave.

She needed courage to be so bold in her actions. Many times she had heard that alcohol bred false courage. Maybe false courage was just what she needed. She looked up at Dave who was wiping away tears.

"Could I have another cup of the special water, David?" she said in a low voice.

Dave immediately brightened up.

"Why of course, Suen, but please, call me Dave. You're Suen, and I'm Dave."

What a hopeless idiot he is, she said to herself.

"Did I ever tell you that I like your name?" Dave said. "In fact, I even like your name better than I like my own. I'm not one bit fond of David. Why, I never even had a sling when I was little. Your name, Suen, reminds me of hopefulness—like a better day will be coming soon. It sure is a pretty name."

Suen looked at Dave in his frilly white shirt and black coat. A wave of hopeless sorrow enveloped her. What a pathetic young man he was. Maybe, if fate were kinder, he could even have been a good man, but he wasn't good, he was mean-spirited and a bully. He seemed weak now, and an idea came to her mind.

She took a deep swig of the whiskey water and said, "I'm tired, David, and my head hurts. I'm going to have to do some thinking about your proposal. I think I feel a bit feverish. I need to lie on that bed until I feel a bit better."

Suen didn't really want to kill Dave. She just wanted to get away. Dave was trying to act kind now, and was vulnerable, but she felt he could turn in a second, try to throw her on the bed and violate her at gunpoint. If he went as far as that, she had a feeling that he could kill her after it was over. He couldn't just let her go—she'd report all this to the authorities, and Dave would go to jail. A bitterness galled her as she reflected on how much longer jail time Dave would get, if he had kidnapped and violated a nice blonde American girl.

She needed to get Dave close to her, relaxed and unaware, so she could try one of the self-defense moves on him. The one that would knock him out was preferable, but if that one didn't work, she was prepared to try to snap his neck. Also, he had to take that gun off. Maybe, if all else failed, she could get the gun herself, she reasoned.

Dave was wide-eyed; he got up and helped Suen over to the bed. He stood transfixed as Suen began to unbutton the front of her long dress, then pull it up over her head and off, letting it slip to the floor. To his speechless astonishment, she removed her bloomers and lay down half-naked on the bed. This was the first time Dave had seen a female's privates, and he was amazed and confused at what he saw. Suen had spread her legs slightly, revealing a large slit, almost like a mouth, but turned sideways and surrounded by a patch of black hair. The mouth even had what looked like lips encircling it! Why, except for the hair and the smaller size, a woman's privates looked not much different than a sheep's, or a horse's! Why, the male member was much more attractive, he decided. After all, it was sleek, well proportioned, and tubular, and stood proud when erect.

Suen was staring wide-eyed at Dave. He just stood there staring, a baffled look on his face. She figured by now he would be on top of her pawing away, giving her the opportunity to get her hands on his skinny neck or head. Conflicting emotions were waging a battle inside Dave. Here was a beautiful woman, half-naked, and the girl of his dreams lying on a bed before him, and nothing was happening to his member. It wasn't even growing!

Surprisingly, Dave wasn't angry; he wasn't even ashamed. He came to the stunning realization that he was simply and proudly a Spartan. One of the older boys in school, who did a lot of extra reading, had told him once that the Spartans, fierce Greek warriors of the era before Christ, preferred men over women when it came to engaging in the sexual act. Sure, the men got married and had kids, the older boy assured him, but when it came to getting really stimulated, the men preferred the company of other naked men.

Dave did enjoy, in a way, the sight of Suen's half-naked body, but it just wasn't having the effect on him as, say, the sight of Pino's large member, or the feel of the large German boy's tool rubbing along his face. *I guess some of us just have to be Spartans,* he figured, somewhat matter-of-factly.

He reached down and picked up Suen's dress and covered her with it.

"You just take a rest, Miss Ling. I'm afraid I made a big mistake bringing you here. You'd never want to marry me. And, as for me, I just realized that I'm a Spartan. It's too late to head back to town, so you just get some sleep, and I'll take you back in the morning. I believe I'll just step outside and get a little fresh air."

Dave closed the door behind him. Suen quickly put her clothes back on and got under the covers. What had just happened was simply amazing and beyond her comprehension. For some reason, she felt mostly at ease, and believed that Dave would leave her alone and actually take her back to town as he had said. Her head hurt, and Dave's behavior and words had made the headache worse. The whiskey, the blow to her head, and Dave Fowler's actions opened the door for sleep.

Chapter 20

For the first time since her capture, Conchetta dared to let herself feel a glimmer of hope. Hope that came in the form of a total stranger who had briefly shouted out her name. She turned quickly and looked longingly back across the bay.

"What are you looking for dear? A knight in shining armor? Turn around and don't fidget. I told you, I need to think," Juan said.

Who was the man, and how did he know me? Conchetta thought to herself. She remembered the fierce look of determination he had on his face as he swam towards the boat, and the clear blue look of his eyes as he tried to reach out and gain hold of the gunwale, before Juan brought the gun down on him. For a while she even thought he had drowned, and the handsome young man who had called out her name was gone forever. She was surprised at the feeling of elation she experienced when she saw him surface and swim weakly back to shore. She felt overjoyed that he was going to survive, and his survival raised in her that glimmer of hope. Someone, possibly some people were looking for her.

The boat was almost across the bay. She glanced at Juan who seemed deep in thought, yet nervous, his crippled leg twitching out now and then in abrupt little kicks.

Juan was on high alert when the boat docked. He quickly grabbed the two larger bags and headed toward the train station, Conchetta walking in front of him carrying her smaller bag. It was awkward and made him limp more, but Juan carried both bags in one hand, leaving his other free to grab either his knife or gun. This fact he mentioned to Conchetta, who was more than used to this threat by now. There may be a time later on for escape, or if she could just manage to stay alive, help might reach her. Somewhere along the way Juan had slipped up. Why else would someone, possibly a law officer, dive into the frigid bay water calling her name?

Reaching the train station, they were greeted by a line of people, all waiting to purchase tickets. The line moved swiftly though, and soon Juan and Conchetta were two people away from the window. From this point Juan could see the back, and part of the sidewalls of the ticket office. His eyes froze at what he saw. There, tacked up along one wall near the ticket agent, was an extremely accurate drawing of Conchetta! There was no mistaking it. Someone had painstakingly recreated her image, probably from a photograph.

Juan immediately grabbed Conchetta by the arm and moved out of line. Several people looked strangely at them, but Juan kept moving, his arm entwined around hers. They turned back the way they had come, towards the waterfront, then down a long side street of mostly fish processing warehouses and old shacks. Juan walked slowly. He needed time to think.

Conchetta hadn't said a word, but it was all she could do to keep from shouting out in glee! At the same time as Juan, she too had seen her picture on the ticket office wall. It was a drawing of her reproduced from the photo that had been taken in Monterey! The fact that it was hanging in a train station ticket office proved undoubtedly that people were looking for her.

Juan knew this too and had already devised a plan. He needed to get on that train. He had to put distance between himself and that swimmer, or anyone else who might be tracking him. It didn't take him long to come up with a solution. All he would have to do was rely on his old friend—disguise.

Walking on a little further, he came to what he needed. A small empty shack stood between two large ware-houses. One of the warehouses was bustling with activity; people and wagons coming and going. The other one seemed to be closed down. Juan and Conchetta loitered for a moment, as he waited for some of the action to cease. At a lull, when no one was looking their way, he urged Conchetta forward and straight towards the empty shack, where a side door was open, held on by one rusty hinge. Except for a few busted up crates the shack was dark and empty, the dirt floor littered with broken wine and beer bottles.

Juan pulled the gun and kept it leveled at Conchetta as he began to remove clothing from one of his traveling bags. At the very bottom he found what was needed. El Zapo had never thrown away the bloody nun's habit he had taken from the dead nun in San Juan Bautista. On a hunch, he thought it might come in handy some day and had done his best one night in San Jose, while Conchetta was sleeping, to wash the blood out of it. A dark stain was still visible on the cloth, but it would have to do. It had been neatly folded, but put away in his bag when still damp, and now when he got it out and handed it to Conchetta. It smelled a little musty.

"Put this souvenir on over your clothes, Gypsy queen. Why, I think you're going to make a stunning-looking nun, and make sure all that hair is properly tucked in," Juan said, pleased with himself.

Conchetta was disgusted, but did as she was told. She wasn't too surprised when Juan pulled from the bag his old seminary student robe and large crucifix and put them on. He also took from the bottom of the bag a long set of rosary beads, which he arranged daintily around Conchetta's neck.

"Now, I do believe that we are ready once again to face the world as two humble children of God. Let's hit the streets, Sister, there's a train awaiting."

Conchetta couldn't help herself, "You're going to burn in hell for all this, but you already know that, don't you?"

"Why, hell yes," Juan shot back happily. "But if I burn, you'll be right beside me to keep me company. I've made prior arrangements with the devil, you see. Come now, Sister Lombardi, out the door with you, and keep in mind this robe is a perfect hiding place for my revolver."

Juan peeked out from the doorway, and seeing no one, urged Conchetta ahead of him and back onto the street. At a rapid pace, they retraced their steps back to the ticket office. The train was getting ready to pull out as they walked up to the window.

"Keep your head down, Sister," Juan whispered. "Remember, Sisters of God are humble, the weight of the world rests heavily upon their shoulders. Two tickets to Healdsburg, please," Juan said, extending some money to the man.

"Sure thing, Father. You and the Sister have a nice trip," he said, handing Juan some change.

"All aboard!" a conductor yelled. "Next stop, San Rafael."

Juan and Conchetta boarded the train, finding empty seats near the back of the car. They stayed inside the train until it stopped at Petaluma. Along the way Juan couldn't stop thinking about Conchetta's picture on display at the Sausalito ticket office. It was really obvious now that she was being hunted. He wondered if all the ticket offices along the line had a similar picture. He began to think back on where things might have gone wrong; when he had slipped up. Introducing the Gypsy queen as Conchetta certainly was one instance. Maybe that was enough right there, he reasoned. Suddenly, a thought came to his mind. Stupidly, in the cabin on Penitencia Creek, he had underlined a few lines in a newspaper concerning the opening of a new church in Healdsburg. If someone was trying to retrace his steps since the performance in Gilroy, displaying a picture of Conchetta along the way, could eventually that someone come to the little cabin on the creek? It seemed next to impossible, he deduced. Surely the planets couldn't be aligned in such a perfect manner. Or could they? Sitting in the train, dressed as a man of God, alongside a woman dressed in the blood-stained robe of a nun, a nun he had raped and murdered, he wondered if Jesus was out to get him. The picture in the bar in San Francisco of Jesus ascending came to him. Of all the saloons in San Francisco, he had to stop in that one for a drink. Saloons usually didn't have religious pictures in them, but that one did.

When the train stopped in Petaluma, he had to chance it and get out. He needed to see something for himself. Rousing Conchetta, who seemed to have been dozing, he prodded her with the tip of his knife.

"Wake up, Sister, we're going to go for a little stroll, but first I need to ask you something. Remember the newspaper we kept by the stove in our little cabin, the ones we used to light the fire. We just left them there, didn't we, or had we burned them all?"

Conchetta was startled. She thought of the paper with the heart and arrow drawn on it with certain words underlined. Juan was trying to retrace his steps, thinking about where he may have slipped up, she realized. If she lied, he might catch her at it.

Nonchalantly she answered, "Papers? Oh, the papers by the woodstove. Yes, some were still there. Why are you thinking about papers?" she added.

Juan stared at her intently.

"A bit of news came to my mind, is all. I was just trying to think back on where I heard it or read it. Could have been in those papers I had delivered back there. Let's get up and walk, Sister. I need to stretch my legs."

They got up and walked out of the car. The afternoon sun was getting low, in a sky filled with gray clouds.

"Keep your head down. Remember, you're chaste. I want to stroll near that ticket office and see if there's a schedule posted."

They moved close to the little office. A man was reading a paper inside. Juan glanced at the walls of the building. Immediately he saw it—a drawing of Conchetta tacked up on the wall!

Conchetta figured out what Juan was up to. He wanted to see if a drawing of her was somewhere inside. She was walking next to him with her head down and was just getting ready to look up and sneak a quick peek at the office walls, when Juan abruptly grabbed her arm, and led her back towards the train. He must have seen the drawing, she guessed.

A man in a suit came towards them on his way to the ticket office. Conchetta quickly raised her head and noticed that he was staring at them. He smiled and touched his hat uttering, "Afternoon," as he passed on by. The man, employed by the railroad, entered the office to relieve the fellow inside who was reading the paper. The first thing he saw when he entered the door was Conchetta's picture on the wall. The face that greeted him was a mirror image of the nun he had just greeted. Then he remembered that the fellow who was distributing the drawings of a missing woman had mentioned that she might be traveling with a thin pale fellow who limped. The priest he had just seen had a limp! The man turned and walked rapidly towards Juan and Conchetta.

"Say, Padre, hold up there for a minute," he said loudly.

Juan immediately sensed that something was wrong. Getting back quickly on the train wouldn't do any good. It wasn't ready yet to pull out. He ignored the man's words and walked fast, with Conchetta in arm, around the back of the ticket office. Luckily, no one was in sight as he drew his revolver and waited for the man to round the building. He pushed Conchetta against the wall, held the gun to her throat, and stood next to her, waiting. The man turned the corner and Juan side armed him to the forehead with the gun. The man staggered and began to fall. Juan caught him with one arm and let him sag to the ground against the back of the building.

"Walk casually back aboard the train, Sister Lombardi. You had better hope no one is the wiser. Remember, rule number one—the first bullet always goes into you."

Conchetta was just glad that Juan hadn't killed the stranger. The man must have recognized her, she hoped. Intentionally, she had raised her head when she saw him coming towards them, dressed in a manner similar to all the other railway office employees. Why else would he have tried to detain them?

Nothing seemed amiss as they boarded the train. Juan shot a glance back at the ticket office, and saw the man inside standing in front of the open doorway looking about. Juan and Conchetta took their seats, and a minute or two later the train pulled out. That had been way to close, Juan thought. Conchetta was sitting next to the window; he was sitting next to her by the aisle. He poked her once or twice in the hip with his knife to remind her of its presence.

Juan now had to do a total reevaluation of procedure. He couldn't just keep on riding the train to Healdsburg. He should probably not even go to that town. So what if there were nuns there? There were nuns all over. A cunning fellow had to be always willing to make a change of plans. He really began to wonder if someone had come upon the paper with the town of Healdsburg underlined. If that were the case, then surely the authorities could be waiting there for him. And, how many places had Conchetta's picture been plastered on a wall?

He pretended to be looking out the window at the golden hills and fields passing by, but actually he was staring at Conchetta. That slut was reminding him more and more of the Madonna, especially with that habit framing her face. Those large innocent eyes, at times they looked so pleading and sorrowful. This could all end right now. He should rape her at the next stop, one more time for good luck, then slit her throat and be done with it. Alone on a fast horse, he could go anywhere. He was angry and in a foul mood. If there was a village nearby, he wanted to pillage it. He had read about pillaging. It meant robbing and laying waste to all that was around. Raping and pillaging always went hand in hand. He didn't know if he was thinking all this, or if Bael was talking to him. It didn't matter by now. He had been confusing the devil with himself for quite a while now. It wasn't important. The final outcome would end with the same results.

What if Conchetta was the Madonna, though? After all, hadn't he met her hanging around a church, an old mission? No, of course not. She had gone there to pray to the Madonna to send her a lover. But wait, he recalled that there at the mission in Carmel, when he had first spoken to her—the fragrance of flowers was so thick in the air that it had almost made him nauseated. He remembered reading somewhere that when saints, angels and the Madonna traveled amongst the living, the aroma of flowers filled the air. He suspiciously sniffed at Conchetta, but all he smelled was the musty black robe, with a washed out bloodstain tainting the stripe of white under the neck.

Looking at Conchetta's eyes, he could imagine the light going out in them. The first time he had seen lights of an eye going out was when he shot a buck at the age of fifteen. He was moving through the forest near his house carrying a fancy Henry lever action .44 his father had bought him for his birthday. There, ahead of him in a clearing, stood a proud-looking forked horn buck, a sleek doe standing next to him. Juan raised the rifle, fired, and brought the animal down with one shot at a distance of about fifty yards. The doe froze for a moment, bewildered, then bounded off. The fallen buck was still moving, weakly kicking its legs. Juan was surprised at how shaken he was, yet exuberant. He pulled his long bladed knife and ran up to the animal, intending to slit its throat. It was good for the meat to let the animal bleed, he had been told. When he reached the deer, he cradled its head in his lap. It was barely struggling now, and Juan just held the animal, watching the lights go out of its eyes. When the lights were extinguished, power seemed to flow into him, course through his veins. It was then that he had learned to love to kill.

For some reason, imagining the lights vanishing from Conchetta's eyes did nothing for him. It wasn't making him excited, and he didn't think it would make him feel powerful. *Curse this witch, she must have put a spell on me*, he said to himself. But that was as far as he could think. For some unexplained reason he knew he just couldn't kill her. He didn't want to kill her, and it galled him to think that this was so.

Conchetta knew that Juan was looking at her, and it made her shiver inside. What was going through that twisted mind? What was he planning next? She didn't want to think about Juan. She wanted to think about her sister, Angelina. Where was she? Had she moved, or had she simply sold the café for some reason.

Conchetta was riding in the same car Angelina and Dom had ridden in weeks ago on their first trip to Healdsburg. Now, the train was nearing Santa Rosa, and Conchetta was less than twenty-five miles from her sister's new home in the Dry Creek Valley. The train slowed as it pulled into the Santa Rosa depot.

"Move fast with me, Lombardi, we're leaving this train," Juan suddenly spoke. "There's not much daylight left, and we need to rent a team and wagon. Hell, I'll buy one if I have to. Who cares. It's only money."

What's with this "we"? Conchetta thought. *He's doing all the insane planning and decision-making, and I'm certainly no part of it.*

"You mean *you* have to rent a team and wagon, I'm just part of the baggage," Conchetta found herself saying.

Juan chuckled and gave her a sideways glance.

"Yea, I guess you are just baggage, Sister. I don't know why I simply can't toss you out."

Conchetta reached out and grabbed Juan's thin wrist. It was the first time that she had willingly made contact with him, and a wave of revulsion coursed through her. She couldn't help but notice that his skin was cold and very soft.

She looked at him fiercely in the eyes and said, "Let me go. Just let me go now. You just walk away and do what you must, just do not kill again. God will catch up with you in the end. You will never have freedom as long as I am with you. Can't you see that? Just leave, leave alone now, and let this nightmare end!"

Juan was taken aback and momentarily shaken. For some reason, he felt moisture coming to his eyes. He had to break away from the look in Conchetta's eyes. He reached out in almost a tender manner and removed her hand from the grip on his wrist.

Struggling to collect himself he said, "What nonsense is this? Leave you? Leave Conchetta, queen of the Gypsies, to fend for herself? Why, my dear, haven't I done nothing but taken the best care of you? Fed you the finest foods. Bedded you down amongst fragrant animal droppings. Introduced you to a most engaging bear, furnished you with the finest of drugs. And, though your face may in a way remind one of Marie Antoinette, not once have I sliced that pretty neck with a blade. Leave you? No, my sweet Sister, that is simply out of the question."

Conchetta slumped back in her seat and took a deep breath. Somehow, she would just have to hold on as she had been trying to do all along. He wasn't about to let her go, even if it made more sense. Why couldn't she get it through her head that the word "sense" had absolutely nothing to do with this devil—the devil with a tear dripping from his eye that she was sitting next to?

Juan hurried Conchetta off the train and away from the busy depot. He stopped a stranger and got directions to the nearest livery stable. While the man was telling Juan which way to go, Conchetta looked down to see a young boy tugging at her robe. The filthy little urchin, dressed in rags, was staring straight up into Conchetta's face.

"Say, Sister," he said in a small scratchy voice. "You look just like a lady who gave me some money once. She gave me money even after I tried to steal her purse. I think she was older than you, though. Will you give me some money too?"

Juan had turned away from the man and was listening to the little boy. Before Conchetta could say a word, Juan reached into a pocket and handed him fifty cents.

"God be with you, young fellow," he said, and hustled Conchetta away.

"What do you think that was about, Sister?" Juan said.

"Evidently, I reminded him of someone," Conchetta answered, bewildered herself.

They reached the livery stable and Juan inquired about buying a sturdy wagon and two horses. The man, a short wiry little fellow, seemed to be nervous that he was dealing with a priest and a nun, but showed Juan some wagons and a few horses, and explained prices. Deciding upon a suitable rig, he paid the man, and questioned him as he hitched up the horses. Juan wanted to know the least traveled way to get over the Mayacama Mountains into Lake County.

While in the cabin on Penitencia Creek, he had studied a map of Northern California. It seemed from the map, which he had retained and was packed away in one of his bags, that from Santa Rosa there were various roads that one could take to do this. Juan had decided to leave California and head on up to Oregon. Ever since he was a youth, the idea of El Norte' had fascinated him. Why, if one went far enough north, the color of a bear's fur changed from black or brown to pure white. Since meeting up with Oso the bear, Juan had a new fascination with the animals. A white bear would be something to see. He was confused as to exactly where the white bears lived, but he thought it might be somewhere in northern Oregon. East of Clear Lake, in Lake County, was a road that stretched through the middle of California, and headed due north into Oregon and beyond. The first white settlers in California called it "The Old Indian Trail." The first pioneers and mountain men into the area had come upon a well-worn path that mostly paralleled the Sacramento River. The path ran north and south through tree-lined forest and open range. Over thousands of years, a path had been worn into the earth by Native Americans on trading missions with the various tribes. This path now had become the main road leading into Oregon. Juan's destination was that road, and he wanted to reach it in a manner the most sparsely traveled.

Sure, there were several ways to get into Lake County, the man was telling him. He explained, in a confusing manner, several of the ways, but these roads were all well traveled, and Juan, now more than ever, sought isolation. Juan thought he remembered from the map a place called The Geysers, and a twisting, isolated road that led to them, and then over the mountain and down into the flat land near Clear Lake. He mentioned this road to the man.

"Oh, sure, you can get to Clear Lake that way. It's a long, round-about way, and few folks go that way, but once you get to The Geysers Hotel you could spend the night, then drop down into the flats the next day."

The man looked at Juan somewhat suspiciously, then glanced over at Conchetta. She sure was pretty for a nun, he thought. Why would she and that young priest be going traveling together in the first place, and why the interest in such an isolated route? The livery stable employee was a practicing Baptist. He didn't have much respect for Catholics in the first place. He had heard tales of nuns and priests running off together and cohabitating. He wondered if these two were such a pair. Why didn't they just take the stage over to Calistoga? It was easy to get to points east from there.

Juan thought he sensed the man's dull mind overtaxing itself. He had seen his eyes appraising Conchetta. Why would a priest and a nun wish to travel together by such remote roads, the man was probably thinking.

Conchetta had been eyeing a crowbar hanging from a nail on a nearby wall. She inched closer to it, contemplating a desperate grab for it, and a shot at bringing it down on Juan's head. Juan noticed her movement and raised a finger at her while the man's back was turned.

"I have to drop the Sister here off at the convent, and then I'll be on my way alone. Solitude and lonely roads leave much time for spiritual reflection. The Bishop says that one so young as myself should seek solitude while contemplating the rapture."

The man had finished his chore and when he turned to Juan, he reached out wide-eyed and took the five-dollar bill that was being extended to him. *What a bunch of mumbo-jumbo those Catholics speak*, he thought to himself, *but this one sure pays good. I don't even know what "rapture" is, nor do I care.*

"Hurry, Sister, get aboard. The mother superior is waiting. Thank you, my friend. You've been most helpful. Oh! Before we leave, isn't there a turn off I could take that leads to The Geysers that's a bit of a shortcut and bypasses Healdsburg?" Juan asked.

"Yea, Chalk Hill Road," the man said. "Take the Redwood Highway north, pass over Mark West Creek, and after a couple of miles you'll see a sign on the right that says 'Chalk Hill Road.' Follow that until you come out into the Alexander Valley. You'll see signs then, pointing to The Geysers. Just follow the signs."

Juan thanked the man again and drove out into the streets of Santa Rosa. He proceeded north out of town, then stopped at what he figured might be the last general store he'd come to for a while. He showed Conchetta the gun under the robe, motioned her down, and the two of them went into the store and purchased some food and supplies that included a can of kerosene and a lantern, extra blankets, and a cast iron skillet. It was dark as they pulled away from the store. The moon was almost full, and the sky was filled with moving clouds. A breeze was kicking up the dry leaves that were just beginning to fall. Autumn was coming on. By October, Juan hoped to see his first white bear.

"Sister Lombardi, I'm going to take you to see a white bear. What do you think of that?" Juan suddenly spoke enthusiastically.

Conchetta had been thinking about the night and what it might bring. They would have to sleep somewhere. She wondered if Juan's privates had truly healed up, and what that might mean. She recoiled at the thought of it. When he started talking about white bears she became confused, and had to wonder what he could be meaning.

"Are you talking about polar bears," she said incredulously. Are you planning on going to Alaska?"

"Of course not," Juan said. "Polar bears run wild all over northern Oregon, everyone knows that. I thought you were a well-educated slut, Lombardi. You should have studied your geography better."

Conchetta had been munching on some dried apricots. If the idiot wanted to think that polar bears lived in Oregon, so what? She just hoped that all this would end way before crossing any borders. She hadn't liked all this talk of isolated roads, but she wasn't that surprised at this new turn of events. People were looking for her. Juan was now, more than ever, a man on the run.

He urged the horses on at a faster pace as they left the outskirts of Santa Rosa. The moon was drifting in and out of clouds, but provided plenty of light to travel by on this dusty well-used road called the Redwood Highway. Seeing no one around him, Juan pulled the wagon off the road and behind a clump of trees.

"Take that habit back off, Miss Conchetta. No longer are you to be a woman of God. Now you shall return once again to the ignorant, uneducated Italian slut that you are," Juan said, pulling off his priest's robe.

He packed both garments neatly away in a bag. Conchetta watched him as he took a packet of white powder, poured some out on the back of his hand and held it to his nose and snorted in deeply. Some type of drug, she deduced. *Now what does this mean?* She wondered fearfully. Juan tilted his head back, eyes up at the moon, then picked the whip up and brought it down hard a time or two on the horses back as they pulled onto the main road.

"On, my swift steeds, the moon is almost full, and the devil roams the earth tonight. Why, I'm not one bit tired. I feel as if I could drive all night. Hold on, Lombardi," Juan said. "You may be in for the ride of your life."

The section of road they were traveling on was fairly straight and Juan made good time. They crossed a wooden bridge over Mark West Creek, a thin willow-lined little stream that sparkled in the moonlight. There were a few houses on either side of the road, including a large two story structure, all lit up, and a sign out front saying "Mark West Boarding House."

Conchetta wished Juan would stop there for the night. People would be inside, and she would feel safer. Juan just cast a glance at the building and passed quickly on by. Conchetta had been thinking about the little boy at the train station that said he knew a woman who looked just like her. Over the years many people had said that she and Angelina, except for the age difference, could have passed for twins. Could the boy have been talking about her sister? And what would Angelina have been doing in Santa Rosa? Aside from a trip now and then to Oakland, Angelina had never left the city. Conchetta was lost in thought, when Juan suddenly slowed down and turned east up a narrow road. A sign at the corner said "Chalk Hill Road" and had an arrow pointing after it. Juan proceeded slowly for a mile or so, then the road turned at the base of some foothills and ran north. At this point a sign said "Alexander Valley" with another arrow pointing after it. This road was very twisty, as well as narrow, and dipped up and down with the contour of the hills. Juan was forced to slow the pace considerably. At times there were sheer drop-offs on either side of the road and the visibility was poor. Large oaks shaded the road, and clouds often hid the moon.

"The country roads around Santiago are better maintained than this rut," Juan complained out loud.

Conchetta didn't say a word. She looked ahead at the desolate road and the twisted branches of the oaks that at times grew over the road from either side, creating a tunnel of sorts to travel through. Occasionally, the lights from a farmhouse could be seen, tucked away from the road, in some narrow ravine or a little clearing. The loneliness of the area, and the fact that she was getting very tired and had little to eat, added to her feeling of hopelessness. Who could ever find her out here? And was Juan really planning on keeping her with him all the way to Oregon? Her future looked as dim as the road ahead. She thought of flinging herself from the wagon, at a point when the road came to one of the sheer drop-offs. But the drop-offs weren't that deep. She'd probably just roll up against a tree bruised and battered, but still alive. Juan would probably just fetch her back up, give her some morphine, and continue on. If she was going to kill herself, she wanted to make sure it was done correctly and once and for all. Whenever these thoughts assailed her, some spark of resistance had always come to her aid in the past. Her depression was suddenly interrupted by Juan's words.

"Say, Lombardi, it's too quiet out here. Why don't you talk to me or at the least, sing me a song?"

The fool amazes me with his stupidity, Conchetta thought. *How could he think that I'd enjoy talking normally to him, let alone breaking out in a song?* She was trying to think of something to say to him, when she felt the tip of the knife poke her ribs.

"Sing, Lombardi, sing now, howl at the moon," Juan said.

Conchetta was surprised to find herself responding with the first song that came to her mind. She began singing in a quiet voice "My Bonnie Lies Over the Ocean."

"Excellent, queen," Juan shouted. "Sing louder."

Conchetta did so, and was surprised when Juan suddenly chimed in and sang along.

When the last verse was sung, he shouted out happily, "Again!"

Conchetta was appalled. Here she was in the middle of the night traveling a desolate road, and singing alongside a demented killer. Why, it almost made her laugh, but her depression had momentarily passed, and now, more than ever, she just felt tired. She hardly ever called Juan, "Juan," but now she felt was a good time to do so.

"Juan, I'm really tired. I need to lie down in the back of the wagon with a blanket and rest. All right?"

Juan was amazed to hear her address him by his name. She must really be tired, he thought, shaking his head at his concern.

"Go ahead, Conchetta," he said, slowing the wagon to a stop. "I'm not one bit tired yet, and I have miles and miles to travel, as the saying goes. I'll try to avoid the chuckholes, but it's almost impossible on this road. I doubt if you'll get much rest."

Conchetta crawled in the back, used her bag for a pillow, and pulled a blanket over her. She was nauseated that he called her "Conchetta." He seldom called her by her first name unless he said it in a sardonic manner. She never should have called him "Juan," she figured.

Juan drove on through the night. The cocaine had worn off. He could have taken some more, but he knew that that too would wear off, and sooner or later he would have to sleep. The more he prolonged the need for sleep, the longer and deeper sleep he would fall into when he finally succumbed. He looked at his pocket watch. It was two o'clock a.m. He should pull off the road now into a thicket and sleep until six o'clock, then move on towards The Geysers. Four hours sleep should leave him somewhat refreshed. He found a suitable pull off, took a small chain and lock out, and secured Conchetta by the ankle to the wagon. She didn't move and continued breathing deeply. For a moment he thought of having his way with her, but he was just too tired. All the bumping up and down on the rutted road had irritated his groin. There'd be plenty of time for pleasures later, he reasoned. He removed his bag, the one he carried a spare revolver in, ammunition and a lever action Winchester he had removed the stock from, so it would fit in the bottom of the bag, and laid it on the ground near the wagon. He secured the horses, gave them some water and a few oats, along with a flake of hay from a bale that he had purchased at the livery stable. He wrapped himself in a blanket, and using his other bag for a pillow, immediately fell asleep.

Conchetta was awake when Juan pulled off and wrapped the chain around her ankle. She listened quietly as he moved about and prepared for sleep. After a time, when she could hear him breathing deeply, she sat up and examined the chain. It was well secured. She could see no way to free herself from it. She lay back down, trying not to think. She needed sleep and pulled the blanket tight around her. She thought of her brother and sister, and the happy times they had shared, until sleep claimed her.

Juan awoke refreshed and eager to get back on the road. He freed Conchetta from the chain, and after she had taken care of her business, told her to climb up again on the front seat. Jerky and dried fruit would have to do for breakfast. It wasn't even light out when they once again got moving. After a while the narrow road ended, and they came out on a large picturesque valley, dotted with fruit trees and grape vineyards. Workers were about at first light, some were on their hands and knees picking prunes from the ground and putting them in buckets. Most of the grapes they saw still had some green berries dotted amongst the purple ones. Juan stopped the wagon, quickly got out and grabbed a couple of bunches. He gave a bunch to Conchetta. They munched on the tangy grapes as they continued on. Quite a bit of activity was going on in the valley, most of it relating to the harvesting of fruit. Besides prunes, pear and peach orchards were plentiful. One vineyard must have ripened early. Men were hustling amongst the rows cutting bunches of grapes and placing them in wood boxes. Some of the boxes were already full with purple grapes, and loaded on to the back of a large wagon pulled by two mules.

Juan didn't like all this activity and speeded up the pace. The road was good and they moved rapidly through the valley. Wagons and riders would pass them now and then. All just waved or nodded and moved on by. As they neared the foothills and the valley got narrower, the orchards were fewer, as were the homes. Oak, madrone, pines, and firs now surrounded them. Finally they came to a turn off, and a road that climbed up into the hills. A sign at the bottom of the road said "The Geysers," one underneath said "Geysers Hotel."

"Well, I guess we start climbing, Lombardi," Juan said.

It was midmorning, and they had moved a couple of miles up the mountain, when they saw two people coming down the road towards them. One was a thin fellow dressed like some type of pistolero; the other was a pretty Chinese girl. *Odd-looking pair,* Juan thought.

The riders looked like they were going to pass on by without a word when Juan pulled up and said, "Say folks, this road eventually drops down into Lake County, doesn't it?"

"Why, sure," Dave said. "Only problem is that there's five or six roads up there that a person could take. Some of them dead-end or lead to quicksilver mines. Only one leads over the mountain and down into Lake County. Tough part is there're no signs up there marking the way. Most folks don't get into Lake County that way. Only a few locals and ranchers. Folks have been known to get lost up there. Maybe someone from the hotel could take you up there and point you in the right direction."

"Do you know the right road?" Juan asked.

"Why, sure," Dave said proudly. "I've hunted these hills since I was old enough to shoot."

"Sir, I'd like to hire you as a guide," Juan said. "I'll pay you well."

Dave's jaw dropped. That would have been easy money, but he knew the quicker he got back to town with Suen, the less trouble he'd be in.

"Sorry, Mister, I can't. I got to get this little lady back to town."

"I'm afraid you're incorrect. You're going to be my guide," Juan said, pulling his revolver and aiming it at Dave.

Chapter 21

Frank Augustino was cold and shivering as he climbed the steps that led to Primo's office. On the coach ride over, he noticed that he had a hard time focusing on a single thought. The blow to the head had placed him in a state of confusion, a territory that he wasn't used to. When he decided to act, it was usually decisively and with vigor. If the blow from Juan's gun hadn't stunned him so much, he would have found a boat, stole one if he had to, and followed Conchetta across the bay. He cursed himself for being so weak as to be unable to. By now, Conchetta was across the bay, and who knew where. Primo would know what to do, he told himself. Getting to Primo's, and the shock of seeing Conchetta in the flesh, were the two thoughts that stood out in his throbbing head. Those eyes, that face, the brief glimpse he had of Conchetta, had made him feel like he had known her forever. She had only spoken one word, "Yes," but that voice sounded as familiar to him as his mother's or father's. This was impossible, and only his imagination soaring he knew, but nonetheless the voice had left a deep imprint on his soul.

At his knock, Primo came to the door and a look of shock came to his face upon seeing Frank, soaking wet, dried blood on his hair and cheek, and a little fresh blood oozing from a gash on his skull. Before Frank could say a word, Primo had ushered him over to a leather sofa, sat him down, and draped his heavy overcoat over his shoulders. He told his secretary to go for the nearest doctor, then took a bottle of brandy from his desk and poured the shivering Frank a tumbler full.

"I saw Conchetta," Frank blurted out. "She was crossing the bay. I swam after her. When I caught the boat, the fellow she was with slammed me in the head with his gun. One of his hands was clamped around Conchetta's mouth. It's got to be a kidnap."

Primo was listening while dabbing a cloth, soaked in brandy, on Frank's wound. He held it there for a while hoping to staunch the bleeding.

"You're going to need some stitches, Frank, but the cut's not that deep. The doc will fix you up in a bit, but a blow like that might have given you a concussion. We'll see what the doc says. Do you feel like telling me the whole story from the beginning?"

"We shouldn't be wasting time talking, Primo. Conchetta's across the bay by now and going who knows where? Maybe Healdsburg's a good guess. We've got to tell the police, now. As soon as the doc bandages me, I'm going after her. Someone in Sausalito has got to have seen them," Frank said.

"As soon as the doc gets here, I'm going to the police myself. I'm going to get more personally involved in this now. I'm going to go home, pack some things, then cross the bay. If the doc says it's OK, you'll come with me. We'll both go after her," Primo said.

Frank was frantic and wanted to do something that instant. That doctor might take forever to arrive. Each moment wasted placed Conchetta further away. He forced himself to remain calm and explained the day's events in more detail to Primo. Moments later, a doctor arrived and began to stitch up his cut. The doctor looked in his eyes and moved his finger around, telling Frank to follow the movement. After asking Frank a few questions, he said he was of the opinion that he had suffered a concussion, and should remain as inactive as possible for a week or two. He gave Frank some headache powder and told him to follow the instructions on the bottle until his head quit throbbing.

When the doctor left, Frank looked at Primo and said, "I'm going to my place and pack a few things, Primo. I'm feeling better every minute. Hell, this isn't the first time I've had a bump on the head. You know I won't be able to just sit around. I need to try and help find Conchetta. Remember, you said we'd go after her together."

"Yea, I said that, if the doctor pronounced you fit. You heard what he said, inactivity. But you are hard headed, and young, and would just go after her on your own, so I'm not going to try to stop you. You're a man who has to be responsible for your own decisions. At least if you're with me, I guess I can catch you if you pass out. Go and pack, then meet me at my house. I'm stopping by the police station first. Within an hour we should be on our way to the waterfront," Primo said.

Frank hurried off to his place, changed into dry clothes, and threw a few things in his traveling bag, including his revolver, a box of ammunition, and his hunting knife. If his parents had lived closer, he would have stopped by and told them what was going on. Just as well, he reflected, they would have seen the bandage on his head and asked questions, and then things would have gotten complicated. He had no idea how long he would be gone, but he'd try to get word to them later.

He hurried to where Tuli was stabled, told one of the stable boys to feed and take care of the horse until he got back, then proceeded to Primo's house.

Pietro answered the door in a heavy overcoat and sturdy boots. He seemed to be dressed for traveling.

"Come in, Frank, we're almost ready. Just a few more things to do."

"Pietro, you're coming too?" Frank said, surprised.

"Of course! Life's been too boring around here, and Dom Londi's a good friend. His wife's sister is in trouble, and I'm thinking the authorities won't be of much help. This man she's with sounds like a mean customer. If he's kidnapped Conchetta, he probably won't give her up without a fight. I have a *Lupara* from Sicily that might be of some help," Pietro said.

"Lupara?" Frank said. "I don't think I know that term."

"It's a sawed-off, double-barrel 10-gauge. Point it in the general direction, and it's bound to hit something," Pietro explained.

"Yea, you'll probably hit your foot, Mafioso. I think you should leave that thing here," Primo said, coming into the room.

"What? You want me to hunt *Bastonates* with only this," Pietro said, opening his coat and revealing a Smith and Wesson pocket 32, nestled in a shoulder holster.

"Good God," Frank said. "I don't think I've brought enough fire power."

"Check this out," Primo said, lifting his pant leg to reveal a Barnes 50-caliber single-shot boot pistol. "Sorry, can't show you the other weapons, Frank. They're already packed away," Primo said matter-of-factly.

"Look what a fancy fellow he is, Frank, a pistol in his boot! And he's talking about me shooting myself in the foot," Pietro said.

Pietro walked over to Frank and put his hand on his shoulder and looked him in the eye.

"Franchesco, from what I hear, you should be at home resting, staring at Conchetta's picture and playing with your knob, instead of chasing after her," he said seriously. "What will we tell your parents if you pass out and fall under a train wheel? Trying to rescue pretty women should be left to more mature men, who aren't marching around at full cock, tripping on their dongs. We'll bring Conchetta back to you and even arrange a formal introduction. Be a good boy now and go home. The Italian army is about to depart," Pietro said, raising his hand.

Frank got so caught up listening to Pietro that he forgot his head hurt. Every time he had met him he had been amazed at the words that came out of Pietro's mouth. He looked over at Primo who was standing calmly, a large grin on his face.

All Frank could think of to say was, "Pietro, I'm half Italian too. A three-man army is better than a two-man army, and don't worry about me falling or tripping on anything. I'm still on your nephew's payroll, and I've got a job to do."

Pietro started to chuckle.

"Frank, you rooster. Who do you think you're kidding? This isn't a job for you. It's romance, plain and simple. You're smitten by a female you've caught one brief glimpse of. But that's OK. We know you were hit by the thunderbolt the moment you laid eyes on her picture. It can happen to the best of us. We forgive you," Pietro said consolingly.

"Come on, enough jabbering," Primo said. "Let's finish up and get out of here."

Maria suddenly rounded the corner and ran straight into Frank.

"Hey, there's that pretty little girl. How are you? I haven't seen you for a while."

Maria looked down shyly and said, "I'm fine, Frank. Are you going with Papa and Pietro? How long are you going to be gone, Papa?" she said, going to her father and holding his hand.

"Yes, Frank's coming along with us too, sweetheart. We'll only be gone a few days. Do what Nella tells you and be good, and don't forget to practice your piano. You and Nella are in charge of things until we get back."

Primo and Pietro finished packing while Frank sat with Maria and talked about her school. Soon they were ready to depart. Frank reached down for his bag and grabbed Primo's by mistake. He was surprised at how heavy it was.

Primo noticed the look on his face, smiled, and said, "Winchester carbine, Colt 44 Peacemaker, with appropriate cartridges."

Frank shook his head in consternation, "Are we going after one kidnapper or a whole pack of desperados?" he said.

"Italians are always prepared, Franchesco," Pietro butted in. "What if this no good has accomplices? Maybe he's part of a gang rounding up pretty girls to sell into slavery or to a wealthy sheik to stock his harem?"

"Good God, Uncle, would you quit reading those adventure romances! But you're right; it never hurts to be prepared. Enough now, let's go," Primo said.

He kissed Maria goodbye, said a few final words to Nella, the governess, and with Pietro and Frank walked out the door to a waiting coach that took them immediately to the waterfront. The timing was precise. A ferry was getting ready to depart. They purchased tickets and soon crossed San Francisco Bay.

At the Sausalito train station, Primo and Pietro pointed to the picture of Conchetta that was tacked on the ticket office wall and inquired if anyone had seen such a woman lately. No one had. Primo was disappointed, after learning that the ticket agent they were talking to was the same one who had been on the job all day. Frank, in the mean time, had returned from a visit to the main livery stable, with no news either of a sighting of Conchetta.

"I'm going to gamble that they boarded the train," Primo said. "This is a busy depot. I don't think that ticket agent is too observant. He seemed surprised when I pointed out Conchetta's picture and why we were there inquiring about it. Maybe someone at one of the smaller depots will remember having seen her."

They bought passage and boarded the train. At each stop they inquired about Conchetta, pointing to the picture. Frank did the same at the livery stables where one could buy or rent transportation. So far, no one had remembered seeing a woman who resembled Conchetta in company with a pale thin fellow who limped.

Their luck changed at the Petaluma depot. The ticket agent they approached had a bandage on his head.

"Hell yes, I've seen her. I'm pretty sure that priest she was with coldcocked me. That picture we got tacked up of her don't show her dressed as a nun though," the agent said.

The three trackers looked at one another, startled.

"You're saying she was dressed like a nun and traveling with a priest?" Primo said. "Please tell us exactly what happened. I'm Primo Nuti, a lawyer, and we're trying to locate this woman. You're telling us some astonishing news."

The man explained the events, adding that when he came to, the train had already pulled out. He wasn't completely positive that the priest had hit him, after he called out and followed after them. But he thought he had seen a flash of a black robe before he went down and blacked out.

"Ben, who was working here too, told me later he saw the priest and nun go back aboard the train. After I came to and told Ben what happened, he went off to tell the police that I got knocked in the head by a priest, who seemed to be traveling with the woman who's been missing, only she was wearing nun's clothes. I've been half expecting an officer to come down here any minute and try to arrest me for being drunk in public. I know this tale sounds pretty farfetched," the agent added.

"Don't feel bad," Pietro said. "The bastard who hit you seems to be good at disguise. One minute he's a Gypsy performer, the next he's a priest. He's shrewd, making Conchetta dress as a nun."

Though the situation was serious, Pietro couldn't resist a dig at Frank.

"Say, Frank, looks like you're out of luck, the woman of your dreams has gone off and joined a convent. Now, what are you going to do?" he said seriously.

"She wasn't dressed like a nun when I got a glimpse of her crossing the bay, but she wasn't dressed like the queen of the Gypsies either. At least a bear didn't try to board the train with them," Frank said.

"Say, we got company policy against such occurrences," the ticket agent spoke, patting the bandage on his head. "Bears and circus animals all have to be properly caged, even if they were being led by a priest and nun. God don't run the railroad. This here's the San Francisco and North Pacific Railroad, and we don't tolerate loose bears."

"Wait a minute. Are you sure you're not drunk, Mister?" Pietro said. "Maybe you just fell down while drinking and thinking about bears and hit your head. I think you might be making all this up," he said, opening his eyes wide at the man.

"Don't pay any attention to him. You've been a great help. You're not the only one with a sore head. Frank here was hit with a gun, also by the priest fellow. You two have matching bandages, and not too fond memories, huh?"

Primo reached into his pocket and handed a five-dollar bill to the man.

"Buy a good bottle of whiskey when you get off work; it might help keep you from thinking about nuns, priests, and bears," Primo said, smiling.

"Glad to be of help, boys. Hope you find this Conchetta. Hope that priest fellow ends up behind bars," the agent said.

The train was getting ready to pull back out and the three men got aboard. They were excited and glad to know that they were on the right track, and not that far behind Conchetta and her abductor. The train was now making frequent stops: at Elys, Goodwin, Cotati Station, Wilfred, and Bell View. Primo inquired about Conchetta at each stop. No one had seen a priest or a nun exit the train. By the time they reached Santa Rosa it was dark. Primo had no luck showing Conchetta's picture and inquiring about a priest and nun. Frank suddenly came running up, breathless.

"A guy at the livery stable sold a couple of horses and a wagon earlier in the day to a priest and a nun. I showed him the picture of Conchetta, and he swears it was the same face. He gave the priest directions for an isolated, roundabout way to get over to Lake County via Geysers Road. The priest seemed intent on going that way, but this livery fellow said that the priest was going on alone, after dropping the nun at a convent. Things are getting a bit confusing again, it seems," Frank added.

"Let's go back to the livery stable. We're going to need horses. The train won't be going north again until morning," Primo said.

After renting three horses and saddles, and questioning the man at the livery further, Primo, Frank, and Pietro rode to the Catholic convent near Saint Rose Church. The men had agreed that most likely this "priest" was lying when he said he would be dropping the "sister" off there, but they felt they should check there just to be safe. It was getting late now, and it took a while before an elderly nun answered the door. It took them only seconds to learn that no one new had arrived at the convent in days.

Back at their horses, they briefly talked things over. Primo concluded that the kidnapper must feel that he was being hunted. Why else would he be seeking such an isolated way into Lake County? Frank, diving into the bay, attempting to reach Conchetta, had to have aroused a sense of suspicion and fear in the man. It dawned on Primo that perhaps while buying train tickets, or looking at departure schedules at one of the depots, the man could have noticed Conchetta's picture tacked up on a wall. That could easily explain the need for a disguise.

A tough decision had to be made: follow the same isolated roads the abductor and Conchetta were taking, or head for the Geysers Road by the quicker route, straight down the Redwood Highway to Healdsburg and out Alexander Valley.

Primo noticed that Frank hadn't been looking too well. His eyes had been drooping and even in the moonlight his face appeared pale. Obviously, he should be sleeping now, not riding through the night on a horse.

"How do you feel, Frank? And, please tell me the truth," Primo inquired.

Frank was impatient to push on after Conchetta, but he had to admit to himself that he was bone tired and could hardly keep his eyes open. He had taken more of the headache powder, but his head still throbbed, especially since he got on a horse.

"I'm tired, Primo, but we've got to keep moving," was all he could think of to say.

"Yea, you're tired all right," Pietro said. "I've been sticking close to you since we got on these horses. Someone's got to be around to catch you when you doze off."

"Here's what I think we should do: ride for Healdsburg by the direct route, tell the police and the Londis what's been going on, then move on to Geysers Road. Depending on how long they stop for the night, and how long we stop, it's possible we could get up the road ahead of them. With the police involved, it will be easier to search the roads," Primo said.

Frank had never been this far north. He had barely even looked at a map of Sonoma County. Primo had traveled this area before; probably he knew what was best.

"Let's get moving then," Frank said. "At least there's a moon out."

"Yea, a lover's moon," Pietro said, slapping a hand on Frank's shoulder.

Frank just shook his head and began to move out.

"Hold up a minute," Primo said, reaching into his travel bag that was strapped clumsily to the horse. "I figured we might have to eat on the run, let's have a bite to eat before we head north."

He produced a narrow loaf of sourdough bread, salami, and a wedge of sharp cheddar cheese. Frank furnished his hunting knife, and soon the men were enjoying the food. As soon as they finished, they rode out of Santa Rosa at a steady pace and on down the Redwood Highway towards Healdsburg.

They were almost to Poor Man's Flats, or Windsor, as some were beginning to call it in hopes of giving it a more dignified name, when Frank slumped in the saddle and slid down to one side. Pietro was right there to catch him and reign in his horse.

"Primo, this young man's all done in. I don't think this riding has been good for his head. We should probably find a place to get a little sleep until morning, huh?" Pietro said.

"You're right, Uncle, I'm pretty done in myself. You too, I'll bet. Let's just pull off the road into that prune orchard and grab a few winks. We can move on at first light," Primo said.

Frank, in the mean time, had reawakened and seemed surprised that they were dismounting.

"Hey, sleepyhead, get your blanket out. I guess it's saddles for pillows tonight. We're stopping for a little rest.

The dirt in this orchard looks pretty soft, just watch out for stray prunes," Pietro said.

"French plums," Primo corrected him. "They are prunes only when dried."

"Mr. Perfection," Pietro said, spreading his blanket out, laying on half and wrapping the rest around him.

The other men did the same. There was no more talk; sleep came to them almost immediately.

Pietro was awakened by a kicking at his feet. He opened his eyes to see a farmer holding two buckets, one in each hand, staring down at him. The man was wearing dusty clothes and an old straw hat, with a not too friendly look on his lined face.

"You folks got to move on now. You ought to know better than to sleep in someone's orchard. This ain't a hotel out here. If it were, I'd be charging rates," the man said.

Primo and Frank awoke at the sound of a voice and sat up rubbing sleep from their eyes.

"Why did you pick my feet to kick?" Pietro inquired.

"'Cause you look the oldest and should know better than to tie horses to a fruit tree with leaves still on it and a plum or two. Look what those horses have done to some of my branches," the farmer said.

The men looked to the trees and saw broken branches near the horse's heads.

"Sorry, Mister," Primo said. "We got so tired we just couldn't ride anymore. If you were charging rates to sleep in your orchard, what would they be, including a damage charge for the branches?"

The man shook his head and suddenly broke into a smile.

"Fill these two buckets with plums and we'll call it even. The orchard's already been harvested, but we left a few green ones on the trees. They look like they're ready to pick by now. With a little yeast and sugar added, plums can turn into good wine. I think I'll make a little for me and the missus," he said.

Frank was surprised the sun was so high. They had slept well into the morning. He was also surprised at how alert he felt. His head didn't pain him at all, except when he felt the wound. He hoped Primo wouldn't want to waste time by picking plums, but the next instant he was watching helplessly as Pietro sprang to his feet and grabbed a bucket from the man's hand.

"I can pick plums probably faster than anyone. I can pick them from the ground or from the tree. We had plums in Italy too," Pietro announced proudly.

"I thought you folks might be Italians," the farmer said. "You've got noses the size of pears, except maybe the young blondish one. His only looks like a large fig."

Primo got up laughing and grabbed the other bucket. Frank got up too and quickly began moving about the trees picking ripe fruit and placing them in his shirttail, then into the nearest bucket. In a manner of minutes both buckets were full of ripe purple plums.

"You fellows are right fast pickers. Could have used you at harvest time. If you need some work, come back next year, but judging by your clothes, I've a feeling you may not need the money," the farmer said.

"We may not need the money, but I always did like working in the fruit. The smell of hot dirt and ripe fruit kind of gets in your blood, and you find you've missed it once you're around it again. Thanks for the opportunity to awaken old memories, sir," Pietro said.

They saddled the horses and took leave of the farmer. Back on the road they ate some of the food Primo had packed along with ripe juicy plums Pietro produced from his pockets.

"At least we'll keep regular on this trip," Pietro said, eating a plum. "Sure do miss a nice cup of morning coffee though," he lamented.

Before leaving Poor Man's Flats, they stopped and watered the horses at a clear little creek. There was good grass nearby, and they paused to let the horses graze for a while.

Frank had a lot of time on the ride to think about Conchetta. Hopefully, they were closing in on her and the abductor. If the chase were to come to a successful ending, with the man captured and Conchetta freed, what would happen next? What could Frank say to her? He couldn't possibly blurt out that he had fallen in love with her picture, and that love had only grown stronger after catching a glimpse of her on the boat. He knew that she was single and had been working in Monterey as a tutor. She had a sister and brother who cared for her, and she was full Italian. His parents, especially his father, would probably think that she would be a perfect wife for him. He was always telling Frank, "Find a good Italian girl and settle down." His mother though would say, "Find a nice Finnish girl and settle down." Frank so far had found neither, and now was mad at himself for thinking of Conchetta in terms of a wife. The woman didn't even know him! All she had seen of him was a wet idiot swimming after a boat. Not a good first impression, he decided. He was feeling a bit down and foolish, when finally in the early afternoon they reached Healdsburg.

They rode straight to the police station, and Primo, after introductions, explained to the officer who said he was assistant chief of police, that they were tracking a kidnapper and could use police help. The officer wanted to know the whole story involving Conchetta, and expressed concern and a desire to help. But Primo wasn't surprised when the man said that chasing after kidnappers, miles away from the city limits, was a job for the county sheriff. Had the sheriff been notified of all this, he asked.

Primo explained that the San Francisco police were going to contact the Sonoma County sheriff's office and tell them the circumstances, but that time was of the essence, so Primo, Pietro, and Frank were following the trail on their own. They had no idea at this point what the county sheriff was doing to aid in locating Conchetta. Primo said he couldn't even be sure if the sheriff's office was treating the case as a serious kidnapping, or simply as a woman over eighteen who had run off with a fellow. That's why the three of them had proceeded on their own.

The assistant chief wished them good luck in their search and said he'd try and find out what, if anything, the sheriff's department was doing to locate Conchetta. He had seen her sister, Angelina, a few times in town. When Primo had showed him the picture of Conchetta, he was stunned by the similarity in appearance. He felt guilty for not being able to provide more help. The chief was escorting a prisoner to San Rafael for trial. So there was no one else to consult with, except maybe Judge Nolan, and this being the weekend, the judge was probably drunk under a grapevine. Procedure, though, dictated that this was a matter for the sheriff's department.

Before leaving the office, Primo mentioned that the town sure looked dead, and asked the officers what was going on.

"There's a baseball game at the new ballpark; most of the town's probably there," the officer answered.

Back out on the street, Primo said, "Remember, Pietro, how Dom was always talking about baseball? I'll bet he's there. I think we ought to check before going all the way out to his place. I'll go back in and ask for directions to the ballpark."

It didn't take them long to reach the ballpark. They bought tickets and were heading towards the bleachers when Dom Londi suddenly came into view, walking rapidly towards them, a smile beaming on his face.

The explanations were made for the Nuti's and Frank's presence in town. Dom immediately walked back to the bleachers and came back with Angelina and a diverse group of other people. Dom introduced Mai and Po, Melanie, Betty Mae, Walter, Fred and Pino to the Nutis and Frank.

Angelina rushed forward and embraced each of the new arrivals, tears streaming down her eyes. In her excitement she found herself talking rapidly in Italian to Primo and Pietro, then caught herself and switched to English when she saw a look of bafflement on Frank's face.

"Frank, apparently it's you I need to thank the most for news of my sister, and here I am going on in Italian. You don't speak it much, right?" Angelina said.

Frank felt weak in the presence of Angelina and hadn't taken his eyes from her since she arrived. Suddenly, it was as if the picture he had been carrying around for weeks had come to life and was standing in front of him talking, only the picture had matured into a strong, no-nonsense, confident woman.

"I speak only a little Italian, Mrs. Londi, and I understand some of what's being said only when it's spoken slowly. I should have paid more attention to my dad when he was trying to teach me. That goes the same for Finnish on my mother's side," Frank said, somewhat shyly.

"Tell me, Frank, do you know my sister well?" Angelina said.

Frank's face turned beet-red. His eyes turned away from Angelina and stared down at his shoes.

"Dio Bono, Angelina, have your intuitive skills diminished since you left Italy?" Pietro butted in. "Can't you see what's happened to the boy?"

"Oh no," Angelina said with a serious look on her face. "It's the thunderbolt! I see now that he's been hit, just like I was the first time I laid eyes on Dom."

She walked up to Frank and gave him a kiss on the cheek.

"We can talk about all this later, but first let's find a place to sit down and you can tell me all you've found out," Angelina said, moving off towards some benches near the entrance to the ballpark.

Everyone listened while Frank told his story, with Primo and Pietro adding their own information, though Pietro's information consisted mostly of ribbing Frank at appropriate places in his narrative.

Pino had been listening quietly, not saying a word, but he noticed that every time Pietro spoke he liked him better. It dawned on him that the man reminded him a little of himself, and they were even both about the same age. Pino liked the way Pietro's eyes sparkled when he talked, and the little lines of amusement that would appear at the corners of his mouth. He would have to get to know him better in order to decide which animal he reminded him of, but so far it was a tossup between the chipmunk and the raccoon, both very powerful spirits.

When all the information was out on the table, Dom spoke.

"Well, it's obvious what needs to be done. Horses, and I guess weapons, need to be procured, then we should start for Geysers Road as soon as possible."

"Exactly," Primo said, and looked around to see everyone, from Po to Mai, to Melanie and Betty Mae, shaking their heads affirmatively.

Walter, who had abruptly left the game when, between innings, Pino had walked over and told him that there was news concerning Angelina's missing sister, now spoke up saying that he and Pino knew the Geysers Road area very well, and even the trail that led down into Lake County. They could go to the livery stable, unhitch their horses from the wagon, leave it there, rent a couple of saddles, and be on their way in minutes.

"I can rent a horse and saddle," Dom said. "Angelina will need the wagon."

Angelina shot Dom a glance, but didn't say anything.

"I too, will need to rent a horse," Po said.

"Me too," chimed in Betty Mae and Melanie.

Mai, who had seldom been on a horse, said nothing but had a perplexed look on her face. Fred just looked dejected. He figured Walter and Pino would say he was too young to go after a kidnapper.

Primo could tell that things were getting a little out of hand. There would be rough riding ahead and events could turn dangerous. He had a feeling he hadn't heard the last out of Angelina yet, but he figured seven grown men should be more than enough to chase after a kidnapper, and his hostage.

He glanced over at Pino, who seemed to be reading his mind, when he spoke out and said, "Melanie, Betty Mae, you girls will need to stay in town. While we're gone, you can pester the police, and check if there's any news about what the sheriff is doing. You can spend the night by the creek where we usually camp," Pino added.

Primo got a smile on his face. He remembered staying at the Healdsburg Hotel on a wine buying trip. The proprietor there seemed somewhat of a bigoted type, the type Primo had little patience with.

He looked at the young Pomo women, who had such disappointed looks on their round smooth faces and said, "Girls, I think it would be better if you stayed at the Healdsburg Hotel. You would be closer to the police station. You wouldn't mind staying there, would you?"

Melanie and Betty Mae looked at each other and giggled, then both said almost at the same time, "No, we wouldn't mind staying there."

"But, I don't think the owner would like it much," Melanie added.

"Oh, he won't mind it one bit," Primo said. "I can almost guarantee you that."

Pino and Walter exchanged a glance, and then Pino just shrugged his shoulders.

"Well, let's get going then," Frank said, suddenly feeling impatient. And back to the center of town they went.

Primo and Pietro went to the general store for some food and supplies. There was no telling how long they would be gone. Po and Mai went back home. Po wanted to pack a few things for the journey. Dom, Walter, and Pino took care of their business at the livery stable. Frank waited outside the general store on a bench, sitting alongside Angelina, Betty Mae, and Melanie.

Angelina could see that Frank was agitated and uncomfortable, just sitting inactive, waiting on the bench. She had instantly been impressed with Frank's demeanor. During his recounting of his search for Conchetta, he had spoken no more than the pertinent facts, in a low even tone with absolutely no hint of swagger. Angelina didn't like swagger. Her first husband had it, especially when drunk. Dom had no swagger whatsoever, one of his finer traits, she concluded. So, Frank had fallen in love with her sister! But evidently he didn't even know her. He certainly was a good-looking young man, she thought, and blonde hair and blue eyes like some northern Italians—only his mother really was from the north. All she knew about Finland was that it was a place of much snow, and was controlled either by Sweden or Russia, she just couldn't remember which. Angelina hoped that there would be plenty of time later, to dwell upon Frank and Conchetta, as a possible match. What she was mostly thinking about was the fact that Dom was planning on leaving her out of the hunt for Conchetta and the son-of-a-bitch who evidently had taken her.

Just then, as she was gazing up the street, she saw Mai and Po running towards them. Everyone on the bench stood up.

When Po got near he blurted out, "Suen's been taken away somewhere by that no-good Davy! A neighbor saw him ride up on his horse, lift her up, and gallop away. Our neighbor, Mrs. Carlson, lives alone and is confined to a wheelchair. She went to the front door and cried for help, but no one came or heard her. Most everyone was at the game. Suen's been gone for several hours now!"

Angelina's eyes hardened, "I knew that Dave Fowler would do something like this some day. He's no good, and he's crazy. Let's hurry, Dom and Primo and the others are at the livery stable. They'll know what to do," Angelina said.

At the livery stable, the men listened wide-eyed as Po explained what had occurred.

Before he had even finished, Walter had his horse saddled and said, "I'm going back to the ballpark. If anyone knows what Davy's up to, or where he might be going, it would be Butch Baylow, his best friend. I'll be back as soon as I can," and off he galloped.

"Pietro, you and Po go to the police and explain what's happened, though the fellow there will probably do nothing more than file a report," Primo said.

"From what I've seen, they don't seem to go out of their way to help Chinese, or anyone else who's not what they consider a true American," Dom added.

"I figured as much," Primo said. "Melanie, Betty Mae, let's walk over to the hotel and get you a room. Looks like you're going to have two people to inquire with the police about now," he added.

"I'll come too," Pino added. "I've got to see this."

The hotel clerk looked startled when Primo and the three Pomos walked in.

Primo walked straight to the counter and said, "Are you the owner or do you work here?

"I'm the owner," the man said, a plump fellow with soft white hands and a few wisps of thin black hair combed sideways over his head. "What can I do for you, sir?" he said in a haughty manner, glaring at the Indians.

"I'd like to rent a room for these two young ladies. Probably for only a night or two, but I'll pay you for a week," Primo said, reaching for his wallet.

The man started laughing.

"Mister, you've got to be kidding, we don't rent rooms to Indians. Everyone knows that."

"Well, I don't," Primo said. "Here's a hundred dollars. My name is Primo Nuti, a lawyer from San Francisco, and a good friend of Judge Nolan's. Give the girls a key to one of your better rooms."

Just to be on the safe side, Primo began to stare about the building, walked to the entrance of the restaurant and peered inside.

When he came back, he said to the owner, who had just stood there, mouth hanging slightly open, "I'm sure the girls will have a fine stay here. If I hear otherwise, I've noticed a few building and safety violations. You do want to remain in business, don't you, sir?" Primo said seriously.

Pino just stood in the background smiling. *This Primo is sharp*, he thought. *He definitely reminds me of the gray fox.* Now, he understood why the white man often referred to lawyers as sly foxes. Evidently some white folks knew their animals too, he concluded.

"Don't we need to sign the register?" Betty Mae inquired.

"Oh, of course," the owner said, pushing forward pen and ink. "Enjoy your stay, ladies," he said, while smiling up at Primo.

The two young ladies carefully signed the register in neat, legible script, "Betty Mae and Melanie—Pomos." They turned to leave; then Melanie stopped, returned to the register, and wrote "Not digger Injuns" after the word *Pomos*. Smiling at the owner, she joined Primo and Betty Mae, who were waiting by the door.

They returned to the livery stable and were discussing the events with the rest of the group, when Walter rode back at full gallop, jumped from his horse, and said, "You won't believe this. Davy may have taken Suen to a cabin up on Geysers Road! Butch said that Davy had been fixing up an old shack somewhere up there, turning it into a hunting cabin. Butch seemed dumbfounded that Davy had run off with Suen. He said he knew that he was sweet on her, and even joked about marrying her some day, but he figured Dave was just day dreaming. Butch mentioned that he had noticed some curtains sticking out of Dave's saddlebags one day when he said he was heading to the shack. Butch had even mentioned, why would anyone bother to hang curtains in a hunting cabin, but Dave had said they were only dusting rags. Butch said he thought it odd, even for Dave. Everyone knows that burlap or old flour sacks make a perfectly decent rag, Butch had said. I've got a strong hunch that Davy fixed that place up with the intention of bringing Suen up there. Suen once told me that Dave's been pestering her since she was a little girl in Modesto," Walter added.

"That's true," Mai said. "He pulled her hair and kissed her, and lately he's been pestering her on the street. Suen's been wary of him since we moved to this town."

Dom suddenly broke in, "Enough talking, if we're all ready, let's go. It's a long ride to Geysers Road."

"I'm packed," Po said. "Just need to rent a horse and saddle. I have an old double-barrel flintlock in my bag. I might have to shoot Davy," he said seriously.

Primo looked around. Counting himself, there were three Italians, middle aged and beyond, a young Italian-Finn, two Pomo Indians, one young, one old, and a small middle-aged Chinese man. In a sense, this was the law that was intent on finding and freeing two kidnapped women, one of them Chinese, the other Italian. *What a delightful country this is*, he mused.

Dom went over and embraced Angelina, kissed her briefly on the lips, then spoke lowly and passionately to her, "Go home. See if Mai wants to come with you. Don't worry; we'll bring Conchetta back. Try to stay calm. I love you," Dom said, turning away towards his horse.

"Dom, be careful," Angelina shouted after him.

"I will," he said, and rode out of town with the rest.

Angelina turned to Mai and said, "Do you want to let them leave us behind, Mai?"

"Angelina, what do you think? Dave has my daughter."

"That's what I thought. Let's buy a few supplies. I see Captain McCraken's horse tied up at the beer garden. I'm sure he'll lend me his revolver," Angelina said.

Chapter 22

Dave sat on the front step of the "Romantic Getaway," gazing up at the stars and thinking about the Spartans, until he got so sleepy that his head began to nod. He quietly went back inside the shack. Suen seemed to be sleeping peacefully. He stretched out on the floor near the wood stove, covering himself with a blanket.

Before falling deep asleep, he went over in his mind all he could remember about the Spartans. What he remembered about Leonidas and the Three Hundred Spartans reinforced his conclusion that one should not be ashamed to be a Spartan. Leonidas certainly wasn't. He was the king of that country and along with three hundred of his finest warriors had held off a huge Persian army that had invaded Greece. Leonidas had fought them at a pass called Thermopolae. The men fought the Persians for hours and died to the last man. The Spartans had excelled in warfare and the use of weapons. Dave was more proficient in the use of his revolver than anyone would have dreamed. There were more ways than one that he was just like a Spartan, he proudly concluded.

In the morning he awoke to the sound of his name being called.

"David Fowler, wake up this instant and take me home," Suen said, standing above him, hands on hips.

Dave sat up rubbing sleep from his eyes. He had been dreaming that he was wearing a golden breastplate, a fine plumed helmet, leather kilt and sandals, his hand gripping a sharp silver sword. He felt a bit irritated that Suen had interrupted such a fine dream and was standing there barking orders at him.

"You silly man," she was saying. "If you take me home right now, without pestering me, I'll tell everyone that this was just all a mistake. I won't even press any charges against you, and probably the police will let you go unpunished. They never aid Chinese people anyway," she added, in a vexed manner.

Dave brightened up at her words.

He got up and began to put some sticks in the wood stove saying, "That sounds good to me, Miss Ling. Can we have a quick breakfast of bacon and eggs first? It's a long ride back to town and we should eat a little something first. This was going to be our honeymoon breakfast," he added sheepishly.

Suen rolled her eyes and tried hard not to let her mouth curl up in a smile. The Fowler boy was way beyond her comprehension. And what was this talk last night about Spartans? All she knew of them was that they were Greeks of old. Somehow though, lying half-naked on the bed, the Spartans seemed in some way to have come to her rescue. Just thinking about the events and David began to give her a headache.

Dave was staring at her, smiling, waiting for an answer.

"Light the fire, David, but you better let me do the cooking. I don't like my eggs hard," she said.

"I'll let you do the cooking on one condition," Dave said. "Just don't keep calling me David. Don't you remember, I told you my name's Dave," he reminded her.

"Yes, Davy," Suen said, grabbing a skillet off a shelf.

After a quick breakfast, Dave got the horses ready, locked the door to the honeymoon cottage, and shortly he and Suen were on Geysers Road heading back toward town.

Why, that place will still make a fine hunting cabin. All I've got to do is remove those frilly curtains, though they do add kind of a nice touch, Dave thought to himself.

The morning had dawned cloudy; a hint of fall was in the air. *Might get one of those late summer storms,* Dave thought, gazing at the sky.

Eating breakfast had been uncomfortable, with few words spoken. Both Dave and Suen wanted to get back to town as quickly as possible, and they hurried the horses on down the road. They were a couple of miles from the bottom of the road, and the flat valley that led to town, when they met a wagon on the way up the mountain. Dave didn't give the wagon much thought. He figured they were probably a couple of tourists on their way up to The Geysers. He was surprised when the man hailed them and began talking, and it took him a second or two to register what was happening, when the thin pale fellow he had been speaking to suddenly pointed a gun at him.

Dave stared at Juan in total disbelief. Here he was, dressed in his gunslinger outfit, and some skinny stranger, who was built a little like him and also dressed in black, had caught him completely off guard and was ordering him about at gunpoint. No one had ever pulled a gun on him, unless you count Captain McCraken when he knocked him in the head with the butt of his pistol, and now here he was miles from town, feeling totally helpless. Dreams of getting Suen home quickly, and getting off scot-free had just vanished.

Dave was angry when he said, "Mister, you better put that gun away; you're breaking the law."

Juan laughed, "Why, one would think that a pistolero like you would understand law breakers. Don't tell me you've never broken any yourself. By the way, unbuckle your gun belt please, and toss it in the back of the wagon.

If you do it carefully, I won't have to shoot you and lose a valuable guide," Juan said.

Suen, in the meantime, couldn't take her eyes off the woman in the wagon. She reminded her so much of Angelina that at first glance she thought that indeed it was Angelina sitting next to the pale, evil-looking man. Looking closer she realized that this woman was younger. Then it dawned on her. She remembered Angelina talking sadly on several occasions about a younger sister she had—Conchetta, she thought her name was. Her sister had suddenly vanished from where she had been living in the town of Monterey. No one had heard from her in months. Could this be Conchetta, here on Geysers Road, traveling with some type of outlaw? She thought of calling out the name Conchetta, but decided against it. The man holding the gun had a look about his eyes, alien to anything she had ever seen. He was looking at Dave, yet there was no light to his eyes, just a vacant stare, cold and lifeless. Suen began to feel paralyzed, looking at those eyes, but her attention was diverted by what happened next.

Dave had unbuckled the gunbelt and tossed it into the back of the wagon. The instant it landed, the dark-haired woman swiveled in her seat and made a desperate lunge for it. She had the revolver by the handle when the man next to her elbowed her in the stomach, knocking the wind out of her and forcing her grip from the gun. All the time his gun had remained pointed at Dave.

"Bad move, Gypsy queen," Juan said. "When are you going to learn to quit making such foolish moves? By now, you should have learned that such foolishness only gets you hurt."

Now Suen was convinced more than ever that this was Conchetta, and that she had been kidnapped by this crazed devil with a gun.

Dave too was amazed at what he had just seen. He had thought the two in the wagon were a couple, probably man and wife. Now, he realized that the woman was under the man's power, just like he and Suen were. Dave hadn't really been paying much attention to the woman until that point. He had been preoccupied talking to Juan, and so startled at what was happening, that he had sort of ignored her. Now, looking at her doubled up in pain, trying to catch her breath, he saw that she looked just like that haughty Italian, Angelina, who lived down the road from him.

He was so stunned that he blurted out, "Say, lady, you look just like a dago in town by the name of Angelina."

Conchetta froze at the name of her sister. She forced herself to catch her breath and sit up.

"Conchetta?" Suen shouted.

"Yes," she answered. "Angelina's my sister."

"Well, well," Juan said in a vaguely amused manner. "It's a small world isn't it? Seems we have a meeting, of sorts, of old acquaintances. Too bad we don't have time for a little tea party, but I don't give a damn about any of this. Time's wasting pistolero. What's your name anyway, hombre?" Juan said.

"Dave Fowler, Mister. Not David."

"OK then, Davy boy, you just get moving back up the road and lead us over and down into Lake County and I just might let you and your Chinese friend live. If we meet anyone, don't say a word. I'll do the talking. If you make any stupid moves a bullet's going to go into you and your girlfriend's back. Tell him I'll do it, Conchetta," Juan said.

"Oh, he'll do it all right. He loves to kill," Conchetta added.

"Now, now, Lombardi. You shouldn't go telling new acquaintances my pleasures. One should be discreet when discussing such personal matters."

Switching suddenly to a loud snarl, Juan said, "Let's get moving. I can smell rain in the air, and I don't like to get wet. I catch cold easily, you see."

Dave and Suen pulled their horses in front of Juan's team and moved off at a steady pace back up Geysers Road.

They hadn't gone far when the first drops of rain began to fall. At first it seemed only to be a brief passing storm, but then the sky quickly darkened and all traces of blue were gone. The rain increased in intensity, and before long the dusty road of fine yellowish gray soil turned to gooey mud. The distant rumble of thunder began to fill the air along with flashes of lightning. A full-fledged storm was approaching, and the wind out of the north pushed the rain straight into the travelers' faces.

Juan didn't like this one bit. He hated lightning and thunder. Since it came from the sky and not the bowels of the earth, he thought, it was probably caused by that bearded God showing off. The earth had often moved in Chile, shaking buildings and bringing down churches, maiming and killing. He was confident that the devil was at work then, reminding people of how weak they were. The lightning and thunder were mere theatrical effects compared to the quaking of the earth. Thunder never killed anyone. Few people were killed by lightning. Usually only when a tree was hit and fell on some poor unfortunate who was standing below it. Once in a blue moon lightning would directly hit a person and they would die, but they were simply in the wrong place at the wrong time. Now when the earth moved, while church was in session, and tons of brick or concrete rained down upon the congregation—that was obviously planned, and not a random occurrence, Juan reasoned. Nonetheless, he hated getting wet, and the thunder and lightning made him nervous.

Davy and Suen rode slowly on, their heads down, their bodies now soaking wet. Conchetta sat in the wagon, hunched over, and actually glad a storm had appeared. This would make it more difficult for Juan, and perhaps a chance for escape or overpowering him would appear.

The horses were having a difficult time pulling the wagon up the steep muddy road. Juan began looking about for some place of shelter where they could wait out the worst of the storm, but the terrain was steep on both sides of the road, offering no protection.

Dave was growing tired of being wet and moving about in a storm. He looked over at Suen, who was shivering. *My God, if she caught pneumonia and died, I'd be in bigger trouble than I already am,* he told himself. The turnoff to the honeymoon shack was just ahead.

Dave turned in his saddle and said in a loud voice over the wind and thunder, "I've got a Romantic Getaway up ahead we could take shelter in, Mister."

"You've got a what?" Juan said. "What's a romantic getaway?"

"A cabin," Dave replied. "A cozy little shack."

Juan brightened up. "Is anyone else there?" he inquired.

"No," Dave said. "We just left from there this morning."

"Lead us there. And this better not be some kind of trick," Juan said.

The turnoff appeared, and shortly the horses were tied to the hitching rail out front, and Dave was turning the black doorknob to the little shack. Juan had herded everyone in front of him at gunpoint and was the last one to enter as the rain poured down incessantly. Dave was not too surprised to find that the little place leaked in several places. He took a bucket and some pots and placed them under the drips.

"Better than being out in that storm," he announced proudly, and began throwing sticks into the wood stove.

The moment Conchetta had entered the shack she looked about her for something to grab as a weapon. All she saw was a heavy black skillet, some chunks of stove wood, and a couple of forks. She saw a box near the forks on the shelf and wondered if any knives were in there.

It hadn't taken long for Dave to get a roaring fire going. Without saying a word, he grabbed Suen by the elbow and led her to a chair he had placed by the fire.

"You just sit there and dry off, Suen. I'll get some coffee going."

Juan had been watching Dave closely. *What a strange bird this one is*, he thought.

"Say, Davy, so this is what you call a romantic getaway, huh?" he said.

"Yes, I find it fits the description, though it would be nicer if it was a little bigger," Dave said.

Juan had carefully taken his coat off and arranged it over the back of the only other chair. He moved the chair to the other side of the stove from Suen and sat down. Conchetta moved to the back of the wall near Suen and sat on the floor close to the warmth of the stove. Steam shortly began to rise from all the wet clothes.

Dave didn't care much for being wet, but figured sooner or later he'd dry off; and storms usually didn't last too long this time of the year. He placed an old coffeepot on the stove, then sat on the floor, his back against the bed. He stared at the man sitting in the chair holding the gun. Being wet was the least of his troubles. The man with the goat's eyes was what he was worrying about.

"Say, Mister, what's your name anyway? Dave said.

"My name is Juan, David, not Juanito or Juancho, just plain Juan."

Dave found he liked that. At least the man was sure of his name.

While the coffee was heating up, an idea came to Juan. He had brought his traveling bag in, as had Conchetta, and now reached into it and brought out a short piece of rope.

"Hey, Lombardi, come over her," he said. "Take this rope and tie Davy's hands to that bed. I've got a little work to do, and I don't trust him. He seems stupid, but he may be fast."

Dave didn't like the stupid part and said, "I ain't stupid, and I don't care to be tied."

"Don't even bother to talk to him," Conchetta said, grabbing the ropes from Juan and doing as she was told.

Juan picked his chair and bag up, and moved to the front of the shack. He sat down, his back to the door, a better vantage point to keep an eye on everyone. He reached into the bottom of his bag and came up with both parts of the Winchester lever action. He laid them on his lap, then reached back in the bag and produced a screwdriver and a small bottle of screws. Within seconds he had the rifle back in one piece and a bullet levered inside the chamber. He moved his chair back by the stove and leaned the rifle against the wall off to his side, within easy reach.

"OK now, untie the coffee maker, Lombardi. That pot's ready to boil over," Juan said, in a matter-of-fact manner. When Dave was free, Juan said, "Well, David, the giant killer, serve us some coffee."

Dave was building a deep dislike for Juan. Since he had entered his life, right from the beginning he had started poking fun at his name. He moved about angrily, finding a spoon and some sugar. He only had two cups, but found a couple of empty cans that weren't too dirty and went to the water bucket and rinsed them out.

"Does everybody want sugar in their coffee?" Dave said.

He looked about. Everyone had shaken their heads affirmatively. Dave handed the two women the coffee cups, he figured he and Juan would drink out of the cans.

"Hey, desperado in black," Juan said, looking at his can of coffee. "Give this one to the Gypsy queen. A man of my dignity does not drink from cans," and held the can out to Dave.

"Mister, you haven't any more feelings than a ten-minute egg," Dave muttered under his breath.

"What's that you say, Davy boy? Eggs? Yes, I could use some eggs," Juan said. "Have you got any?"

It was well past noon now, and Dave was hungry. The rain was still coming down in buckets and the wind was stronger than ever.

"Yea, I've got a few eggs. A slab of bacon too and some blackberry jelly. No more bread though. We ate it up this morning," Dave said.

"Why, that's no problem," Juan said. "I've got soda crackers tucked away in my bag. I'm sure your jelly will be delicious on them. Up, up, Conchetta, give Master Davy a hand at preparing our meal. A pistolero such as he should not have to labor alone."

Conchetta rose reluctantly. She felt miserable being so wet. Her dress was heavy, and she would have to sit by a fire for hours before it dried out. She had another dress in her bag that probably hadn't gotten wet. By this time, she didn't give a damn about modesty. She was tired of being miserable and she figured that if she felt more comfortable her spirits would brighten. Some food and a dry dress might keep her more alert.

"I need to change into a dry dress. There's one in my bag," she said, looking at Juan.

"What? Here in front of everyone? I don't see another room here, Lombardi, do you?" Juan exclaimed in an exaggerated manner.

"I don't care. It will only take a moment. This dress will never dry."

She looked over at Suen who was wearing a light-weight oriental style shift. Suen had risen from her chair and had been standing by the stove and the hot black pipe. She seemed to be drying out quickly.

"Davy won't care," Suen said quietly to her.

Conchetta wasn't sure what that meant, but just stood there staring at Juan.

"Oh, go ahead, Lombardi, if you don't care, I don't. Just be quick about it. I'm getting hungry," Juan said.

Conchetta reached into her bag and brought out her other black dress. It was barely wet. She quickly got the wet one off and momentarily stood there in her wet bloomers and camisole. The wet garments clung to her, revealing her shapely figure.

Juan looked over at Dave who had not so much as looked up, but was intent on cracking eggs into a bowl.

Conchetta slipped the dry dress on, regretting that she still would be damp underneath, but at least she was warmer and her undergarments would dry out sooner. She hung her wet dress from a nail on the wall near the stovepipe, and walked to where Dave was.

Juan thought this whole scene quite strange. Dave had paid absolutely no attention to a scantily clad, beautiful female! Odd indeed, he concluded.

"Say, Davy, what's with you? You didn't even glance over at Conchetta! What are you, a mariposa, a maricon, some type of queer?" Juan said.

Dave didn't know the first two words, but he knew what queer was, and even though maybe he fit the bill, he didn't like to be called one.

"Hell no, I'm a Spartan," Dave said proudly.

"Yea, and this dumpy shack's a romantic getaway. What's that supposed to mean, you're a Spartan?" Juan asked incredulously.

"It means I'm a warrior who likes brave men," Dave said matter-of-factly.

"Yeah, a limp wrist who doesn't like women," Juan shot back. "Oh well, to each his own," he added.

Conchetta cast a glance back at Suen, who looked at her and shrugged her shoulders.

"I need a knife to slice up some of this bacon," Conchetta said in a low voice to Dave.

"I heard that. Don't you dare give that woman a knife, David, my man. She will have your balls slit in a second, and then you won't be anything. You cut the bacon and be quick about it. Remember, a bullet's faster than a knife, and there's one aimed right at you, so be careful with that slicer," Juan said.

At Juan's mention of a fast bullet, a thought was triggered in Dave's head. When Juan showed up and started ordering him around at gunpoint, and the storm broke with all its intensity, Dave had become so startled and confused that he forgot that the little single-shot derringer still rested snugly in his inner coat pocket.

My bullet's probably just as fast as your bullet at close range, Mr. Smart-Aleck, Dave thought to himself. Finding the correct opportunity to use the little pistol was what he now began to think about. Dave sliced up some bacon and returned the knife to a shelf where it was in plain sight.

Juan rose from his chair and retrieved the knife saying, "Hum, not bad balance, might even make a good throwing knife."

Still holding the revolver in one hand, he abruptly swiveled and threw the knife at the far wall where it buried itself in the middle of Conchetta's wet dress. While Juan stood for a moment admiring his throw and getting ready to speak, Dave reached inside his coat for the little derringer. He had trouble getting it out of his pocket. He imagined it being so simple and easy, but it wasn't. It seemed it had taken an eternity for him to wrap his fingers around the handle.

"Stop right there, David," Juan said.

He had seen Dave's clumsy move out of the corner of his eye and had instantly taken two steps toward him and now stood close to Dave with his arm extended, the barrel of the revolver inches away from Dave's forehead.

"Bring an empty hand out of that coat pocket, David," Juan barked, moving closer and jamming the gun in Dave's stomach.

Dave dejectedly did as told, and Juan quickly reached inside his coat and removed the derringer.

"My, what a nice little toy. Too bad you hadn't practiced getting it out faster. Who knows what damage you may have done? You see, David, practice makes perfect. Surely you noticed how fluid and accurate my knife throwing is," Juan said while going over to the knife, retrieving it and tucking it into his belt. "Why, think of how accurate your namesake was when he hit Goliath in the forehead with a rock flung from his sling. Now that was a true demonstration of skill. Though I don't believe any of it. The bible, I mean. Nothing more than wives' tales intended to keep people docile. Have you noticed how the devil always looses in the bible, David? Why do you think that's so, my Spartan friend?" Juan said.

Dave reluctantly glanced up at Juan's eyes. For a split second he thought he saw a tiny flame in each of Juan's pupils, then the flame vanished, and all he saw were two eyes devoid of life. Dave didn't like that Juan seemed to be making fun of the bible. His Ma was always reading the bible, and she seemed to enjoy it.

He thought for a moment and said, "The devil always loses 'cause he's evil and bad. Why, he's nothing more than a fallen angel, as I recall," Dave said knowingly.

"No, no, no, David, that's wrong too. The devil was around way before any angels. The devil was the bearded god's twin brother. They were still inside the womb of the world, but some fluke of nature occurred, probably a comet. The comet struck the womb of the world on the side where one of the twins rested; causing that twin to be born with uncontrollable power, though his leg shriveled a bit from the heat, so he came out limping," Juan said sadly.

Continuing, he said, "The devil only loses because he wants to. He tricks everyone into thinking he's the weak one. One day he will return in the form of a man and walk the earth, displaying his power and annihilating the bearded god's disciples."

Juan straightened his body; a full smile came to his face revealing a mouth full of yellowish teeth. He seemed to grow in stature, and the large shadow he cast on the wall seemed to be moving and shimmering, though Juan was standing quite still.

Suen had been watching and listening carefully to all this, and couldn't believe what she was hearing. The skinny, pale young man was obviously crazy. He seemed to have invented his own twisted creation myth. It certainly had nothing to do with Christianity or Buddhism, nor any other religion she was familiar with. *Twins inside the womb of the world struck by a comet! Incredible,* she said to herself. *Why, I thought David was dangerous and crazy, but he's a saint compared to this nut, Juan.*

My, my, Conchetta thought. So, now he believes he's the devil returned to walk the earth. Why didn't he say 'limp around the earth' and be more precise. He constantly tries to show off, but his powers are failing, I can feel it, she told herself.

"Well, the show is over folks. This exercise has increased my appetite. Here Lombardi," he said, returning to his bag and tossing a sack of soda crackers at her. "Busy yourself at spreading some jelly on these. David, get that skillet full of bacon on the stove. Notice I haven't shot you. I still would like you for my guide, though my feelings are some-what hurt by your rude behavior. I would have thought that a Spartan would have been more courteous than to try and shoot a friend," Juan said.

"You ain't my friend," Dave mumbled, and proceeded to cook the bacon.

When the bacon was done, he set it on a plate, drained some of the grease, dumped the eggs in the pan, and began scrambling them. Soon everyone was eating as the rain continued to pour down. Juan was vexed by the storm. Though he had taken back roads and had avoided Healdsburg, he had a nagging feeling that someone was trailing him. The storm was a bad turn of events, and now in a while it would be getting dark. After eating, he tucked the revolver in his belt and grabbed the rifle. He threatened everyone not to move an inch, and walked out the front door to look at the sky, while keeping a sharp eye on everyone inside. There was no let up in the rain. Every inch of sky he saw was filled with grayish black clouds. The horses looked miserable tied out front, their heads hung low. He would need strong, rested horses to make it over this mountain, he realized. He looked quickly around and noticed a corral of sorts in back of the shack. He went inside and told Conchetta and Suen to sit on the floor near the bed. He gave Dave some rope and told him to tie the women securely to the bed. This done, he ordered Dave to unhitch the horses and lead them to the corral. The same was done with Dave and Suen's horses once the saddles were removed and brought to the porch. Dave gave the horses some of the hay Juan had in the wagon, and Juan motioned him back inside with a wave of his gun.

"Go ahead and untie the women, David. Looks like we'll have to spend the night here, in which case all of you will have to be tied if I'm to get any sleep," Juan said.

Once untied, Conchetta and Suen returned to their seats near the fire. Dave walked over to the stove and added more wood. His leg hurt where the ragged man had bitten him the previous day. In spite of his current predicament, thoughts of rabies once again entered Dave's head. Juan had returned to the chair near the door and sat calmly observing everyone, revolver in lap.

"Say, Mister Juan, I got bit yesterday by a ragged man who popped out from under a bridge and bit me on the leg. It feels like it's festering. I don't know if whiskey would help, but I'd be grateful if you'd let me get the bottle and pour some of it on those teeth marks," Dave said.

"Why, by all means, David! Troll bites can be quite dangerous. I hope the troll you ran into was not rabid. If that's the case, I'll have to take you outside like a dog and shoot you," Juan said seriously.

Dave grabbed the almost full whiskey bottle from the shelf, pulled up his pant leg and doused the bite with a little whiskey. The bite didn't look that bad, but it got Dave to start thinking about trolls.

"This man weren't no troll. Why, he fought for General Winfield Scott, even skewered some Mexican kid like a sausage from his bayonet. I think the war made him crazy," Dave added.

"Oh," Juan said. "I see. Skewering boys with a bayonet. What a fine idea. If one were to substitute nuns and priests for boys, I would love to indulge in such pleasures myself.

"You'd skewer a nun or a priest? Why you'd go straight to hell, Mister," Dave said wide-eyed.

"David, David, where do you think I've come from? Now be a good fellow and pour out some of your whiskey. You and I shall ride the storm out while slowly drinking. The women can catch up on their beauty rest. Have you any cards, Davy boy?" Juan said.

Dave grabbed a deck of cards from the shelf. Juan moved with his weapons to the floor in front of the make shift table. He told Dave to sit opposite him, and bring the bottle. Juan and Dave played cards until dark. The wind and the rain never let up and continued battering away at the isolated little shack.

Chapter 23

Angelina and Mai walked straight to the beer garden and entered the open doorway, Angelina leading. She went up to McCraken, who was seated on a stool at the bar with a mug of beer and said, "Captain, I need to borrow that Navy Colt you whacked Davy in the head with."

Besides the bartender, there were only two other men in the beer garden, but they stopped drinking and looked, astonished, at the two bold women who had suddenly entered.

"Why, Angelina, good to see you. Sure, you can borrow it, but why do you need a revolver? Dom said you had gotten quite accurate knocking down ducks with a shotgun. That's a far better weapon to use than a revolver," McCraken said.

"She's not going to shoot ducks. We need it to go shoot Davy and another kidnapper. Davy rode off with my daughter, Suen, and some other snake kidnapped Angelina's sister," Mai said, in a breathless rush of words.

Angelina quickly added more details to Mai's explanation. She told McCraken, and everyone else who now had crowded around them that the man who had her sister was evidently headed up Geysers Road, as was Dave. A posse of sorts had gone after them, was even now out searching, Angelina added.

Captain McCraken stood up and unbuckled the heavy Colt, wrapped the belt around the holster, and handed it to Angelina.

"I'd go with you, Angelina, but the doc and my son would frown on it. I'm supposed to keep calm and not do much riding. If the doc weren't out of town, I wouldn't dare be sitting here drinking a beer. He'd tell my son he saw me up at the garden enjoying a drink, and next thing they'd do is take away old Parker. I've had Parker since he was a colt. Named him after my Parker shotgun. Parker would probably pine away if I didn't ride him now and then. Besides, if there's a posse already after them, that ought to do. Davy shouldn't be much trouble. By the way, Mrs. Ling, I don't think you need to worry much about Davy harming your daughter. Davy don't even like girls. He just hasn't figured it out yet. He probably grabbed Suen to do a little experimenting is all. It's about time he came to the realization that he's partial to males instead of females. Had a few of them in the army we did. Some of them made damn good soldiers. Took a lot of ribbing, though, they did. Davy's mean and can be nasty, but he wouldn't harm a woman. I can almost guarantee you that," Captain McCraken said.

"I hope you're right, Captain. I've already lost a son to stupidity. I hope David's reckless behavior won't result in harm to my daughter," Mai said.

"Thanks for the loan of the gun, Captain," Angelina said, reaching out and squeezing the old man's arm. "We've got to go now; it will be getting dark shortly."

"Be careful, Angelina. It's obvious you're headstrong and determined to follow that posse. Gossip makes the rounds in a small town. I heard your sister was missing; I hope you get her back. Just you girls keep your heads down if bullets start flying. If you end up using my Colt, keep a firm grip on it. It's got a good jump to it. Good luck, ladies," McCraken added.

When Angelina and Mai left, Al the bartender said, "I knew that Davy was up to something. I talked to him earlier. He came riding through town dressed up like some fancy gunslinger in one of them dime novels he's always reading. Said he was going to a shooting contest over your way in Poor Man's Flats." Al looked quizzically at McCraken.

"There's no shooting contest in the Flats. Dave was trying to create some type of alibi is all; looks like he's finally gone and got himself in deep trouble now," McCraken said.

"What? Because he ran off with that cute little China Mary? No one cares what happens to them foreigners around here. Why, if she fell off Dave's horse and split her skull, it would only mean that a few less China brats would be born around here," Al said.

The captain shook his head and stuck his grizzled face closer to Al.

"Al, where were your folks born?" he inquired.

"The Old Country. One in Scotland, the other in Ireland," Al said matter-of-factly.

"And you've got a son, Tim, right?" the captain said.

"What are you talking about? You know Tim," the bartender said.

"Well, what if someone hit Tim over the head and killed him, and I said, 'Good, who gives a damn about them foreign Scotch-Irish? Guess there will be one less young stud to sire a brood of them foreigners,'" the old man said, rubbing his chin.

"McCraken, you're daft! Everyone knows Scotch-Irish ain't foreigners," Al said in an offended manner.

"Al, you just don't see the point, do you? People is people—they all bleed red. Oh, why do I even talk to you? Sometimes you seem too dumb to scratch fleas," McCraken said. He finished his beer and left the bar.

Now that a weapon had been procured and a few supplies purchased, Angelina and Mai rode out of town in the wagonette. Angelina didn't want to try to catch up with the men. She knew Dom and the others would think it foolish and dangerous to allow two women in a pursuit. Her plan was to stay out of sight from the men, but close enough to hear any gunshots and arrive at any meeting of the kidnappers and the posse in less than ten minutes. Angelina was the only one there who knew Conchetta and how impulsive, and at times rash, she could be. If there were to be some kind of standoff she wanted to be within shouting distance of Conchetta. She had no idea of what she might say, but she figured she would know when the time came.

It was dark when they reached the bridge that spanned the Russian River in Alexander Valley. The moon was out, but clouds covered it most of the time. Angelina led the wagonette over the wooden bridge, and had not continued on for more than a quarter of a mile when she saw a campfire off the road in a grove of trees that separated two orchards. She could see a group of men moving about the fire, and figured it was Dom and the others. She stopped, handed the reins to Mai, got down and walked quietly closer to make sure that it was Dom and the group. She returned shortly and announced to Mai that indeed it was the men, and evidently they had decided to stop for the night. Dom and Po seemed to be doing the cooking, she told Mai. There was no suitable spot to camp nearby, so they decided to go back to the river and spend the night in a sandy clearing amongst the willows.

Before long they had their own little fire going, and the women began to prepare a meal. Mai filled a pot with river water and put it on the grate to boil. Angelina chopped up garlic, onion, and some dried mushrooms. Just before the water was ready to boil, she poured a good amount of olive oil into a pan, added her ingredients, along with dried oregano and rosemary, and sprinkled in some salt and pepper. In no time, a wonderful aroma began to fill the air. Mai dropped a package of dried macaroni into the boiling water and when it was cooked al dente, as Angelina had taught her, she drained the water and poured the contents of the other pan over the noodles. She mixed it all together, then spooned it into two wooden bowls they had purchased at the general store.

They sat cross-legged on the packed sand near the fire to enjoy the food, and had only tasted a few mouthfuls when the dark figure of a man appeared before them. He stepped closer to the fire, and the light revealed a filthy, ragged-looking man, gaunt with an unkempt beard. His beak-like nose was twitching, and he looked straight at the pot of food sitting on the grate.

Angelina had the revolver nearby, but for some reason made no move to grab it. Instead, she stood up, grabbed the pot that still held a spoon and walked towards the man saying, "Sit by the fire, Joe. You look like you're hungry. Try some of this. It's not too fancy, but it's all we've got tonight."

"Why, thank you, ma'am. That's very hospitable of you. I could smell your cooking a hundred yards away. I can't quite remember smelling anything so good lately. In fact, I can't remember much of anything. I can remember eating fish, carp mostly, but once I speared a salmon. By far a superior fish taste wise, but a fellow can live on carp if he has to."

The filthy man squatted on his haunches by the fire, spooning large mouthfuls of macaroni into his mouth. He ate the first few bites so fast that it spilled from his lips and collected on his beard alongside the thistles.

Realizing he was wasting food, he slowed down and said between mouthfuls, "I reckon you ladies are looking for a Celestial girl. Well, I've seen her. Some no-count dressed like a Jim Dandy had her slung over his horse. I met him this afternoon. Bit his leg, I did. Leg smelled like dog piss. I imagine the boy's been up to no good. He said the gal was his dead sister, but I seen her breathing under the blanket he had her wrapped in. Knew she was a China Mary by the smell. She smelled just like you ma'am," the old man said, nodding to Mai.

Mai stood up and wagged her finger at the man saying, "We are not China Mary. You saw my daughter, Suen, and my name is Mai."

"My, my, you're a touchy one. I meant no disrespect. It's just that I'm not used to talking much to people anymore, and sometimes I choose the wrong words."

"What do you mean you saw her breathing under a blanket? And what is your name anyway?" Mai asked.

"Name's Oliver Platte, veteran Mexican American War, served under General Winfield Scott. Skewered a boy at Chapultepec. That Jim Dandy fellow probably cold-cocked your daughter to keep her under control. She was slung over his horse, but like I said—she was breathing. The son-of-a-bitch coldcocked me too. Didn't have much of an effect though. Us Plattes are hard headed, and now I'm dim witted," Oliver said.

Mai sat back down and stared into the fire. Evidently, Suen had been knocked unconscious. Her son, Mat, had been hit in the head by a horse and killed. Suen was breathing, but for how long? Mai began to feel so agitated, sad, and angry, that she wanted to run out into the night, run until she found Suen and saw for herself that she was breathing. The thought of Suen not breathing, but still and cold like Mat, placed a dark shadow in front of the fire, and Mai felt like she was going to vomit. Her head began spinning and she lay over on her side, her face touching the hard sand. Quiet sobs began convulsing her body.

Angelina rose to go to Mai, but Oliver Platte beat her to it. The ragged man, stinking of fish, put his arm under her shoulder and sat her up. He stroked her head with his large bony hand and said, "Mai, your daughter's going to be all right. I've seen terrible things in war and have known men who have done terrible things. I'm one of them. That Jim Dandy ain't. He's just stupid. Knew it as soon as I laid eyes on him. He couldn't hit your daughter very hard. It's not in him. Why, he's too busy being confused to do much damage. I saw a strange-looking group of men crossing the bridge earlier. One of them was a Chinese fellow. Your husband, I'd guess. I know a posse when I see one. I'll wager those men are out to get your daughter back, and I've a feeling they will."

Mai looked into Oliver Platte's eyes and saw years of weariness, but she also saw a determined look of conviction. He had his arm draped around her shoulder and the reassuring hug he gave her made her forget about how terrible he smelled. His hug made her remember how strong Suen could be, and how determined she was to hold her head high, in a land that often bred people who tried to make Chinese feel so low. She reached out and patted Oliver's bony hand.

"You really think my daughter is going to be fine?" Mai asked.

"Of course. Us addled folk know certain things. A Jim Dandy who lets a dog piss on him is too stupid to hurt anyone bad," Oliver Platte said.

Angelina began to laugh, so too did Mai.

"Say, Spaniard, you've got a mighty fine laugh. I have a feeling I'm a lucky man. I do believe that if I'd been a meaner sort you wouldn't have hesitated to shoot me with that Colt you've got next to you," Oliver Platte said to Angelina.

"Hey, watch it, Joe. I'm an Italian, not a Spaniard. You sure do smell, but I figured you weren't a bad sort. The moon whispered it into my ear," Angelina said, smiling, her white teeth gleaming in the darkness.

"Hum. I've a feeling you're a strange one. Italian you say. Well, I'll not call you a Spaniard, if you quit calling me Joe. You know, you remind me a little of that old saying, 'Most women are half devil and half angel—that's the sugar in the coffee.' By the way, what kind of spices did you put in that macaroni?" Oliver asked.

"A little *rosemarino*, a little oregano. Fresh is better, but dry works too. Say, Oliver, I haven't seen you around town. Why don't you find a shack in Healdsburg? I'll bring you some macaroni or some ravioli now and then. What have you been doing? Living under the bridge?" Angelina inquired.

"Well, yes. For a little while anyway. I became mesmerized looking at fish. Ate a lot of them too. Down at the bottom of a deep pool, I saw a fish that had a head as large as a man's with a mustache curling out as it swam. I could see its eyes. They never blinked. It moved slow and kept to the bottom. Don't tell a soul, but I think I saw a man-fish," Oliver Platte said in a low voice.

"Oh, you only saw a big old catfish. In the morning, you better start on your way to town. Camp down by Foss Creek. When I get back I'll help you find a cozy little shack. There's catfish in the river near town. I'll show you where to find them. I'll teach you how to do some good cooking, and at night you can dream of fish. How does that sound?" Angelina said.

"You would teach me how to cook macaroni and find them spices? You think I could dream of fish instead of bloody boys? Say, what's your name anyway? And how do I know that you're not a witch? Witches can be beautiful, I hear tell," Oliver said.

"I'm Angelina Londi, and what if I was a witch? Why would you care as long as I helped you quit dreaming about bloody boys? I can do that you know."

Angelina rose, walked over to Oliver Platte, and put her hands on either side of his temples. She gazed into his face with half-closed eyes, and then she opened them wide and said, "No more bloody dreams. The river is peaceful, and the fish are calm. Dream of the river and the blood shall be washed away."

Oliver Platte's eyes filled with tears. Great sobs racked his body. Angelina still held his head. Mai came over and hugged him. They held him like that until the sobbing ceased.

"My, my, I think I'll go to town in the morning. Maybe even look for a job. Don't know what come over me, but I feel like I'm breathing a little better. The air seems fresher." Oliver Platte stood and shook his head. "Say, Angelina, you don't happen to have a bar of soap in that wagon? I'd like to go back to my camp and clean up some. Gotta look good if I'm gonna go to town," he said.

Angelina rummaged in the wagon, then handed him some soap. "Keep it, Oliver. I've got extra. That's a good idea. You go clean up. We're tired and may have a big morning ahead. Remember, camp by Foss Creek. You might find some Indians there, but don't worry about them. Tell them you're Angelina's friend. Maybe they'll befriend you," she said.

"Good night, ladies," Oliver said, looking up at the moon that had popped out from behind a cloud. "I have a feeling that today was my lucky day, running into you two. You girls are going to be all right. The moon just told me," Oliver Platte said, and he walked out into the night.

"Mai, let's finish eating. It's cold food now, but we need it. Are you very tired, or do you feel like taking a little walk? Those clouds have parted for a while, and I think we could sneak up on the men and see what's going on. What do you think?" Angelina inquired.

Mai was all for it. The two women put on coats and began walking down Alexander Valley Road. After a while, Angelina decided it was wiser to get off the road and proceed through the orchards and fields instead. It would be better not to have to explain to anyone who might pass by what they were doing walking a lonely road at night-time. Occasionally, night birds would cry out and a frog would bellow, but mostly it was the cicadas they heard as they cut through an orchard, straight for the glow of a fire that they could see in the distance, flickering behind a grove of trees.

"I'll bet you those rascals are drinking," Angelina quietly said as they approached the cover of the trees that separated them from the men gathered about the fire.

Sure enough, most of them were drinking from tin cups. A gallon jug wrapped in burlap was sitting on a stump. Some of the men were still eating. Angelina saw Dom walk over to a pot suspended above the fire and spoon what looked and smelled like beans with bacon onto his plate. A long loaf of bread was on the stump next to the jug. Dom cut off a slice of it and went to his saddle and sat. The men had arranged their saddles around the fire and were sitting either on them or on the ground in front of them with the saddles as a back support.

Mai and Angelina exchanged glances, both shaking their heads side to side.

"Look at those knuckleheads. There's serious and dangerous business ahead, and all they care about is their stomachs and what's in that jug. Great rescuers they'll make, all hung over in the morning," Angelina whispered.

Mai just smiled. She was looking at Po. The women were crouched behind a thick valley oak about sixty feet away from the men, and Mai could see Po quite clearly. He too was sitting on his saddle, holding a plate of food and talking to Pino, who sat to his left. The men were talking to one another, except for Frank, who stood away from the fire and was staring out at the road.

"I think if we creep to that next tree we can hear clearer what they're talking about," Mai whispered.

The women moved closer, carefully placing their feet down slowly and gently on the dry grass and leaves. No one noticed. Now they were in earshot, crouched behind another large oak. Mai's eyes opened wide when she heard what Pino was saying.

"Po, you mean you haven't noticed how Walter's been behaving around Suen? I'm afraid the king of baseball is smitten by your daughter. You're going to have to watch him. When we get her back from Davy, Walter's probably going to try and run off with her next."

"Pino, would you mind your own business," Walter said from his position on the ground next to him, his back leaning against the saddle. "Po, you know I have nothing but respect for Suen, but Pino's right, in a way. I have been thinking about asking your permission to come calling. I do enjoy talking with Suen whenever I get the chance," Walter admitted.

In a way, Mai wasn't surprised to hear this. She had noticed that when Suen was around Walter she seemed at ease and not reserved and defensive, as she was around most other young men. Mai liked Walter. She was impressed with his intelligence and his sound opinions on almost any subject. He was good looking too. If only he could find a way to make some good money, she lamented.

Po picked up his cup, walked to the jug, and poured a little of its content into it. He liked Walter and appreciated the honest and forthright way he had spoken. Someday, he hoped Suen would marry and have children, but he always imagined the lucky man to be Chinese. Life would just be easier that way, he figured. What problems and difficulties might arise between a union of a Pomo Indian and a Chinese girl? Just the thought of it produced a nervous feeling inside his stomach. He had heard of a few wealthy landowners taking a Chinese bride. These were usually older men who treated their wives like concubines.

Walter and Suen were almost the same age, and Walter certainly wasn't wealthy.

Po knew that Walter was expecting some type of comment, but couldn't think of what to say without hurting the boy's feelings. In exasperation he said, "Why, if you just want to talk to Suen, I see no harm in that, Walter. But if you were to expect more than that, I'm sure you must realize the difficulties that would ensue."

Dom had been standing off to the side listening. He walked up behind Po, laid his hand on his shoulder, and said, "Po, my friend, you know that there are no difficulties that are stronger than love. What if Walter and Suen were to fall in love? Possibly they already have, for all we know. Could you stand in the way of their happiness?"

Behind the tree, a big smile came to Angelina's face. *Dominico Londi, you hopeless romantic,* she thought. *Oh well. I would have said much the same myself,* she admitted.

Mai was waiting for Po to speak. She knew this would be a difficult question for him to answer. She knew, though, how she would answer it.

Po took a reflective sip from the cup; then a smile came to his face. He thought of when he first laid eyes on Mai in the laundry in Sacramento. He barely had a cent to his name and smelled like a livery stable. True, Mai was Chinese like him, but what if she weren't? What if she had been a pretty Indian girl of his same age, and something about her had filled him with a burning attraction and desire? Would he have acted any differently?

"Dom, I must be getting old. Probably out of caution, my thoughts of late are conservative, but I'm not such a fool to stand in the way of love. If love blooms between Suen and Walter, what right would I have to cut it off?" Po said.

Walter felt his face flush. He hadn't drunk from the jug, but all of a sudden he felt giddy.

"Po, you old romantic poet. Well said!" Dom added, bringing the jug over and splashing a little more into Po's cup.

Frank, though standing apart, was near enough that he overheard the interchange. On the ride from town he had an opportunity to talk to Walter and immediately liked him. He had been amazed at Walter's vocabulary and choice of words. Frank had studied while at university, but talking to Walter made him wish he had studied even harder. This Suen was probably a real nice girl, he reasoned. Walter was lucky to find someone that he was interested in and possibly in love with.

All this talk made him think about nothing but Conchetta. He was infuriated when the men decided to stop for the night. He had even told Primo that he could ride on alone by moonlight. There was a chance he could come upon Conchetta and the man who held her.

Primo had noticed that Frank still wasn't quite himself. As the day wore on, he had noticed the young man's eyes growing heavy, and at times he almost looked as if he would nod off on his horse. Aside from Frank, the impromptu posse was made up of mostly older men, some of them not too experienced at riding, let alone riding in the dark. Primo had consulted with the others, and the conclusion had been reached that more could be accomplished if they got a good night's sleep, and continued the hunt in the morning. Pino had mentioned that he didn't like the way the sky looked or the air smelled. A storm could come by morning, he thought.

Frank stared out at the empty road, deep in thought. He should have ignored the others and proceeded on his own. He had to force his mind to stop imagining what the man who held Conchetta may have done to her. She had been under the man's control now for quite some time. The brief glimpse he had of her told him nothing. All he knew was that her cry had sounded desperate, and her eyes held a mixture of both hope and fear.

Gazing up at the moon, he allowed himself to imagine a day when this was all over and Conchetta was free and safe. At least Walter and Suen knew one another. This was not so with Conchetta and he. What if they got to know one another and nothing happened. What if Conchetta showed no more interest in him than that of a helpful stranger? What if she didn't like men with blonde hair and blue eyes? What if the man who held her captive had used her cruelly and left her in a broken, shattered state, forever hateful of men? Frank had heard tales of women that had been abused by men. Some of them never got over it. What if something so terrible had happened to Conchetta that she would never even want to look at another man? The thought of it made him tremble.

Suddenly, Frank realized that he was very tired. Primo had probably been right. All he felt like doing now was sleeping and not thinking. He turned towards the campfire just as Primo was walking up to him.

"Frank, quit worrying. We'll get Conchetta back. Go lie down, get some rest. You've certainly done your part. Remember, none of us would even be here if you hadn't successfully done your job. Say, that reminds me," Primo added. "When this is all over, you are going to law school, aren't you?"

"I am, Primo. I've already spent too many years running around a bit aimlessly. Thanks, by the way, for all your encouragement and help," Frank said.

"Why, Franchesco, use your head. Maybe I have selfish reasons. My caseload is getting so big that soon I could use a partner. Could be I'm trying to hand pick and groom a partner. What do you think?" Primo said smiling.

Frank saw a quick vision of himself as a successful lawyer, with Conchetta by his side, dressed in fine clothes.

"I guess I had better take it one step at a time, Primo. First I've got to pass that damn bar exam," Frank said.

"You will," Primo said as they walked back towards the fire.

Frank lay near his saddle and wrapped a blanket around himself. He wished the others would quiet down, but he couldn't help but listen closely to what Pino was saying. He was telling the others that not all of them were needed to go after one kidnapper and Davy.

"You men should stay here and wait. If only Walter and I went, there would be less commotion. There's too many guns around here. Walter and I don't need guns. I will guide Walter to this kidnapper and he will use a good solid rock for a baseball and fling it at his head. One throw, no shots—that's all it will take," Pino assured everyone.

"What about Davy? A rock too?" Po asked.

"Po, David doesn't know what he's doing. When he finally realizes it, he'll probably decide to face the music and bring Suen back on his own. I have a feeling I even know which shack he may have fixed up and carried her off to. It's probably Fandango Bob's old place. It's the only shack up there worth fixing up," Pino said.

"Who's Fandango Bob?" Walter asked. "I don't think you've ever mentioned him."

"Bob was the Pomo who traveled the farthest. His real name was Running Quail, because he would never stop moving. Once he moved all the way to Mexico with a bag of gold nuggets, hoping to trade them for turquoise. When he returned, no one wanted the turquoise. So he moved up this mountain where he and a white friend, Jack Ass Ray, built a cabin. They trapped animals and raised a few horses. Fandango Bob used to say that he taught a rattle snake to guard the place when he was gone," Pino said.

"Why did they call him Fandango?" Walter asked.

"Because, while down in Mexico, he learned a special dance called the Fandango. When he got back up here, he spent most of his time showing the dance to anyone who would watch. An elder called him Fandango Bob and the name just stuck," Pino said.

"What happened to him? I like a good dancer," Pietro chimed in.

"His friend, Jack Ass Ray, said the rattle snake bit him. He died, and Ray buried him somewhere near the cabin. He taught that snake to guard the place, but he forgot to explain to it who the owner was. Ray left after that and moved into town. One day, a few years later, he returned to look at the old place. He carefully opened the door, and sure enough, there was the snake waiting. He shut the door and never went back."

"And you think Davy took Suen there?" Po asked.

"Yes, I do, Po. But don't be concerned. If that snake was still there, Davy would just shoot it and eat it. He doesn't know it, but I've seen him practicing with his gun. He's very accurate with it. Once, I saw him shoot a rattler and cook and eat it on the spot. I admit I have a fondness for them too," Pino added.

Angelina and Mai, crouched behind the tree, had clearly heard the story. They looked at each other and exchanged shrugs. Mai didn't like the story about the snake. David was a big enough snake already. A real rattler was just one more thing she would have to worry about.

Pietro, who had been drinking liberally from the jug, grabbed his Lupara and said, "If we go up to that cabin and the snake is still around, there won't be any of it left to eat after I blast it with this. I think Fandango Bob and I could have been good friends," he said, a slight slur to his voice.

"Don't be angry at the snake, Pietro. It was just doing its job. Ray said that Bob named the snake 'Doom.' And you know what they say about doom—when it's got your mark, you're already dead," Pino pronounced solemnly.

The men were silent for a moment, listening to the crackle of the fire. Except for Pino, all of them had been making trips to the jug. It was getting late now, the moon hidden mostly in clouds. High in the sky, a large flock of ducks could be heard moving south. The men started to wander off into the bushes to water the ground.

Angelina was taken aback when she saw Dom coming toward the tree to relieve himself. She pulled Mai close to her and covered her eyes. "Don't look," she whispered. "That thing of Dom's might scare you to death." Mai began to laugh and snort in Angelina's hand. She quickly controlled herself, lest Dom hear.

The men returned to the fire and covered up in the blankets. Pietro poured a last shot into his cup and sat by Pino, who was still up staring at the clouds.

Pino turned to him and said, "Do you know about the Etruscans too? Dom's been telling me about them."

"Why, of course. They were the masters at predicting the future. Some of them did it by looking at livers," Pietro said.

"Livers?" Pino said, amazed. "Why didn't they just ask the large red ants? Everyone knows that they are the wise ones. They only stay so busy because they've seen the future, and they know that there is much to do in their time allotted."

"But how do you talk to them?" Pietro asked.

"Simple," Pino said. "You place one in your ear and let him walk through your head and come out the other side. By the time he's accomplished that you will know all you need to know. Didn't the Etruscans do that?" Pino inquired.

"Perhaps," Pietro said seriously. "I'll ask Primo in the morning. At times, I've seen him busy as an ant. I should check on the horses one last time," Pietro said, and stumbled a little as he walked away from the fire.

"Let's go," Angelina whispered. "We need sleep too."

The women crept away soundlessly. When out of hearing distance, they walked at a rapid pace back to the river and their camp. Along the way they were startled by a large raccoon and its babies that passed near them in the shadowy moonlit field. Now and then flocks of ducks continued moving through the sky. While listening to the men and their silly talk, Angelina had slipped into a light mood. But now, moving towards camp, thoughts of Conchetta and the seriousness of the situation returned to her. She felt tired and almost wanted to cry, but when they reached the camp she was amazed at what she saw. The campsite had been all tidied up! The horses had been unhitched and were tied on long leads, quietly grazing. Some of the oats that were in a sack in the back of the wagon were spread out around them.

Their fire was burning nicely and something fragrant and steaming was in a can over the grate. Their blankets had been spread near the fire and thick ferns had been piled up for pillows and covered with sackcloth. Angelina walked to the can over the fire and took a deep whiff.

"Why, it's chamomile, chamomile tea!" she said.

"Angelina look!" Mai said, pointing.

Away from the fire a hole had been scooped out of the damp sand. It was lined with bracken fern. Mai walked over and moved away some of the ferns revealing four nice sized silvery trout, cleaned and ready to cook.

"Oliver Platte," Angelina said. Mai nodded her head. "Those trout will make a good breakfast. Let's have some of the tea. It's good for sleeping," Angelina said.

The moon continued drifting in and out of clouds as Angelina and Mai curled up in their blankets. A quarter of a mile away from them, when the morning dawned, the men couldn't find their horses.

Chapter 24

The Big Swede, his real name was Erick Soderholm, and Butch Baylow occasionally passed a bottle back and forth as they rode. They were traveling through Alexander Valley, heading for the Soderholm farm. After the baseball game, Erick and Butch talked about doing some salmon fishing the next day. The river ran in back of the Soderholm's place, and Erick had seen a few salmon moving up the shallow riffles. Their plan was to sit by a promising riffle, sip some whiskey, and have a couple of pitchforks nearby. Why bother with hook and line when it was easier to jam the sharp tines of a fork into the fish?

Along the way, they talked about the game and about how Walter had abruptly left and then returned with the astonishing news that Dave had run off with Suen Ling. Big Swede and Butch found this hilarious. They agreed that Dave must have either been dead drunk or had finally lost his marbles. Erick was glad that Walter had left the game. He had made him look silly, striking him out so easily. The pitcher who replaced Walter had given up a home run to the powerful swing of Erick's bat. As they rode and passed the bottle, the conversation focused mainly on how Indians shouldn't be so uppity or even allowed to play baseball, which should purely be a white man's sport, and how old Dave was gonna have a passel of fun with a China Mary.

It was dark now, and instead of crossing the wooden bridge, they cut straight through an orchard and crossed the river at a shallow spot. They hadn't gone far when they saw a group of men milling about a fire and setting up camp. Butch immediately recognized that Walter was part of the group. They dismounted and moved closer through some tree cover to have a better look. Butch and Erick not only saw Walter, but also the owner of the Chinese laundry and that fancy Italian, Dom Londi. A moment later, Walter's crazy old Indian friend, Pino, stepped into view. Three other men were there, none of whom they recognized. Two of the men looked a little like Londi, with big noses and stern-looking, craggy features. Foreigners, Butch concluded.

"Would you look at all them foreigners and Injuns. I'll bet you I know what they're up to, Swede," Butch said.

"Why, I only see one foreigner, Butch—that little chink who runs the laundry," Erick said.

"What do you think Londi is, and those others he's talking to? I'll bet you they're just like him, a garlic-eating wop. Wait a minute, there's a younger one there; blondish hair, but would you look at the beak on him. I'll bet he's a half breed," Butch concluded.

"Butch, how come you and Dave don't call me a foreigner? My folks were from the old country too," Erick asked.

"Why, we know you're a foreigner, Swede, but you're alright. You got blonde hair, blue eyes, and two pretty sisters. Besides, you like 'taters and gravy and your ma makes the best buttermilk around. Hell, you can hit the ball farther than anyone else. But most of all you ain't uppity. Why, you realize you're only a Swede and are grateful us Americans tolerate you. You're a good old boy," Butch said, slapping the Swede on his meaty shoulder.

Erick scratched his head, not sure what to make out of what Butch had just said.

"You know what that is, Swede? That's a posse going after Dave. What else could it be with that Chinaman around? He's found a bunch of losers to try and help him get his daughter back. Why, we oughta do something about this. Give Dave more time to have a little sport with her," Butch concluded.

They peered at the group and watched as Walter strung a rope between two trees and tied the horses to it.

"I've got an idea," Butch said. "Let's go to your house and have some of your ma's fried chicken. I'll try to tickle one of your sisters, then we'll do a little more drinking out in your barn—then when it's late and them yahoos are sleeping, we'll sneak up and untie their horses. That ought to buy old Davy boy a little time. What do you say, Swede?" Butch asked.

"Why, OK Butch. You know I'm glad you don't care that I'm a foreigner. Why, a fellow couldn't have better friends than you and Dave. But, Butch, I have to warn you, if my pa catches you trying to tickle one of my sisters, he'll jam you with a pitch fork," Erick said seriously.

"Oh, I was just joking," Butch said, taking a swig off the bottle. "Let's go get some of that chicken."

At the Soderholm farm, Butch made no attempt at tickling. Mr. Soderholm was stern at the dinner table, and Butch could tell that the man didn't care much for him. He tried his hardest to act like he hadn't been drinking and concentrated on politely filling himself up on the tasty meal. After a huge slice of fresh apple pie, he and Butch excused themselves, and Erick told his pa that they might ride out and do a little coon hunting.

They sat in the barn and drank for a while, then rode out to where the men were camped. They left the horses and quietly sneaked closer. The fire had mostly died out, and everyone looked asleep, wrapped tightly in blankets. Butch decided that the horses would be less spooked if only one of them approached them. Big Swede was so big that just the sight of him might scare a horse, Butch concluded. So, Butch walked soundlessly to the horses and one by one untied the knots that held them to the rope. Each horse knew where to go. A couple hundred yards away, an apple orchard was ripening nicely, and a cold little creek flowed next to it. Butch returned to his horse and watched for a moment as the horses vanished into the night.

"Well, let's get out of here Swede. Someone might wake up," Butch said.

The two rode quickly back to the farm. Butch pulled a fresh bottle from his saddlebag. They stayed up late, sitting amongst the straw, drinking and congratulating themselves on their handiwork.

A hint of light was in the sky. Walter had been awake for a while thinking about Suen. The thought of what Davy might have done to her riled him so that he couldn't wait to find him. He knew everyone would at least like to have some coffee, and was about to rise and get a fire going, when Pino, who had been lying next to him, nudged him and said, "Walter, you've got to remember, Davy doesn't like girls. He likes my member, or as you know, possibly any good upstanding member. I can't blame him. Betty Mae likes it too."

Walter couldn't help but burst out laughing. By now, it didn't surprise him to find that Pino had guessed what he was thinking. It was the look on Davy's face that appeared vividly to him, the times when Pino had revealed himself, that caused him to laugh. Nonetheless, he still didn't trust Dave, even if it was true that he preferred males to females. Why did he have to pick on Suen to experiment with? He should just have gone to the whorehouse in Santa Rosa if he desired to find his true nature. That place, he had been told, even had a few boys and men available for those who flew in a crooked manner.

Walter's laughter had awakened Dom, who immediately rose and began stirring the fire to see if there were any live coals. Walter got up and walked away from the camp to check on the horses. Only there weren't any horses. The rope between the two trees was still in place, but the horses were nowhere in sight.

They had been tied securely. Someone must have come during the night and untied them, Walter thought. Remembering who lived fairly close by, he cursed himself for not suggesting they tie the horses closer to the camp. Possibly anyone, for a variety of reasons, could have done such a thing, but Walter figured it was Butch Baylow and Big Swede. After the game, they were probably heading for the Soderholms and had spotted them setting up camp. He could just see the delight in Butch's pimply face when he watched the horses scatter in the night.

The other men were beginning to stir and rub sleep from their eyes when Walter came back to camp and announced that the horses were missing.

"Uncle, I thought you were going to check on them before turning in," Primo said, a touch of anger in his voice. "I knew you were visiting that jug too often," he added.

Before he could answer, Walter came to Pietro's defense saying, "The horses were all there when we turned in, and were tightly secured. I checked on them myself a little while before Pietro did. Someone came while we were sleeping and turned them loose, and I have a feeling I know who it was," Walter said.

Walter explained about Butch and Big Swede and their dislike for Indians and anyone else they didn't view as "true Americans," and how Butch was Davy's best friend.

"I don't get it," Pietro said. "This Big Swede is a 'true American'?"

"Oh, the way a lot of idiots around here think is too non-sensical to try and explain. Big Swede, Erick Soderholm, is so eager to have some so-called friends, that he goes along with anything," Walter explained.

"Let's quit jabbering and go find the horses. Maybe they haven't wandered very far," Frank said, disgusted that there would be a delay in the hunt.

Po had been looking up at the sky, which was clouding over, and said, "Yes, we had better hurry. I think a storm might be coming. That would make them harder to catch."

They all agreed, and not waiting for coffee, went off in search of the horses. Walter saw where the dry grass was trampled in a westerly direction and figured that the horses were probably headed for an apple orchard and a small creek nearby. Sure enough, some of the horses were there, contentedly munching away at fallen apples. Walter and Frank caught them and lead them back to camp and tied them, with Po staying in camp to keep an eye on things. The rest of the party spread out in different directions searching for the remaining horses.

Dom and Pietro walked in a northerly direction. They passed through the apple orchard and came to an open field of dry grass up to their knees. The grass had been recently trampled, probably by the horses, they figured. Moving through the field, Dom thought of Angelina. Every day he looked forward just to getting up so he could look at her. The way she cocked her head at times, the many expressions that came to her face, the funny things she would say, made him want to live more than ever. And, now he was on the trail, once they found the horses, of a man who had kidnapped her sister; a man who was obviously desperate and no doubt dangerous. Dom had borrowed an old pistol while at the livery stable. He would have preferred a shotgun or a rifle, something he was more familiar with, but the rusty six-shooter would have to do should some type of fight ensue. He wasn't one bit afraid or hesitant about going after and confronting the kidnapper. What he worried about was the idea of the man putting up a fight to keep Conchetta. The idea of his life ending by one of the bastard's bullets angered him. Not because he was afraid of death, but because his eyes would no longer bask on Angelina. He was thankful he got a good night's sleep and had not made overuse of the jug. From now on, he would have to be on his toes and alert to danger. No way, while he was so happy, did he want to lose sight of Angelina.

Pietro wasn't talking much. He had a slight hangover and was a little peeved about his nephew questioning him about the horses in front of the others. He was grateful to Walter for speaking up for him, and as his head began to clear a bit on the walk, he realized that Primo was just tired from so much riding and not enough sleep. Last night around the campfire, Po, Dom, Pietro, and Primo had all been complaining about how sore their asses were. They were all men past forty and not used to much riding. Primo and Pietro were especially sore, having been mostly on a horse since leaving Santa Rosa.

The field they were moving in was long. After a while, it slowly curved and began to parallel the river. Several times, large coveys of quail had taken flight in front of them, their wings beating in a low-pitched whoosh. Off in the distance, the horses finally came into sight. They were standing away from the field, close to the river, grazing on some green grass that bordered a trickle of a creek that spilled into the river. Two gray herons suddenly took to flight, slow to gain altitude, their long wings flailing the air.

Dom and Pietro quietly moved closer to the three horses. When they were twenty feet or so away, a large skunk, leading four babies, came up from the river and crossed between the men and the horses. The horses, more startled at the presence of the skunks than the men, began fidgeting and neighing. This must have startled the mother skunk, who lifted her tail and let loose her fine aromatic blast. The horses didn't wait around, but took off at a gallop for the riverbank. They climbed down it, and soon were moving rapidly towards the river bar.

Dom and Pietro had been close enough to the skunk, who had simply vanished with her brood into the tall grass, to get a partial affect. The odor had filled their nostrils and their eyes stung a little. Not wishing to dawdle, the men took off at a run after the horses.

For over a mile, they played cat and mouse with the horses, moving upstream on the gravel bar, criss-crossing the shallow river several times. Finally, the horses allowed themselves to be caught. Somewhat tired and smelly, but relieved, Dom and Pietro grabbed the leads and headed back towards camp. The sky was filled with ducks and Canadian geese, flying below the moving clouds. By the time they returned, the rain began to fall. And now, October had come, and when the water touched the dry earth, the mushrooms would grow, and the land would begin its big change.

"What took you so long?" Frank said, then instantly regretted that he had questioned the older men. He couldn't believe that a matter of stray horses would ever have become so important. But now, all the horses were accounted for, and the men could continue the chase for Conchetta and Suen. They broke camp and continued on through Alexander Valley, towards Geysers Road.

Around noon, the rain began to increase in intensity, and it was about that time that they reached the road that climbed up to The Geysers. Another road that hugged the foothills to the east also came to the base of Geysers Road at this point. It was the road that Juan and Conchetta had been traveling on only hours earlier.

Walter and Pino had exchanged words as the men paused for a discussion. Walter suggested that he should backtrack on the eastern road in the chance that they had arrived at the junction ahead of Conchetta and the kidnapper. Most likely, they were probably well ahead of them and already moving towards The Geysers, but there was the chance that they could have been delayed for some reason. The men agreed that if Walter didn't come upon them within four or five miles, he should turn around and try to catch up with the others.

"If this storm gets much worse, we'll probably wait it out at the cave," Pino said. "Check for us there, before you continue on up the road," he added.

Oh shit, Frank thought to himself. Why am I continuing to travel on with these old men? Now, there's talk of a delay because of a little rain. He decided that he wasn't going to hole up in some cave, and would continue on alone if he had to.

Walter turned his horse and headed back south alone. The rest of the men began to climb up Geysers Road. Now the sky had grown grayish black and the rain came down in sheets. The wind gained in velocity and the thunder and lightning began. Evidently, the rented horses weren't used to traveling much in storms, for they began to balk and turn skittish. At one blast of thunder, Dom's horse reared up and almost threw him. The progress they made was slow as the road turned to mud, with rivulets of water cascading down it. Frank's horse was acting like the others, skittish at every flash of lightning or roar of thunder. He wished he were riding Tuli. Tuli had been in many a storm up in the Sierra Foothills and just ignored them.

The men were soaked to the bone, but still they rode on. No one wanted to be the first to talk in favor of this "cave" that Pino had mentioned, but all now began to think of a dry cave and maybe a warm fire. They struggled on a couple of more miles, hoping that the storm would break up, but it didn't. The rain continued on steady and it was ever harder to get the horses to advance.

Finally, Pino shouted out over the wind and the thunder, "There's a cave just ahead. We should get out of this storm and let the horses rest. Maybe it will break up in a little while."

All of the men, even Frank, nodded in agreement. He patted his horse and said, "Good thing you're not Tuli, because if you were, there would be no rest for you, I'm afraid."

But, follow the others he did, as they turned off the road onto an overgrown trail, no longer even wide enough for a wagon. They didn't have to traverse it long, when a dark cave, hollowed into the side of a hill, appeared.

"This was the beginning of a quicksilver mine. The owner died, and no one ever continued digging. Everyone says that this elevation is too low to strike quicksilver. Most of it's found on The Geysers ridge or on Pine Flat ridge," Pino explained.

The cave, braced in places with thick redwood timbers, only went about forty feet back into the hillside. There were some oaks and madrones nearby that offered a little protection, and Frank soon had a rope strung and the horses securely tied. Pino mentioned the possibility of animals inside the cave, possibly bear or mountain lion, and began throwing rocks into the cave while Pietro stood ready with his Lupara 10-gauge.

"Watch a pack of skunks run out," Dom said, nudging Pietro.

No animals ran out, but Pino cautioned that there still could be rattlesnakes inside, and began searching under the trees for a long sturdy stick. Finding one, he entered the cave alone, the rest of the men standing near the horses under the slight protection of the trees. Seconds after Pino entered, two large rattlers slithered out of the cave and vanished into the wet grass. Pino followed after them and motioned the men over.

"Just like herding sheep. They need a little coaxing now and then with a stick. Keep your eyes open in there. Could still be some babies hiding under loose rocks," Pino cautioned.

Everyone entered the cave—cold, shivering, and soaked to the bone. Some dry debris was scattered about, and it didn't take them long to get a fire going, near the entrance where the smoke could escape. Frank and Primo went back out in the rain and searched under the trees for larger wood to throw on the fire. They returned shortly with armfuls of wet wood, but the fire was hot enough to burn it after a while. Quickly though, the cave began to get smoky. The wind at times would blow the smoke back into the cave, and the wet wood itself put out lots of smoke before it got hot enough to burn. Frank and Primo went back out and brought in more wood, which they piled by the fire, giving it time to dry out a bit. The cave got pretty smoky, but not bad enough that they couldn't breathe.

Dom and Po ventured out to the horses and returned with the fire grate, and some cooking utensils and food. The men stood around the fire trying to dry out, while Dom got some water boiling for coffee.

There was no sign of let up in the rain. The thunder and lightning had passed on to the south, but the wind was stronger than ever. All the men could do was to dry out and wait for the rain to end.

Dom, as well as the others, felt frustrated by yet another unexpected delay, but the weather was just too vile to move about in. It was doubtful if Conchetta and the kid-napper were moving on in such a storm, they all reasoned.

"Davy and Suen are probably riding this out in Fandango Bob's place," Pino mentioned.

Po wished Pino hadn't spoken. The thought of Davy alone with Suen in some deserted shack had filled his thoughts since Suen was taken. Thinking about it made him feel helpless, angry, and sad all at once, but thinking about it was all he could do.

While everyone stood around the fire and drank coffee, Dom rummaged around in one of the packs and produced two huge steaks and some flour tortillas, all of it wrapped tightly in paper.

"Let's eat this fresh food first," Dom announced. "If we're gone much longer, it will mostly be beans."

The smell of steaks grilling over the fire soon filled the cave and whetted the men's appetites. When they were done, he cut the meat into strips while Po took care of warming up the tortillas. A can of Mexican tomatoes spiced with jalapeno peppers and onions was opened, and presently the men were wrapping the savory meat in the tortillas, and covering them with some of the mixture from the can.

"Dom, when you and Angelina get tired of living out here in the wilds, you should move back to San Francisco and open a restaurant, or at least move into our house and come and cook for me," Primo said, eating heartily.

Indeed, all the men agreed how exceptional the food tasted prepared in a cave with a storm howling out front.

Walter had strung a rope between two of the support timbers towards the back of the cave and the men had hung their wet coats from it. Now, after eating, they sat around the fire and tried to get the rest of their clothes dry.

Pino laughed when he saw the men turning themselves every few minutes trying to dry out one side or another. "Hey, I know a quick way to dry out. Let's just put a little more wood on the fire and move that rope closer to it and get out of these wet clothes," he said.

This seemed like a sound idea and soon there were six naked men standing or sitting around the fire.

"I hope one of those baby rattlers doesn't sneak up on me," Pietro said from a sitting position. "He might mistake my peter for another rattler and try and pick a fight with it."

The men started howling with laughter, but those who had been sitting on the ground causally got up and began casting glances around a little warily.

As steam rose from Dom and Pietro's clothing, the pungent odor of skunk began to displace the pleasant cooking smells.

"Hey, Pietro," Pino said. "I think you and Dom should just burn your clothes and begin working on making some *tule* or leather skirts, or you could even use the inner bark from redwoods, like my people used to. Who knows? Maybe you could start a new style around town," Pino added.

"Don't put that idea in their heads, Pino. A style like that might take hold, and then I'd lose business," Po said, mock seriously.

"Say, Pietro. Did I ever tell you that I like yours and Primo's names? They start with a *P* and sound a little like mine," Pino said. "You could even say 'Pietro, Primo, Pino' and people might think you're talking nasty. I think our names are fine sounding," he added.

The fact that they were all sitting around naked had put the men in a lighthearted mood. They talked amongst themselves, and Frank, then after a while Dom, moved to the side of the cave and sat with their backs against it and their eyes closed, trying to sneak a little nap.

The rain continued on unabated, and shortly before dark, Walter returned to find the men sitting or sleeping around the fire.

"Wow, would you look at this," he said. "I hope Davy doesn't stumble upon this cave. Who knows what he might do."

Walter had barely seen a soul all day. No one was venturing out in such weather. He was soaked and hungry, and in no time had his clothes off and was enjoying some of the food that had been set aside for him.

Before total darkness, the men went out and got more wood. Some beans were prepared and another loaf of the bread eaten. The jug was brought out, but no one seemed in the mood to pull off it regularly. Pino said he would be surprised if the rain wouldn't have stopped by morning, and after awhile, the men got out their bedrolls and one by one drifted off to sleep.

That morning, Angelina and Mai had their trout cooked and the camp broken down shortly after first light. They saw no sign of Oliver Platte, but thoughts of the strange old fellow remained fresh in their minds. Thinking that the men were probably on the road, they continued on in the wagon. When they got close enough to spot the camp, they were surprised to find that the men hadn't left. They were milling around talking, and both women noticed at about the same time that the horses were gone.

"Those drunkards probably didn't tie their horses good. Dio Bono, now how much time is going to be wasted? And would you look at that sky? It's probably going to start raining any time," Angelina said, disgusted.

From their vantage point, they watched as the men began to scatter in different directions, obviously to look for the horses.

"We better turn back," Mai said. "Some of them are walking this way."

They had no choice but to turn the wagon and head back to the river. Angelina and Mai were incensed. They would have liked to proceed on their own, but they would have to go right by the men's camp. At any moment some of the men could return and spot them. Under the circumstances, all they could do was wait about until the men caught the horses and began to continue on.

After a while, Mai went out on foot to check on the men. Some of the horses were back in camp, and a smile came to her face when she saw Po milling about, evidently guarding them and the campsite. She returned and told Angelina, who had a small fire going and some coffee brewing, the news.

Time passed, and then the rain began to fall. This time Angelina ventured out on her own to check on the men. They were breaking camp and all the horses were in plain view. She quickly returned, and once again they were back on Alexander Valley Road, moving towards The Geysers.

On one long straight away they could actually see the men ahead of them about a quarter mile. They kept behind them at this distance as they wound on through the valley, and the rain increased along with the wind. By the time they began the climb up Geysers Road they could see that a full-fledged storm was approaching. The wagonette had a good solid top and the women were staying relatively dry until the wind began to swirl and blow the rain in on them.

Before leaving Healdsburg, Angelina had been watching the sky and had guessed the possibility of a storm. At the general store she had wisely purchased a large oiled canvas slicker. She paused the wagonette, unfolded the canvas, and wrapped it securely around Mai and herself. All now that was getting wet was the women's faces, which began to sting with the coldness of the slanting rain.

When the thunder and lightning began, they too began having trouble with the horses. They made slow progress moving up the now muddy road. They could plainly see the tracks of the men's horses and began to wonder how long the men would continue on in the increasing violence of the storm. As the road got muddier, Angelina began to wonder if a wheel would bog down in it, but so far, beneath the slush, the road seemed hard packed.

Angelina and Mai climbed on in the storm. Both women were wondering what their loved ones, who had been taken, were doing during the storm. If Suen ended up getting pneumonia because of that stupid Davy's actions, Mai would shoot him herself, she decided. Angelina had no idea what Conchetta could be doing or thinking. All she knew was that somewhere ahead of them on this mountain road was the sister that she had struggled for so many years to help raise. Aside from missing the opportunity to meet Dom, she almost wished that they had stayed in Italy. Then she remembered the bandits who often roamed the Italian countryside and at times would venture into the towns and run off with a pretty girl. She remembered how fate, and some unexpected turn of events, often entered one's lives. Who would have dreamed that her first husband, so strong and relatively young, would die in a construction accident? Her brother, Mario, had struck it lucky and was happily married and a successful fisherman. Why, and for what reason, had such a hard destiny wrapped itself around Conchetta? She knew that there were no answers to such questions. All she could do was press forward and hope for a break in luck.

Suddenly, she noticed that the men's tracks had veered off the road and continued on down a narrow trail between some trees.

"They must have pulled in over there to get out of the rain. We need to find a bit of shelter too," Angelina said to Mai.

It was too narrow where they were to immediately turn around, but Angelina could see a wider area ahead. Upon reaching the spot, they turned the wagonette around and went back down the road until they spotted a turn off close to the one the men had taken. Traversing down this, they continued on a ways through a small field that gave way to a thick forest canopy. They stopped the wagon under a partial protection of firs, intermingled with some pine, madrones, and oaks. The wind was not as harsh as out on the open road, and the cover of the overhanging branches blocked some of the rain, as did the hillside to the west of them.

"We might as well go spy on the men. Who knows what they might be up to," Angelina said.

"Probably already drinking," Mai added.

They tied the horses, then folded the slicker until it was smaller and could be draped over their shoulders. Walking close together, they stayed relatively dry as they reached the main road and began walking up it. Both women, surprisingly, were in good spirits. The power of the storm made them feel exhilarated and very much alive, and the prospect of spying on the men excited them.

They turned down the trail the men had taken and after a short while a cave came into view. The horses were tied off a ways under some trees.

"They found a cave to get out of the rain," Mai said.

"Yea, if we sneak around in back of the horses and stay behind those trees, we can look directly in and see what they're up to," Angelina said.

The women backtracked and cut through the trees until they had a full frontal shot of the cave opening. The men were standing around a fire, and then all of a sudden began taking off their clothes.

"Oh, no!" Angelina said. "They're going to have an orgy!"

Mai couldn't help it and let out a short laugh before catching herself. The wind must have been blowing towards the cave at that moment, because a naked Po appeared at the very entrance and peered out towards the trees. He moved his head from side to side, and Mai could even see the quizzical look on his face. Then they saw what the men were doing. They had taken off their wet clothes and were now draping them over a rope that was strung near the fire.

For a moment they felt like young girls spying on a group of boys skinny-dipping in a warm, lazy river—then

Pietro stepped into view with his almost seventy-year-old body and the image from their youth was shattered.

"Well, at least they're using common sense," Angelina whispered. "Why stand around in wet clothes?"

The women had seen enough and were ready to leave when, taking one last look, they saw Pino approach the cave opening where Po had stood and stare out towards the trees.

"Oh, my God! It's a donkey," Angelina cried.

"No," Mai said. "It must be a snake crawling down his back and dangling between his legs."

"Poor Betty Mae. I think she's sweet on that old buzzard," Angelina added.

Straining to hold back laughter, the women turned into the trees and made their way out to the main road. It didn't seem that there was to be any let up in the rain, and obviously the men had no intention of moving about in it, so when they got back to the wagonette, they began to make preparations for spending the night. They thought about attaching the canvas slicker to the roof of the wagonette and then stretching it out and tying it to two close by trees. At least then they could sit under it and get a fire going. But, that was the problem—getting a fire going. There was nothing really dry in the wagon to burn long enough to kindle wet wood, and all that was within sight was soaking wet wood. Even if they could manage to get a fire going, it would smoke so much that perhaps the men would spot the smoke and venture out to investigate.

Instead, they decided to forsake a fire and use the canvas in another manner. They spread it over the top of the wagonette and let it drape long on the sides. Taking some rope and some string, they secured the canvas to the wagonette, which now was enclosed on two sides. Now, if they sat or lay down in the back, they could remain almost perfectly dry. They dug into the supplies and dined on salami and cheese along with some crusty bread. They talked for a while until the wind and the rain began to make them groggy and urge them to sleep. The women lay down in the back and soon were asleep, covered in blankets and quite dry.

They awoke shortly before dark, ate some more, and took care of the horses. Angelina produced one of two bottles of the Massoni zinfandel she had packed, and the women sipped the delicious wine and talked on into the night. When the bottle was empty, they curled back up under the blankets and lay still, listening to the rain pour down on the cover that protected them.

A quarter mile away, the men, now back in dry clothes, began spreading their bedrolls, and Dom and Po dreamed about how much more pleasant it would be to be sleeping in a warm bed with the women they loved.

Chapter 25

The Geysers. There are many places in the world that share this name. Iceland is said to have awe-inspiring geysers.

The Geysers Juan would have to pass by if he hoped to cross over into Lake County were situated within the western front of the Mayacamas Mountains—part of the California coastal range, in a region of rugged topography.

Alexander Valley was situated at about two hundred feet above sea level. The Geysers sat at seventeen hundred feet. Looming over The Geysers was Black Mountain, its summit formed of igneous rocks, was the highest peak in the immediate surroundings.

Weird, eerie, uncanny, and awesome are words often used when trying to describe The Geysers area. The Geysers phenomena was formed eons ago in a volcanic area, where subterranean streams of water continuously mixed with chemical elements of the earth's crust, and caused heat and boiling, thus producing a pressure that forced this mixture to the surface.

For centuries, The Geysers had held the intrigue of the eastern band of Wappo Indians. Before the coming of the white man, they would build scaffolds over certain steaming geysers and place the sick there, either to be cured or to pass on.

Viewed at one time as second only to Yosemite in California's natural wonders, The Geysers would come to inspire poets and writers, who took the long and arduous stagecoach or wagon ride, so they could tell their readers of this wonder of the west.

While exploring the wilds in 1842, Joel Walker and John Ransford were probably the first white men to set eyes on The Geysers. But most folks credit Wild Bill Elliot as the actual "discoverer" of The Geysers, or Devil's Cauldron, as it later would be called. A member of the "Bear Flag Revolt Party," who lived near Mark West Creek, Elliot had been with a party of Americans who seized the pueblo of Sonoma, then controlled by Mexico when rumors were rampant that all Americans were to be expelled from Mexican California.

The group of rag-tag, but well-armed, settlers and adventurers who made up the "Bear Flag Band" invaded General Mariano Vallejo's home—held him and his family captive, and helped themselves to the general's fine wines.

Vallejo was the founder of the pueblo of Sonoma. In 1838, Vallejo was made Commandante General of Alta California—this included all lands north of San Francisco Bay. Thus, for a period of time—until the "Bear Flaggers" took over Sonoma and raised a flag with a crudely drawn bear on it, and proclaimed that they had freed the area from Mexican rule, and even went further to claim that California was now a republic—Mariano Vallejo, a descendent from Spanish nobility, was overseer of all affairs that occurred in what soon would be Sonoma County.

In 1847, Bill Elliot and his son were hunting bear in the rugged hills northeast of what later would be called Healdsburg. They had just killed a grizzly bear when they noticed some smoke rising from a distant canyon. Thinking that they had stumbled upon an Indian village, they investigated and were amazed at what they saw. Sulphur springs, some of them shooting high into the blue sky, along with other areas of geothermal activity, unfolded before them at the bottom of a gorge. The Geysers, so to speak, had been discovered.

As Sonoma County began to fill with settlers, and word got out of this impressive natural phenomenon, a company was formed by three men who built a toll road from Ray's Station in Alexander Valley over Hog's Back Ridge to The Geysers.

In 1861, with R. C. Flournoy at the reins, the first double team and buggy carried a man and a woman over the road to The Geysers Hotel, formerly only accessible by horseback. The first house at The Geysers was built by M. Levy, alongside a wild grapevine that measured twelve inches in diameter. The hotel was built in the 1850's from lumber milled at a sawmill near the site. The hotel often changed ownership, at times, almost yearly. Now, in 1871, J.C. Susenbeth was proprietor. Susenbeth rented it from the owners, Coe, Baxter, and Foss. The first hotel register in 1854 had twenty names on it. In 1870 alone, over two thousand visitors had signed in at the hotel.

Over the Hog's Back was the most picturesque route to The Geysers, though they could be accessed by other roads. The Hog's Back ridge separated the waters of Big and Little Sulphur creeks, both alive with ocean-going rainbow trout, and passed close under the shadow of Geysers Peak. From there, one could see the Russian River Valley, and on a clear day, the ocean far away.

Tourists were mostly interested in the steaming and shooting geysers that were within a half-mile of the hotel in a gorge called "The Devil's Canyon." Pluton Creek flowed nearby. A concrete bathhouse trapped the bubbling, warm sulphur waters, where tourists emerged themselves in the steaming waters, hoping to cure all that ailed them. A series of caves were situated in the hillside near the bathhouse. These caves contained the element radium, and the vapor issuing from them was around one hundred degrees. Some of the caves issued steam, others only vapor. Entrances to Hell, some concluded.

Wild flowers growing near these caves were of gigantic proportion. Stems that normally would be four or five inches tall attained the length of three or four feet. Early hotel owners had planted fig trees nearby. These trees grew unbelievable leaves almost the size of elephant's ears. One leaf was actually measured at twenty-eight inches long. Watches stopped working in the vicinity of the caves.

The sulphurous region around Devil's Canyon boiled, steamed, roared, hissed and gurgled, and one was drawn to the conclusion that the whole area could suddenly erupt in volcanic activity. Mineral springs were all over, some furnished clear, sweet tasting water—others flowed liquid black as ink. All over, steam issued from vents and fumaroles. One gulch was blackened with a never-ending spray of chemical vapors—this was called "The Mountain of Fire." Next to a spring that bubbled water hot enough to boil food, was another spring, with water too cold even to drink.

In an area called "Proserpine's Grotto," the canyon wall was covered with Epsom salt crystals. At the "Devil's Machine Shop," the stones and the ground were hot, and the soil varied in color from the chemical action. One walked on dirt that at times was black, then green, brown, yellow, gray and red. Along a path that wound above "Proserpine's Grotto," a large rock was hollowed out by nature to resemble a chair—the "Devil's Armchair." A little ways past this was the "Devil's Kitchen," a recess in the walls of a ravine covered with sulphur and iron stalactites. From the wall, an opening hissed steam and was called the "Devil's Oven." Near this was another orifice of the same type called the "Devil's Teakettle."

The "Devil's Inkwell" was also near, with its bubbling black water. Further along the path was the "Devil's

Canopy"—a ledge with overhanging iron and sulphur stalactites. Close by was the "Witches' Cauldron"—a depression in the bottom of the gorge bubbling with an inky solution of iron, alum salts and sulphur, hotter than boiling water.

Overlooking this vision of hell, up and on the other side of the canyon, sat the "Devil's Pulpit"—where one had a view of it all. Perhaps the most impressive of all was the "Steamboat Geyser," which was nearby, continuously discharging its sulphurous steam, hissing and roaring and often exploding to a height of two or three hundred feet.

This was where the madman Juan was taking Conchetta, with Davy and Suen leading the way.

Juan rose before early daylight. The moon was now full to the west. The storm had passed, but the sky was gray with billowy white clouds, looking like tufts of cotton circled around the edges with the glow of moonlight.

Juan stared up at the sky and began thinking about Dave and Suen. Obviously, he would have to kill them. It would be impossible for him to allow them to live, and spread the news that Conchetta Lombardi's kidnapper was headed for Lake County with his captive. Once Dave had shown him the correct trail into Lake County, he would quickly eliminate him with a bullet to the head and hide his body. But it was that pretty Chinese girl, Suen, that mainly occupied his thoughts. She was just a few steps away, sleeping on the bed next to that fake Madonna— both women securely tied.

The best thing to do, he decided, was take care of her now. It would be simple to quietly go to the bed, clamp a hand over her mouth, and slit her throat. He could just imagine the look Lombardi would have on her face when she woke up next to a pool of fresh blood. Juan concluded that this would be too simple and devoid of pleasure. He should take Suen outside, make use of her slender white body in the moonlight, and then slit her throat—the same style he used on nuns and those given to religion.

Reaching into his pocket for his bandana, he reentered the shack and quickly gagged a sleeping Suen. She snapped awake in terror to find Juan untying her. Suen instantly began struggling and woke Conchetta, who immediately began kicking out at Juan.

The ruckus woke Dave, who had been sleeping on the floor and tied to the bed. With difficulty, he sat up to find Suen engaged in a struggle with Juan.

"Hey, Mister, what's going on? Leave her alone!" Dave yelled.

"Go back to sleep, and mind your own business, Davy boy. I'm only going to take your lady friend outside for a little stroll in the moonlight," Juan said, managing to jerk Suen to her feet.

Dave knew at times he was slow to pick up on things, but he felt he had a pretty good idea what strolling in the moonlight with Suen might turn into. At one time, he had entertained similar thoughts himself—thoughts that included killing Suen if she refused to cooperate. He had been dreading something similar to what was occurring. Before drifting off into sleep, he had tried to imagine reasons for Juan to continue to allow Suen to live. He hadn't been able to think of any, unless Juan decided to be good-natured and turn Suen loose; not caring what she would tell folks back in town. Dave had gotten her in this fix, and now that he had a change of heart and was totally reevaluating his life, the prospect of helping to bring about Suen's death was intolerable to him.

"Juan, I swear, if you hurt Suen, I won't guide you anywhere. You may find someone at the Geyser's Hotel who will help you, and then again you may not. And I've a feeling a man like you is in a hurry. Why, there's probably people tracking you right now, I'd imagine," Dave said, grasping at straws. "I know a trail that bypasses the hotel. If you follow my lead, you won't have to run into a lot of people. Why, that hotel is probably packed with sightseers who couldn't leave during the storm. And, if it's clear in the morning, the stage and who knows how many wagons filled with tourists, will be climbing this road tomorrow. If you kill Suen, you might as well kill me too on the spot, because I won't give you one bit of help," Dave said forcefully.

It was the most meaningful bit of talking that Dave had ever done. In his wildest dreams he had never imagined that the words he could speak might be the difference between life and death.

Conchetta listened to Dave's speech and was grateful for his quick thinking. She imagined she knew what Juan had in store for the Chinese girl and could only lie there helpless, and hope that Dave's words would buy Suen some time.

Suen was surprised more than anyone at Dave's words. He was actually trying to save her, and she realized Juan had no reason to let her live. She could easily imagine what Juan would probably do to her before killing her. She had noticed earlier that night how at times he had looked at her, as if those sinister, dead-looking eyes could bore right through her clothes. Once she had looked up and found Juan staring at her with a smile while licking his lips.

For an instant, her mind registered amazement that here in a desolate shack, the boy who many years ago had pulled her hair was trying to bargain for her life.

Juan was disappointed. He had imagined quietly slipping out with Suen and having his way. Now people were glaring at him, not one of the three even had a terrified look on their face. All he saw was hatred. He could even see hatred hidden behind the stupid look plastered on the dim-witted Spartan. Just the thought of Dave as a Spartan made him want to laugh. Evidently though, there was some grit about the fellow. He seemed willing to sacrifice himself in order to keep the Chinese slut alive. And slut she was—no different than Lombardi or any other woman, including his mother.

Oh well, I can always have a little fun and kill her later, Juan said to himself. He decided that in a way Dave was right. He didn't want to go to a hotel where there was a bunch of people, and someone probably was trailing him. He had a guide right now—finding a new one could prove dangerous and time consuming.

"Why, David, I had no idea you were such a brilliant orator. I do think you may have plead a successful case for the sparing of your Chinese friend's life. What a resourceful Spartan you are!" Juan added. "Well the fun is postponed for now. Go back to sleep, all of you. There's only a couple more hours until daylight. At first light we leave this 'romantic getaway' and journey up the road. I can't wait to see these famed geysers. I have read one account that described the place as a 'vision of hell.' An area worthy of such a name indeed must be truly remarkable," Juan said.

He removed Suen's gag and moved to his chair by the door and sat down—his revolver resting in his lap. Conchetta, Suen, and Dave lay back down—each one of them thinking and dreading what the morning would bring. None of them could really get back to sleep, and before long the glow of sunlight could be seen outside the windows.

Since there was coffee available, Juan was moving about before light stoking up the fire he had managed to keep barely going. He put the pot on the stove and untied Conchetta while he sat back down and held the gun on her as she went about freeing Suen and Dave's wrists. After everyone drank some coffee and had a few mouthfuls of food, Juan helped himself to some of Dave's supplies. He threw some beans, the rest of the bacon, and the coffee into his bag and ordered everyone out the door.

The sun was burning bright and not a cloud in the sky. The smell of the air was unbelievably fresh and clean after the storm, and a hint of fall was present. Juan led everyone to the corral in back and told Dave to hitch up his wagon. When this was done he had him saddle the horses.

While Juan was engaged in watching Dave, Conchetta discreetly used her heel and gouged out two letters in the muddy earth near the corral. Within moments they were leaving Dave's "Romantic Getaway" behind and once again climbing the road to The Geysers—only this time Dave was driving the wagon, with Suen by his side. Conchetta and Juan were on the horses following behind.

Juan reminded everyone that his revolver was within easy reach, and if they met anyone on the road, they were just four people traveling together on their way to see one of nature's spectacular wonders.

Conchetta was having a hard time getting used to riding the horse. Her body was stiff from often being tied, and the position her leg was in while astride the horse aggravated the injured area where Juan had struck her up on Penitencia Creek. Her face was unusually thin and pale, and her long hair was a tangled mess, but the morning was so bright and the scenery so gorgeous that her spirits were uplifted a bit as she told herself to stay alert for any opportunity to escape or to incapacitate Juan.

The road was a muddy mess, and the wagon could only make slow progress. The wheels were soon caked with sticky mud, as were the horses' hoofs. The rain had cut gouges in the road where rivulets of water had crossed from one side of the road to the other, and some of them were deep, causing the wagon to creep over them slowly.

Dave felt lower than he had at any point of his life. A chain of events had landed him in so much hot water that he figured he'd be boiled alive in it—just the same as if he fell into one of those steaming geysers that awaited them on the road ahead. He had lied to Juan when he told him that he knew of a road they could take that would bypass the Geyser's Hotel. Sure, a couple of horses could probably cut through the brush and trees and avoid the main road, but a wagon certainly couldn't. He resigned himself to having to deal with Juan's reaction when the time came, and glumly concentrated on guiding the horses up the muddy road.

Dave was surprised when Suen began speaking quietly to him. "David, thank you for helping me out back there in the cabin. I think you may have saved my life, momentarily anyway. It was a brave thing you did, speaking out to that madman."

"Oh, it wasn't much, Suen. I didn't really do much of anything, except get you into some big trouble. I just can't believe all this is for being so stupid, but you sure don't deserve any of this. If I'd just gone to the whorehouse in Santa Rosa with some of the other fellas, none of this would be happening," Dave said between clenched teeth.

Suen was a bit confused concerning the last part of what Dave said, but didn't spend a lot of time thinking about it.

"You realize that once you show him the road that leads over to Lake County he's probably going to kill us. Don't you?" Suen whispered. "We have to be alert for a way to escape or a way to attack him. I would rather die fighting him than let him shoot us like a couple of meek sheep," Suen added.

"I know. I hear you, Suen," was all Dave could think of to say.

Juan was watching Dave and Suen talking. He had ridden off to the side of the road a bit and could just see their mouths moving. *How strange life is, he reflected. In a little while he would have to kill a dimwitted, sexually confused idiot, and what appeared to be an intelligent, pretty, young Chinese woman—and all of it happening thousands of miles away from Santiago.*

I should just kill the Lombardi slut along with them, he began telling himself. The game with her had lasted long enough. There was no sensible reason to keep her alive. Sooner or later she would slow him down enough, or participate in some other fashion that would result in his death or capture. He glanced over at her riding somewhat stiffly on the horse. Her black dress had ridden up, revealing her white bloomers, now splattered with mud. A morning breeze had picked up and her mass of hair fluttered out behind her. Her face had become so white and thin, and her once gleaming eyes were sunken and dull. Once again he was amazed to find that for some reason he felt a sense of compassion towards her. At the old mission in Carmel, all she had been doing was praying to meet a nice man—and what had she got for her effort—an emissary of the devil.

He had tortured her long enough. The only right thing to do was to put her out of her misery. Then he noticed the crucifix. Conchetta was wearing the crucifix he had taken from his bloody victim in San Juan Bautista. At some point she must have slipped in on and had kept it hidden under her dress. Now, it gleamed in the sun and flopped on her bosom with the motion of the horse.

For some reason, Conchetta, at this point, looked directly over at Juan. She had a slight smile on her face and her eyes, once dull and vacant a moment ago, now seemed filled with compassion and understanding.

Damn it! It's the Madonna on horseback—back again to guide the world and challenge me, Juan said to himself and turned his eyes away.

Just then a loud voice, coming from behind them and from a distance, called out saying, "You people ahead. Hold up. There's trouble on the road ahead!"

Frank Augustino had been impatient since first light. There had been enough delays, and he had a feeling that there was a crisis coming to a head. A sense of urgency gnawed at him and he felt a helpless concern for Conchetta's safety.

After some quick coffee and a little food, the men were back on the road. They urged the horses on through the mud and before long arrived at the turnoff to Fandango Bob's old place.

Immediately, they noticed fresh wagon tracks as well as those left my two separate horses. With weapons ready they approached the little shack. They weren't surprised at not seeing any horses or a wagon—the recent tracks they had spotted all had been leading away from the shack and out onto the main road. A slight wisp of smoke was still coming from the rusty chimney. Possibly someone could still be inside, but most likely the occupants had just left, they all concluded.

"Just as I thought," Pino said, dismounting. "Davy's been here, I recognized those curtains he's hung up. They used to hang from his house until a couple of years ago. I wonder if he cooked and ate the snake?" he mused out loud.

All the men now had dismounted. With drawn gun, Primo walked up and rapped on the door.

"Anyone inside?" he called out.

When there was no response, he tried the black doorknob. The door opened and he peered inside. The shack was empty. Tin cups and some empty cans were scattered about. Then he noticed what he had been hoping for. He counted four metal plates, all of which held a few crumbs.

"Looks like four people have been here," he announced to the men in back of him.

Everyone squeezed inside and began looking around. The empty cups and cans still held a little coffee and the coffeepot was still warm, sitting on the wood stove.

"Looks like we just missed them," Dom said. "And it does appear that there were four people. Look at these forks—four of them, unwashed and covered with what looks like eggs. I guess Davy and Suen made the horse tracks and there must be two others in the wagon. Do you think it's possible they could have stayed here with Conchetta and the kidnapper? No, not possible—too wild of a coincidence," Dom concluded.

"Don't discount coincidence, Dom. Many strange things happen in the world. Some possibly for a reason, others a whim of fate," Po chimed in.

After quickly peering inside, Frank inspected the grounds outside the shack. He saw where the horses had been kept in the makeshift corral in back. Glancing about he noticed what appeared to be letters gouged into the mud. Walking closer, it immediately became apparent that indeed they were letters—CL.

"Conchetta Lombardi," he said out loud. "Hey, look back here!" Frank cried.

Frank quickly pointed at the ground when the men arrived.

"Conchetta Lombardi," Dom instantly concluded.

"Right," Frank said. "And they're probably not that far ahead."

Mounting his horse ahead of the others, he said over his shoulder, "I can probably ride the fastest. Now's the time for hard riding. If I spot them, don't worry, I'll try and wait for you to catch up."

Frank took off like a shot and was galloping up Geysers Road, mud flying from his horse's hooves, before the other men were comfortably mounted.

"Dom, I hope he doesn't do anything rash," Primo said. "He's wound up tighter than a spring."

"This Conchetta is sharp, like Angelina. She left us her spoor," Pino said.

"You mean she left us her calling card," Pietro said.

The older men followed after Frank as best they could on the muddy road; already he was nowhere in sight.

Po was thoroughly bewildered by what was happening. Apparently Suen and Dave were traveling with a kidnapper and Angelina's sister! But why? It just didn't make much sense. Unless, of course, the kidnapper, for some reason, was forcing Dave and Suen to accompany him. He knew the man had a gun and wasn't afraid to use it. He had hit young Frank Augustino so hard that he had almost drowned in the frigid waters of San Francisco Bay. Po began to be more frightened at what type of man was moving up the mountain road with his daughter.

Before long, Frank caught sight of a wagon with two people aboard and two riders trailing behind. In this area, the road climbed steeply like a giant snake. He was too far away to make out features on the people ahead. Nervously, his heart beating fast, he reached into his saddlebag for the binoculars within. As a second thought, he had thrown them in with his revolver and hunting knife. The binoculars had always come in handy when scanning for deer in the Sierra foothills.

As he held them up and began to focus them, he was surprised to find that his hands were shaking. He took several deep breaths and abruptly the focus was there. The woman whose picture he had fallen in love with. The woman whom he had seen only once briefly, moving away from him on San Francisco Bay, was less than a quarter mile ahead of him, astride one of the horses. Upon the other horse sat the man who had lashed out and wounded him with the barrel of a gun. Holding the reins of the wagon was a skinny fellow dressed all in black, and sitting next to him was a young Chinese woman—Suen Ling, he concluded.

Mai Ling's spirits weren't brightened by the brilliant sun; there had just been too many heartaches, and she was not yet fifty years old. The vibrant trees, the lush ferns, and the golden hills radiated nothing but beauty. The red-tailed hawk that flew in the deep blue sky above and called out a joyous greeting to the day could not buoy the sinking feeling that assailed her.

She looked over at Angelina, who had a serious look on her face as she was preparing the wagonette for departure. She was struck with the thought that Angelina was a little like her, though they had come from two distinct cultures, a world apart. She too had been born in a land thousands of miles away from California. For most of her young life, Angelina hadn't even had the warmth of a mother around. She had in effect been mother to her brother and sister, and now her sister was missing, probably somewhere on this road ahead of them in the hands of a kidnapper. Angelina was familiar with the vacancy of never having born a child. Mai was familiar with the vacancy brought about by a child losing its young life senselessly. Both women had found strength and solace in the men they loved, and now both of them were on a desperate chase to regain those they loved.

Mai walked over and ate a little of the bread and cheese Angelina had sliced up and left sitting on a rock. She didn't know how this day would end, but she had a feeling that strange forces were about. The sky was just too clear. The birds and the crickets too loud. And, unlike yesterday and most of the night, there was no wind. Not one blade of grass or leaf moved.

Angelina too was in a somber, reflective mood. She hadn't slept well during the night. They were dry and warm enough in the back of the wagon, but she kept waking up and listening to the wind and the rain and thinking about her sister. For a few years now they had always joked about men. Angelina hadn't had good luck with them. Conchetta was having a hard time just meeting a nice one, and feared if her luck didn't change soon, she would turn into a spinster.

"At least you'll be a pretty spinster," Angelina had teased her.

Now, in Conchetta's absence, Angelina had met and married a good man, a very good man, one whom she was deeply in love with. She couldn't wait for this to all be over, and she would have her sister safely back. She couldn't wait to introduce her to Dom and tease her as to what good luck she had to land such a fine catch. But a dark sense of foreboding colored her thoughts. What if something was to happen to Conchetta? What had already happened to Conchetta? And, what if something was to happen to Dom? All night such thoughts went through her mind. She awoke tired, but resolved to see things out to the end and hoped that good luck and the powers above would bless her and her sister.

The women boarded the wagonette. Angelina had placed a folded blanket on the seat between them; wrapped in the folds was Captain McCraken's loaded revolver.

After a short while, they came upon the new tracks. They saw where they had turned off on a narrow side road, but they also saw where the tracks continued on up the main road ahead; tracks that obviously were made after the storm. Angelina urged the horses on. The road got steeper and before long was nothing but a continuous series of curves. As they rounded one curve, the men suddenly came into view. They were not more than five minutes ahead of them, moving at a steady pace up the mountain. Angelina pulled the wagonette closer to the bank. If the men looked back and down they probably would see them. From this distance, Dom would surely recognize his recent purchase and guess who was driving it.

Just then, the morning was shattered by the sound of a gunshot, followed closely by another. Angelina saw the men break out in a gallop. Her heart leaped to her mouth, and again she urged the horses forward. Mai began to shake, and tears rose to her eyes.

Chapter 26

Before Frank had really thought the situation over and formulated some type of plan, he found himself calling out to the people higher up on the road ahead of him. The sight of Conchetta so startled him that he forgot tactics and caution. An overpowering need to make some type of contact with her, even if only a verbal shout, ruled his brain. He needed to get the group ahead to stop moving, as he now continued on at a fast trot.

Words came to his mouth, seemingly without him having to think, and he cried out at the top of his voice, "The road's washed out ahead. There's been a huge slide."

Juan found this preposterous. If the road were washed out, they'd find out soon enough on their own. Why would a lone rider frantically yell at them? And, why now would he be racing his horse towards them? This just didn't seem natural; something was wrong. The devil Bael was sending him warnings. He had to keep a distance between his party and the lone rider, and he needed time to think and plan a course of action. Reaching into his coat, he drew his revolver.

"Get that wagon moving, Davy boy, full speed and no tricks, or a bullet goes into your sweetie's back," Juan said.

Dave wasn't sure what was going on, but he flicked the reins hard and the wagon moved up the twisty road at a fast pace. If the road was washed out—washed out just around a curve—at this speed he wouldn't be able to stop in time. They would probably plunge over a cliff or run right into a wall of rock and dirt—but, with Juan threatening to shoot, he had no choice.

Conchetta thought she recognized the voice that had called out. Since crossing the bay, she had spent many hours thinking about that voice—the voice that had spoken one word, "Conchetta," the voice of a blonde young man who had plunged into San Francisco Bay in an attempt to reach her. She dared to let herself imagine that the rider on the mountain below was that same young man. And now, looking over at the cunning face of Juan holding a gun, she feared for the rider's safety.

Frank was closing the gap between himself and Conchetta. Eventually, he knew that he would catch the wagon. What he was afraid of was that the kidnapper would take off at full gallop and force Conchetta to do the same. With Tuli's superior speed and endurance, it would only be a matter of time before he caught up with the horseback riders. But Tuli wasn't here, and the rented horse he was astride seemed sorely lacking.

Rounding one of the S curves, a bullet landed in the mud inches in front of his horse. He looked up and saw the wagon still moving, but the two riders had paused and the kidnapper had a rifle out and aimed at him. By now the gap had closed to within two hundred yards. Frank heard another report of the gun, and the next thing he knew his horse was going down in a heap, throwing him roughly to the muddy road.

"That should slow your rescuer down a bit, Gypsy queen. I do believe that hombre had blonde hair. I must say that I fired off an excellent shot for around two hundred yards. At that distance I cannot be sure, but if I was to venture to speculate, I do believe that's the same fellow down there who foolishly dove into the bay after you. What do you think, Lombardi? Is that the man of your dreams down there? Is that the one you were praying for to that ineffectual virgin back in Carmel?" Juan said, shoving the rifle back in the scabbard.

Conchetta was intent, staring down at the rider. The moment his horse had collapsed and thrown him, the man was back on his feet and reaching into his saddlebag. Juan was right, at that distance it was hard to make a positive identification, but the man who was now running up the road did have blonde hair, and she was convinced that his voice was the same she had heard that day on the bay.

"Answer me, Conchetta dear. Do you think that's your dream lover down there, running up the road like a little kid?" Juan snarled.

"Oh, go to hell, brave man! You shot a horse. You're probably so scared you shit yourself," Conchetta said, for some reason in Italian.

Juan just looked at her and laughed.

"What's the matter, Lombardi, not in a good mood?" he said, speaking back in Italian. "Come on, ride hard. The wagon's getting too far ahead. Who knows what that idiot *maricon* might be doing," Juan said, switching back to English.

At the sound of shots, Dave slowed the wagon down. Evidently Juan was shooting at the man who had yelled out a warning to them. He turned and looked back, but saw no one. He moved the wagon closer to the edge of the road and looked down to see if he could see the rider who had yelled, but the area where he had last seen him was blocked by a think stand of trees.

Dave tried to think fast. Now might be a chance for some kind of escape—but how, on this narrow, twisty road? There was nowhere to go. On one side of the road was a steep bank, and on the other, a sheer drop off. He thought about stopping the wagon, grabbing Suen, and running somewhere to hide—but there was nowhere to hide. The bank was too steep to scale, and the drop off was too sheer to climb down.

Thoughts of escape vanished as Dave heard the sound of approaching horses, and Juan and Conchetta were once again directly behind the wagon.

"Haste! We need to make haste! Onward brave Spartan. Put the lash to your steeds. Get that wagon moving. It seems a chase is afoot. Why, there's a poor soul back down the mountain who is afoot this moment. Some avid marksman just shot his horse out from under him," Juan spoke, excited and pleased with himself.

Suddenly, he had a brilliant idea. Now would be the perfect time for one last boost, he decided. Reaching into his inner coat pocket, he withdrew the last of his cocaine that was in a vile next to the little derringer he had taken from Dave. Pausing for a moment, it was gone in an instant, and shortly the drug was bolstering his confidence and supporting his crazed ego.

"Geysers, here we come! Faster, Davy, faster!" Juan shouted.

At the sound of the gunshots, the men following Frank picked up the pace; each urging their horse forward, and each with different results. Walter's horse was the fastest. It was his own horse and used to climbing mountains, and it excelled in endurance. Pietro's was the slowest, and Pietro wasn't the best of riders. The rest of the men were scattered in between.

It didn't take Walter long to find out what the shooting had been about. Rounding a bend, he came upon Frank's dead horse, but Frank was nowhere in sight. Figuring him to be somewhere on the road ahead, he kept a fast pace and soon saw Frank, carrying a box of ammo, running up the muddy road. Frank, hearing a horse, stopped and turned, and in a moment Walter was reaching down and giving him a hand up on back of his horse.

"That dirty bastard's a good shot. He must have been almost two hundred yards away when he fired," Frank said.

"Keep an eye up on the mountain. He might try something like that again," Walter said.

"Suen and Dave are with the shooter. So is Conchetta Lombardi. I got a good look at all of them through the field glasses. The kidnapper and Conchetta have been riding in back of the wagon. I have a feeling he's forcing Suen and Dave forward at gunpoint. I wonder what he wants with Suen and Dave," Frank speculated.

"If he wants to get down to Lake County, he'd need a guide to point out the right roads. Dave's hunted this area for years. All I can figure is he's using Dave for a guide and Suen just got dragged into it," Walter said.

Frank was now more anxious than ever. Not only was the kidnapper a good shot, but he was cunning. Looking down on a target and firing from a distance would be a difficult shot, to hit a human astride a moving horse. But the horse was a bigger target, and that's what the shooter went for. Also, evidently he had easily influenced Dave to guide him, though probably at gunpoint. Eventually, the man would notice other riders coming up the road. He might decide to make a go of it alone. A true killer then could even decide to eliminate Conchetta and the others. Frank had no way of being sure, but he had a feeling, now that his horse had been so easily shot out from under him, that the man ahead was not afraid to kill.

As they were crossing the bridge over Little Sulphur Creek, Walter and Frank heard Primo shouting out to them. Walter stopped the horse and soon Frank was explaining to Primo what had happened and what he had seen. Before they finished talking, Dom and the others arrived.

It was decided that it might be best if Frank switched to Pietro's horse and Pietro ride with Pino.

"Come on up, Pietro. Us old buzzards will ride together. Just don't let your friend the Lupara go off by accident and blast me into Lake County," Pino said.

Pietro patted Pino on the shoulder, and tucked the sawed-off shotgun in the saddle scabbard alongside Pino's old single shot.

"Careful now. I had that gun in the wagon when we drove into town for the baseball game. It's always loaded in case we stop for lunch and encounter a rattler that likes to stage a surprise. I've never used it for that, but who knows, that day might someday come," Pino said.

"That day might be here. A man that would shoot a horse could well be a snake," Pietro said.

"I think the man we are chasing is worse than a snake. I think when he was young he may have listened to a crooked owl. A crooked owl is worse than a snake," Pino proclaimed.

"What do you mean, a crooked owl? An owl who is deformed, or an owl who can't be trusted?" Pietro inquired.

"I mean an owl who eats its young the moment they are born, an owl who enjoys the taste of their own flesh. I have a feeling that the man above, who shot Frank's horse, was young when he met the crooked owl. The owl may have spoken for days into his ear. And now he is just as crooked as that silly bird," Pino said.

"Oh shit, we never trusted owls in Italy. My great-grandfather was trying to shoot an owl that had been killing chickens. He fell in mud and crashed his head into a tree. When he regained his senses, the only word he could say was 'owl.' My great-grandmother used to have to clean up his stool," Pietro spoke sadly.

"You should get Walter to talk to you sometime about owls. Some of his relatives have turned into them and live high up in some rocks. Walter has problems every time he goes and visits them," Pino said.

The men were now moving up the mountain road relatively close together. They proceeded with caution and kept glancing above them. At times the road was still a series of curves, exposing them to the eyes of anyone at a higher elevation.

Dom and Primo were riding close together discussing the willingness of the man above to shoot.

"That son of a bitch's given me an idea. We can shoot horses too. Maybe we can shoot his, or shoot one of the horses pulling the wagon. That would certainly slow them down and give us some time to catch up. The road would have to curve just right, giving me a good side view of the horses," Primo said.

"Conchetta and Suen can't be too close by. I guess if you missed and hit Dave, no one would be too sad. He's certainly been nothing but trouble since I met him, but I guess I wouldn't wish death on him. Pino knows him better, and insists he's just mixed up and stupid," Dom said.

"I'd only take a shot if I were sure of it, Dom, and we'd have to get a little closer. We've got to be gaining on them, as long as they stay with that wagon, they can't move that fast," Primo said.

Below on the mountain, Dom's wife and Mai were in his wagonette moving as fast as safety and the strength of the horses would allow. After hearing the shots and seeing the men move out fast, Angelina threw caution to the wind. She didn't care if the men looked down and spotted them. She just wanted to be close to Dom and close to Conchetta. She thought she could feel the presence of her sister, on this day with the breathtaking scenery around them. Each rounding of a curve brought in a new vista. On a more normal day, she would have been thrilled with such sights. They were coming to a sparkling little creek, narrow and deep in places, filled with rocky boulders worn smooth by ages of passing water. Alders and a few aspen with yellow leaves grew next to the fern-lined creek. The road here had leveled out momentarily, but now, after crossing a narrow bridge, it began to climb again. Angelina looked far above her and for a moment caught a glimpse of a wagon and two riders behind it, and then the scene vanished as the riders rounded a bend.

"Mai, did you see that wagon far above?" Angelina asked.

"Yes, I've been looking up trying to get a glimpse of the men, but for a moment I did see a wagon and some horses behind it. They were too far away. All I could see were forms," Mai said.

"I wish I had that telescope Dom bought. He goes out on clear nights and pretends he's Galileo. He sips wine and looks at the moon and stars. I like to do it too," Angelina reluctantly admitted. "But I sure wish I had it now. I'd like to see who's in that wagon, and who's riding behind it."

She turned her head and looked directly at Mai.

"Do you think we may have seen Conchetta or Suen?" Mai said, reading her thoughts.

"I'm hoping it may have been, but I'm so wound up I think I can imagine anything," Angelina said.

When Angelina and Mai were looking up, Conchetta was looking down. She saw a group of riders come briefly into view, then vanish into the trees. Hope, desperate wild hope, filled her. The lone rider wasn't alone. Others were riding fast up the road. She dared to imagine that they were pursuing Juan and her, but even if they were only a group riding towards The Geysers, at least she wasn't alone. Surely the riders would catch up with them, and then what would happen?

Then, further below the riders, a wagon suddenly rounded a curve. Conchetta couldn't be sure, but she thought she could make out long dark hair on the driver and a passenger. The wagon had a top on it and only for an instant had the figures come into view.

Juan too had seen the same thing: six horses, one carrying two men, and further below, a wagon pulled by two horses. Juan quickly glanced at Conchetta, who was still looking down the mountain.

"Well, Lombardi. This seems to be a busy road. I wonder who all those people are down there. Do you suppose they're tourists going to The Geysers, or perhaps they're on a mission of sorts? Do you think it could have anything to do with us?" Juan said quizzically.

"The riders are after you, Juan. They're going to catch you and kill you. They're moving fast, and we're moving slowly. They'll be on us in a moment and then what will you do? Shoot them all?" Conchetta said.

"Why not? I have enough bullets, and you know what an excellent shot I am, Conchetta dear. I think your rescuer is down there with them. I would so enjoy planting a bullet into that blonde head," Juan said.

They were now traveling along the crest of the Hog's Back Ridge. Miles to the west, they could see where the land ended and the ocean began. In spite of the situation, Conchetta thought she had never seen such a beautiful view. She thought about what Juan had said. He was actually planning on killing all the riders below. She wanted desperately to yell out a warning to them, but knew that Juan would shut her up before more than several words escaped from her mouth. But maybe several words would be enough. On the top of this ridge, surely her voice would carry for a great distance.

She decided to risk it, and suddenly looked back and shouted at the top of her lungs, "He's a killer!"

She just managed to get the last word out when Juan backhanded her in the mouth so hard she almost fell off her horse. The blow hurt and she wasn't surprised when blood began to fill her mouth, but she had done it! She had gotten three words out, loud and clear. But had the riders heard? And what would it mean to them?

Down below, the men were riding fast, but above the sound of galloping horses, they heard the three words.

"It's Conchetta! She's warning us," Frank shouted.

"By God, what else could it be?" Primo said, slowing down, as did the others.

Dom felt a surge of emotion. What had Angelina's sister been through? And, how brave she must be to call out a warning! In spite of the seriousness, he smiled inwardly, thinking about how like Angelina she probably was. This girl was strong, and obviously not about to give up. He didn't want to dwell on what the bold warning may have cost her.

"We need to keep pushing the horses, but we need to watch out too. A bullet could be waiting for us around any bend," Dom mentioned to the others.

Dave and Suen too, had seen the horsemen below, and a glimmer of hope flashed before them.

It wouldn't be long now until the road ascended down into the Devil's Canyon, and The Geysers Hotel. At the rate they were moving, Dave figured that the riders would catch up with them somewhere on the descent. He began to wonder if he knew the riders. They had been too far away for him to make out much, but one of the men seemed to have long gray hair and reminded him a little of that strange Indian, Pino. Once he thought of Pino he thought about that smart aleck, Walter. Dave wished he could get another look at the horsemen following. When Conchetta had yelled out her warning, Dave felt sure the riders must have heard it. The words had sounded sharp and clear at this high elevation and had practically echoed off the canyon walls. She had paid for it though— he had glanced back and seen her take the blow Juan had given her. She was bold, he had to admit; just like that sister of hers back in Dry Creek.

For a while, the windy road continued on along the crest of the ridge through twisted oaks and shiny red-barked madrones. Then the road began to dip and start the final descent through another series of curves to Big Sulphur Creek, or Pluton River as some called it.

Juan looked back and above and saw a man poised, still on a horse, pointing a rifle. The next instant a shot rang out, and a bullet crashed into one of the horses that was pulling the wagon. Dave hauled back on the reins as the animal crumpled and fell, almost upsetting the wagon. An instant later, a second bullet hit the fallen horse square in the head, and it ceased to move.

"Oh, good idea! Someone wants to be just like me and enjoys shooting horses," Juan spoke in a maniacal voice. "Quick, David. Get down off that wagon and unhitch the live horse. You're going to have to ride it bareback. How much longer to that turnoff you said bypasses the hotel?" Juan said.

Before Dave could answer, Suen leaped from the wagon and onto the steep hillside alongside the road. She fell when her feet touched the ground and began rolling and sliding downward.

Juan, who had his revolver drawn since he heard the first shot, fired two rounds in rapid succession at the tumbling Suen. Both shots landed in the ground behind her.

Suen hadn't had much time to think. When the horse went down and the wagon was useless, she figured Juan now had no reason to keep her alive—people were closing in on him. He would be desperate for speed. She felt that now he would no longer care about Dave's threat to refuse to lead him if she were to be harmed. And the coldness of Juan's eyes made her feel that he wouldn't just let her stay there by the wagon and wait for the riders. So she decided to jump. She figured that if she could survive the jump and still be able to run, she would have a chance to vanish into the trees and brush. She thought

Juan wouldn't take time to pursue her, and she was right. After tumbling and rolling and crashing into several rocks, she managed to skid on her rear to a halt, gain her footing, and run into thick cover quite a distance from the curves of the road.

Conchetta was amazed at what Suen had done. She thought for sure she would crash into a tree and be knocked senseless, but somehow Suen had avoided the trees and seemed to have made a clean escape. She looked over at Juan who was looking nervously at Dave, fumbling with the harness, and glancing back in the next instant over his shoulder.

"What's the matter, Gypsy king? Things not going quite as planned? Why don't you just give up? Or better yet, if you don't want to get caught, put a bullet in your head. I'm sure your devil friend will be glad to welcome you," Conchetta said.

"Shut up, bitch. If I had more time to waste I'd love to play hide and seek with the Chinese slut. What a jump! I didn't think she had it in her. She seemed well behaved—the quiet type. Not like you, Lombardi. You've got a big mouth. But don't worry, you and me are going to stick it out to the end. We started out on this little journey together, and we're going to go out together," Juan said.

Dave finally got the horse free and mounted it bareback.

"Davy boy, you didn't answer me. How much further to the bypass?"

Dave didn't know what to say. There was no bypass. The road continued twisting downward for several miles and pretty much brought you straight to The Geysers Hotel. Now that the wagon was being left behind, he supposed he could look for some type of trail that would stay clear of the hotel and head up and out of the canyon towards Lake County, but he wasn't sure he could find any such trail. He was so taken aback by what was happening, that he had trouble thinking at all. When he saw Suen jump and tumble down the steep hill, he was sure she had committed suicide. Some of the villains he had encountered in the dime novels were Orientals, and if the going got tough, and there was no way out, they weren't afraid to commit something called Hari-Kari. That usually involved jabbing a sword in your gut and holding it there until you died. Suen was Oriental, Dave reasoned, but there weren't no sword around, so maybe she decided to use a tree to commit Hari-Kari, Dave reflected. In any case, she was gone. And, if she hadn't killed herself, she had made a successful escape, which was more than he could see himself doing.

"There's less than a couple of miles to the bypass trail," Dave said, hoping to buy a little time to figure some way out of the dire straits he was in.

"Good. Lead the way, David. There's cruel men who shoot horses behind us. Careful though. Without a saddle you might slip off that horse. I wouldn't like to lose a valuable guide at this point," Juan said, and keeping his revolver out, herded Conchetta and Dave quickly down the road.

When a side view of the wagon and horses came briefly into sight, Primo had been ready. He knew he couldn't afford to miss, and he had taken careful aim. When the horse went down, he didn't linger, but urged his horse on, the others right behind him. He had been riding ahead of the others and when he paused to shoot, he also had his first glimpse of the woman he had sent Frank out to gather information about and try and locate. Conchetta Lombardi looked just like her picture, and strikingly like Angelina. Frank and Walter rode up shortly after Primo fired. They too got a glimpse of Conchetta, as well as Suen, sitting in the wagon. When Primo took off they didn't linger either, but rushed on down the road rounding a bend, and once more losing sight of those they pursued.

Suen Ling was battered and bruised. She was bleeding from a cut on her leg where she had smashed into a jagged rock. A blade of dry grass had jabbed into her eye during the tumble, and that bothered her more than anything else. She had never experienced such pain in her eye and felt like rubbing it and rubbing it, but knew she shouldn't. Maybe something had broken off in her eye. Rubbing it would make it worse. She knew somewhere below was The Geysers Hotel and people. She hid behind a tree surrounded by scrub brush and watched the road with her one good eye, the other blurred with tears. She was breathing hard and just glad to be alive. She carefully patted at the moisture running from her eye and was glad to find that it was not blood. She heard horses and suddenly Dave, Conchetta, and Juan were in sight, riding hard down the road, and then they vanished around one of the curves.

She crept from tree to tree, just to be safe, and made her way closer to the road. The riders should be coming up shortly, she figured. Years of caution were ingrained upon her. She wanted to at least have a look at these riders before she drew attention to herself. A group of men, men who had shot a horse, could have many natures about them. A pack of men could at times be as ruthless as a pack of dogs. She hoped her fears would be groundless, but nonetheless, she approached the road with caution.

She was now close to the road and around a hundred yards below the wagon and the dead horse. From behind a tree she watched as the riders slowed and maneuvered around them. The lead rider was a fairly big man with a stern-looking face. Then, to her surprise, Dom Londi came into view, followed by none other than her father. Now tears filled both of Suen's eyes and she rushed out onto the road.

"Father, Father!" she cried, and though sore and bruised and barely able to see, she began running up the steep road.

Overjoyed and amazed to see Suen, Po dismounted and ran down the road towards his daughter. He reached her and swept her up into his arms, tears too streaming down his face. She buried her face in her father's shoulder and desperately held him for a moment. She heard hoof beats and looked up to see Walter riding up. And presently, Pino was there, smiling at her.

Po held his daughter away at arm's length. Her right eye was swollen and red. He saw bruises on her forehead, and blood was dripping down on the ground at her feet. Her dress was covered with stickers and burrs and torn in places. But there she was, standing in front of him and trying to smile.

"Suen, you're bleeding. Where are you cut?" Po asked frantically.

"I cut my leg Father, but I don't think it's too deep. Look into my eye though. Is there something sticking out of it?"

Po came close and gently opened Suen's almost closed eye. It was red and irritated, but he could see nothing in it.

"I think your eye will be all right, but what has happened to you? How did you get like this?" Po asked.

"I jumped from the wagon. I thought this monster, Juan, was going to kill me. He's the one who's kidnapped Angelina's sister, Conchetta," Suen said, overwhelmed with emotion.

"Po, you stay here for now and take care of your daughter. When you're ready, continue on down to The Geysers Hotel. Be careful though, and look about you. This Juan could be anywhere," Dom said, patting his friend on the shoulder.

"I want to hear about all this later," Pino said. "Did Dave hurt you?"

"Yes, did Dave hurt you, Suen?" Walter repeated.

"No, well, he kidnapped me in a way, and hit me on the head, but he also saved my life when Juan wanted to shoot me. Dave thought he wanted to marry me, but then he decided he was a Spartan," Suen explained, a sense of mirth suddenly coming back into her life.

Then a strange-looking, large-nosed older man, who was sharing the horse with Pino, suddenly spoke to her and said, "A Spartan! They were brave, but I think they mostly liked other men!"

Pino turned his head, saying over his shoulder, "If you get to meet David, believe me, it will all fit into place."

At this point, Frank rode forward.

"I'm glad you're safe, Miss Ling. I'm Frank Augustino. I've been searching for Conchetta. Is she hurt? Is she all right?"

"Juan slapped her in the face when she yelled out, but she's tough. She talks back to Juan. She fears him, but she won't give in to him. She seems healthy, but she looks very tired. She has a hurt leg, and she limps a little," Suen said.

"Thanks, Miss Ling. Goodbye," Frank said and rode on down the road, the others, except Po, following.

Po couldn't stop beaming, he was so glad to get his daughter back. He had Suen sit on the bank alongside the road and examined the cut on her leg. It was fairly deep and oozing blood and probably needed stitching. He cleaned the dirt out of the cut as best he could and wrapped his handkerchief securely around her leg. He looked again in her eye, and again saw nothing.

"Something must have scratched your eye, Suen. When that happens, it can feel like something is in there, but I don't see a thing. I think it will just go away in time," Po said, picking burrs out of his daughter's hair.

Then Po heard noises coming from the road above. So had Suen. They looked up and saw a wagon slowly maneuvering around the dead horse and abandoned wagon. Po and Suen were stunned when they realized it was Angelina Lombardi driving the wagon and Mai Ling was sitting on the seat next to her!

Mai almost fainted when she saw the people on the road ahead. Tears of joy began streaming down her face.

"Suen! Po!" she cried.

"Mother!" Suen shouted, and once again tears began to fill her eyes.

Seconds later, the wagon was there. Angelina halted the horses, and Mai got down and ran to her daughter. She knew she must be all right when she looked at Po, who was just standing there grinning like a happy idiot.

"What are you doing here?" he said, forcing sternness into his voice, but still grinning. "You and Angelina are supposed to be at home, not up on this mountain."

Mai was hugging her daughter and examining the bruise on her forehead and peering into her red eye. She wanted to joke with Po, and make some kind of snappy remark, like Angelina probably would with Dom, but she just couldn't. She was just too happy and grateful to find Suen safe.

All she could think of to say was, "I'm so grateful to see our daughter again; I don't think I can talk, Po." Po reached out and encircled Suen and Mai in his arms.

Angelina was still sitting in the wagon looking at the three. Her eyes too were wet with tears.

"Suen, you were in that wagon back there?" Angelina said, venturing a guess.

"Yes," Suen said. "David and I were in the wagon, and your sister was riding a horse alongside Juan. Juan is crazy. He kidnapped Conchetta."

Finally the mystery was being revealed and the pieces falling into place. A madman had indeed run off with her sister. Angelina wanted to hurry and continue on, but she also wanted to talk more with Suen.

"Why don't you all get back in the wagon. That Geysers Hotel can't be much further, and I need to be with Dom and get my sister back," Angelina said.

The Lings climbed aboard the wagonette. Po had to help Suen in. She winced in pain with certain movements of her legs and arms.

"Suen, do you think you have any broken bones, or are you just sore?" Mai inquired.

"No broken bones, Mother. I'm just sore all over. I don't know how far I rolled down that hill. Mother, Father, you don't know how glad I am to see you, and just be alive. That Juan was going to kill me," Suen said, filled with emotion.

As the Lings talked quietly amongst themselves, Angelina drove on. She was overjoyed that Suen was safe and reunited with her parents. She heard when Suen said Juan was going to kill her. She knew Suen to be strong-willed and not prone to exaggeration as some young women her age were. What kind of man would want to kill Suen Ling? And, what for? Now Angelina feared more than ever the man who held her sister captive.

The road was still steep, and seemed to be winding downward with no end. Where could Conchetta be now? Surely The Geysers couldn't be much further ahead.

Just then, Angelina was shocked into heightened awareness. Gunshots began echoing off the wooded canyon walls.

Chapter 27

"Well, Davy, where's this bypass?" Juan said, slowing down to a trot, and motioning to Conchetta and Dave to do the same.

They had reached the bottom of Devil's Canyon and the road paralleled the Pluton River. A well-worn path ran alongside the stream that had swelled with the recent rain.

"Looks like we must be approaching the famed geysers. Get us out of here, David. I sense people ahead," Juan said.

For Dave Fowler, the ruse was up. He had been searching desperately for some type of trail to turn off on and convince Juan that it bypassed the hotel, but all he saw were thick stands of trees and tangled manzanita bushes, and nothing that even resembled a path cutting through them.

Dave had developed an intense hatred for Juan—hatred mixed with fear. Dave had never met a killer, but he knew he'd have to answer to the words of one now.

Shortly, they probably would be encountering people. The sun was almost directly overhead and the day was exceptionally clear and beautiful.

Since Suen made her leap, Dave had been reevaluating his thoughts. Suen was Chinese. All of his life he'd hated Chinese; been taught by many to hate Chinese. But now he didn't hate Suen one bit. He admired her and thought she was as courageous as anyone he had ever met. And the woman riding next to him was probably the best-looking creature he had ever seen. She was one of them Italians—a dirty wop! She was dirty all right. But that was because there wasn't much of an opportunity to wash up. Her hair was all tangled up and he could see it badly needed a combing, but this woman, like Suen, had been incredibly brave. Dave didn't know what Juan may have done to her since he had kidnapped her, but the woman didn't seem broken one bit. She had even smiled at Dave a time or two. The smiles had given him a sense of encouragement and optimism. He was supposed to hate Italians. But he didn't hate this one. And he was surprised to find himself thinking that he shouldn't have been mean to her sister, or her sister's husband for that matter. What had either of them ever really done to him? Nothing. He had just been blind and ignorant, and now that he finally realized this, he was probably about to die.

They had been moving through a sylvan setting; the stream gurgling loudly near them. Dave could hear the hissing of the Steamboat Geyser ahead. If they could just ride on a little further, they probably would run into tourists.

Juan looked over at Dave. *What a moron,* he said to himself. *He looks like a daydreaming cow.*

"Davy boy, you've been lying to me, haven't you? There's no bypass, is there?" Juan said, a strange singsong lilt to his voice.

Conchetta figured out what was probably going to happen next. When Juan began to raise his gun, Conchetta, who was quite close to him, hurled from her saddle and crashed into Juan. She fell awkwardly to the ground, but it had bought time for Dave to act. Dave charged his horse into Juan and desperately reached out for the gun. He got his hand on the barrel and at that instant Juan pulled the trigger. A bullet tore into Dave's shoulder, but he held on to the gun and forced the barrel into the air as Juan squeezed off another shot. There was a thud and a splintering of bark as the bullet slammed into an overhanging branch. With his good arm, Dave lashed out a wild punch at Juan and connected on the side of his head.

In the meantime, Conchetta, who narrowly avoided being trampled by the frantic horses, made a run for the creek, hoping to cross it and seek cover in the trees.

Juan, still struggling with Dave over the gun, grew more desperate than ever when he saw Conchetta up and running out of the corner of his eye.

Dave was stronger than he looked, even with a shoulder running blood. Dave was holding onto the barrel of Juan's gun and succeeding in keeping it pointed in the air. Juan was weakened by Dave's blow to the head. It was all he could do to tussle with Dave and still cling to the handle of the gun. He couldn't afford to waste time struggling with this idiot maricon. The riders trailing him would certainly arrive at any moment.

Juan, desperate to wrest the gun away from Dave, freed one of his hands from the struggle and reached into his inner coat pocket for the derringer. Just as Dave's hand had fumbled for the derringer back at the honeymoon shack, Juan too had a hard time producing the little gun. For an instant, his hand grabbed the empty vial of cocaine instead.

Dave's whole shoulder was growing numb. When Juan reached into his coat, Dave figured he was after the derringer or a knife, but there was not much he could do. One arm was now useless. He still held on to Juan's revolver, but it was as if in slow motion he watched as Juan's arm moved up and outward from inside his jacket.

Just then, a bullet hit Juan's horse and it fell, blood pumping from a wound to the heart.

Primo and Frank had been riding side-by-side, faster than what would normally be safe, down the steep, twisty road. Coming to level ground, they heard two shots close by. Riding at full gallop, ahead of them they saw Juan and Dave astride their entwined horses and struggling over a gun. Primo didn't hesitate. He reined in his horse and jumped down instantly, freeing the Winchester from his scabbard. He had decided in a moment to once again shoot a horse. Trying to hit Juan was just too risky a shot. Dave and Juan were struggling too violently, and changing positions every instant. Once again, from this distance, the horse was simply a bigger target, and Juan's was mostly standing sideways and at a good angle. He took careful aim and fired. The horse went down. Quickly, he mounted his, and rode after Frank, who hadn't paused, but kept on riding hard towards Juan.

When Juan's horse fell, Dave fell with it. All he could manage to do was try and cling to the barrel of the gun. He fell sideways out of his saddle, but he wouldn't let go of Juan's gun.

Juan fell awkwardly, Davy on top of him. He succeeded in freeing the derringer, and swung the arm that held the little gun, hoping to plant it right into Dave's chest and squeeze the trigger, but Dave, in a desperate move, flung his leg up and back. The gun went off and the bullet, at point blank range, exploded into Dave's leg a little above the knee. Juan yanked his revolver free from Dave's grasp. Dave had a startled look on his face. He stared up into Juan's maniacal eyes and saw his own death. Before Juan could finish him off and pull the trigger, a bullet passed clean through Juan's side. He turned and saw a man no more than fifty yards away approaching swiftly on horseback.

For some reason, all Juan thought of was Conchetta. He looked off in the direction of the creek and saw her floundering in it, trying desperately to wade across. There were now three people he could try to shoot: finish off Dave, kill Conchetta, or try for the galloping rider. His instinct for survival told him the rider was the only immediate threat. He tucked the revolver in his belt, grabbed the rifle off the dead horse, took quick aim, and fired from less than twenty-five yards at the blonde-headed man who had just put a bullet through him from the fast moving horse.

Juan's bullet hit Frank just below the collarbone and he fell from his horse roughly onto the ground. But Frank had gotten off a second round before he fell; his bullet caught Juan in the left forearm as he held the rifle up. Juan tried to lever another round into the chamber, but found he was unable to do so. He couldn't make his arm move and blood was running fast from it. He reached for his revolver, snapped off a shot at the fallen rider, and ran as fast as his limp would allow after Conchetta. He saw a second rider approaching and knew his only chance at staying alive was to regain Conchetta and use her as a hostage.

Juan left a trail of blood from his two wounds, but he didn't hesitate, and he didn't look back. Where Conchetta was trying to cross, the water was deep and swift and the rocks slippery. The combination caused her to lose her footing, and she fell, the current pushing her downstream. The wet dress made it difficult for her to rise to her feet. Finally she was able to gain her balance and stand, just as a hand reached out, grabbed hers and yanked her out of the water and onto the bank. Juan pushed her to the ground and kneeled on her. With his good hand he held the revolver, the barrel poking into her back.

Primo had stopped his horse when he reached his young friend. The last round that Juan had fired at Frank had missed. Primo took a quick look at the wound below Frank's collarbone. It certainly looked a mess, but it probably wasn't life threatening. He helped Frank to his feet.

Frank was wobbly and a bit stunned, but his wound wasn't bleeding too badly and he told Primo that he was all right.

Primo and Frank, guns drawn, walked slowly and cautiously towards Juan, who wasn't moving, but just kneeling by the stream like an animal on top of its prey. From a distance they could see he had a gun pointed at Conchetta's back. They could also see the look on the man's face. Both men were mesmerized as they drew closer and gazed upon the most hideous, crazed-looking picture of cruelty and hate that either one of them had ever imagined seeing.

Frank and Primo quickly glanced over their shoulders at the sound of approaching horses. Walter, Dom, Pino, and Pietro rode slowly forward. The Lupara was dangling from Pietro's right arm. Dom was holding the revolver and the reins at the same time.

When the horsemen drew even with Primo and Frank, their eyes transfixed on the man and the woman at the water's edge, Pino said in a loud voice, "Well, what have we here? Looks a little like wounded eagle trying to hold down a rabbit."

"No, Pino, looks more like a stinking buzzard covered in blood, pounced on a dead rabbit, only the rabbit's not dead," Pietro corrected.

"Good observation, my friend. I stand corrected," Pino said.

Juan suddenly rose, jerking Conchetta to her feet by the back of her dress. He was bleeding fast from the wound in his side, but a little life had come back to his arm. That wound wasn't bleeding much and he was able to grip a little with hand.

"Hey, Indio, you've got a big mouth. So does that old hook-beak in back of you. None of you come any closer or a bullet goes into the Madonna here," Juan shouted.

Dom and Primo exchanged glances.

"He's absolutely crazy," Primo said. "Before you guys came up, he had a look on his face that was purely insane."

"Let's end this now, Mister. You're wounded. You can't get away. Let Conchetta alone. We'll get you to a doctor," Dom said.

"No doctor for me, senor. I see by your accent, you're Italian too. Perhaps you're related to this Madonna slut, no?" Juan said.

"She's my wife's sister, and you've harmed her enough. Let her go. Put the gun down, and we'll help you," Dom said, trying to remain calm.

Conchetta, who had been trying to struggle out from somewhat of a state of shock, snapped alert at the words that the man had just spoken. She focused her eyes on the speaker and saw a trim gray-haired man with a thick mustache and a large straight nose, hooked a bit at the end. At the sight of him a brief smile came to her face.

"How's Angelina?" she shouted out.

"Fine," Dom said. "She's worried about you," thinking it best to keep it brief.

When Conchetta shouted out, Juan poked her roughly in the back with the gun and whispered, "Shut up, Lombardi. There will be no family reunion for you."

At this point, Dave had managed to get to his feet and came limping towards the group of men. He had found a strong stick and was propelling himself forward, blood running from his shoulder wound and his leg.

"Walter, be careful, he's a crazy killer," Dave said as he got closer.

Walter, seeing Dave bleeding badly from his wounds, walked quickly towards him and began to administer aid. He took his belt off and wrapped it tight above the wound in Dave's leg. Then he removed Dave's jacket and the frilly white shirt now soaked in blood. Walter tore some cloth from the shirt and pressed it over the shoulder wound. With the rest of the shirt, he tied it tight under Dave's arm and over his shoulder.

"Hold it tight, David. That's about all we can do for now. Keep pressure on your shoulder wound. You've got to stop losing blood. You shouldn't be moving. Let's go sit you by that tree," Walter said, leading Dave to a large madrone.

Dave needed to talk. He had never really been hurt badly. Possibly these wounds would kill him, he thought. Walter was turning to leave and rejoin the others. Dave reached out and pulled on Walter's pant leg.

"Walter, I'm sorry for the way I've behaved. I was just stupid, that's all," Dave said in a weak voice.

Walter couldn't believe what he was hearing. He looked down at Dave who was looking up at him with a bashful smile, a couple of his yellow buckteeth exposed.

"Wow, Dave, I guess a couple of bullet holes have done you some good. Why, you should have gotten shot much earlier," Walter teased, and patted Dave on the good shoulder, then walked away.

When Walter rejoined the group, Juan shouted out, "How's our Spartan friend? He's tougher to kill than I thought. I think he was sweet on the Chinese slut until he realized he was a mariposa," Juan cackled and began to cough.

"Mariposa? It sounds familiar. It's *butterfly* isn't it?" Pietro said.

"Yes. He's using it as slang for queer," Pino volunteered.

Primo now spoke. "Juan, your name's Juan, isn't it? What do you want? What will it take for you to let Conchetta go? If it's money you want, I'll wire a bank of your choice. Come, let us negotiate."

"You sound like a lawyer, big man. Another Italian, huh? What is this, the Italian and Indian army coming to the rescue? Say, you're probably the cruel man who likes to shoot horses, huh?" Juan said, noticing the rifle slung over Primo's shoulder. "Only a lawyer would be cruel enough to shoot horses," Juan added. "No. I don't want money. I have plenty of my own. I want to go sightseeing. I want to tour The Geysers and be alone with my Gypsy queen, my Madonna slut, the *putah* Lombardi. She has many names you know. She has dared to challenge the devil, and in this place, Devil's Canyon, the signs say, I plan to show her all of Satan's wonders. Leave us alone. You wouldn't interrupt a couple of honeymooners on a tour, would you?" Juan spoke between coughs.

Pietro quietly slipped off the back of Pino's horse. He was itchy to use the Lupara on the crazy man, but obviously couldn't.

Frank had been standing by, feeling totally useless and helpless. He was pressing his handkerchief over the bullet wound, his revolver dangling from the other hand. Even if he had been a master marksman, there was no way to shoot Juan without endangering Conchetta. Juan held the gun right on her. A bullet in Juan would probably trigger a reflex and the gun would fire point blank into her. Here was the woman of his dreams, so close by, yet so far away. The centerpiece of a long torturous drama, she was soaking wet, covered with mud and blood, but Frank had never seen anything so brave and lovely in all his life.

At that moment, Conchetta was staring at the wounded man who had swum after her on San Francisco Bay. It was definitely him. There was no mistaking it now. In spite of her predicament, she couldn't help but realize how handsome he was. He even looked like he might have some Italian in him. Most blondes she had seen had small noses. Many of them even had small ones that turned up at the end. Not this man. Even from a distance she could see that his was large and curved down a bit. The young man seemed to be staring straight at her with a terrible sad look on his face. More than anyone she had ever met in her life—Conchetta wanted to get to know this man. She wanted to be clean and happy and have on a new dress.

She wanted to walk around the old mission in Carmel with this man when the roses were in bloom. She wanted to know all about him, and tell him all about herself.

Then the light went out of her thoughts. Tell him about herself? Tell him what? Tell him about being drugged and raped? Tell him about spending days alone with an insane murderer? Tears began to fill her eyes and she cast them down and gazed unfocused at the wet earth. Then she felt a light breeze blowing at her, coming from the direction where the young man was standing. She looked up and could see that the man was smiling at her. A moment ago he had been holding a gun. Now he was cautiously waving at her, his hand held low near his waist. The gun, she saw, was tucked in his belt.

Conchetta waved back, and for a second she felt a bond was formed between the two of them. The next instant, Juan slapped her hand down.

"Hey you, blondie, quit waving at my woman. I should have shot you instead of hitting you that day on the bay. Hey, you like Lombardi so much, why don't you come on over here. I won't hurt you. We'll just walk around and see the sights until we both bleed to death. Well? Are you game, blondie? Oh, that's right, you better throw your gun away. Give it a good toss in back of you. Guns can be dangerous you know," Juan said, his body quivering a bit as he spoke.

Frank pulled the gun from his belt, tossed it behind him and immediately began to walk towards Juan. Primo reached out and grabbed him by the arm.

"Whoa, Frank. That's not a good idea. You'd just be walking into a trap. Stop and think. We'll get Conchetta out of this somehow."

Primo, though, really had no idea what to do. He wasn't sure at all about how to go about freeing Conchetta or killing Juan. He had faced stalemates in the courtroom, but nothing there had prepared him for what was occurring now at the bottom of this canyon.

"Primo, let me go. I can at least get close to him. Maybe I can get the gun away or trip him up somehow. I'm certainly not doing a bit of good here. Let me go, it may be Conchetta's only chance," Frank pleaded.

Primo could see the sense in this. Frank was wounded, but he had plenty of game left in him. He mostly was afraid that Juan would simply shoot him when he got close and nothing would have changed, except Frank now would be dead.

Dom and the others heard the conversation. None of them could think of a good course of action, and none of them doubted that Juan would shoot Conchetta at the blink of an eye.

Dom was unbelievably filled with anger. As a young man in Italy he had been capable of feeling rage, but he had not felt rage in years. The helplessness he now felt had brought his anger to a crescendo. No one on the face of the earth should be acting like the evil-looking man with the gun. In his anger he cursed the day that weapons were brought to the world, but then he saw the folly of this. After all, wasn't the human hand one of the best weapons of them all?

"Frank, are you sure you want to try this? You could be throwing your life away for nothing," Dom cautioned, catching Frank's eye.

"Dom, I don't want to live if I don't try," Frank quietly said.

Before anyone could say another word, Frank started walking towards Juan and Conchetta.

When Angelina reached the bottom of the road and turned onto the flat stretch that led to The Geysers, she slowed the wagonette down. The gunshots she had heard had to have come from somewhere close by. Spotting a well-worn path alongside the rushing creek, and noticing that the forest looked manicured in the vicinity, she figured the geyser attractions to be near. She pulled the wagonette to a halt and turned to the Lings.

"Po, you and your family should get out and wait. Maybe stay somewhere hidden for a while. That shooting must mean Juan's somewhere ahead and close by. Who knows what he might do next. I've got to go on and see if I can help my sister. You've got your family to worry about. You need to stay here for now and protect them, right?" Angelina said.

Po agreed. Now that he was reunited with his daughter and Mai, he wasn't about to expose them to further danger.

"We'll wait near those thick trees," Po said, pointing.

"Come back to us when you can, Angelina, and be careful, don't do anything rash," Mai said.

"I'll come back. Remember, The Geysers Hotel is somewhere just ahead on this road," Angelina said and flicked the reins.

She proceeded at a slow trot and hadn't gone far when she spotted the men standing in a group off to the side of the road. They were all looking towards the creek, their backs turned towards her. She pulled the wagonette off the road and got down. Obviously, something was going on. There was no longer any shooting, but the men were just standing in a bunch, evidently looking at something. She moved cautiously from tree to tree, McCraken's heavy Colt in her right hand. The trees were thick here alongside the creek. It was easy to stay hidden. She crept closer, and then rounding a little bend she saw what all the men were looking at. Her sister, Conchetta, was standing next to a man who held a gun at her back. They were right next to the creek. Even from a distance, she could see that the man appeared to be a lunatic. A hideous grin occupied his thin, pale face. His tongue lolled out from time to time and licked his lips as if he was thirsty.

So, this was the animal who had taken her sister. How had God allowed something like this to happen? Conchetta had done nothing to deserve such fate. Her musings ended when she noticed a man moving through the trees towards Juan and her sister. It was that young Frank Augustino! He didn't appear to have a gun, and Angelina had no idea what was going on. She was too far away. She needed to get closer. Crouching low and using the trees for cover, she crept along the creek until she was within earshot. Now she could hear that Juan was speaking to Frank.

"Hey, blondie. If we're going to die together, you should at least tell me your name, and I should introduce myself. I am Juan Fuentes from Santiago, Chile. And you?"

"Frank Augostino, San Francisco."

As Frank drew close, he could see Juan was bleeding badly, especially from the wound on his side. His face was ghostly white, and he quivered like a leaf from time to time. *If I can just keep him from shooting Conchetta, he might drop soon from loss of blood,* Frank hoped.

"Augostino! I might have known. A blonde Italian, huh?" Juan said, coughing a little.

"My mother is Finnish. You've heard of Finland, haven't you, Juan?" Frank said, hoping that talking would buy some time.

"Of course, asshole. It's that northern country where they sit naked in hot houses until they can't stand it. Then they go and plunge into an icy lake or some snow bank. What idiots! I'll bet your mother likes to get naked, eh Frank?" Juan said.

"Oh yea," Frank said. "My whole family hates clothes. The temperature is pretty constant in San Francisco. We run around naked all the time."

"Oh, wow, a funny boy. Well, you won't be joking much longer, big shot. Whatever happens, I'm taking you with me. You're the son-of-a-bitch who's put these holes in me, and this is going to be your last day on earth, Franky. Lombardi's too, for that matter. By the way, do you two know each other? I can tell you're sweet on this slut, aren't you, Frankie boy," Juan said.

"I've never been formally introduced to Miss Lombardi, though I would deem it a pleasure and an honor," Frank said, looking at Conchetta.

Conchetta gazed up into Frank's blue eyes. He had a smile on his face; a smile that hinted of optimism, but also reminded her of one of those stiff-upper-lip smiles—the ones that, she imagined, some people had on their faces when they were trying to be brave when facing certain death. Studying his face briefly, she detected something else. His eyes sparkled and seemed to be full of life. He was looking at her as if they were old friends. And then she had a sudden realization—he was looking at her with the eyes of a lover, as one who desired her.

Conchetta began to blush. Her clothes were wet and she was soaked to the bone, but she felt a heat rising to her face. For an instant, she wanted to throw herself into the man's arms—to lose herself in his embrace until the memories of all she had gone through turned into dust and once again she was herself. Before that day at Mission Carmel when the animal, masquerading as a man of faith, entered her life.

She smiled shyly at Frank, then turned her eyes away. She had been inventing things, daydreaming and wishful thinking. The tension of the circumstance had clouded her thinking and was leading her down a dangerous path. Now was not the time for romantic nonsense. For her, possibly there would never be love and romance. Juan was poised to end such notions. Anyway, why would that handsome man standing next to her want anything to do with her—a woman tainted and used? She had been mistaken. The look in his eyes was only one of pity. But yet, who was he? And why at this moment was he risking his life? Why had he called out her name and swum towards her on the bay? Why had he trailed her all this way?

Her thoughts ended at the sound of Juan's voice.

"Enough sappy looks at one another. We aren't at a ballroom. So forget any ideas of asking her for a dance, Augostino. Let's see, Augostino and Lombardi, sounds like an olive oil company, or a winery," Juan said. "Well, are we all ready? Let the final tour begin then. We're off to see The Geysers. You and Conchetta lead the way, Frankie boy. I'll follow close behind with my gun aimed right at the little lady's back. Move out! There are sights of wonder to see and time is of a premium," Juan said, trying to swagger, but shaking instead.

Frank and Conchetta led the way down the well-worn path. They came to a post buried alongside the stream with a hand carved sign on it that read "Pluton River, or Big Sulphur Creek."

"Oh boy, Pluton River. That must mean Pluto or Hades is nearby, God of the underworld, a true Renaissance man, and a master of darkness. Maybe we'll meet him soon, hey, Frankie boy," Juan said.

Frank glanced sideways at Conchetta, who he was surprised to find, was looking at him. She rolled her large eyes up and around. Frank was amazed that in spite of their predicament, Conchetta was obviously making fun of Juan. In spite of her muddy, wet appearance and tangled hair, Frank ached at the sight of her beauty. He had to take out Juan, or die trying, even if it was only to hear Conchetta laugh when he told her how he felt about her, and how at first sight he had fallen in love with her picture.

They came around a bend and saw a group of tourists peering cautiously in their direction. Everyone who was in The Geysers area that morning had heard shooting. Most people thought it to be hunters or someone engaged in target practice. One of The Geysers employees, though, had found this odd. Game was scarce in the immediate area. Too many people about, and no one with a lick of sense should be target practicing near people. Just to be on the safe side the employee, old Carl Filbert, urged the tourists to stay near the hotel until the shooting was investigated. Most people heeded his warning, but some couldn't be deterred and wandered off towards the attractions. One such group, Carl amongst them, had stumbled upon Juan and his captives and the group of men watching them from a distance.

When Juan spotted the tourists, he fired a shot in their direction and yelled, "Get the hell out of here! There's a private tour going on today!"

"Quick, back to the hotel!" Carl urged. "Looks like something serious."

No one needed to be told twice, and soon Juan had The Geysers all to himself. They kept going on the path and saw a gulch across the creek that was blackened by chemical vapor. A sulphurous stink permeated the air. A sign with an arrow pointed at the gulch read, "Mountain of Fire." Small flames rose from the bottom of the gulch, burned for a moment, and then went out.

"My, that's a nice little trick, and I do like that smell. Rotten eggs are a wonderful thing. It means that the gooey mess inside won't grow up to be a chicken, and one day end up on the dinner table. No suffering for that life. It never even got a start," Juan said, laughing weakly.

Dom and the men were cautiously following along on the road, keeping some distance, as when they first encountered Juan. When they tried to narrow the gap, Juan ordered them back, saying they were welcome to watch and join the tour, but only from a distance. The creek and the path were now winding away from the road, and the men had to enter the trees and proceed through forest to keep sight of Juan and the captives. All the horses were now tied. The men carried their weapons, but no one saw an opportunity to use them. Juan was still walking directly in back of Conchetta, the barrel of the gun at times touching her back.

Primo, like the others, had been keeping his eyes glued on Juan, but now he noticed that it had been just too quiet. He turned to look for Pietro, but didn't see him.

"Pino, where's Pietro?" Primo inquired.

Pino looked about and was at a loss.

"He was here a minute ago. He slipped off the horse before I dismounted and tied it. Come to think of it, I hadn't noticed him then, I was too busy keeping an eye on that rabid fox and trying to figure out a way of dispatching him. Pietro must be pretty sly himself to sneak off in such a manner," Pino said.

"Oh, he's sly all right. I just hope he's not going to do anything stupid. He must be off in the trees somewhere. He certainly can't do much with that shotgun. I don't know what he's up to," Primo admitted.

Juan urged Conchetta and Frank forward. Away from the path a sign read, "Devil's Machine Shop."

"Let's go look at that. I do like the sound of that," Juan said.

Frank was even surprised at what presently he was looking at. The ground in front of them was of different colors, and it was steaming. The earth was so hot that he could feel it through his shoes. There were stones amongst the dirt, and they were so hot that surely that would burn through the sole of a shoe in seconds.

"Wow, we better get out of this place. I like it hot, and look forward to burning, but not just yet. Onward, Augostino! I hear something ahead," Juan said.

Pietro Nuti was crouched behind a manzanita bush no more than thirty yards away from Juan. The moment he had slipped off the back of Pino's horse, he vanished silently behind a tree. Using the horse and then the trees as a shield, he backed away from the others until he crossed to the far side of the road. Then, using brush and trees for cover, back-tracked for almost a hundred yards, then crossed the road and gained the path that bordered the creek—the same one that Juan was on. Always keeping a tree in front of him, he moved closer and closer, until now he was as close as he dared to get. He had no grand plan in mind. He just felt that if he were to be of any aid at all, he would need to be closer to Juan and the captives.

Angelina Lombardi was right behind him. She too had moved quietly from tree to tree. She had been down low and crouched behind the little bank that bordered the creek when she saw Pietro sneak in front of her, carrying the Lupara. For an instant, she thought of quietly signaling Pietro. He had passed within a few feet of her and hadn't seen her. Then she decided against it. She might startle him and end up exposing him to Juan. As everyone continued to move forward, so would she, a short distance behind Pietro.

"Well, would you look at this. The Devil's Oven."

Juan and his group were staring at a ravine. Part of it was covered with icy stalactites, but not far away from it an opening in a wall of the ravine hissed hot steam. A sign nearby called it "Devil's Oven."

"Boy, the devil sure likes this place. I've never seen so many attractions honoring the old boy. By God, or should I say, by devil, this is my kind of place," Juan announced. "What can possibly be next?" he wondered aloud.

They walked on and came to a section of the canyon wall that was gleaming and sparkling, covered with shiny crystals of some sort. The sign proclaimed this spot to be "Proserpine's Grotto."

"Obviously, they like Roman terminology around here—Pluto, Proserpine. Me, I prefer the Greek. Persephone sounds much more melodic than Proserpine. Don't you agree, Lombardi?"

"Why, of course, Juanito. By the way, how are you feeling? You're ruining this nice path. No one's ever going to want to walk on the blood you're dripping all over. Perhaps you should climb up there and take a little rest. I think it's quite fitting for you," Conchetta said, pointing ahead.

Juan gave her a nasty look, then looked towards where she was pointing. Somehow, nature had hollowed out from solid rock a depression that resembled a chair complete with armrests. The sign called it "Devil's Armchair."

"Yes, I would like to try that chair out. Some other time, perhaps. Now, that's where I would like to go, Conchetta dear. That high spot over there, where there's a view of it all."

Juan was referring to a trail that wound up the canyon and across the creek. At the base of the trail a sign with an arrow pointing up said "Devil's Pulpit."

"Now listen, children. How good do you remember your bible? Why, as I recall, it's Mathew IV, or Luke IV, or maybe both, where the devil takes the weakling, Christ, high up on a mountain and shows him all the kingdoms of the world, and all their glory in a moment of time. He tells the idiot that he can have it all. Only he must bow down to him and worship him—the great devil. The fool refuses. And what did it get him? Nailed to a post. Just like one of these signs. What do you say we all go up there, and I'll give you a chance to bow down to me. Who knows? If you do it, maybe I'll even let you both live," Juan said, trembling more than ever.

They walked a little further and were about to cross over a footbridge when Juan heard a noise, and he turned to see Pietro running towards a tree. Juan aimed and fired in an instant. The bullet caught Pietro below the knee, and he fell.

Before Juan could turn his gun back on Conchetta, Frank sprang at him. He took a step towards Juan, caught his foot on an exposed root, and ended up falling at Juan, arms extended. His momentum pushed Juan backwards and off to the side. Juan stumbled, but didn't fall.

The instant Pietro fell and Frank rushed at Juan, Angelina made her move. Not trusting her skills with a revolver, she dropped it and ran through the trees along the path. Pietro had dropped the shotgun, but was reaching out for it. Angelina now rushed up, grabbed it without breaking stride, and ran at Juan. Juan had regained his balance and was concentrating on Frank. He decided to kill him right then, but as he turned to level the gun he caught a glimpse and heard someone coming towards him. It was a woman dressed in black, hair flying behind her.

Conchetta, he thought, and turned. Angelina ran with all her strength. When Juan realized it wasn't Conchetta and raised the gun to fire, she had the Lupara aimed squarely at him. She jerked the trigger, and the heavy shot drove straight into Juan, blowing his light body off the ground and depositing him backward and off the path. He landed in a depression near the creek at the bottom of a gorge filled with bubbling black boiling water. The sign next to it read, "Witches' Cauldron."

Juan's gun lay on the path near Conchetta's feet. She quickly picked it up and made her way down into the gorge. Frank called her name, but she didn't stop. He had twisted his ankle, but he followed after her, Angelina soon by his side.

When Conchetta reached Juan, he was still breathing. The bottom half of him was submerged in the inky boiling water, cooking like a crab or a lobster in a pot. Somehow he was propping himself up on his arms. His chest was a raw, bloody mess. The blast of the powerful shotgun had ripped most of his shirt and coat away.

Conchetta needed to do one thing. She had to look in his eyes once more before he died. Several times since he had kidnapped her, she had thought that she had detected a glimmer of humanity trying to emerge from those cold, often vacant, cruel eyes. She wondered if now, at the moment of his death, Juan would become human.

"Juan," Conchetta said, and leaned forward, her eyes looking into his.

Juan's eyes were filled with tears, but they were indeed the eyes of a human. He looked at Conchetta and blinked, a softness crinkled the corners of his eyes. For a moment, he seemed as if he were about to smile; not a sardonic smile, but a real smile, Conchetta thought. Then his eyes moved away from her and gazed downward. A look of fear transfixed his whole face.

The last thing Juan Fuentes saw as he let out a final, painful scream was Conchetta's golden crucifix dangling from her neck and gleaming in the warm sun—the crucifix he had taken from the nun he had raped and killed in San Juan Bautista.

Chapter 28

Conchetta Lombardi felt arms around her. She turned away from Juan and looked straight into the eyes of her sister.

When the shotgun blast tore through the air and sent Juan flying, Conchetta never looked back to see where it came from. She had kept her eyes glued on Juan. She picked his gun up and scrambled down the gorge after him. She didn't believe he could be dead. If he wasn't, she wanted to place a bullet in the center of his head. She wouldn't shoot him in the chest, because she doubted that there really was a heart in there. It was his evil mind she wanted to explode. Also, she needed to look once more into his eyes.

Before she stopped his brain, she hoped to see that little spark of humanity that had peaked out several times, for if she saw it, then a seed of goodness could survive within even the darkest evil. But it was too late for the lonely seed to grow.

When Conchetta saw Juan, she knew he was finished. Half of him was boiling away, but he didn't seem to even notice. For a moment, she had seen the little seed struggle to grow, but in an instant it was gone, as he screamed in pain and horror, and she watched the light go out of his eyes.

Now, she was suddenly seeing her sister's face smiling at her, tears falling from her eyes. Conchetta's senses fluttered. She became dizzy and felt she was going to faint. Was she dreaming, or was this real?

Angelina saw her sister's eyes fluttering and losing focus. She shook her and said, "Conchetta, everything's all right; he's dead. It's me. I've been following after you. You're going to be all right. You're alive, and the sun is shining."

At the sound of the familiar voice, Conchetta clung to her sister and broke into deep sobs that shook her whole body. She wasn't dreaming. She was clinging to a real body, her head buried in her sister's neck.

Angelina held her and stroked her head. "Cry, cry. It's all over. It's good to cry. But soon you'll cry out of happiness. You don't know how much I worried about you and how I missed you. But I never gave up on you. I never thought you were dead. And you're not. That monster is. It's October, and it's warm and sunny. You always liked it when the leaves changed color. You used to collect them, remember?" Angelina said in a rush of words.

The thought of the changing leaves triggered something in Conchetta. She moved out of Angelina's embrace, controlled her sobbing, and looked once again at her sister. She reached her hand out and touched her face. Angelina grabbed her hand and held it. She just smiled at her sister and shook her head up and down.

Conchetta noticed a man's legs a few feet away. She looked up and saw Frank. He smiled at her and tears too were running from his eyes. He walked forward, reached down, and gently helped Conchetta to her feet. Her sister aided her from the other side.

"Come on, let's get out of here. There's a hotel nearby, and we've got to get you some dry clothes," Frank said, kindly, but business-like. Conchetta just nodded her head, took a deep breath, and turned with Angelina toward the path out of the gorge.

When their backs were turned, Frank grabbed Juan by the arms and pulled his body from the inky, bubbling water. He didn't want to look at his face, so he turned the body on its stomach and followed after the women.

The searching, the chase was finally over. Conchetta was safe. Frank had seen more shooting than he ever wanted to see. When Angelina fired the Lupara, he had been so close to Juan that he could feel the air the large pellets displaced as they sped by him and smashed into Juan. In the excitement and confusion he had forgotten about his own wound. He put his hand to it and it came away wet with blood. Primo's handkerchief was stuck to the wound, but it was soaked through and he realized he needed attention. The pain wasn't that bad, but he was losing blood. Thinking of Conchetta, he hoped he had a lot to live for; wanted to have a lot to live for.

They climbed out of the gorge and were met near the top by the men. Dom climbed down a ways and extended his hand to Angelina. He didn't say a word until everyone was once more on the path away from the gorge. Then he embraced Angelina and wrapped her in his arms. He could have held her forever, but Conchetta was there, and he wanted to say something to her.

"Conchetta Lombardi, my name is Dom Londi. I love your sister, and I married her. But I love you too, and I'm so glad to meet you," Dom said. He stepped forward, hugged Conchetta, and kissed her on the cheek.

Conchetta had to smile just looking at this man. He seemed so happy and full of life. His eyes were moist, and she could feel a kindness and compassion exuding from within him. His gayness and enthusiasm rubbed off on her. She looked at Angelina who was staring at Dom. She had never seen her sister look at a man this way. She had never looked at her former husband, Roger, this way.

"Adoration" was the only word Conchetta could think of to describe the look.

"Well, Dom Londi, I'm so glad to meet you. And if you love my sister, then I love you too. And I'm glad that you married her. She can be a handful, though. And she's stubborn," Conchetta said, the last words in a whisper.

"She's stubborn all right. She's not even supposed to be here. But since everything turned out all right—Dio Bono! I can't believe it! The crazy woman saved you and Frank," Dom said, shaking his fist under Angelina's jaw.

"Oh, pipe down, big mouth. I couldn't have done a thing if Pietro hadn't made a move allowing the *animale* to be distracted. And then Frank pushed him away, allowing me to get off a shot. How's Pietro? He was hit in the leg, no?" Angelina looked about and saw Pietro leaning on Pino, and he was smiling.

"*Il Bruto animale* hurt me, but only a little. You hurt him worse, Angelina," Pietro said.

"We can all talk later. We have wounded. Let's get to the hotel, and we're going to need a doctor," Angelina said.

"Frank, Dave, can you make it to the hotel? We'll help," Primo said, peering at Frank's wound.

Dave had limped over and joined the group. Conchetta looked at him and smiled.

"Miss Lombardi, you saved my life back there. Juan was going to plug me when you went for him. I'm grateful to you, ma'am. I'll be grateful to you forever," Dave said bashfully.

"You're a good man, David. You helped Suen. Please call me Conchetta. We know each other pretty good now. Right?"

"It is a pleasure to know you, Conchetta," Dave said, and meaning every word of it.

"Wait a minute. Sis, you're OK right now?" Angelina said.

Conchetta nodded her head.

"I'll go get the wagonette. Dave, Frank, and Pietro can ride in the back. My sister's exhausted. It's not too far away," Angelina said.

"So, that's how you got here! You came in the wagonette? And in the storm? And alone?" Dom exclaimed.

"I wasn't alone. Mai was with me," Angelina said and walked off. Dom followed right after her, talking in Italian and motioning with his hands.

Now that Angelina was gone, Conchetta felt alone and awkward. For a moment it was quiet, and she could hear the sound of the rushing creek. She only felt that way for a moment though. Suddenly, everyone seemed to start talking to her at once and introducing themselves.

The large Italian man spoke first. "Conchetta, I'm Primo Nuti. The rascal with the wounded leg over there is my uncle, Pietro. We're Dom's friends and your sister's too. Are you all right? Are you hurt anywhere?"

Conchetta was sore and bruised in places, but it was nothing. Nothing at all compared to what she had been through.

"I'm all right. A little sore and bruised," Conchetta answered, smiling a little.

"Conchetta. You don't know me, but I feel like I know you. From this day on you will always have me for a friend. My name's Pino and this is Walter," he said, slapping Walter on the shoulder. "We're your sister and Dom's friends. Can you cook good like your sister and make the long white worms covered with red sauce?" Pino inquired.

"He means spaghetti with tomato sauce, Conchetta. He knows what it's called. He's just trying to act like an Indian," Walter said, smiling.

In spite of her mixed emotions, Conchetta let out a cautious laugh. So many things had happened since she had been gone. Her sister had gotten married, and evidently had made friends with very unique and amazing people. And they were all looking at her with nothing but kindness and sympathy in their eyes. She wanted to start crying again, but forced herself to get a grip.

"I'm glad to meet all of you. There's so much I don't know," Conchetta said, shaking her head sadly.

For a moment, a hollowness stole over her eyes, and an image of Juan flashed in front of her. Memories of her ordeal assailed her, and she felt unclean and unworthy. For an instant, she just wanted to run, run to a dark place and hide until she sorted out her thoughts. Everything was happening so fast. For the most part, she was standing amidst total strangers. Who was Dave? Who was Frank? Dave, she had met only the day before and his acquaintance had occurred only because of Juan. Frank had swum after her and called her name. Her feelings regarding Frank were laced with confusion, but for some reason the confusion wasn't upsetting or displeasing. The other men standing there, she had just met. What were all these men thinking about her?

Suddenly, she felt a blanket draped around her shoulders. She hadn't noticed, but Walter had walked to his horse, grabbed a blanket, and had handed it to Frank. Frank was carefully arranging it and folding it tight in front of her.

"You're going to be warm and clean in no time, Miss Lombardi. One of the main attractions about this place is the bathhouse. Clean, hot, bubbly water comes from out of the ground. I hear it's caught in a large concrete pool. People relax in it, and it's said to cure all that ails you. Once I get bandaged, I'm going to try it too," Frank said.

"Me too!" Primo, Walter, and Pino said all at once.

"I probably won't go in," Pietro said. "I've got a hole in my leg."

"Me neither. I've got two holes," Dave said.

"Shit! That reminds me. Someone should be going for a doctor. It probably wouldn't be good for all you wounded to ride back to town on a bumpy wagon until a doc looks at you and tends to you. My horse is the fastest and strongest. I'm going off now. I'll be back as soon as possible. Meet you at the hotel with the Doc," Walter said, and he ran for his horse.

"He's right," Primo said. "As soon as we get to the hotel, we'll fix everyone up as best we can until the doctor arrives."

Conchetta looked at the three wounded. They didn't realize how lucky they were just to be alive. Juan was out to kill each one of them. Only his unusually poor shooting had saved them.

The sound of an approaching wagon made everyone turn and look. Dom was driving the wagonette, Angelina alongside, and in the back sat Po, Mai, and Suen. Dom pulled up, and the wounded were helped in. Conchetta climbed up front next to her sister. Primo and Pino followed behind on the horses.

Before they reached the hotel, they were met by a group of tourists and Carl Filbert. "What the hell went on back there?" the old man inquired.

"There's a man dead back there, lying by the Witches' Cauldron. A kidnapper and probably more," Primo said.

"A lot more. I know of at least four people he's killed, including a priest and a nun," Conchetta said, surprised at the violence in her voice.

"What?" Angelina said and hugged her sister to her.

"I've got so much to tell you, but I can't even talk about it now. Later," Conchetta said, tears once again rising to her eyes.

"I'm a lawyer, Primo Nuti, from San Francisco. Is your stage back to town leaving soon? We haven't met anyone else on the road. The sheriff needs to be notified as to what went on up here," Primo said.

"It's due to leave any minute. Come on, let's get to the hotel," Carl Filbert said.

The hotel was filled with confusion upon the arrival of the newcomers. Within moments, a brief sketch of the occurrences had spread through the guests and staff.

Primo and Dom took charge. A large room with three separate beds was provided, and Frank, Dave, and Pietro were soon lying down, their wounds being cleaned and bandaged by Angelina, Po, and Mai. Dom ordered food for everyone. A thick venison and vegetable soup was served to the wounded, and everyone was soon eating. Conchetta found herself unbelievably hungry and asked for a second helping after finishing off her first bowl.

"Well, I see you haven't lost your appetite. Good, you're too skinny. You're coming back home later with Dom and me. We'll have you looking your old self again. Oh, that's right. You don't even know that Dom is probably the finest chef of them all, back in Florence," Angelina said.

"Cook," Dom said from a nearby chair.

Though the caregivers were amateurs, all were of the opinion that no one's wounds appeared life threatening. Dave's shoulder wound seemed the worst. He complained that the whole area was kind of numb. Nerves must have been damaged, was the general consensus. Most of everyone's bleeding had been stopped. Now, it was just a matter of resting and waiting until the doctor arrived.

While Conchetta was eating and quietly talking to her sister, Dom got an idea. Conchetta's dress was torn in places, and wet and muddy. He sought out the proprietor and asked him if there were any spare clothing around, especially women's dresses. Since the isolated hotel had opened, many guests had stayed there, and it was just as Dom had figured, a whole closet was filled with articles of clothing left behind by guests over the years.

"Help yourself, Mr. Londi. Anything for the little lady, after what she's been through," the proprietor said.

Dom picked out a clean green dress of what he guessed was Conchetta's size. He returned to the dining area and held up the prize.

"Conchetta, look! A clean dress! Why don't we all go to those baths and relax. Outside of Florence there were hot springs also. I've been to them. It's a refreshing experience and very relaxing. What do you say?" Dom inquired.

After the food, Conchetta felt tired and mainly wanted to rest and be alone, but the idea of relaxing in warm water and getting into clean clothes swayed her, as did Dom's enthusiasm. She had to admit that he had come up with a great-looking dress, and probably just her size too, she thought.

"You found a nice dress, Dom. I've never been in a hot spring. It's nice you say?" Conchetta said.

"The best! Let's all go. I'll go find the others."

A short time later, a motley crew, as some already at the bathhouse thought, assembled at the dressing rooms. Pino, Primo, Dom, Po, and Frank went to the men's side and changed into bathing clothes. Angelina, Conchetta, Suen, and Mai went to the women's.

The bathing pool was a large concrete square, about three feet deep and roofed over with exposed redwood beams. It was humid and steamy inside and smelled lightly of sulphur. Some of the bathers, upon seeing a large older Indian and three Chinese, quickly got out of the water and headed for the dressing rooms.

"Well, I never!" one woman said to her bald husband when passing the group. "Evidently they let riff-raff of all types into this place. Wait until I find the manager," she said and walked off in a huff.

"Maybe we should leave," Po whispered to Dom.

"Not in a million years, Po," Dom said.

Before the woman went very far, Angelina called out in a strict voice, "Hey lady, hold on there!"

The woman froze in her tracks. Angelina walked up, looked the woman straight in the eyes and calmly and quietly said, "I just killed a man back there who kidnapped and harmed my sister. All these people here are my friends and helped me get my sister back. And I mean, all these people. Do you have a problem with that?" Angelina said, and moved her stern face within inches of the startled woman.

"Oh! Why, no. No problem at all. I was just a little surprised that's all. Excuse me, please. I'm so sorry. I didn't mean anything. Excuse me, please, we were just leaving," the woman said, and followed her retreating husband out of the bathhouse.

Pino walked over to Angelina. The rest were just looking at her and smiling. Dom had put his hands to his head and rolled his eyes up to the ceiling.

"Good work, Angelina. At least you didn't push her back in the water," Pino said, patting her on the shoulder.

Primo started laughing, and surprisingly, so did Conchetta. It felt so good to laugh that for a moment she couldn't stop. She stepped into the hot bubbling water and submerged herself in it, trying to contain her laughter. Finally, she controlled herself, at the realization that her laughter may have been hysterical. The water felt wonderful, though. She held her nose and submerged her head. When she came up, everyone was in the pool. Angelina was next to her with a bar of soap and began soaping her hair.

Frank was in the water nearby, smiling at Conchetta. He had insisted on coming, assuring everyone he wouldn't get his wound wet, and that the relaxing water would probably do him good. Conchetta rubbed water from her eyes and turned to see Frank smiling at her. She smiled back, then felt self-conscious and turned away, instantly confused at her reaction. She should be enormously grateful to this man and let him know her appreciation for what he had done. Instead, when she looked at him, shyness and nervousness assailed her and her face felt flush.

Frank was disappointed when Conchetta averted her eyes and turned away. The only reason he forced himself from the bed and ignored the aching wound was to be near Conchetta, and she seemed to want to have nothing to do with him. But he had come too far in his pursuit of her to give up easily. *She's just tired and traumatized,* he told himself. *After what she's been through, striking up a relationship with a man is probably the furthest thing from her mind.*

After Angelina was finished with Conchetta's hair, Dom waded over, took the bar of soap, and began washing his wife's hair. Conchetta backed off a ways in the direction of Frank, who casually moved a little closer towards her.

"Mr. Augostino, you should probably be lying down and resting. You've lost a lot of blood," Conchetta said in a concerned voice.

"Oh, I don't feel too bad, and this hot water and the steam help take my mind off the pain. Besides, you're here," Frank boldly decided to add.

When he said the last words the temperature of the hot water felt substantially cooler than the rush of heat that rose to Conchetta's face.

"I've not had the opportunity to thank you properly for all that you've done. That day on the bay when you shouted out my name was what made me not want to give up hope. You gave me a reason to live. When Juan hit you, and you went under, I was so worried. I thought you were going to drown. Then you surfaced and swam back to shore. I can't tell you how relieved I was. We've never met, sir. You must have recognized me from my picture. Correct?" Conchetta inquired.

Frank couldn't keep from beaming at Conchetta. He was standing fairly close to her. She was clean and fresh, with wet dripping hair, and her beauty dazzled him.

For a moment he thought he was going to be tongue-tied, but then he said, "Conchetta, if I may call you that, please call me Frank. I feel we know each other in a way, too well to address one another as sir or miss. Yes, I knew you from your picture. I've carried it for weeks. When I saw you moving away from me across the bay, saw you in the flesh for the first time, I felt that I had known you forever. I know that must sound stupid, but it's true. If I told you how many times I've taken out your picture and looked at it, you'd think I was crazy," Frank said, shaking his head.

Conchetta looked up at the man and momentarily searched his face. No, he wasn't crazy. He had been speaking words to her, and behaving in a manner that she had hoped her whole life some man would. But, the elation that she felt at what he was saying, was quickly shattered by visions of Juan, and remembrances of things past.

Dom and Angelina had been watching the two, while pretending not to. They moved away a little further so they could talk.

"My sister's been through hell and who knows what, and is just lucky to be alive. And, of all the times of her life, she meets someone who's obviously head-over-heels for her. Why couldn't she have met Frank before, and under different circumstances? He seems like just the type of man she's been hoping to meet her whole life. It's not fair. None of it's fair," Angelina said.

"No, it's not fair. It's just life. Why Conchetta had to travel such a path is anyone's guess. Some things have no logical explanation, and just plain don't make sense. You know that, Angie. What brought you and me together? Coincidence, or fate? Who can know? And does it matter? All that matters is that we're together. And maybe it's going to be the same for Conchetta and Frank. Your sister's going to need a lot of kindness and loving understanding. I'm sure you'll give her that, but wouldn't it be wonderful if a loving man her age could also be there for her, and help her to forget, or at least put behind the past?" Dom spoke quietly.

Angelina leaned forward and gave Dom a quick kiss on the lips. He scooped her off her feet and playfully threw her with a splash in the bubbling water.

Conchetta and Frank turned and looked. Conchetta laughed at the sight of her sister coughing up a little water. Frank put his hand out and caressed her cheek.

"Someday you and I are going to be just like those two," he said as they met one another's eyes. "By the way, did I tell you I fell in love with your picture?" Frank said.

Chapter 29

Conchetta was standing under the redwood tree at her sister's house. She had just heard a squirrel, and seen it scampering in an oak tree off to the side of the house, making noise. And the noise sounded like, "Chetta, Chetta." She looked in the direction, but saw nothing.

Conchetta had been remembering that weak little seed she thought she had seen in the corner of Juan's eye. It looked like a little seed, cracking and beginning to germinate, but upon seeing the light, instead of opening up and embracing it—it hid from the heat and brightness and folded back in on itself, never to grow. And the seed didn't care. Oh, it was so hard to realize that she had met a soul who didn't care. Several times she had thought that Juan cared. And, as hard as it was to accept the realization, she had to admit and remember that the times she had seen him act like he might have cared, it was her that he seemed to care about.

She heard the screen door slam, and turned to see Dom walking towards her.

"Hey, Lombardi, come on inside, everyone's here."

"Don't call me Lombardi," Conchetta said. "He used to always call me that. Oh, I'm sorry, Dom. I guess I'm just not in a good mood today. I know, it's my birthday, and I should be happy, but I just can't get Juan out of my mind. It's bad luck," Conchetta said, holding back tears.

Dom wasn't sure what to say. Conchetta had been living with them for around a month now, and much of the time she had been moody and somewhat distant, even to her sister. Each day when the weather was nice, she would walk by herself along the gravel bar near the creek. Sometimes Angelina would go with her, but Conchetta had made it clear that, for the most part, she preferred to be alone.

Dom and Angelina both felt helpless in regards to cheering Conchetta up. They had tried buying her little things in town, and had taken her on the train to Santa Rosa for a shopping spree, and then to a nice restaurant, and after dinner to a play—a light-hearted comedy. For a while, Conchetta would act cheerful and seem to actually enjoy herself, but sooner or later, a shroud of melancholy would drape over her, and her vibrant eyes would turn listless.

At a loss for words, Dom just said, "Come, let's go in. There are people here whom you haven't seen for quite awhile. Primo and Pietro just arrived. And guess who they brought with them? That Augostino fellow, Fred, Freddy, Forest—what's his first name? I can never remember," Dom deadpanned.

Conchetta's eyes lit up a bit, and she slugged Dom in the shoulder.

"OK, OK, I get the point. Just don't expect me to be the life of the party, Dom. I don't think I have it in me," and grabbing Dom by the arm they walked back to the house.

Quite a lot had transpired since that afternoon in the hot springs up at The Geysers. Walter had returned that evening with the doctor. They were lucky to have found Clark Foss in town working on one of his wagons at the livery stable. When Walter explained to him what had occurred, and how they needed to get back to The Geysers Hotel as fast as possible with the doctor, he was more than willing to help. He quickly harnessed up his six fastest horses and before long the three of them were off—hell bent for The Geysers; careening around curves at a breakneck pace.

Once at the hotel, the doctor treated Dave first. He was in the worst shape, weak from loss of blood. His shoulder wound was nasty and was already starting to look infected. The doctor disinfected it and cleaned it up as best he could and bandaged it loosely. Dave's leg wound wasn't bad, but the shoulder would have to be watched carefully.

Frank was tended to next. The bullet had passed clean through him, and once he recovered from loss of blood and the wound was kept free from infection—the doctor thought he would heal up just fine.

Pietro was the luckiest. The bullet slamming into him had knocked him off his feet, but in actuality had done little damage as it tore into the fatty part of his calf. The doctor was of the opinion that after a good night's rest, the wounded could be made as comfortable as possible in the wagon, and depart in the morning for town, as long as Mr. Foss took his time and tried to avoid the ruts and bumps.

In the morning, at first light, the sheriff arrived. Conchetta briefly explained to him all that had happened. Father Donovan, the nun in San Juan Bautista, and the two ranch hands outside of San Jose, were all dead at the hands of Juan. The sheriff wanted more details, but Primo spared Conchetta any further recounting and assured the sheriff that he would act as spokesman for Miss Lombardi, and that in the next day or two would meet with the sheriff and discuss the matter further. This satisfied the sheriff. Juan's body had been brought to a shed near the hotel. The sheriff wrapped it securely in blankets, strapped it over the back of a spare horse, and departed quickly for Healdsburg.

Later on that morning, all the others got in wagons or on horses and headed back toward town. Dom drove the wagonette, with Angelina and Conchetta riding next to him on the front seat. Mai, Suen, and Po rode in the back. The wounded returned with the doctor and Clark Foss. Pino, Walter, and Primo followed behind the wagonette.

The folks at the hotel had furnished the group with some boiled eggs, venison jerky, a wedge of cheese, and some fresh baked bread.

"I don't know about anyone else, but I'm getting a little hungry," Dom announced when they were over halfway down the road. "Maybe we ought to pull off the road and have a little bite, huh?" he suggested.

Suen, who was in exceptional spirits and simply over-joyed at just being alive said, "Let's pull into the 'romantic getaway' and eat. I'd like to see that dump one more time."

Conchetta, who had been experiencing both elation and depression, burst out laughing.

"Yea, what the hell, might as well look at the old roman-tic getaway again. I swear—that David is really something. Did he really want to marry you, Suen?"

"I think he did, at least until he decided that he was a Spartan," Suen said and began to giggle.

Walter, Primo, and Pino had ridden up close and were listening to the conversation.

"Suen, did you say that Dave thinks he's a Spartan?" Pino questioned.

Suen shook her head affirmatively.

"Well, good for him! At least he finally knows who he is. Walter, oh Walter. I remember what you told me about Spartans. It all makes perfect sense to me, don't you think?" Pino said.

Primo began to chuckle. He too remembered a thing or two about the Spartans, including their sexual preferences. He had a feeling he knew what everyone was talking about.

They turned off the main road and there it was, the Honeymoon Shack, the Romantic Getaway, or as Pino called it, Fandango Bob's old place. Everyone took a peek inside. Angelina and Mai looked the longest, never having seen the place.

"You mean Dave actually fixed this shack up just so he could take you here and propose to you?" Mai queried Suen.

"It's true, Mother. He even hung those lovely curtains and set up that beautiful table with those delicate flowers in that priceless vase. Why, he'd make a great decorator, don't you think?" Suen said, straight faced.

Mai and Angelina burst out laughing. Conchetta had briefly looked in, then quickly turned and walked back to the wagonette. Her wet dress was still hanging from the nail in back of the stove. She saw the tear in it where Juan's knife had struck it. It made her think of the nun's blood stained robe and the gaudy Gypsy clothes she had fouled while tied down in a drugged state, and discarded in a little creek outside San Jose.

Angelina quickly followed after her.

"Come, let's have some food. This was probably not a good place to stop, but we're here now, and the sun is shining, and the surroundings are quite pretty, if you don't look at that shack. Come on, *manga, manga*."

Angelina got the basket out, lowered the backboard of the wagonette, and placed the food there. Everyone gathered around and had a little snack.

After eating, Pino walked around a bit and spotted the remains of the fire where Dave cooked the huge rattlesnake. Looking around further, he stopped and held up the skin of the great reptile, and called out to the group.

"Hey, look at this. Have you ever seen a snake so big? This was probably Fandango Bob's guardian snake. Dave killed it and ate it. Oh, I'd hate to imagine what dreams could come to a person who ate such a powerful spirit. I'll bet Dave saw Rah-Ah-Rohna, the snake woman with the rat's arms and claws in his dreams. I see now why Dave became stronger and more sure of himself, and a better person too, from what Walter says. That snake gave him power and clarity and showed him the path to the Spartans. Fandango Bob would be happy," Pino said.

Conchetta listened to Pino in wonderment. Her sister and the others evidently were used to hearing Pino talk, but she certainly wasn't. The old man said everything so confidently and matter-of-factly, but a lot of it sounded like nonsense to her. She decided, though, that she would like to hear some more of this strange Indian's opinions. For some reason, Pino reminded her a little of Father Donovan at Carmel. Like clockwork, tears filled her eyes when she thought of the old priest, who had told her to come back when the roses were in bloom.

It didn't take long to eat, and once again they were continuing on down Geysers Road. By the late afternoon they reached the Healdsburg Hotel, where they had all agreed to meet.

Pino and Primo went inside the hotel and inquired about Melanie and Betty Mae. News of what had occurred at The Geysers had already spread through town, after Walter had arrived at the livery stable. The clerk treated Primo and Pino like conquering heroes who had rescued damsels in distress and had rid the world of a bad man.

"Walter never said how you guys took that kidnapper down," the clerk said.

"Oh, Angelina Londi blew him to bits with a Lupara, a sawed-off shotgun. He shouldn't have messed with her sister," Primo added nonchalantly.

"I trust the Pomo girls received fine treatment and enjoyed their stay?" Primo inquired.

"Oh yes, sir. The little ladies have had a fine time. They even left me these for a little snack," the man said, and reached under the counter and held up a glass jar filled with roasted grasshoppers.

"Good for you!" Pino said. "The more you eat of those, the more youthful and virile you become. Isn't that right, Primo?"

"You're the doctor, Pino."

They turned and left after hearing that the girls were probably at the creek where some other Indians had camped for the night.

Po, Mai, and Suen went home, after some heartfelt thank-yous and tearful good-byes. Primo and Pietro spent the night in the hotel, and they left for San Francisco with Frank on the train the following day. Pino and Walter camped for the night by the creek along with the other Pomos.

Angelina insisted that Frank come back home with them and spend the night, where she could feed him some good soup and change his dressing. Dave spent the night at the doctor's office, and the next day his parents loaded him up in their wagon and took him home for a watchful recuperation.

Once back at the house near Dry Creek, Angelina quickly killed a chicken herself, and in no time had it cut up and boiling on the stove. After removing the bones and cutting it up further, she added fresh vegetables and herbs, and some barley. By dark, Conchetta was feeding Frank hot soup as he lay in bed, at Angelina's insistence.

Now that Frank was alone in a room and close to Conchetta, he had become tongue-tied and nervous and disliked the sound of his own voice. What he really wanted to do was ask Conchetta to marry him, right then and there. He wanted to get the words out and be done with it, but he could see it just wasn't the right time.

Up at The Geysers, he had practically told Conchetta that he loved her, or more precisely that he had fallen in love with her picture. She, in turn, hadn't expressed much in regards to this. He could see that she cared for him, and appreciated his efforts in helping rescue her. But in all reality, how could she love him? She didn't even know him. And he could see that now wasn't the time for light-hearted banter and romantic talks and sharing feelings that were a necessary step for building a loving relationship. Conchetta was just too important to him. He had waited a long time to find a woman like her. He would just have to wait a little longer, and let time heal some of Conchetta's wounds. The wound he had was superficial, compared to the wounded look that at times came over Conchetta's face.

The moment Conchetta stepped into the living room, everyone shouted "Happy Birthday" in unison. The little house was full. Besides Primo and Pietro, Walter, Pino, Betty Mae, and Melanie were smiling at her, holding tall glasses of lemonade. Po, Mai, and Suen were there standing around Dave, who still was in bandages, relaxing in a chair, bashfully waving at Conchetta. Dave had become somewhat of a hero around town. The fact that he had run off with Suen and put her in jeopardy in the first place, had been quickly forgotten in light of the bravery he had shown in dealing with Juan. After all, who could blame a hot-blooded young man like Dave for becoming infatuated with the beautiful Celestial girl? Dave never told folks around town about the conclusion that he had drawn in regards to being a Spartan. Some day he might, but for now he was content to bask in his newfound popularity.

Conchetta watched as a man she had never seen before moved from in back of Pino. It was a Pomo male about Dave's age. The man had sleek black hair pulled into a ponytail, held together by some type of shiny bone clasp. His eyes were highlighted with dye applied in a manner similar to that of some women who pursued certain pastimes. Bracelets adorned his wrists, and two large gold earrings framed his angular face.

"Dave, I want you to meet Rodney. Walter and I have been talking about the Spartans with him, and he has expressed much interest in meeting you. You two may find you have a lot in common," Pino said, draping a hand on Dave's shoulder.

Dave wasn't sure what to do. He just stared up at the Indian, Rodney, thinking he had never seen such a handsome fellow.

"Hi, Rodney," Dave said, grinning his bucked-tooth smile.

"Hello there, David. I have heard many nice things about you and have been looking forward to meeting you," Rodney crooned.

Pino slyly nudged Walter in the ribs and rolled his eyes. It was all Walter could do to keep from bursting out laughing.

Conchetta watched as Suen came up to Walter and slipped her arm under his. Within the last month Suen and Walter had been spending much time together, and in spite of Po's misgivings and doubts, the two had become engaged. Once again, Walter had been living in San Francisco. He was attending university and planning, on Primo's suggestion, on becoming a lawyer. The long-term plans were for him and Suen to marry and live in San Francisco, where Walter could finish up his classes while working part-time for Primo. Suen also planned on working part-time in a Chinese grocery to help make ends meet. Primo had assured Walter that once he had become a lawyer, there would be plenty of work for him amongst the Chinese community. With Suen as his wife, many doors now would be open. Walter also spoke Spanish well, and Primo felt that many in the Latin community would seek out Walter's professional help too.

Conchetta could just see, by the way they looked at one another, that they were truly in love. Conchetta felt a little sorry though for Melanie. She had been told how Melanie had hoped to be Walter's sweetheart and some day to marry. Pino once had patiently explained to her that Walter just couldn't be totally happy with Melanie. He had just become too cosmopolitan. San Francisco did that to people, Pino had explained.

Just then, a man in an old blue army uniform burst through the door carrying a keg of beer.

"Cavalry's here folks, Oliver Platte to the rescue. Angelina invited me to the party, and I figured some of you folks might be kind of thirsty," he said, and placed the keg on the table.

Oliver looked around and spotted Dave deeply engaged in conversation with Rodney. Dave saw him at the same time, and a slight look of fear transfixed his face.

Oliver Platte marched boldly across the room to Dave, kneeled down in front of him, and began sniffing his leg.

"Good, no dog piss. Guess you're finally learning boy, so there's no need to bite you. Say! Who's your friend here? Reminds me a little of a fellow we had in the army. Best dancer in our unit he was," Oliver announced.

"Why, I'm a very fine dancer too. When Dave's better I'm going to teach him some moves," Rodney said, tousling Dave's wispy hair.

What a bunch, Conchetta said to herself. Most of them reminded her of a bunch of circus performers. Unfortunately, as soon as she thought of circus performers, she had a vision of Juan and her dressed in the Gypsy costumes, parading around with a twirling bear.

Suddenly, she felt like bolting back out the door and heading off alone towards the creek. At that moment, she felt a hand on her shoulder. She turned and stared into the pale blue eyes of Frank Augostino. He was smiling at her and had grabbed hold of her hand.

"Conchetta Lombardi, you and I are going to need to talk. It can either be now, or maybe later after we all eat. But sometime today we have to go off alone. I have a few things I want to tell you," Frank said, looking deeply into Conchetta's dark eyes.

Angelina had been standing in the kitchen doorway, watching her sister. She was holding a wooden spoon she had been using to stir the sauce. She had made a savory tomato-based sauce with lots of garlic, fresh herbs, and chanterelle mushrooms. Dom had offered to get some robins for the sauce, but she had refused.

"If every Italian around here keeps adding robins to the sauce, pretty soon there won't be any more robins," she scolded him.

Besides, she didn't need any robins for flavor. She had a huge wedge of *parmesiano*, along with several fresh loaves of sourdough French bread that Primo had brought from San Francisco. The pungent cheese she would grate over her sauce that would cover the spaghetti.

Angelina had been having nightmares. They occurred almost once a week, and mostly she just saw herself in them running at Juan, clutching the Lupara, then firing and blowing him off his feet. She figured that eventually the vision would go away, but now, more than ever she could identify with some of Oliver Platte's feelings and his memories of war.

The sight of Conchetta and Frank looking intently at one another cheered her, though. Things would turn out just fine in the end, she told herself.

Conchetta was starting to say something to Frank when Angelina walked up and interrupted her saying,

"Hey, now that there's a keg of beer here the men aren't going to be in a hurry to eat. You two would probably like to go for a little walk. Frank hasn't been here for a while. Why don't you show him around, birthday girl?"

"Sounds good to me," Frank said. "It's certainly a beautiful day here. No fog, and this November sun is brilliant."

Turning to Conchetta he said, "Yes, do show me around, birthday girl, before the sun goes down. We won't be gone too long, Angelina. The smell of your sauce is making me hungry. You must have just added some fresh basilico. My father always had a few plants out back, but they didn't do all that well in San Francisco fog," Frank added.

"No, the plants like lots of sun and heat, and we get plenty of both here. You two go now, before Pietro tries to bog you down with drinking beer with him, Frank. Hurry, go now," Angelina said, and scooted them out the back door.

Conchetta felt self-conscious, and for some reason, somewhat reluctant to be alone with Frank. Frank had been writing her once a week since he returned to San Francisco. The letters mostly centered on what his plans for the future were. His wound was almost healed, and after the first of the year, he would be finishing up his university classes. He had also been accepted into law school. Conchetta had noticed that his letters, for the most part, were light-hearted and never too serious of a nature. He always inquired about her health and well being and what she had been doing to occupy her time, and how all the people he had met in Healdsburg were doing. She looked forward to his letters and promptly wrote him back in somewhat of a similar light-hearted vein. Conchetta was a little disappointed though. In spite of bouts with depression and memories of Juan flashing in front of her, she secretly hoped that Frank's letters would contain more of the tone of an ardent passionate lover. Part of her yearned for flowery romantic prose, similar to something the Bronte sisters wrote, or Elizabeth Barrett Browning in "Sonnets from the Portuguese," or even William Shakespeare. Frank's letters were rather plain and matter-of-fact. For a man who had told her that he had fallen in love with her picture, he certainly never sounded like a dreamy, sensitive lover in his letters. She knew Frank cared for her, but she wondered at times if he felt that way only because of her looks. After all, he had said he had fallen in love with her picture, not her. He barely knew her. He had said that he felt like he had known her forever, and she had felt the same way about him. And this, she thought, was true.

Walking out the door with Frank, Conchetta glanced up at him. He certainly was a handsome man and always was considerate and caring. But, if she gave herself to Frank— gave him all her love—might not he, or any other man, one day when the freshness of new love has lost its bloom, come to resent her or question her due to her involvement with Juan? These misgivings tore at Conchetta as she and Frank walked out into the late afternoon sun.

"Let's walk along the creek," Conchetta suggested. "Wild ducks sometimes fly up it this time of day."

"Sounds good to me, but Dom said that there's a trail across the road that climbs up to the top of a hill where there's a great view. Do you know that trail, Conchetta?" Frank asked.

"Oh, yes. I've only been up there once, but it is beautiful up there. I'm not exactly dressed for hiking, but who cares, it's only clothes," Conchetta said, and a vision of herself sitting naked in a little creek staring at her Gypsy outfit snagged on a branch fluttering in the water assailed her.

"Speaking of clothes, I've got something of yours that I bet you would like to burn. When I was trying to retrace your steps, or track you down, as one might say, I found a red and blue outfit snagged on a branch in a little creek. I thought it might be yours. I tucked it away in my saddlebag. It was yours, or it was something he made you wear, wasn't it, Conchetta?" Frank asked, his brow knotted in seriousness.

Good God, Conchetta thought. *Can he read my mind?*

"I can't believe you found that! Yes, he made me wear it. I was drugged and tied in the back of a manure wagon. I was lying in my own excrement!"

Conchetta had nearly screamed the last words. She took off at a run, crossed the road, and vanished up a trail, upward into thick woods.

Frank was a little stunned, but ran after her. The only way for Conchetta to heal and for them to have a normal life together was for Conchetta to face her demons and talk about them. And Frank was in this for the long haul. He knew that time was the best healer, but by God he was determined to be with Conchetta every step of the way. He entered the thick forest and began climbing the narrow path. Conchetta had stopped running. She was paused on the path, looking down at him. She was wearing a white dress with light blue squares, gathered at the waist. Her long black hair was parted in the middle, and the luxuriant waves framed her face as she struggled to regain composure.

"You shouldn't make me remember. I don't want to remember. I want to forget. Don't you understand?" she said in a voice filled with emotion.

Frank walked up to her and placed his hands on her shoulders and looked her straight in the face. He knew what he wanted to say, but with his hand upon her and her dark beauty lighting up the forest path, all he wanted to do was embrace her and smother her in kisses.

He fought this urge and forced himself to speak, "Yes, I know you want to forget. I know you wish this had been a nightmare and none of it had happened. But it's not a nightmare. It did happen, and I know it was terrible, and I know that it's tearing at your soul and filling you with con-fusion—but you're going to have to talk about it. And, I want you to talk about it with me. Sure, Angelina and any-one else, but mostly I want you to talk about it with me. You see, I love you, Conchetta Lombardi, and I want to make you Conchetta Augostino. And, I hope to have a whole lifetime together in which you can share everything with me. And, don't you dare think that you'll shock me, disappoint me, or make me turn away. Nothing you can ever tell me will dampen my love for you. You want to forget. Well, that's impossible. It can fade away. In time it can become an unpleasant memory, but I'm afraid it's always going to be something that you're going to have to live with. Think of it as a fresh scar that slowly fades with time. And you know who's going to help it to fade? Me! I'll make it fade by loving you so much that you won't have time for bad thoughts, and I'm going to start right now!"

Frank carefully encircled his arms around Conchetta and pulled her to him. He was surprised to find that she had a slight smile on her face. Her lips were parted, and he kissed them gently. He kissed her eyes and cheeks, her hair, her neck, and then returned to her mouth. Conchetta pressed closer to him and passionately returned his kiss.

Suddenly, she broke away from him. Tears of relief and love were streaming down her cheeks.

"You better mean what you just said, because if you mean it, then I think everything is going to be all right. I can get through this, but you're going to have to help me. And you had better never stop loving me. Do you under-stand, Mr. Augostino?"

As soon as Frank saw Conchetta's tears, tears filled his own eyes, but her words bored into his soul and filled him with a happiness he had only dreamed of.

"I understand you. But tell me, will you be Mrs. Augostino? And, the sooner the better as far as I'm con-cerned," Frank said.

Conchetta had controlled her tears, and now her eyes were sparkling, and her face exuded a dazzling radiance.

"Yes, I'll marry you. In spite of all that's happened, I began loving you the moment I saw you swimming towards me in the bay. My sister's always talking about being struck by the thunderbolt. It's a version of Cupid and his arrow, I guess. Did you shoot me with an arrow, Frank?" Conchetta inquired.

"No. But something sure hit me, and it felt like an arrow or a thunderbolt, the moment I saw your picture. When I saw you for the first time, moving away from me on the water, I could hardly breathe from desiring you so much. I hope you're prepared for the fact that I'm never going to let you float away from me again, my lovely Conchetta," Frank said, caressing her cheek.

"Oh Frank, that's what I need to hear. Don't ever let me float away again," she said, and threw herself in his arms.

They kissed passionately and lovingly for what seemed like an eternity. Frank found himself so aroused that he felt the danger point had been reached. By Conchetta's abandonment and quickening breath, he knew that she too was approaching the point of no return.

This wasn't the time, though. That time should come later. More than he had ever hoped for had just occurred. They had taken the first step in what he hoped would be many, until the day would come when the steps would vanish into nothing. He forced himself to pull away from the woman he desperately loved.

"I love you. You're making me dizzy. Let's get to the top of the hill before the sun sets. I want to see the sun go down on the happiest day of my life," Frank said.

They climbed hand in hand up the winding steep path. At times it was narrow, and Frank urged Conchetta to take the lead. Finally the path ended. The trees thinned, and they emerged at the top of a round hill. They looked out to the east and could see the Alexander Valley way in the distance below them and the Russian River cutting through it like a snake. Geysers Peak and the Hog's Back Ridge loomed above the valley.

Conchetta stood transfixed, then took a deep breath, turned and faced the west. The sun was setting in a brilliant blaze of orange behind one of California's golden hills. She looked down at her feet. Fresh blades of grass were beginning to emerge from the earth, pushing their way through the older dry blades. And not for one instant did she think of that seed that failed to grow from the corner of Juan's eye.

"What a view," Frank said, breaking the silence. "Calls for a little bonfire, I'd say."

Conchetta watched quizzically as Frank moved to a rocky bare area of the hill. He kicked away any dry grass, then reached in back of him. Hidden by his coat, and tucked into the back of his pants was Conchetta's red and blue outfit. He brought it forward and unceremoniously tossed it on the ground. Conchetta watched, almost mesmerized, as he reached into his coat pocket and produced a little bottle of clear liquid. He sprinkled the contents on the clothes, then lit a match and flung it down. The clothing instantly ignited with a whoosh. Frank moved to Conchetta and hugged her.

"Feel a little better now?" he asked.

Conchetta just looked at him and smiled, nodding her head, and watched the smoke drift off to the west.

Made in the USA
Lexington, KY
20 July 2011